THE
IRON KHAN

THE
IRON KHAN

A Detective Inspector Chen Novel

LIZ WILLIAMS

OPEN ROAD

INTEGRATED MEDIA

NEW YORK

This is a work of fiction. Names, characters, places, events, and incidents either are the product of the author's imagination or are used fictitiously. Any resemblance to actual persons, living or dead, businesses, companies, events, or locales is entirely coincidental.

Copyright © 2010 by Liz Williams

Cover design by Barbara Brown

ISBN 978-1-4804-3822-4

This edition published in 2013 by Open Road Integrated Media, Inc.
345 Hudson Street
New York, NY 10014
www.openroadmedia.com

THE
IRON KHAN

1

The ghost horde swept out of the east, moving fast across the black sands. Standing on the rise, legs braced and bow drawn, Omi could see a train in the distance, racing over the desert toward Urumchi. The horde was moving faster than that, quite silent, though in life, Omi reflected, the hooves would have sounded like thunder on the stones. They were heading straight for him. His fingers tightened on the bow and he spoke, also silently, to the Buddha, thinking of those images which still swam out of the shadows of the caves so many miles to the east. The memory gave him courage.

The horde was close enough now for him to see their faces. Not at all Chinese, though he knew that some with local blood had ridden under the Khan. Flat-faced men, black eyes below their topknots, which streamed like horse-tails from the back of their helmets. In the front of the horde rode the Khan, in armor the color of night: a man with a thin face, a narrow beard, all angles. He was riding hard up the slope and Omi drew back the arrow, thinking: *Not yet, not yet—now!* He fired. The arrow sang through the air but the Khan was coming, expressionless, as though he could not see the archer, but Omi knew he had come for this and he leaped forward, springing down the stones of the slope as the arrow sang on. At the last moment the Khan's pony swerved. The arrow sailed by, nicking the Khan's face. A single drop of dark blood flew out and Omi had the cup ready: he caught it. It sizzled into the metal cup and Omi snapped shut the lid. But the Khan had turned in the saddle with a bow of his own and as Omi met his blank night eyes the Khan, in turn, loosed an arrow.

"Now!" Omi cried. "Make it now!"—and the desert was ripped away from under his boots into the shadows of a cave and a pair of huge, calm eyes, looking down at him.

2

"Missing?" Chen said, into the phone. Behind him, Miss Qi sat with neatly crossed legs, exuding a delicate perfume of cherry blossom. She sat up a little straighter at the tone of Chen's voice. "When did you last see it?"

On the other end of the receiver, a very long way away, Mhara the Emperor of Heaven answered, "A week ago. We had its annual honoring ceremony to celebrate the time of its writing, if one can say that. The Book wasn't so much written, as wrote itself."

"You'll have to forgive me," Chen said. "I don't know anything about all this."

"It's kept as secret as possible," Mhara explained. "Not even all the denizens of Heaven know that it's a real text. You'll meet people who think it's no more than a creation myth."

5

Chen caught Miss Qi's glance and, ever tactful, the Celestial warrior rose and glided from the room, closing the door behind her. "From what you've told me," Chen said, "This isn't so much a creation myth as a creation manual."

"Exactly. The words it contains are the blueprint for Heaven. If they're tampered with—deconstructed—then Heaven itself could begin to unravel. Of course," Mhara added thoughtfully, "there are those who might say that this is no bad thing."

After the loss of both of Mhara's parents—an Emperor gone mad and an Empress turned wicked—Chen couldn't blame him for those sentiments. "Things are stable now," he reassured Mhara, "now that you've been crowned."

"Ruling has become somewhat more achievable than it initially appeared," the current Emperor agreed. "At least, so I thought until yesterday. Then the curator appeared in a flat panic and told me that the Book was gone."

"And it's definitely been stolen? Could it have—I don't know— taken itself off? Does it have a will of its own?"

There was a short pause on the other end of the line. "I don't really know," Mhara said slowly. "I've never heard anyone mention it. But often these magical artifacts have some degree of consciousness. What a depressing thought, that things might have become so lousy in its own creation that it's removed itself."

"Is there any way we can find out?" Chen asked.

Mhara sighed. "That's why I called you. Sorry, Chen. I know you've got a lot on your plate at the moment . . ."

Chen smiled. This was characteristic of Mhara: to be concerned, but also omniscient. In this instance, however, the Emperor of Heaven was simply being courteous. "I *have* got a lot to do. But it's all good stuff, as well you know."

He could almost feel the Emperor's smile. "Robin has spoken to Inari, I know. She told her that things are going well with the pregnancy."

"Yes, it's been four months now," Chen mused. He still couldn't quite believe it. He'd always wanted a child, of course, but never thought it would actually happen. Humans and demons could breed, but it wasn't always an easy process. And this child . . . well, they were all special, weren't they? But it seemed that this child might be more special than most. Not a comfortable thought.

"Inari has hopes," he confided, "that this might bring herself and her family back together. Children often do reconcile warring relations."

"And what do you think?" Mhara was being very patient with him, as usual. A theft that could threaten the very foundations of the Celestial Realm and here was Chen waffling on about his family.

"To be honest, I doubt it. I've seen rather too much of Hell's attitude toward family life."

"How is Zhu Irzh?"

"Actually, he's fine as far as I know. Jhai had business in the Far West, so she's out there now. Zhu Irzh chose to cash in some vacation time and go with her. Spoke to him last night. Says there are some nice restaurants. But you didn't call me to talk about all this, Mhara."

The Emperor of Heaven sighed. "I wish I had. Everyday life is so relaxing. It would be nice to have more of it."

"About this book," Chen said. "I'll do my best, you know that. I've got a fairly light caseload at the moment. For a change."

"In that case," Mhara said, "could you come to Heaven for a day or so? To look at the scene of the crime?"

"I'll be glad to," Chen said.

*　　*　　*

Later, the trip arranged, he walked with Miss Qi alongside the harbor wall. Out in the bay, the boats bobbed beyond the barriers of the typhoon shelter; it was autumn now, the air mercifully cooler after the summer's steaming heat, with a salt breeze stirring up from the ocean. In a week or so, Chen knew, that breeze would grow stronger, heralding the storms that lashed at the south China coast. His son or daughter would be a winter child: it was not, Chen considered, all that surprising.

"Jhai didn't ask you to go west with her?" he asked Miss Qi now.

"I'm on standby," the Celestial warrior said. "I know I was hired as her bodyguard, but she said she just wanted to get away from it all for a bit."

Trust Jhai to think that the Gobi Desert was the ideal place to "get away from it." But she was probably right.

"Well, Inari appreciates you being around," Chen said. His wife had suggested they ask Miss Qi to dinner that night and Chen had agreed. Their social circle had expanded since the worlds began opening up: a handful of years ago, Chen wouldn't have been able to mention his otherworldly pursuits without people coughing nervously and heading in the opposite direction. Or phoning a psychiatrist. Just look at Sergeant Ma, whose view of the supernatural had started out as raw fear and now was close to resembling a healthy interest, or an unhealthy one, depending on how you looked at it. These days, they often entertained all manner of people and Chen had to admit that his wife had blossomed because of it, unless that was simply a product of the pregnancy. He hated to think how lonely she must have been in the earlier days of their marriage: separated from her admittedly vile relatives, torn from the only home she'd ever known, and living incognito in a city in which half the inhabitants couldn't see her and the other half were likely to summon an exorcist as soon as she came into view. Sure, Inari had the badger to look after her, but the badger had his limits.

But things were changing, as the presence of the quiet, pale warrior by Chen's side attested to. Miss Qi looked up at the rose and turquoise of the evening sky and smiled.

"It's quite lovely sometimes, this human realm," she said.

Chen returned the smile. "It's not as beautiful as Heaven, I'm afraid."

"Heaven can get a bit . . . cloying," Miss Qi said, frowning as though she'd said something disloyal. "I never thought so until I lived *here,* and then I started looking at Heaven with a different eye. I suppose that's what travel does."

"There's a Western saying I heard in a movie once," Chen told her. "'You can't go home again.'"

"Well, you *can* go home," Miss Qi said, "it just won't be the same."

Perhaps she was right, Chen thought as they crossed the makeshift bridge of other people's sampans to one of the little rowing boats that was used whenever the houseboat was moored further out in the harbor. Miss Qi took one oar, Chen the other, and they rowed the short distance to the houseboat. But it was certainly good to be coming home this evening, seeing the old-fashioned lamp that swung from the prow of the houseboat and the lights in the kitchen. A familiar striped shape was waiting at the top of the rope ladder.

"Hello, badger," Chen said. The badger grunted, bowing his head to Miss Qi. She'd learned not to try to pat him. Badger had been uncharacteristically patient.

9

"Good evening, spirit of earth," Miss Qi said. Badger preferred formality.

"Good evening, warrior of Heaven. Mistress will be pleased that you've come." The badger trundled inside.

"You must be one of the only people I've ever met who has a badger for a butler," Miss Qi remarked.

Chen laughed. "He's a little more than that." They followed the earth spirit inside, to where Inari was bending over a steamer on the stove. Looking at her, one would never have known she was pregnant. Chen had not known what to expect of a demon gestation, and Inari had not reassured him by saying vaguely that it took all manner of forms. Much more helpful had been the explanation given by the midwife. They'd been very lucky in finding Mrs Wo: demon health professionals weren't common in Singapore Three, even under the new and more relaxed immigration policies. Half of Heaven seemed to have decamped to the city after Mhara had insisted that his personnel take a greater role in human affairs, and all of them seemed to want to be healers. Well and good, thought Chen, but they'd all balked at treating a demon, even one who was a personal friend of the Emperor himself. It wasn't a political issue, they'd taken pains to explain: it was simply that they lacked the relevant obstetrical knowledge.

Then, one evening, he'd come out of the police station to find a hunched figure sitting on a bench in the shadows, veiled by an enormous hat. Chen had thought there was something odd about her at the time, and moments later, when he felt a tug on his sleeve and looked down into little green eyes, like chips of jade, set in a coal-black face, he realized that beneath the hat was a demon.

"Sorry to trouble you," the demon had said, gripping the handle of her capacious handbag, "but this might be of interest."

She proffered a large, ornate business card, on which the words *Mrs Wo, Midwife* were written in gold.

"I have references," Mrs Wo said. "I know you'll be wary of trusting a demon. But you'll need someone, at least, when the time comes."

Inari, when asked, had requested a meeting and she had, rather unexpectedly, taken a liking to Mrs Wo. Chen checked out the references with all the capability of a police department that deals extensively with Hell, and they were excellent. So Mrs Wo had been hired as a midwife to the Chen's forthcoming child and, thus far, had proved invaluable.

Now, Inari straightened up from the stove and smiled at Chen and Miss Qi.

"It's good to see you," she said to the Celestial warrior.

"Thank you," Miss Qi said, gravely, and Chen watched with a quiet satisfaction as his wife served tea to their friend.

3

Urumchi was not an unpleasant city, Zhu Irzh thought as he stood on the hotel balcony. There was a park, situated on a greenly wooded hill, with a pagoda rising from it. Streams of morning traffic wound around the base of the hotel, some twenty floors below: the sound of distant horns floated up through the hazy air as impatient drivers utilized what Zhu Irzh had heard referred to as the "sixth gear." Beyond the road, a jumble of restaurants and shops led to a bridge, and beyond all that, lay the endless dusty expanse of the steppes, and Central Asia.

Zhu Irzh had never been so far west before, and somehow he'd expected it to be much more primitive than this thriving metropolis. But this part of the country had proved interesting. They had already been to an official dinner at a restaurant in the mountains, which rose up at the back of Urumchi in a massive, white-capped wall.

And Hell was a little different here, too. He could feel it. It had appeared to him in dreams—a liminal space, the gap between the Chinese and the Islamic Hells, and the hint of something much older yet. These were not Han lands: the people here were Uighur, Turkish, as well as Chinese. They looked different. Their food was different. And their beliefs were different. It made Zhu Irzh feel slightly disoriented, as though the ground was literally changing beneath his feet. He'd not had cause yet to discuss this with Jhai, but he planned to. In the meantime, she was busy, here to discuss the construction of a new chemical plant out on the barren steppe. She was in a business meeting right now, leaving Zhu Irzh to enjoy the hotel. With that in mind, the demon realized it was now eleven o'clock, almost time for the bar to open. He slipped on a pair of sunglasses, to hide his eyes, and wandered downstairs. They'd know he wasn't local, but hopefully they wouldn't realize *quite* how local he wasn't.

The main lobby was occupied by a wedding. The bride, in full Western bridal gear that made her look like a gigantic cake, was nearly six feet tall. Behind her veil, the eyes that glided incuriously over Zhu Irzh were a bright green. Not at all Chinese, Zhu Irzh felt, with a pleasant frisson of being abroad. He headed into the plush red velvet opulence of the bar and ordered a local beer.

Not bad. Looking at the range of wines featured above the bar made the demon feel provincial: he hadn't realized quite how many vintages the Gobi and its environs produced. There had always been attempts throughout China's long history, to encourage settlement out here. But no one wanted to leave the comforts of the east for this difficult and still dangerous land, a place where

13

sandstorms scoured the desert and the land stretched red and black for miles. Not unlike Hell, really, but without the crowds. Reflecting on similarities, Zhu Irzh sipped his beer and watched the wedding party proceed into the dining area. *Oh god.* That was another thing to think about—his own wedding. Jhai had set the date for the following summer. It was to be a big affair, befitting the marriage of the stepson of the Emperor of Hell (China) and a scion of the royal family of Hell (India), not to mention Jhai's role as a leading industrialist.

Their mothers had been in close correspondence. That in itself was enough to strike fear into a demon's heart. Mind you, Zhu Irzh thought, at the rate at which they had both been casting out family members, give it another few months and there wouldn't be anyone left to invite.

And there was his own bride-to-be now, striding in through the swing doors of the lobby. With a crimson sari billowing out behind her and her out-size designer sunglasses, Jhai looked like an exotic and venomous moth. Zhu Irzh raised a hand.

"Hello, darling!" Jhai slid onto the barstool beside him.

"How was your meeting?"

"They were all imbeciles, quite frankly, but anxious to please. I think we've got a few things resolved. We're supposed to be going out this afternoon to look at the site—you can come with us if you want. I'll have to change my clothes first."

"Why not?" the demon mused aloud. "Might be interesting to see a bit of the actual desert now we're here."

"It'll be the middle of nowhere," Jhai warned. "Like Lop Nur. You don't want to put a chemical plant anywhere that matters."

"What's that—Lop Nur?"

"One of the country's big nuclear plants. Remember the one in Hell? It's like that. They were doing atmospheric testing until recently. So I don't think a few chemicals are likely to make much difference."

One thing you couldn't accuse Jhai of being was ecologically sensitive. Zhu Irzh once more felt that faint, strange tremor of unease that he'd learned to identify as his conscience. After seeing what had become of Hell's main nuclear plant, he wasn't so sure that siting a chemical factory in even such a remote place was a good idea. But for the sake of peace, he said, "Probably not. Want a drink?"

Jhai accepted a mineral water. "What's going on in there?" she asked, gesturing in the direction of the dining room.

"Wedding reception."

"It's very *loud* for a lunchtime reception, isn't it?"

Jhai was right. Zhu Irzh hadn't really been paying attention and had initially taken the noise for the congratulatory shouts of happy revelers. But what he was now hearing were screams.

He ran for the dining room, dimly aware that beside him, Jhai had gathered up the skirts of her sari and was sprinting along. The bar staff were similarly responsive, but the demon was first through the door.

The dining room was in chaos. Overturned tables and chairs littered the floor, along with canapés and glasses. One of the ushers slipped on a pool of spilled champagne and fell flat; Zhu Irzh had to swerve to avoid falling over him. Someone, possibly the bride's mother, was emitting a series of ear-splitting shrieks. Then somebody stumbled onto the dance floor, leaving the way clear and revealing the source of the commotion.

At first, Zhu Irzh thought that some hippy had wandered in off the street. The figure was tall, with a streaming mane of red hair and bright blue eyes. His torso was bare and covered in a swirl of tattoos, and he wore a pair of baggy tartan trousers. At first glance, he looked like some of the Western backpackers that thronged the streets of Singapore Three in the summer, but they were, on the whole, alive.

This man wasn't.

He was heading for the bride. Unlike some of the reanimated dead that Zhu Irzh had previously encountered, this one neither lurched nor hopped. He moved with a sinister fluidity, much faster than a human, if not as swift as demonkind. He carried a curious weapon, a long staff with a bulbous head, like a truncated spear. The bride stood stock-still, her mouth gaping, as if paralyzed. The man swung the staff up and over his head, twirling it like the cheerleaders Zhu Irzh had seen in American films. But before he had time to strike down the bride, the demon was striding forward, ducking under the spinning staff and slamming a hand into the center of the zombie's bare chest. Cool and hard, more like stone than flesh. Contact had to be made for Zhu Irzh to speak the necessary spell, a basic piece of magic for one born in Hell, designed for the inconvenient human dead. He'd never tried it on Earth, and had a moment of doubt, for magic differed between the worlds and Chen had sometimes experienced reversals in his own spellcraft when visiting Hell. But luck, or locality, was with the demon. He felt, rather than saw, the zombie slacken and crumple, then watched as the unnatural spark in those blue eyes faded to a pinpoint star and was gone. But at the moment of its departure, just before the connection between them snapped, the demon saw the zombie's last thoughts.

Desert. High and arid, a long ridge of sandstone, red in the last light of the setting sun. Below, the village huddled around its wells, the meager foliage still green in the early summer heat. Soon the ground would bake, hot enough to fry an egg, and the wicked sand would spin up from the deep desert, whipped on by devils riding skeleton ponies.

They'd had a message from the west, from long-lost kin: a spoken tale of somewhere gray and mist-ridden, sea crashing into thunder on the rocks. The blue-eyed man had never seen the sea, had ventured once to a lake in the mountains and thought it must be the same. Join us, the message had said. Whatever the reason for the separation, it is your ancestors' wrong, not yours. And the blue-eyed man looked out across dryness, to where the small people were waiting and hating, and wondered if they should leave.

After that, there was nothing, only a terrified blur of wind and sand and choking death. The blue-eyed man fell at Zhu Irzh's feet, stiff in desiccated atrophy.

4

On the slab in the local Urumchi morgue, the man had clearly been dead for centuries. Zhu Irzh stood looking down at him in wonder.

"We're considering it as theft, rather than a murder attempt," Inspector Turgun said, mildly. Tall and thick-set where Chen was short and round, Turgun nonetheless reminded the demon of his absent colleague. He was visibly Uighur rather than Han: a leathery face, with slanted, opaque eyes and a small, thin nose like a beak.

"Theft?" Jhai echoed, frowning.

"This gentleman is actually the property of the local museum," Turgun said. "A very famous exhibit. I remember being taken to see him and the others when I was a child."

"But who is he?"

"Well, no one knows his name, obviously. Much too long ago for that, and they didn't keep written records."

"He's not Chinese, though," Jhai said. "Or Uighur, is he? He looks like a Westerner."

Turgun nodded. "Essentially, he's a Celt. Or a proto-Celt. That's what the history professors tell us, but maybe in a few years they'll have changed their minds. I believe the theory is that many thousands of years ago, when the people who became the Celts migrated from northern India, some of them turned left and a handful turned right. They ended up here, in the Gobi, and set up a civilization. They were called the Tokarians, and this is what this man was. As you can see, he bears no resemblance to any of the Chinese peoples, because he simply isn't one of them."

"So if he was in the museum, he must have been—what? Dug up? I suppose the atmosphere in this area must be very dry."

"That's right," Turgun said. "He was mummified, probably in a sandstorm. The others in the museum are the same."

"Might be worth giving the museum a ring, if you haven't done so already. Find out who else might be missing."

Turgun gave the demon an unhappy glance. "It's already being done. I suspect the worst."

"If I may say so, Inspector, you're taking this very calmly. Do you have much, uh, supernatural activity in Urumchi?"

"You'd be surprised," Turgun said. "Or given where you come from, perhaps not. Remember, Seneschal Irzh, this is a border country. Islam meets Chinese beliefs, with more than a dash of Buddhism thrown in. That means many Hells and many peoples: there are ifrits out in the deep desert, and demons here in the city. Sometimes they meet, and it isn't pretty. We've had a lot of trouble, which we try to keep quiet. If you were both Han, I'd be much more careful what I said to you, but as it is—we have enough suspicion from the Chinese government, and trouble with terrorists, too."

"I'd heard about that," Jhai said. "Of course everyone's paranoid about Islamic terrorism these days."

"Especially the government in Beijing," Turgun responded. "Of course, we have a few extremists—they're to be found everywhere. But in the main, the Uighur people here, myself included, just want a quiet life." He sighed, looking down at the mummified, ancient corpse. "Some chance of *that.*"

Turgun was right. When they left the morgue and returned to Turgun's office, they learned that the call had been made to the museum.

"How badly is the custodian hurt?" Jhai asked, when she heard the news.

"She's shaken, but not physically damaged apart from a few bruises. It knocked her out." Turgun replaced the receiver. "I suppose I should say 'she,' rather than 'it.'"

"Some of the Tokarian mummies were female, then?" Zhu Irzh asked.

"Yes. Two women, two men—one was old, even by today's standards. He didn't get far. The younger man smashed his way out of his case and so did the women. One of them collapsed in the courtyard after attacking the custodian, but the youngest woman is still at large."

"I suppose three out of four isn't too bad," the demon said, optimistically.

"It could be a lot worse. But it's the youngest woman I'd be inclined to be worried about, to be honest. We don't really know what she was, but she had a pouch at her belt containing amulets and I know some of the museum staff think she was a shaman. A reanimated magic-practitioner is likely to be more dangerous than even a warrior."

Zhu Irzh remembered the vision he'd shared with the blue-eyed mummy, that hot harsh place. Magic hadn't helped the girl, when the sand swept in. But given a second chance, who knew what she might do? Hard, too, not to wonder about the state of their souls: the zombies he'd met in China had been simple vessels of flesh, with little of the original personality and none of the original soul. They had been dispatched to Heaven or Hell, there to await reincarnation. But here in this borderland, who knew what the Tokarians had believed, and who knew where their souls might be? Summoned back from some ancient limbo, perhaps, or crouching in their dried-out bodies, awaiting life?

"Any idea where she might have gone?"

"No. Back to the desert, maybe?" Turgun's expression was hopeful.

"The gent in the morgue didn't," Zhu Irzh reminded him. "So far, they've attacked two people. Either they're fully animate or someone has programmed them to do it."

Turgun sighed. "You're right, of course. But we've had no further reports and she's been missing for two hours now. I'll get units out and searching."

"I'll help if I can," Zhu Irzh said diffidently. He knew that other police forces sometimes objected to outsiders coming into their patch, especially, perhaps, Easterners, though Turgun seemed extremely accommodating so far.

"Thank you," the Uighur inspector said. "We've got our own forensic team on it—they might be able to pick up a trace of our missing mummy. I'll call you if there's any news."

Released into the midday flurry of Urumchi's traffic, Zhu Irzh and Jhai returned to the hotel, which had done an admirable job of soothing shattered bridal nerves and re-hosting the disrupted reception in a non-mummy-infested part of the hotel. Zhu Irzh ordered room service while Jhai changed into more desert-friendly clothes, and after a quick lunch, they went back down to the lobby where Jhai's car was pulling up.

"How far is this factory site of yours?" Zhu Irzh asked.

"About a hundred kilometers out. Local government insisted."

Zhu Irzh watched with interest as the shabby suburbs and industrial estates of outer Urumchi fell away as they approached the desert: first, flat fields and irrigation plants, then a huge wind farm, outlined like striding ghosts against the faint blue bulk of the mountains, and then miles of salt pans. As the city receded, the desert began to take hold in earnest. This, according to Zhu Irzh's guide book, was not the Gobi itself, but a region known as the Taklamakan: a name that, roughly translated, meant *if you go in, you don't come out.*

Reassuring. But he could see what the guide book meant. It was like the lowest reaches of Hell: bleak and lunar-arid, more stone than sand, with ridges of exposed rock striking up through the surface as though the earth was in revolt. You could hide a dozen chemical plants out here and no one would notice. The last sign of habitation—a small military-style hut—had been passed miles before and now there was nothing. He said as much.

"Yeah, it's certainly empty," Jhai remarked with satisfaction. She studied her cellphone. "You can still get a signal, though."

The road on which they were traveling was tarmacked, but soil and sand had blown across it, making it seem more of a track. Then they turned off the road and started bumping down a real track, toward a tumble of rocks.

"This is it?" Zhu Irzh asked.

"This is where it's going to be." Jhai pointed to an expanse of flattened earth, glistening white with salt. A collection of four-by-fours stood at its edge, accompanied by a small huddle of people.

The car slowed to a halt and Jhai jumped out, scattering greetings. The demon followed more slowly, and was struck by a sudden weight of silence, despite the voices of Jhai and her companions. The heat burst up out of the ground like a fist, searing even lungs accustomed to the airs of Hell, and the place smelled dry, an old bone odor. If the Tokarians had managed to eke out a civilization here, they were worthy of some respect.

Jhai was studying architectural plans. Two of the men, in hard hats and stout boots, were evidently surveyors.

"Sorry about this, Zhu," Jhai said. "Dragging you out to the middle of nowhere. I've got to go through this. It's probably going to take an hour or so."

"No problem," the demon replied loyally. "Always interesting, to see new places. I might go for a stroll."

"Don't get into trouble," Jhai said, with a sideways glance at miles of empty world.

The demon grinned. "Thanks for the vote of confidence."

Much as he wanted to support Jhai, he'd actually been telling no more than the truth. Since his arrival on Earth, he'd seen relatively little of it: his duties had largely been confined to Singapore Three, with occasional visits to various Hells, and apart from a weekend trip to Shanghai, also courtesy of Jhai, he'd experienced almost nothing of China itself. Empty though the Gobi might be, it was still different. He set off across the salt flats with some enthusiasm. The tower blocks of Urumchi were no longer visible from this distance, but the eastern end of the mountains—the demon did not know what they were called—was clear against the pale sky. With the heat shimmering the air, earth and sky merged into one another, creating a world of mirage. Jhai, the surveyors, and their vehicles were a small black patch against the rocks. But as he walked, Zhu Irzh realized that he'd been wrong about the lack of habitation. He could see something up ahead, a collection of buildings. Jhai had mentioned military activity out here in the desert, so perhaps these were not houses, but something to do with that. Initially, he wasn't even sure that the buildings were real—a product of the shivering air—but drawing closer he saw that they were quite solid, a thick wall of baked clay, reaching up some twenty feet, with a gate set into it. The place looked like some organic fortress. He'd seen a documentary about Central Asia, where there were similar towns.

Maybe, Zhu Irzh thought hopefully, there would be a bar.

The gate itself, of a wood so old and dried that it resembled stone, hung open, so the demon walked through and found himself in a narrow street. Houses stretched on either side, small-windowed places with doors that would have been accommodating if one were a hobbit. And with a sudden disjointed shock, Zhu Irzh realized where he was. This was the village he'd seen through the mind of the mummy, back in Urumchi. The tiny doorways were to keep out the encroaching sand; you had to duck to enter them. The memory, not his own, returned with the force of a physical blow and that was when Zhu Irzh understood that the link with the blue-eyed mummy, generated through the connection of the banishing spell, was still there.

But the village couldn't still be standing, could it? It was over four thousand years old and though the desert air preserved, Zhu Irzh doubted that it would keep a place so intact. Then he glimpsed the glint of coals inside a beehive-shaped bread oven, and knew. This village was still occupied. Either it had come forward in time, or he'd gone back.

He was not immediately worried. It was unlikely that a supernatural creature such as himself could be trapped in the past, but it was disconcerting, all the same. Equally unnerving was the fact that the place seemed deserted, in spite of the glowing bread oven. He walked quickly around the little maze of streets, finding a well with a bucket drawn over its lip and a small plantation of vines, but no sign of human life.

Interesting, but unproductive. Zhu Irzh went back through the gate and stopped.

Someone was coming across the sand, a bundled figure on a small, quick pony. The demon did not have time to duck back under the gateway. The figure raised a hand in greeting, and Zhu Irzh stood, waiting, until it drew nearer. He was, somehow, expecting the blue-eyed man, but when the figure dismounted and unwrapped the protective scarf from his face, the demon saw that this was someone else entirely.

Also a Westerner, but with something oriental in the brown eyes and the darkness of his skin. A thin, clever face, black-bearded, smiling. His head was shaved, like a monk's.

"Good afternoon," the figure said, in accented Mandarin. He looked a little more closely at Zhu Irzh. "Ah, I see you are not human. From Hell? But you are not an ifrit, I think."

"No, I'm from the Chinese version," Zhu Irzh said, obscurely relieved. This man seemed so matter-of-fact about the demon's origins that it would, at least, save explanations.

"I don't suppose you have any cigarettes?" was the man's next remark.

"Sure." The demon rummaged in his pocket. "Here you go." He proffered a lighter.

"Thank you," the man said. "May I?" He took the lighter, which was a disposable plastic one dispensed by a local restaurant, and examined it. "Unusual. May I ask when you are from?"

"When? Twenty-first century."

The man's black eyebrows rose. "Indeed? I died in the 1920s, myself. How interesting."

It was the demon's turn to be surprised. "You're a ghost?" There was little sense of it.

"Not . . . exactly. Perhaps a ghost in the same way that this village is a ghost. You know what *Taklamakan* means?"

Thanks to the guide book, Zhu Irzh did.

"Sometimes those that go into it, *really* don't come out. Ever. I'm luckier than most, due to—well, never mind that now."

"In my day," Zhu Irzh said, taking a chance, "someone's just brought some of these people back to life."

"Reanimation?" The man looked thoughtful. "The Tokarians have been gone for many centuries. It would have to be someone well-versed in desert magic to restore them." He glanced over his shoulder. "You and I had best return to our respective points of origin, I think."

"Why?"

"The sand." The dark man pointed. Far on the horizon, but approaching quickly, was a boiling red wall.

"Shit!"

"Stand clear of the gate," the man instructed. Zhu Irzh did so and the man raised a hand, inscribing a long sparkling arabesque in the dry air. It looked like Arabic and the whisper of magic was suddenly all around. Zhu Irzh could sense things changing.

"Wait!" he said, as the sand boiled closer and the wind whipped grains of it about his boots. "What's your name?"

The stranger's lips moved, but only half a name came to the demon on the rising wind. "Nicholas—" And then he, and the village, and the sand were gone, leaving Zhu Irzh in the clear calm light of a late desert afternoon.

5

"He didn't look at all familiar?" Jhai said, biting her lip as the car bumped across the desert back to Urumchi.

"No. But he was a magician, and a powerful one." Zhu Irzh had seen, and done, enough magic to be accustomed to the ease with which an accomplished magician can act, and this man had drawn a gap in time and the world as easily as Zhu Irzh himself might open a door.

"If you're going to be snatched back to the Tokarian era, maybe we shouldn't bring you out to the desert again," was Jhai's next comment.

"Fine with me. I'll stay in Urumchi next time." Next time, there might not be an obliging magical stranger to help him get back: the memory of that deadly wall of on-rushing sand was a chilling one. Then his cellphone hummed.

"Zhu Irzh?" Turgun's voice was strained. "We've found her."

*   *   *

High on the roof of the apartment block, Turgun and the demon watched as the dead woman stood, balancing, on the very edge of the building. The street lay below her, some thirty stories down. Jhai had ordered the driver to speed up as soon as Turgun's call had come through, and it was not yet quite dark when they reached Urumchi. A vivid green strip of sky showed in the west, over the mountains, and the mummy was outlined against it. She wore a long blue dress, the skirts snapping out behind her as the wind snatched at them. Here in the heart of the city, the wind smelled of the desert. Zhu Irzh tasted salt on his tongue.

"What's she doing?" Turgun whispered. The forensic team had, so he'd informed the demon, failed to pick up any trace of the missing mummy. They'd finally tracked her down as a result of another phone call, a panicky one made by someone working late in the office block on which they now stood. This time, the mummy hadn't injured anyone, or sought to do so.

"She can't surely be trying to kill herself," Turgun said. "She's already dead."

"Hard to say what's going on in her mind," Zhu Irzh replied. The mummy raised her arms, so that the draperies of her dress left them bare. Tattoos snaked up them and, in the floodlights of the roof, the tattoos looked alive, and crawling. The flesh on which they moved appeared young. The woman's dark hair whipped out behind her and Zhu Irzh felt the prickle of magic. This, he believed, was someone in full possession of their faculties, for all she may have been dead for thousands of years and in a glass case for decades. And now she was speaking in a language as dead as she, in words that the demon had never heard but recognized as ancient: the root words of his own tongue of Hell, the spell-speech which could create and then uncreate again. In the empty air above the evening streets of the city, something started to form.

"We've got to stop this," Turgun murmured.

"I'm not sure we can." The spell felt completely different to the one by which Nicholas had sent him back to his own time, and yet had that same sense of assurance, of ease. Death hadn't altered this woman's abilities. With caution, Zhu Irzh left the doorway and walked out onto the roof. Something was coalescing, swirling in currents through the air. The woman brought her hands abruptly down, spoke a word. Zhu Irzh stared. A bird hovered before her, enormous, its feathers glittering in jewel-colors of sapphire and emerald. It had a long curving beak. The woman stepped lithely off the roof, onto its waiting back. Bare feet braced, her arms slightly outstretched for balance, she looked Zhu Irzh directly in the face. She was remarkably beautiful, but it wasn't an Eastern face: angular, with a delicate, arched nose. In the floodlights, her eyes were as blue as the sky. She smiled when she saw Zhu Irzh, whispered something that could have been a promise. Then the bird soared outward, flying down through the canyons of the city with the shaman on its back.

"Well," the demon remarked to an open-mouthed Turgun. "There's something you don't see every day."

"Short of scrambling the air force," Turgun remarked a short while later, back in the hotel bar, "there's not a lot I can do. And I don't think the government would take kindly to a phone call telling them to send out aircraft to look for a lady on a giant chicken."

"Actually, it was more like a crane," Zhu Irzh said, choosing to be pedantic. "But I agree with you. There's a limit to what you can expect people to believe." He was having a hard enough time evaluating recent events himself; ironic, given what he'd been through. "I suppose you'll just have to wait and see if she shows up again." But privately, he was wondering if that conjured crane wasn't taking the shaman out to the salt flats of the Taklamakan, taking her back to that hot, bright world, taking her home.

That night, Zhu Irzh had a dream. This was unusual enough—demons rarely dream—but the content was enough to make him wake and sit upright, sweating and yet cold.

He was standing in a street, by a high stone wall with a fret-worked pattern running along the top. Zhu Irzh did not know what lay behind the wall, but it filled him with fear all the same, a clammy sense of anticipation and dread. There was nothing to explain this: all he could see over the summit of the wall was the fronds of trees. The road on which he stood was dusty, a fine, soft dust, unlike the sandy grit of the desert city. There was an orange glow to the sky which suggested streetlighting, and the wall looked like something from the nineteenth century.

Zhu Irzh walked around the wall and found a gateway. Like the gate to the Tokarian village, this was half-open. The demon looked inside, into a courtyard with a fountain. A faint splash of water greeted him, and with it, a wave of horror.

What the fuck? I'm from Hell. I don't do horror.

Whatever it was, it was not connected to him, the demon understood, but was some property of the place itself. An ornamental building, constructed in the shape of an "E" without the central bar, lay within: an odd mix of architectural styles. It looked Chinese, but with painted shutters and an intricately carved roof.

He didn't want to go inside, but curiosity won. The demon

stepped through the gate and into the courtyard. The fountain seemed to be blocked and when he examined it more closely, Zhu Irzh saw that it was running not with water, but with blood. He straightened up, aware that someone was watching him from the shuttered windows of the villa. As soon as he looked at them, they withdrew.

"Who's there?" the demon asked. No reply. Zhu Irzh bounded up the steps to the door and went in, determined not to be out-mastered by some spirit. But as he entered a plastered hallway, something came through the door behind him, with a scimitar upraised, and a weight of bursting psychic pressure descended upon Zhu Irzh's head.

He staggered. Next moment, there was a blast of fresh cold air and the presence was dispelled. Zhu Irzh found himself standing outside, gripping the rim of the fountain. The magician he knew as Nicholas was there, holding out a hand.

"What the—where are we?" Zhu Irzh asked.

"This is where you must come. This is where he originates." Nicholas' saturnine mouth turned down in distaste. "This is where he kept me prisoner. This is Kashgar."

"Who is 'he'?"

"The one they call the Iron Khan. A magus who has lived through centuries, dining off lives."

"A vampire?"

"More than that. A ruler born, who will not die. Help me, Zhu Irzh. Come to Kashgar, and help me."

"I—" Zhu Irzh began, but the dream was fading, Nicholas' face diminishing to a spark of light . . . and then he was awake and shivering, with the word echoing around the walls of the hotel room.

Kashgar . . .

6

Patiently, Omi drew a sigil in the ashes of the fire and waited for it to take form. Here in the heights, the air was cold and crisp, heralding snow. The scent of fir was refreshing after the endless blasting heat of the desert; Omi felt that he could breathe again. This was enough like Fuji to feel like home . . . Omi took a breath, remembering early morning at the monastery, walking out into the formal garden, its artfully placed rocks changed to a miniature mountain range of their own by the rime of frost. The distant ring of a bell through the clear air, the smell of pine . . .

Very familiar. Omi was conscious of a weight lifting from him. He shifted the sword on his shoulder and stood. The sigil formed slowly out of the ashes of the fire: the bright burn of the sign that meant *Hell*. Omi gave a grim smile; it was no more than he'd expected. He looked south, over the vast expanse of the desert, to where forces were gathering.

Not easy, being here, aware of ancient wrongs. Omi was pledged to give his life for his country, his Path. That didn't mean he had to like it, or even to agree. The Chinese hated his people and he couldn't blame them. There was honor, and then there was the mask of it. Important to know which one was which. And now he'd been sent here, to a place that was barely even China, to combat an ancient enemy and a wrong yet older than that.

Where are you? Omi whispered to the night wind. *Where are you, this time?* Enduring through the ages, always at the heart of battle and, lately in a more sophisticated age, intrigue.

"You won't know him when you meet him," the sensei had said, handing back Omi's newly blessed sword. "He is always different."

Omi had bowed his head, thinking: *You are wrong.* Grandfather would tell him, he knew, and with that memory he murmured it aloud: "Grandfather?"

"I am here." The old man spoke out of the trunk of a nearby pine, the bark twisting into shadowy mist to form the familiar face. "What is it, my son's son?"

"He is here, not Hell. Yet the sigil says Hell. What does it mean?"

"The sigil is your helper," Grandfather said. "And therefore, so is Hell itself."

Omi frowned. "How can that be?"

"Look for one from Hell. Don't judge. Don't assume. Be careful!"

Well-trained as he was, it took a moment for Omi to realize that the last remark was not part of the same advice, but was directed at his present condition. Reacting instinctively, he swung the katana over and up, gripping it in both hands as the ascending mass sped overhead, aiming low, then coming around for another attack. Omi recognized it: one of the lesser ifrits, but directed to kill and potentially deadly. He struck out as the ifrit swept back, leathery wings outspread and exhaling poisonous heat. He could see its eyes: small and interested and blood-red. He'd missed, that first time, the ifrit moving with unnatural speed, but the second sword-strike hit home. The ifrit's head parted from its long neck in a shower of fiery blood, and the ifrit exploded with a thunderclap.

He hadn't killed it. There was only one way to do that, and Omi was not magician enough, though Grandfather had been. It would have re-manifested in the wide deserts and domed cities of its own Hell, but for the moment, it was gone, and Omi could be well enough satisfied with that.

He crouched on his heels with his back to the tree from which Grandfather had appeared, and closed his eyes. The proximity of his grandfather's spirit steadied him, as had the dispatch of the ifrit. He had wondered, so many times, whether he was really cut out for all this, but the sensei had been adamant: *It is your bloodline they're after, and it is you who must do what has to be done.* His father had tried, and failed, had met a grisly end in the Taklamakan at the claws of one of the Khan's succubi. And Grandfather himself had died in the Khan's dungeons.

How long, Omi had ventured to ask the sensei, has this been going on?

Long enough, was the answer to that. The Khan was ancient, Omi knew, using the blood and spirits of his enemies to rejuvenate himself in the manner of a magic so old it had become a cliché. And Omi's family were themselves of the Royal House of Japan, a minor branch these days, but still moving secretly through the bloodlines of the aristocracy, a proud heritage. There was nothing to be done except duty, and Omi would honor that; despite his doubts of himself, he was determined to see an end to it. He wanted to marry, when the time came, and he wanted a child. That was it, really; he had no great desire for wealth or status, only for a family of his own and for that son or daughter—it did not matter which—not to have to face the same battles.

If that meant consorting with Hell, Omi thought, straightening up and setting about his makeshift camp, then fine. That's what he'd do.

7

"It's looking very dark over there," Inari remarked, shading her eyes with her hand and staring out to sea. Beside her, Miss Qi frowned. She had been persuaded to stay overnight after the dinner. Chen had departed to work.

"Is Earth often like this? I've never seen such a sky in Heaven."

That didn't surprise Inari. Miss Qi had not been on Earth for very long, and Inari understood from her heavenly friend that Mhara's delegation to the human world was forbidden from interfering with the weather. Out along the horizon, a mass of cloud was gathering, inky and shot with bronze where the sun made its last feeble attempts to push through.

"Everyone was startled at the weather-working ban," Miss Qi said, echoing Inari's own thoughts. "No one could understand it. Hurricanes and earthquakes and typhoons—why would anyone want to put up with that?"

"Don't you have any weather in Heaven?" Inari said, rather timidly. She did not want her friend to think that she was criticizing her, or cause her to lose face.

"Sometimes there are breezes. And the occasional shower of rain in the spring, just for contrast. But it's extremely gentle." Miss Qi gave a very human shiver.

"I'm afraid you're not likely to find this weather 'extremely gentle,'" Inari said grimly. The ominous bank of clouds reminded her of Hell. "If Wei Chen were here, I'd—" but her thought was cut off by a high-pitched wail from the shore.

Miss Qi jumped and her hand flew to the hilt of her sword. "What is *that?*"

It sounded like a cat being tortured, but Inari had heard the noise before. "It's the typhoon warning siren! We need to move the boat."

Miss Qi gaped at her. "Can this boat be moved?" Of course, Inari reflected, Miss Qi had only ever seen the houseboat in its current position and, like a lot of people, must have assumed it to be stationary.

"Yes. This has happened twice before, but Wei Chen was here each time. We'll have to do it ourselves." She found that her hand had crept to her stomach, unconsciously protecting the growing child. She did not relish the prospect of steering the boat all the way around the point to the typhoon shelter, but it would have to be done: the harbor was too exposed and all around them people were scrambling with mooring ropes and starting their engines.

"We'll have to bring the anchor up," Inari said.

"*I'll* have to bring it up," Miss Qi retorted. "You're pregnant."

37

"Demons are more robust than humans," Inari said.

"But it's half a human baby!" Miss Qi said over her shoulder, running along the deck to where the anchor rope strained over the side. Inari cast an anxious look toward the horizon, where the cloud was beginning to boil. As she did so, a mammoth crack of thunder rolled across the sea, followed by a bolt of lightning as bright and sharp as a razor. Inari frowned. That wasn't the right way round . . . The wind was starting to rise, too, stirring her hair and the hem of her skirt with a salty, electric breath. She looked back along the deck. It seemed that Heaven's warriors were more robust than humans as well, for the seemingly delicate Miss Qi had already got the anchor up to the railing and was heaving it over the side. As quickly as she could, Inari ran up the stairs to the little wheel-house. This was an old-fashioned boat, which Chen had modernized over the years so that the controls were relatively slick. Inari knew how to steer, but the sea was growing increasingly choppy; and besides, there were all the other boats around her, some of them quite a lot longer, all making for the typhoon shelter. Well, she had no choice.

"Ready?" she shouted down to Miss Qi.

"Nearly!" Miss Qi replied. "Get going!" Inari started the engine and after a few sputters, the old houseboat roared into life.

"Mistress!" Inari looked down to see the badger. "I can offer little assistance," the badger said, reluctantly.

"Perhaps you could help Miss Qi with the mooring ropes," Inari said, forbearing to add, "And please don't fall in."

By now, the sea was churning inward, driven before the oncoming storm. Inari looked out the window of the wheel-house and her courage almost failed her. The clouds were coming at a tremendous pace, whipped on by a dimly glimpsed, whirling mass at their heart: the typhoon itself. A sudden gust threw rain across the window of the wheel-house; Inari felt as though the storm had spat at her. This didn't feel like a normal storm: the way the clouds moved, the way the wind was rising. Inari swallowed panic as Miss Qi called up, "We're no longer moored!"

Inari spun the wheel, checking the position of the boats on either side of her, a commercial barge and a much smaller sampan crewed by an elderly couple. There was little time for maritime etiquette: the barge waved her on and Inari took the houseboat out into what was becoming a shipping channel. The boat wallowed in the swell, lurching from side to side. Miss Qi leaped nimbly up the stairs and into the wheel-house, her pale hair starred with rain.

"It's *cold*," she said.

"Miss Qi, I don't think this is the usual type of typhoon. I don't know what it is, but it's not like the typhoons we've had before." She steadied the wheel. "And we had so little warning. Normally, they know days before if the weather's starting to change—they want everyone in the shelters well before it hits."

There was, she thought, little chance of that now. The houseboat was rounding the point now—she could see the ridge of pine trees at the far end of the spit—and the typhoon shelter was visible as a series of barriers bobbing in the water of the next harbor. But they were at the tail end of the queue, and given the number of boats trying to get into the bottleneck of the shelter, Inari thought they were unlikely to make it.

She wouldn't abandon ship. But she might not have any choice. A series of possibilities, none of them pleasant, flashed through her mind: drowning, in which case she'd return to Hell. Swimming to shore, but losing the houseboat, the only true home she'd ever known. And what would she say to Wei Chen on his return from Heaven? *Sorry, dear, home sank.* She had to make it to the shelter, but the houseboat, chugging along, could not be made to go any faster. It was already at its limit and the storm was lashing the coast now, blurring the lights of the city through the rain-speckled glass, and causing the boat to heave in the water. Good thing demons were not easily afflicted with seasickness, but she was not certain that the same could be said for poor Miss Qi, who was now so pale that her skin had a faint gleam of green.

"Sit down!" Inari commanded the Celestial.

"I've never thrown up in my life," Miss Qi protested. "I don't know how!"

"I think you'll find it comes quite naturally," Inari said, with sympathy. The badger had wedged himself into a corner of the wheel-house like a cork in a bottle and showed no signs of budging. Then a blast of wind struck the houseboat broadside and caused it to lurch. The wheel was ripped out of Inari's hands and freely spun. She grabbed it, losing skin, and managed to regain control of the craft, but only for a moment. They were yards from the entrance to the typhoon shelter—she saw the sampan glide safely through—when the storm struck full on.

The wheel was once again torn out of Inari's hands. The house-boat spun violently into a right-angled turn, throwing Inari and Miss Qi into a heap on the deck. The wind hit them with a sound like an express train. Inari had a sudden, confused glance of the barriers of the typhoon shelter far below them, as they were carried up on a wall of water that should have deposited them in the middle of the sheltering boats. Instead, the wave dropped, letting the boat fall and fall and fall, until Inari could see not sea, but stars.

8

"If you want to go," Jhai said, not yet impatient but verging on it, "then we'll go. The surveyors are getting on with what they have to do. You've still got leave. And I could use a proper break."

"It might not be much of a vacation," Zhu Irzh said, thinking of that sinister villa. "And it's not like me to be influenced by dreams."

Jhai shot him a curious glance. "No, it isn't, is it? This must have been some dream."

"Something's seeking me out," Zhu Irzh said. "I'm not used to that." It was true. Usually, he was peripheral to events, along for the ride. He might have been involved in some of the major upheavals of the last few years, but only as a participant, not as someone whom others tried to rope in. Yet there had been something about Nicholas' dark gaze that Zhu Irzh felt oddly reluctant to ignore.

"This man who came to you," Jhai said, as if she had read his thoughts. Zhu Irzh blinked. For a moment, it was almost as though Nicholas was standing in the room. "What exactly did he say to you?"

"He mentioned someone called the Iron Khan," the demon reported. "I don't know who or what he meant by that—I've never heard of such a person. But that's not so surprising. Out here, the Hells are so close that they overlap with one another: he might be a figure from the Islamic version. I've never been there, don't know much about it. Nicholas said that the Khan is like a *jiang shi*, a vampire."

"Have you met many *jiang shis?*"

"No, never. I've met a couple of zombies, but they weren't life-force leeches. There aren't any in Hell, for obvious reasons—they come about because the soul fails to leave a human body properly, and Hell is, by definition, a place of souls."

"I've heard theories that they don't really exist," Jhai said. "That they're demonized forms of the Manchu—that's why they all wear those Qing Dynasty clothes. There's another belief that they were invented by smugglers, who dressed up to scare off locals from investigating their activities."

"That may be so," Zhu Irzh said, "but I wouldn't rule them out, all the same. Especially not after what happened at that wedding downstairs."

Jhai laughed. "If I see any furry people with long black finger-nails hopping about, I'll let you know. Better go around holding your breath. Or we could get some sticky rice from room service. That's a sure-fire cure for *jiang shis*."

"I think you've been watching too many movies," Zhu Irzh said.

But all the same, next morning, Jhai booked flights for Kashgar.

"Have you heard anything more from Turgun?" Jhai asked as they waited in line at the airport. It would, doubtless, have been easier to commission Paugeng's own jet, but the runway at Kashgar was apparently not up to the task. So here they were, standing in line with grandmothers and small children and dogs and crates of chickens, in Urumchi's new and surprisingly glossy airport terminal.

"I called him while you were packing," Zhu Irzh said. "He's heard nothing more about the female mummy. He said that the male's been returned to the museum and has shown no further signs of life. Turgun's got armed guards on duty, but there's a limit to how long he'll be able to keep them there—the authorities have been asking awkward questions, apparently."

"Can't blame them," Jhai said. "When is this line going to start moving? Ah. Here we go."

They shuffled through the security channels, which were tightly controlled: Turgun had not been joking about the government's concerns regarding terrorism. Soldiers armed with machine guns swarmed around the little terminal and even Jhai's baggage was searched, which she bore without comment. Zhu Irzh himself, resplendent in a pair of designer sunglasses to hide non-human eyes, attracted no comment.

"Good thing we're not going out of the country," Jhai said in an undertone. "If they'd needed to see your passport, you'd have to take those off."

43

Zhu Irzh could not help wondering about Mhara's Long March, whether the Celestials who had come down to Earth would really be able to have that much of an effect on human problems, on terrorism, on war. With the Ministries of Hell still doing their best to carry out their remits, Mhara's people would have their work cut out.

Together, he and Jhai made their way out onto the tarmac. At noon, the airport was baking in the heat, a desert in itself, and behind them the terminal shimmered in the haze until rendered almost spectral. The plane itself was a small, squat vehicle, bearing an Air China logo. Jhai and Zhu Irzh took their seats and awaited take-off.

You certainly got a sense of China's size, flying over it like this. The demon squinted out of the little window while Jhai concentrated on her laptop. They'd opted for first class, so the facilities were somewhat better, but not by much. Zhu Irzh watched as the landscape scrolled beneath: wave upon wave of high, bleached hill interspersed with dark stripes and red washes, the stark colors of the deep Taklamakan. No trees, nothing that was green. Occasionally, there was the glitter of salt in the harsh sunlight. Given recent events, the demon would not have been surprised to see a woman on a blue crane flying alongside the plane, but none appeared. Was she now in some Hell of her own, he wondered, flying between the worlds? The woman intrigued him, as did the entire situation. The Tokarian, the shaman. She had not looked like a *jiang shi*, stiff and hopping. She'd looked *alive*.

Movement at the front of the cabin attracted his attention and Zhu Irzh looked up from the window. The pilot, smart in his official uniform, had come out of the cockpit, accompanied by his co-pilot. Both were beaming.

"Who's flying the plane?" Zhu Irzh asked uneasily. He was

aware that technology was not his strong point. Magic was much simpler, somehow. Jhai glanced up.

"What? Oh, it must be on autopilot. Perfectly safe." She returned to her spreadsheet. The demon watched with interest as two bureaucratic men at the front of the plane were greeted fulsomely by the aircrew, while a smiling stewardess looked on. Local government officials, probably. Both the men wore designer suits and were clearly of some importance.

Then the plane gently veered to the left, heading southwest over the desert, and the cockpit door slammed shut. The co-pilot gave a frown of irritation and reached for the handle. But the door did not open. The pilot himself had not yet noticed that anything was amiss as he continued chatting with the two dignitaries. The co-pilot bent over the door mechanism, gave it a surreptitious wrench. No one else, while reading their in-flight magazines or investigating the contents of their snack boxes, seemed to have realized that things were not well. Glancing out of the window, Zhu Irzh saw that the ground was rather closer than it had been. Far away to the left—but drawing rapidly closer—were a range of mountain peaks, impossibly high: Tibet, and the northernmost heights of the Himalayas.

By now the co-pilot had given up any attempt at subterfuge and was hammering at the door mechanism with his fist. Jhai looked up sharply from her laptop. Everyone else was now watching, too, and a mutter of consternation was spreading through the aircraft.

"What the hell?"

"He's locked himself out," Zhu Irzh said. "How good is this autopilot thing, anyway? Can it land the plane?"

"Yes, but only if they set it up first, and I doubt whether they've done that yet—we're only halfway through the flight. But this shouldn't be happening on autopilot regardless!"

"We'll be at the end of it in a minute if he doesn't get the door open," Zhu Irzh said, rising from his seat.

The pilot proved a little more decisive, or reckless, than his deputy. Opening a cupboard on the wall, he wrenched out a small axe and began beating at the door.

"God!" Jhai said. "I don't think that's—"

Tibet loomed prettily to the south, close enough to glimpse glaciers snaking their way down the mountain wall. A woman screamed and that started off others in the plane. Zhu Irzh was fighting his way past Jhai and another passenger who had made his way into the aisle.

"Stand back!" the demon ordered. He had a vague idea that magic wasn't permitted on public aircraft, any more than weaponry, but he didn't fancy a trip down to Hell quite so soon and neither, he could be fairly certain, would the majority of the passengers. The pilot, astonished, stepped quickly away and Zhu Irzh, raising a hand and murmuring a speedy invocation, sent a bolt of energy straight down the aisle. It hit the door square on and the door shattered. The pilot, recovering quickly, fought his way through the splinters into the cockpit and a moment later the plane, which had been turning disastrously toward the nearest glacier, righted itself. Zhu Irzh sank back into his seat and watched as Tibet mercifully receded. There was a scattering of grateful, if disconcerted, applause and Zhu Irzh fought the urge to bow.

"Well done, darling" said Jhai. She picked up her laptop, rather shakily, and went back to work. The panicky noises in the cabin died away, to be replaced by whispers, but Zhu Irzh, looking up the aisle toward his handiwork, saw one of the dignitaries staring back at him with an expression of frank curiosity and speculation on his face.

Damn, thought the demon. There was an old Chinese curse he'd once heard: *May you come to the attention of those in authority.* It looked as though that curse might be coming true and that wasn't reassuring.

Forty minutes later, they touched down in Kashgar. The other passengers stood back, to let Zhu Irzh off the plane first. He tried to tell himself it was a measure of their appreciation, but couldn't quite manage it. Jhai, in an unusually subdued frame of mind, accompanied him out to the taxi rank and thence to their hotel.

That afternoon, they walked out into Kashgar. It felt even hotter than the desert itself: a frontier town, China to the east, Central Asia to the west. Zhu Irzh had learned from one of the hotel's leaflets that Kashgar was essentially a way station, an oasis. Not too far away, the Torogurt Pass led up into the mountains and over to the far east of Kyrgyzstan and Uzbekistan, and from there, down into the Ferghana Valley, a hotbed of Islamic radicalism provoked by the repressive Uzbek regime. The pass was therefore rigorously controlled, but it was still open and some of the other guests in the hotel had come down through it that morning, so the hotel clerk informed Jhai. Not a tourist destination, then, Kashgar, but an ancient outpost of the Silk Road, a crossroad of East and West.

"It's a very interesting town, even if it isn't very big," the clerk said. "There's the mausoleum of Abakh Hoja, who to us is a prophet, and we also have the biggest mosque in China, and the biggest statue of Chairman Mao, also."

Jhai, with the demon lingering in earshot, expressed polite interest but said that what she really wanted to see was the market. A map was duly procured and they set off. It was by now late afternoon and the sun was sliding down over the western mountains, casting long shadows into the merging shade of trees. The old oasis city was very much in evidence: thick walls of clay hiding courtyards and secret entrances, a winding labyrinth of ancient stone in the heart of the modern network of roads and traffic. The faces that they passed were Uighur, not Chinese, the difference far more marked than in Urumchi, and as they made their way further into the old part of the city, the flowered dresses and jeans of the local girls gave way to coffee-colored shrouds, so thickly woven that it would have been impossible to tell which way a stationary woman was facing. Jhai grimaced, but said only, "It's a personal choice. I wear saris, after all."

Zhu Irzh looked about him. No one had reacted to his presence, and he wondered if they could even see him: many of the Chinese could not and these folk were presumably devoutly Islamic, with a Hell and a Paradise of their own. Little room there for a Chinese demon . . . He watched a young man sitting back on his heels and beating a huge copper dish into shape. Other copper wares hung from hooks all along the store front. The scene reminded him of Hell; here on Earth, it must be like going back in time. Then there was the unmistakable sound of a Nokia ringtone and the young man took his cellphone out of his pocket without missing a beat of the hammer, and answered it. Well, almost like going back in time.

Zhu Irzh and Jhai wandered past shops that sold caged birds, past butchers and grocers and ironmongers. At the end of a street lay a tea garden with a shaded balcony, but they decided to return to the hotel and harder liquor instead.

"No sign of your mysterious stranger?" Jhai asked with a smile.

"No, though I've been looking out for him." Zhu Irzh had,

indeed, half-expected to see Nicholas stepping out of one of those shadowy doorways. He could feel the man's presence, like a ghost at the shoulder: a curious sensation, given that he'd only met the man twice, and one of those meetings had been in a dream. "Frankly—and I never thought I'd say this—I've had quite enough excitement for one day."

"Hell, yeah," was all that Jhai had to say about the matter.

At the end of the road, the old city stopped abruptly. A gateway led through a wall of packed yellow bricks, onto a more modern street.

More modern, but still not contemporary. Zhu Irzh looked with interest at the handsome villas, partly obscured by fronds of greenery.

"So when do these date from, do you think?"

"Nineteenth century, I would think. They're more Central Asian than Chinese—I went over the border once to a trade fair in Almaty, in Kazakhstan, and there were some houses there like these. Pretty. I like that ornamental woodwork."

Zhu Irzh agreed. They were pleasant. At least the ones that didn't have a seeping sense of horror permeating through their walls. He tried to tell himself that it had just been a dream, but somehow, his internal protestations were not convincing. Very probably, the villa in the dream did not even exist.

And then they turned a corner and there it was—much bigger than the other properties, and surprisingly, more exposed. The trees that fringed the path that led up to it looked as though they were dead, or dying. Fawn leaves littered the path like beetles' wings and the blue panels of the house were stained with a creeping rust.

Zhu Irzh stopped dead. Jhai gave him a questioning look. "Don't tell me. That's it."

"That's the place."

In the late afternoon sunlight, the villa held no apparent menace, and yet there was something wrong. The villa was dilapidated, as though it had been long abandoned, whereas the places on either side—at quite some distance—were obviously inhabited.

"Do you want to take a closer look?" Jhai asked.

He was inclined to say *no*. But he was a demon, the stepson now of the Emperor of Hell itself. A house and some ghosts couldn't hold any real terrors, in the middle of the sunlit day.

"I'm going in," Zhu Irzh replied.

9

"It was kept in here," Mhara said, as they came to the huge double doors of an inner chamber. Somehow, Chen thought, the doors did not look in keeping with the rest of the Imperial Palace of Heaven: whereas the Palace was filled with rich shades of gold and red, or pastels, the doors were made of a silvery-gold substance that could have been either stone or wood. Carvings shifted and flowed across their surface; meaningless symbols to Chen, yet in some way alive. The doors looked wrong too, as though they had been appropriated from some other building entirely. He said as much, hoping that he was not giving offense. He thought he knew the mild-mannered Mhara well enough by now not to cause him to lose face by witless remarks, but one could always be wrong.

But indeed, Mhara took no offense. "You're quite right, of

course. And how astute of you. The doors come from another Heaven—I'm not sure which one, perhaps one of the Western paradises. They're ancient—even more ancient than this palace."

"How could they be Western, in that case? China is far older than that, so the Palace must have come first."

"They cannot be Christian," Mhara agreed. "But there were peoples in the western lands before that, and they had a belief in an afterlife. I believe these doors were an exchange—I don't know what we gave for them, however."

"Fascinating," Chen said, wondering who those ancient peoples could have been. This was sophisticated work and now that he looked more closely, he could see the faces of animals peering out at him from the door frame: cats and hares and foxes. And a badger. Well, well. He'd have to tell Inari's familiar about that, when he got home. "But why keep the Book of Chinese Heaven behind someone else's doors?"

"It's written into the guarding spell," Mhara said. "Technically, because these doors are foreign, they are not subject to the same magic as the rest of Heaven, and because the magic to which they belonged has been lost—apart from the guarding spell itself—our own magic cannot be used to open them. It was an extra safeguard, against attempts to steal the Book."

"Which may now have stolen itself."

"Apparently so."

Chen stood back a pace and looked at the doors. Foreign magic, running clear and cold like a mountain river, with nothing that was redolent of evil. "And behind them?" he asked.

"I'll show you." Mhara extended a hand and a stream of light reached out from it, blue and bright, flooding the doors with its brilliance. Slowly, the doors began to open, with the creatures that roamed their surfaces creeping back into the foliage of the door frame. Then the doors stood fully open and the light began to die.

At first, Chen thought that the chamber was empty. He had the impression of somewhere immensely high and cavernous, resembling a cave rather than a room. The chamber was circular and bones of stone held up its ceiling, arching up like branches.

"Like being in a forest," he murmured.

"I think that was the idea," Mhara replied. "Best let me go first. I need to introduce you to it."

An odd turn of phrase, Chen thought, but as soon as Mhara motioned for him to enter the room and he crossed the threshold, he understood what the Emperor had meant. The chamber was not merely beautiful and strange; it was alive. He'd mentioned a forest and this was exactly like stepping into a wood: filled with whispers, a distant echo of something that could have been birdsong, or running water, or music. Things flitted out of sight, glimpsed only from the corners of the eye.

Welcome, the room said to him, inside his head. *You are welcome here.* Mhara smiled as though he'd overheard, which perhaps he had. "It was designed to recognize evil. It won't let it enter."

"What would happen to an evildoer, if one did come here?"

"They would not be destroyed. Simply removed, to a remote area on Earth. It has only happened once in the Palace's history—a thousand years ago now, with a very clever thief. He found himself down in the desert and the shock was so great that he gave up his ways and became a holy monk."

"A nice story," Chen said.

"Sometimes things do work out."

The nature of the place gave fuel to the speculation that the Book of the landscape of Heaven had abducted itself, but this was still not sufficient evidence for the theory to be proved, Chen reflected. "If someone who was not wicked, whose intentions were entirely pure, came here to steal the book, could they succeed? Presumably so."

"That's my concern," Mhara said. "Now that the Emperor my father is dead, and with him the dictate that all Heaven must think exactly as the Emperor does, agreeing with all his proclamations, it is feasible that someone with ideas other than myself, with the best of intentions, might have gained access to this room and taken the Book. For what purpose, I do not know. But if this was the case, then one must consider that it was probable that the Book agreed to its abduction. It has its own protections, after all, just as the room does."

"So in such a case, would book and thief be in the right?" Chen asked.

"That's what worries me," Mhara replied. He beckoned to Chen. "Look at this."

Chen obeyed the instruction and found himself standing before a lectern, made of so clear a crystal that it was almost invisible, had it not been for a glitter of light on its polished surface. "This was where the Book was placed?" he asked.

"Yes. You can see how easy it would be to leave a fingerprint, if one were careless."

A print would show up on this surface like a blot of soot. But this thief had been wary, if indeed, a thief there had been. The surface of the lectern was pristine.

"Are there any recording devices, magical or otherwise, in here?"

Mhara pointed up to an owlish face looking out of carved greenery. The face winked, making Chen jump.

"It sees everything and projects it onto a crystal screen in an adjoining chamber."

"Remarkably modern," Chen said.

"Yes, even Heaven occasionally adopts ideas from the human world," Mhara said wryly. "As you might have noticed . . . Anyway, the screen shows nothing. One moment the book is there, the next it is not."

"If there's this magical transportation system, then that lends some weight to the hypothesis that the Book simply removed itself—took itself down to the mountains, perhaps."

"I'd considered that," Mhara said. "But what would it do then? It has no legs of its own and its ability to transport itself on Earth would be very limited."

"So the Book might have an accomplice, then?"

"Possibly. Maybe it approached someone in a dream. Such things have been known."

"This job doesn't always lend itself to the likeliest explanation," Chen said. "Is there any way the recording device could have been tampered with? You can alter the footage on CCTV cameras, after all."

"No!" came an irritated protest from high on the wall. "Nothing changes me! I am a guardian of the Book."

Chen did not want the device to lose face and therefore did not say that it had not proved a very effective guardian, given what had happened. But he thought he might point something out, all the same. "Could the Book itself have changed you?"

A long silence, then, very grudgingly, "It's a possibility."

"I don't mean to criticize," Chen was quick to add. "But if we know it's a possibility, then it gives weight to our hypothesis."

The device lapsed into ruminative quiet as Mhara and Chen explored the rest of the chamber. There, the Emperor declared, nothing amiss, and Chen had to accept this, given the Emperor's familiarity with the room. They left soon after that—

an empty chamber, guarding nothing—but Mhara was careful to seal the doors behind him. After the room, the rest of the Palace seemed lifeless and stale.

"At least we have a working hypothesis," Chen said. "The next thing, I'd suggest, is to go to the place where that thief-turned-monk was sent, and see if the Book is there."

Mhara sighed. "I was afraid you'd suggest that. The problem is that the location is rather extensive."

"What's it called? The region where he found himself?"

"The Gobi Desert."

10

Omi spent most of that night in meditation, emerging to find a pale rosy dawn firing the sky beyond the pines. He was being watched. He could feel it at the back of his neck, as palpable as a touch upon his skin. Yet it did not feel like an enemy—it was more akin to being watched by an animal, a wolf or bear.

There were both in these mountains of northwestern China, and Omi was immediately wary. The skills in which he'd been trained were effective against ifrit or human, but he doubted whether they'd prove as efficient if he were confronted with a bear. His hand stole to the shaft of the bow and closed around it. Slowly, he rose to his feet and turned.

Both she and the bird looked as though they were made from mist. The blue tattoos that ringed her arms coiled and snaked with a life of their own and the feathers of the crane's wing fell across her shoulder, merging and shifting as the mist itself curled up the mountainside. She was watching him with an unblinking gaze, also blue, and the hair that trailed down her back was shot with indigo.

Omi's skin prickled all over again. "Who are you?"

"I am called No-one," the woman said. She was human, not ifrit or, he thought, demon.

"What kind of name is that?" Omi asked.

The woman smiled. "I traded my name for power," she said.

"That's an old magic," Omi commented.

"I'm an old magician. You may call me Raksha, if you wish. That means the same thing in my language."

"You don't look that old," Omi said gallantly, but he knew at once that she was telling the truth: there was the sense of a great presence to her, as if she carried far more than the obvious weight of her years.

"I came to find you," Raksha said. "Your name is Omi, is that not right? And you are a warrior, from Japan, trying to avenge the murder of your father at the hands of a man who should by rights be dead."

Omi grew very still. "How do you know all this?" The details of his father's murder were known, so he'd believed, to only three people: Grandfather, his sensei, and Omi himself. Now here was this supernatural stranger commenting as casually upon the core of his life as if remarking upon the weather.

"Do not worry," the woman said. "I didn't learn this from any-one living."

"How did you learn it, then?"

"I can't tell you. I made a promise."

"Are you a demon?" Omi said. He didn't think so, but after the vision of the sigil he had had earlier, it was worth checking.

"No. Well, not really. I've been—out of circulation for rather a long time. I've been sent to help you."

"By whom? Another 'no one'?"

A curious expression crossed the woman's face, half-amused, half-dismayed. "I can't tell you. I made a promise. Do you think you can trust me? My people had vows of honor, once. They're dead, but the vows remain, written on the world."

Omi considered. It wasn't a question of trust—how could he do that?—but he thought he could best her in a fight, even though she was a magician. After all, so was he, and so was Grandfather. It was two against one . . .

"What did you have in mind?" he asked.

An hour later, flying high over the glaciated summits, Omi was wishing he'd never asked. He'd flown in planes before now, but never on the back of a magical crane, holding tightly to the sinuous waist of an ancient magician and hoping he wouldn't fall off. It was, he supposed, quibbling to wonder why they both didn't freeze, although there was a rime of ice along the soles of his boots and an icicle depended from the tip of the bow like a small glass spear.

"Where are we going?" he asked, but the wind swallowed his words and Raksha did not turn her head. She had bound up her long black hair into a topknot and occasionally her sharp profile turned to the right, staring down into the mill of the clouds. When he dared follow her gaze, Omi caught glimpses of the mountains far below, but they were traveling down the range now, toward the desert: a place he had no wish to go. It seemed, however, that he'd have little say in the matter. The crane, prompted by some invisible or inaudible command of its mistress, was veering south, until the chill of the mountains ebbed and a smack of heat arose from the dry lands below. The clouds were gone, leaving a fierce blue sky. Below, Omi could see a dried-up riverbed snaking across the surface of the desert, and they were following it, still flying high, but close enough for Omi to see the patterns of the rocks and, weaving between them, the almost undetectable tracks left by the ifrits' infrequent migrations. He thought of saying something but, not knowing where Raksha's allegiances might lie, decided against it.

Raksha raised a thin hand and pointed. "Do you see?"

Omi squinted into the day. There was a smudge of gray-green on the horizon that could have been illusion or oasis.

"What is it?" Raksha did not reply. But the crane was flying fast and soon he could see the outline of groves of trees lying in the midst of humps of dry brown earth. The earth had split, leaving a cliff face rearing up over the river. Here there was a trickle of water and a series of regular rectangular holes in the face of the cliff, and all at once Omi knew where this must be.

"This is Dun Huang!" he said. A figure in saffron robes was crossing the river on a narrow bridge and this reassured him: this was a holy place, where monks lived. If Raksha was evil, then she wouldn't be coming to such a place as this. Beyond the cliff, Omi could see, incongruously, a car park. A bus was trundling out onto the dirt road that ran parallel with the river. The crane glided overhead but none of the passengers looked up, and although they passed close enough to the monk that the beat of the crane's wings would have been clearly audible, the monk continued on his serene way, smiling gently to himself.

The crane glided to a landing at the edge of a grove of trees and Omi stepped gratefully down into sudden silence. It was warm, but a breeze stirred the leaves of acacia and oak. A cuckoo called, precise and close at hand.

"It's a long time since I've been here," Raksha said. She murmured to the crane and it took off once more and sailed up into the branches, folding itself up like an origami bird.

"I've never been," Omi said, staring up at the cliff face. "I've seen photos. It's a tourist attraction now."

Raksha looked at him, puzzled. "'Tourist'?"

"Travelers."

"Ah. Pilgrims."

"More or less."

Raksha strode down to the bank of the stream and ran a hand through the clear water. Omi got the impression that she had, in some manner, learned something from it, for her expression when she straightened up was thoughtful. "Interesting," she said. "They're still here. I thought they were. I could feel them."

"Who?" Omi asked.

"The old," she said. "There's a new religion here now."

"This is a Buddhist center," Omi said. "There are some very famous statues up in those caves."

Raksha smiled. "I've heard of 'Buddhist.' When I was in Hell once, someone told me about the new faith."

"It's not all that new," Omi said, thinking, *Then how old are you?*

"The akashi were here first," Raksha said. "My cousins."

"Akashi?"

"Oasis spirits. You'll meet them, maybe. If we're lucky. Or unlucky."

"Tell me," Omi said, struck by sudden suspicion, "are these akashi the same as ifrits?"

Raksha laughed. "Oh no. They're old enemies of the ifrits." She turned and began walking along the bank of the stream. Her feet were clad in soft leather shoes, Omi noticed, and she left no footprints. He believed her in this, at least: Dun Huang was one of the holiest places of the Buddhist faith—powerful enough, surely, to keep out the ifrits.

The cuckoo called again from the trees, a clear bell-note. The monk was nowhere to be seen, though Omi glimpsed buildings through the branches. The sun was setting now, going down in burnished bronze behind the wall of the cliff. Raksha was heading toward a narrow walkway that led up to the caves. Omi followed her, not without misgivings.

11

Zhu Irzh suggested that Jhai remain at the gates of the villa and watch for anyone who might come in or out. He did not tell her that she might also need to raise the alarm if he didn't return, but Jhai flatly refused to stay behind.

"I want to see what's in there," she said. "Don't treat me as though I'm in need of protection. It's very sweet but I'm a demon, too, you know."

"A demon who has recently been seriously injured."

Jhai snorted. "What, by Lara? My cousin couldn't fight her way out of a paper bag."

Zhu Irzh forbore to mention that Lara, tiger demon turned Bollywood star turned, well, tiger, had come close to disemboweling her relative. Jhai didn't take well to tactlessness and he knew better by now than to argue with her once she'd made up her mind. "Okay," he said. "We'll both go."

They made their way cautiously down the path to the villa. No alarms sounded, nothing stirred in the dense undergrowth that had once been a formal garden. Roses twined in profusion up through the tangles of bramble, winding their coils around the overhanging branches of trees, but when Zhu Irzh came close enough to smell one, there was no odor at all, only a faint and unpleasant scent of rotting meat.

Funny, that. In fact, the whole villa had an air of decay. And there must be some reason why this prime piece of Kashgarian real estate had not been snapped up by some rising entrepreneur. The number of Mercs and BMWs cruising the streets near the hotel had told Zhu Irzh that at least some of the residents weren't poverty stricken.

When the demon reached the front steps, he paused. The veranda was sagging and the wooden boards didn't look all that safe. He picked his way gingerly up the steps. The front door was ajar.

"Want me to go first?" Jhai asked. That decided him; he still had some pride, after all.

"I'll go," Zhu Irzh replied. He pushed the door open and stepped into the hall.

Anticlimax. There was no sense of any brooding evil, no ghosts.

"Musty," said Jhai, close behind. The hall smelled as though whatever freshness might be in the air outside had failed to penetrate the building. Damp, rot, mold. Just as it had been in the dream, the hall was wallpapered in an old-fashioned floral print, interspersed with pale blue panels. But dark red stains spread upward from the skirting board and seeped over the paper like lichen.

"I can hear something," Jhai whispered, prodding the demon's arm. Zhu Irzh listened. There was a faint, low murmuring, coming from a room at the end of the hall. Zhu Irzh's skin prickled. As in the dream, he couldn't understand why this place should affect him so badly: he'd grown up in a far more sinister mansion, for Hell's sake.

At the door to the room, which was shut, Zhu Irzh stopped and listened. The whispering was louder, a susurrus like the rush and hush of the sea.

"Are you going to open it?"

He couldn't come this far and turn back now. Besides, he was curious. There was no handle, not even a keyhole. Zhu Irzh took a step back, made up his mind and kicked open the door.

The smell hit him first. It was like opening the door of a charnel house, and even the demon gagged. The room itself was dimly lit, with gas lamps burning along the walls. A long dining table extended the length of the room. Bodies lay slumped in their seats, men in military uniform, their heads shot away. Brains and scraps of flesh spattered the walls. Zhu Irzh had seen worse, but it still froze him for an instant. Then, looking down the table, he saw a man sitting at the head of it. Black eyes, a pointed black beard above a red leather tunic. The man was holding a human bone in one hand and roaring with laughter.

"Look!" he cried in accented Mandarin. "New guests for my table! Come and sit down!"

"I don't think so," the demon retorted. He grabbed Jhai by the arm and dragged her backward, just as the man reached out a hand and cast a black glowing web through the air toward them. Zhu Irzh slammed the door shut.

"Jesus!" Jhai said. "What was that all about? Didn't you like the décor or something?"

Zhu Irzh stared at her. "Didn't you see him?"

"See who? All I saw was another dusty old room in an abandoned house."

"We're leaving," Zhu Irzh said, and marched her out. He fully expected the door to burst open but it did not. They stumbled out into the early evening light, and the fetid air of the garden was, in comparison, relatively fresh. The demon leaned on the gatepost, laboring for breath.

"Are you all right?" Jhai asked. Zhu Irzh nodded, unable to speak. "This isn't like you."

"I saw a human head with an apple in its mouth served up at a table in your cousin's palace," Zhu Irzh managed to say, coughing. *"That's* normal. He's doing something, I can feel it."

"Who's doing something?"

"The bloke at the dinner table."

"What?"

"The Khan," said a voice. Zhu Irzh glanced up and was filled with relief. Nicholas stood at the gate. Despite the heat of the day, he wore a long black coat, old-fashioned in cut.

"Who *are* you?" Jhai demanded.

"My name is Nicholas," the man said. "Nicholas Roerich."

Rather to Zhu Irzh's surprise, Roerich ordered tea when they got back to the hotel, and drank it.

"I thought you were a ghost," he said.

"In a manner of speaking. I'm no longer alive, put it that way. Then again, technically, neither are you."

"I've heard your name," Jhai said. She regarded Roerich narrowly. "Weren't you an explorer?"

Roerich laughed. "Yes, I was. You might say I still am, although my field of exploration is rather wider than it used to be. When I was alive, which was in the late nineteenth century and beyond, I made a series of expeditions to Siberia, to Tibet, and to the Himalayas. I am Russian, you see. They used to describe me as a mystic, which is one way of explaining someone who does things you can't understand. In fact, I made a study of meditative disciplines and had a certain degree of experience in magic, though I kept that as quiet as I could. I painted a few things, as well."

Jhai snapped her fingers in realization. "That's it! More than a few things, I think, Mr Roerich. Your work is famous. I've seen some of it in New York."

Roerich looked modestly pleased. "Really? Yes, there is a small gallery there. It's odd, to think of one's work surviving after one's lifespan."

"Go and see it for yourself," Jhai suggested.

"I don't think that would work . . . On this plane, the Masters have confined me to the parts I knew in life. There's always other planes, however."

"The Masters?"

Roerich looked at her. "You're Indian, I think? And you, Zhu Irzh, are of Chinese origin. Some of the Masters come from your parts of the world, but they don't participate in your Heavens and Hells. They have their own realm, Shambhala. I wasted a lot of time searching for it in my youth. I should have just waited. I work for them now. I am not, you understand, a Master myself. They are those who have transcended into the other realm without dying first."

"I thought they were a myth," Jhai said, frowning. "I always associate them with dodgy old Victorians in England."

"I've never heard of them," said Zhu Irzh, feeling ignorant. "Sorry."

Roerich shrugged. "They keep themselves a secret these days, except to initiates. They've learned from their earlier experiences."

"The man in the villa," Zhu Irzh said. "This Khan. Who is he?"

"An old enemy of the Masters. He calls himself a Khan, but he was born centuries before Islam came to Central Asia. He dates from the time of the Tokarians. When you told me that someone had reanimated them, I immediately thought of the Khan."

"You came to me in a dream, didn't you?" Zhu Irzh said. He was aware of the beginnings of a powerful headache, which he resented. Demons don't get headaches, any more than they are overcome by fear and revulsion.

"Yes. The Khan's marked you."

"Oh great! How?"

"He seeks followers, throughout the centuries. Wears down their resistance until they agree to serve him. Ambitious, to try it with a demon of Mandarin Hell."

"Why does he need servants?" Jhai asked.

"Like me, he's confined to this part of the world—I understand it was a condition of his living on. You see, the Khan is like me: he was granted ascendance by the Masters, but he turned against them. They cannot rescind their gift once it's given, but that gift had the same terms that my own did—stay in the lands you knew in life. When I was a living man, before I was granted the gift, I was held prisoner here in Kashgar by the Khan. He tried to force me to obey him. I resisted, with the meditative techniques I'd learned from my Tibetan contacts. Eventually I managed to escape, but not without great difficulty. At what would have been the end of my life, the Masters came to me and told me that because of what I had done, they wished to offer me employment, against the Khan."

"If you know where he is," Zhu Irzh said, "why can't you just—I don't know, burn the villa down? Dispatch him to a Hell? It didn't seem all that well-defended to me."

Roerich smiled. "If I were to set foot in that villa now, Zhu Irzh, I would find only a deserted house with dusty rooms and a kingdom of mice. So would most people. Whatever you saw, you did so because the Khan wanted you to see it."

"I saw the Khan at dinner," Zhu Irzh said. "Eating human flesh. There were soldiers all around, all of them dead. If I'd come across it in Hell, it would have been less of a shock."

"I didn't see any of this," Jhai qualified.

"The Khan relives edited highlights of his existence. He conjures them from the astral—essentially he creates a private hell all of his own. What you saw was an episode back in the late nineteenth century when, posing simply as a local potentate, he invited a Russian general and his men to dine with him and then had them shot at the dinner table."

"What did they do—criticize the soup?"

"They did nothing at all," Roerich explained. "The Khan has acted on whim for a long time."

"And you want me to stop him?" Zhu Irzh asked. "How?"

"That's the problem. I don't know. A lot of people have gone after the Khan over the centuries but none of them have succeeded and most of them have died in the attempt. The last one was a Samurai, a Japanese warrior who managed to destroy the Khan's mountain palace, but who died at the hands of the Khan. Initially, like myself, the Khan's power came from the Masters, but they withdrew their support long, long ago, and now no one knows where he draws his power from."

"But why should he mark me?" Zhu Irzh asked. "I'm just another minor demon."

"Not anymore, you're not," Jhai said. "You're the stepson of the Emperor of Hell."

"I need your help," Roerich said. "You have access to the Khan now. You can see him, for a start. We need to find out what the Khan is planning."

The demon sighed. "You want me to go back to that villa, don't you?"

"It was the Khan's home throughout the nineteenth century. It seems he's taken up residence there once more."

"All right," Zhu Irzh said, although he wanted to say no. Perhaps it was that Roerich reminded him slightly of Chen, or simply some quality possessed by the Russian that was all his own: a kind of steely serenity. "I'll do my best."

12

The houseboat rocked and spun, as if caught on some great tidal eddy, but Inari, holding onto the wheel column for dear life and glancing down the tilting deck, could see the city outlined below them: a map of Singapore Three drawn in lights. Yet though they were high in the air, with the Earth falling swiftly away from them, all around was the sound of the sea. Immense invisible waves broke over the blunt prow of the houseboat, spattering Inari and Miss Qi with cold saltwater that just as suddenly dissipated. There was a strange smell of hollowness. All Inari could think of was the baby, but she couldn't even wrap her arms around herself to protect it; she had to hold on.

Then the city was nothing more than a line of light on the horizon and the houseboat started to shudder and shake with such force that Inari was convinced that it would be torn apart.

LIZ WILLIAMS

"We've got to abandon ship!" Miss Qi cried.

"Where to? There's no 'overboard' left!" Inari shrieked over the noise. She could see only blackness beyond the railing of the houseboat: thick and empty and cloudless. Even mist would have been a relief. But something about it was familiar, all the same.

Eventually the noise began to subside. The houseboat gave a final groan, as if in protest, and stopped, gently turning on an invisible tide. Inari and Miss Qi struggled to their feet. To Inari's intense relief, she felt reasonably well, if somewhat bruised. She didn't know what it would feel like to miscarry, but there were no internal pains. She waited for a moment, to see if anything happened, but she seemed to be all right. Miss Qi was looking at her with concern.

"Is everything well, Inari?"

"I think so." Cautiously, she made her way to the railing and looked over. A swirling cloudy dark was rushing around the sides of the boat. "This is the Sea of Night," Inari said in dismay. "What are we doing here?"

"I can't see a thing," Miss Qi called from the other side of the boat.

Inari realized Miss Qi was right. They must be very far out into the Sea: normally one could glimpse the shores of at least one of the worlds. But there was formless nothingness as far as Inari could see. And that wasn't all that was worrying her.

"Badger!"

"I am still here," the familiar said. It trundled out from behind the wheel-house, took a look over the side, and spat.

"I know how you feel," said Inari.

"But how could an ordinary typhoon take us all the way into the Sea of Night?" Miss Qi asked, then answered her own question. "So it wasn't an ordinary typhoon."

"It remains to be seen whether we've been cast adrift," Inari said grimly. "Or kidnapped."

An hour or so later, they were still calmly afloat, though it was difficult to judge here: technically they had been cast outside time. They had seen no other craft and Inari was beginning to feel prickly about this. It looked as though they had been singled out and she did not like it. Besides, the Sea of Night was much closer to Hell than Earth was, and she had no wish to see the shores of her home.

They'd tried to power up the houseboat, but without success, and Inari had not really expected any. Anger was starting to build, too, an anger that, some years ago, she would have been incapable of feeling. But only a short while ago, she had been beheaded, her spirit kidnapped into another realm, then rescued and restored to what passed for a demon for life. She did not relish the prospect of a similar thing happening again, and she was growing very tired of the fact that she and Chen and the people around them— like poor Miss Qi—were constantly being used as pawns in some greater game.

How do you think I feel? said a voice from within, and with a start Inari realized it was the voice of her unborn child. *You're not the only pawn.*

Who are you? Inari asked, thinking of transmigrating souls. The assassin Lord Lady Seijin, her own slayer, had died at last, his/her soul fled, but where to? Inside the child that Inari now carried? She did not like the thought that she might be bearing the Assassin of Worlds, Seijin's ancient title, passed down from carrier to carrier.

I will be a warrior, the child said. *You may be sure of that.*

Not reassuring in any sense. *A warrior, or just another of those pawns?* Inari asked, but the child was silent and she could feel its

73

spirit withdrawing. But it was a legitimate question. Even Mhara wasn't exempt, and look what Mhara was. Inari fought down futility and turned to Miss Qi.

"We've got to try *something*. We can't sit here forever."

"I agree," said the Celestial. "If the engines won't work, then what do we have? Magic?"

Inari nodded. "Not much choice, is there?"

They debated what to use, eventually coming up with a location spell. They already knew where they were, but the Sea of Night was vast and if they could pinpoint their location more accurately, Miss Qi suggested, then they might be able to send out a call for help. This would depend on whether they were closer to Heaven or Hell: Earth wasn't as yet much good at answering mayday calls from the great beyond.

"Although things *are* different now," Miss Qi mused. "With so many members of the Emperor's March in Singapore Three, someone might actually hear us."

"Someone might actually help, as well," Inari added. A little more hopeful, they began their preparations.

A drop of blood, from each. They watched as the Celestial's silvery life force and Inari's much darker demon blood hissed and mingled in a bowl borrowed from the kitchen. There was some comfort, Inari reflected, in being abducted along with her own home. They took a drop of night, brought up in a bucket from the Sea below and rolling around in the bottom of the bowl like a bead of thundercloud. Then, together, Inari and Miss Qi spread their hands over the bowl and spoke the spell. Blood and darkness mingled, to form a thin, blurred shape over the surface of the bowl, constantly changing: the Sea of Night itself. A tiny drop of silver showed their position, close to the exact center of the Sea. And there was something else, too, a blacker spot.

"What's that?" Inari asked.

"It's another boat!" Miss Qi said. "Maybe one of the boats that takes souls to their destination—they might be able to help us."

They peered at the spot. It was moving. Abandoning the bowl, Inari and Miss Qi ran to the railing and looked out. At first, through the swirling mist which covered the insubstantial waves of the Sea, they could see nothing. But then it appeared, its high prow carving through the mist. Unlike the craft which carried souls, it had no sails, no sign of a crew. Its sides were black and glistening, like wet stone. Traceries of gold snaked over the prow, gleaming in the light of the lantern that hung from it.

"That's one of Heaven's boats," Miss Qi said. Inari was aware of an overwhelming relief, spared from having to deal with Hell.

"Hail it—I don't want to leave the houseboat, but perhaps they could help us, or take a message—*you* could go, I don't want you to be stranded here."

"That's very kind," Miss Qi said. "But I don't want to leave you, either."

"I won't be on my own—I have the badger."

They shouted to the boat, but no one appeared on its deck. It glided in, coming closer and closer, until Inari became uneasy: it did not look as though the boat was going to stop. Maybe it, too, was adrift—perhaps the storm that had snatched the houseboat had stolen away this other craft, also, and its crew was missing. But she was becoming afraid that it would ram the houseboat.

It did not. Instead, it pulled up alongside, only three or four feet away. Now that she could see the boat more closely, it looked old. The sides were scraped and scarred, shadowy barnacles ornamented its lower reaches. It did not feel like a vessel from Heaven and when Inari stole a glance at Miss Qi's face, the Celestial's expression mirrored her own doubts.

"Maybe they've realized we're in trouble," Miss Qi said doubtfully.

"But who are they?" Inari had heard stories of pirates on the Sea of Night. Had some of these stolen a boat, taken it over? No one had appeared on its decks so far.

"There's only one way to find out," the Celestial warrior said. The boats had moved close enough together for her to step over onto the other's deck.

"I'm coming with you," Inari said. For all her brave words about the badger, she did not want to be on her own until she was sure that this strange vessel meant no harm. She thought Miss Qi might protest, but after a moment's pause the warrior said, "Very well. Be careful."

Miss Qi hopped over onto the other deck and assisted Inari's slower progress. The baby didn't greatly impede her so far but she was still very conscious of its safety.

There was a scrambling at the rail and the badger joined them. Inari was glad of its presence, but not entirely happy about leaving the houseboat uninhabited. Standing on the deck of the strange vessel, she looked about her. There was a general air of decay, but it was slight, and yet the boat had moved with such purpose . . . Was it possible that the boat itself was alive? She'd heard of such things.

Then Miss Qi dropped to one knee, her bow drawn. Inari, not being a warrior, took a moment to register that a sound had come from the interior of the wheel-house. But no further movement occurred and Miss Qi stood.

"Someone's inside."

"Or *something*."

With Inari close behind, Miss Qi strode to the wheel-house. She paused before the door for a second, listening, then kicked the door open. It opened easily, suggesting that it had not been locked. Ahead stretched a shadowy passage. Inari and Miss Qi glanced at one another and then, with the badger at their heels, went inside.

Whispers. And echoes, that sounded like snatches of old conversations, endlessly replayed. From what Inari could catch, they sounded trivial: gossipy murmurs, expressions of delight.

Miss Qi frowned. "Those sound like Celestial voices."

"You said you thought this was a Celestial ship. Could they be—well, not ghosts, but similar?" If the ship's crew had been abducted, or had to abandon the ship, maybe they'd left some trace of themselves behind. But these voices sounded more like ladies at lunch than the crew of a boat.

Then the sound came again, a scratchy shuffling. Miss Qi pointed to a door at the far end of the passage. Inari nodded and together they crept toward the door. Once more, Miss Qi flung it open, but here there was no empty hallway. A luxuriously appointed chamber lay within, smothered in heavy velvet draperies, the air thick with incense. Two glistening eyes looked out at them from a masklike face above a costume so opulent Inari wondered how the wearer could stand.

Miss Qi's mouth dropped open. She said a single word: "*Empress.*"

13

It was not entirely dark inside the cave. At some point, someone had installed electricity and now a light gleamed high on the wall, not enough to fade the irreplaceable murals, but enough for tourists to be able to see them.

"These are beautiful," Omi said. He stood, staring up at the girls and tigers and deer that danced and arched their way across the wall.

"They are akashi," Raksha said. "A time when the world was one and deer and tigers were friends."

"Has there ever been such a world?"

"There still is," Raksha said. "The afterlife of my people. I've seen it once, but only for a little while." She sounded wistful.

"But—you were dead, weren't you?"

"Our killers sent us first to Hell, then trapped our souls in our bodies. We lay there like seeds, until someone gave us the power of movement again. Some of us are still there."

"That is a terrible thing to do," Omi said.

"It was the Khan who slew us and the Khan who brought us back." Raksha looked as though she might spit. "I am tired of doing the Khan's bidding."

Omi couldn't blame her. He studied the akashi, who looked more like the erotic sculptures from Indian carvings—all breasts and pointed toes and sly knowing eyes—than Buddhist nuns, before walking on.

In the next cave, Omi found himself confronted by a face: an immense, placid, golden visage. He recognized it.

"Buddha!"

"Yes. He's the guardian of this place, so I understand. He's kept it free of the Khan's influence."

"He is lord of all," said a new voice, fluting and happy. A girl stepped out from the shadows surrounding the giant head. She wore diaphanous trousers and a short-sleeved silk top that left her jeweled midriff bare. Her long hair was piled on top of her head and decorated with scarves. Rubies winked in the light, decorating wrists and neck and ears. Smiling at Omi, she walked past him and put out a hand. Omi saw Raksha flinch, but she stood her ground.

"Like us, but not," the akashi said. She smelled of unknown magic, Omi thought, something spicy and unfamiliar, like a dust in the air.

"We have not met," Raksha said. "I am a cousin of yours."

The akashi studied Raksha, with her head to one side. "You are a Tokarian, aren't you? I thought you were all dead." She looked a little closer: Omi got the impression that she was smelling Raksha. "Ah, I see you are. My commiserations."

"I have recently been reanimated," Raksha said. "By an old enemy, the Khan."

A rumbling sound came from the giant head and Omi turned. The head was as before, quite peaceful. The akashi was frowning, but in the manner of someone who seeks to solve a problem. "Do you seek sanctuary here? You would be welcome."

"I seek aid, but not sanctuary," Raksha said. "I'm trying to take down the Khan."

"Ambitious," the akashi said. She turned to Omi. "And you. You are a Buddhist?"

"Yes. I am Japanese. I trained as a warrior. My grandfather was a Samurai, killed by the Khan. My mother raised me as a Buddhist, but I have a duty of vengeance."

"Sometimes one must fight," the akashi said.

"Sometimes, one must. Raksha has come here asking for help. Can you help us?"

"We are held here," the akashi said, sighing. "All of us desert spirits are closely attached to place; we are woven into the landscape. We akashi are bound to this temple complex, for instance. We cannot leave it—we would wither and die. If we could be freed, we could act."

"It's the same for all of us," Raksha said. "Including the Khan. You're right. Except for you, Omi."

Except for me, and someone from Hell.

"Is there a way of freeing you?" Omi asked. "It seems to me that your goals and those of the Khan are the same, but from opposite sides. He seeks warriors to do his bidding, and so do you, except that the warriors you need are yourselves."

"Believe me, we've tried," the akashi said. "This temple holds many archives—some of them were ransacked and stolen by people from the West over a hundred years ago now. But documents still remain and my sisters and I have spent years going through them in search of a spell, or anything that might liberate us. The only thing we've ever found is a mention of a charm, very far away."

"Do you know where?" Omi asked.

"There is a map," the akashi said. "It is not clear. Mice ate part of it. But I can show it to you, if you like."

Omi agreed. He was not optimistic: it seemed to him that the constant shift and change of the desert over the centuries was not conducive to information remaining the same. With Raksha in close attendance, he followed the akashi down a ladder that traversed the length of the Buddha's body. The statue was at least thirty feet high and Omi took a moment to admire its builders, their dedication in this lonely place.

The archive was housed in the back of the caves, via a passage which led through into a modern office. It was strange to see Raksha and the akashi in this contemporary setting and Omi, fearing tactlessness, was nonetheless compelled to say as much.

"Do the monks know you are here?"

The akashi smiled. "They know our likenesses adorn their walls—and even the t-shirts that they sell."

"That wasn't quite what I meant."

"They may glimpse us out of the corners of their eyes, or in their dreams," the akashi said. "But you know, these are holy men. Celibates. If they see us—well. The human mind is prone to conjuring fantasies. Especially—no disrespect—the male mind."

"I see."

"Our very nature hides us. Many years ago—more than two hundred—one of my sisters fell in love with a monk." The akashi's beautiful face betrayed sadness. "They ran away together. They did not get far. She was killed by the spell that binds us here and he pined away. Their bones lie hidden by the sand."

"A tragic story," Omi said.

"If you find a way to break this spell, Omi, you will not be the only one who is thankful for it," the akashi said. She took a handful of scrolls out of a cabinet, the parchment so fragile and ancient that Omi feared they would disintegrate within the minute. The akashi unscrolled one of the documents onto the table as Omi and Raksha looked over her shoulder.

The temple complex was outlined in a series of small black boxes. There was also a hole and, spread out across the map, scratches which indicated the desert and its environs. Omi saw hills he did not know, and finally, at the bottom of the map, faint marks.

"Those are dunes," the akashi said.

"How do you know?"

"A bird told us, on its way north." The akashi's face was sad. "They still come to speak to us, but there are fewer of them these days. The climate is changing, even in these lands."

"If they are dunes," Omi said, "they will almost certainly have altered over the years."

"That is so. The charm is held here—" She pointed to a small indigo dot. "But the oasis this represents has been here for hundreds of years—many people know about it. There is a chance that it still remains."

Raksha took Omi's arm. "You can borrow my crane, if you wish. Faster than going on foot, and safer."

He did not want to show her how afraid this idea made him. But she was right. "Thank you," he said, swallowing. "I will."

14

At night, the villa belonging to the Khan was substantially more sinister than it was by day. This cliché annoyed Zhu Irzh, who was hoping that he could use irritation to carry him through his nerves. If there was anything "sinister" around here, he thought, it ought to be him. All the same, he hesitated at the gate, trying to work out exactly what it was that had so disturbed him about this place. It wasn't that image of the Khan, seated, roaring over his dinner of human flesh, that had got to him, but some quality of the Khan himself—reanimate or whatever he might be—a voraciousness that Zhu Irzh had rarely encountered, even in Hell, where spirits could afford to be more laid-back. After all, once you were already dead, a certain degree of urgency was lacking, whereas the Khan clung to life . . .

Better get on with it. Zhu Irzh spoke the words of the concealment mantra with which Roerich had provided him.

"It's very old," Roerich had said, "but not as old as the Khan, so he might know a way round it. I'm hoping he doesn't. It's a Buddhist spell, so be careful with it, given that you're a demon."

His instructions had been precise and meticulous, and Zhu Irzh, mindful of consequences, followed them to the letter. When the mantra had been spoken the requisite three times, he waited for a moment. He felt no different, but the air smelled of an unfamiliar magic. This was encouraging; so once more, the demon made his way down the path. This time, the front door was closed and Zhu Irzh could find no way to open it. It was very tempting to give up the entire idea, go back and tell Roerich that he'd been unsuccessful. But the demon found, to his considerable frustration and annoyance, that he was as incapable of letting Roerich down as he was with Chen.

Damn.

It would be easier to let *Jhai* down. She might not forgive him, but he knew she'd understand. It was other people's disappointment that he had such a hard time with. When he got back to Singapore Three, Zhu Irzh told himself, he was going to get the number of a good demon psychiatrist and stick to therapy, even if it meant weekly visits back to Hell.

But he could see the newspaper headline now: *Emperor's Stepson Seeks Psychiatric Treatment for Attacks of Conscience.* "*I try to be evil,*" *Seneschal Zhu Irzh, aged 372, formerly of Bone Avenue, told this reporter. "But I keep suffering from attacks of sheer decency. My life's a living—oh, wait.*"

And imaginary press persecution notwithstanding, he knew he wouldn't do it, any more than he'd sought therapy after leaving Hell and taking up a new life as Chen's right hand. Time to grow up?

At this depressing thought, Zhu Irzh marched around to the

back of the building, looking for another means of ingress. He finally found it in the form of what appeared to be a scullery window, which was closed but yielded to force when shoved.

The demon wasn't remotely stout, but it was a tight squeeze all the same. He landed on the scullery floor some minutes later and looked around him. Nothing unusual. Rows of pots and plates were arranged along the shelves and the place smelled of mold. Zhu Irzh opened the door and saw a long, dark hallway, similar to the main hall of the house, but narrower.

The Khan was home. The demon could feel him. But he wasn't sure whether the Khan could sense him in return: he hoped that Roerich's spell was working. He hadn't liked to ask Roerich if anyone had tried the spell before—if it was that old, then they almost certainly had. And had almost certainly failed.

Walking on, the demon heard a faint sound to his left. He paused, listening. It came again: a knocking. But the pastel wooden panels of the hallway seemed unbroken. Mice? No, it was too loud. Cautiously, Zhu Irzh rapped on one of the panels and was rewarded with another knock.

"Push the rose!" a voice said in accented Mandarin.

Zhu Irzh looked. The panels were decorated with plaster flowers, and one of them could have been a rose. He poked it with his finger and the panel slid to the side.

"Thanks!" said the voice. A young man stepped out into the passage. A Westerner, obviously so, even in the dim light. He wore gaiters and a cream-colored jacket, and sported a luxuriant moustache. He was, from his complexion and the stains on his jacket, also fairly obviously dead.

"You're welcome," the demon said. "What are you doing here?"

"One of the Khan's guests," the ghost said. He grimaced. "Was given the chance to move on, actually, but thought I'd best stay and find out what the old monster was up to. Told the rest of the chappies I'd join them later."

"Chappies?"

"My regiment. Was with the—well, I don't suppose it matters now. Ran into the Khan's men outside Khokand. Nasty business. Most of them died. Some of us were brought here. Wasn't too pleasant after that, but luckily I don't remember much. And spying was my profession, you might say—all along the northeast frontier. So I thought I'd hang on, Queen and country and all that."

"Quite," said Zhu Irzh, who had only the faintest idea what the ghost was talking about. "And did you find anything?"

"Well, not all that much. Khan spends some of his time here, some of it in other places—Khokand, Khotan, out in the desert. Looks for victims, mainly. I've seen a good few folk come through these doors and I'm afraid very few of them have made it out again. You're not human, are you?"

"No. Demon. From Mandarin Hell."

"Yes, I've met a few of you chaps before. India was more my field of ops, though. Some funny buggers out there—four arms and all that. At least you've got the usual complement of limbs. Don't get me wrong. Not unduly prejudiced against Johnny Foreigner. Known some damn fine fellows, in fact."

"My name's Zhu Irzh," the demon said. Sometimes you had to be careful in giving people your name, but he had an instinct that in this case, it would be all right. "What were you doing in the wall?"

"Khan found me snooping about on his last visit. Normally I keep out of the way, but he lost his temper. Had me shut up there—this place is riddled with secret passages. I'd have found my way out eventually. Appreciate your help, though." He held out his hand and Zhu Irzh took it. "Name's Foyle. Rodney Foyle. So, what are *you* doing here?"

"Same as you, more or less. Can I ask you something? You can see me, yes?"

"Clear as daylight, old boy. That's a Buddhist spell you're using, of course?"

"Yes. How did you know?"

"Spent some months in a monastery up in Lhasa. Pretty much converted. Didn't tell the pater—he was very high church, you know, all bells and smells—kept it to myself. But they taught me magic. Don't know that you'd be visible to anyone else."

"I'm hoping not. I need to find the Khan. And not be visible."

"Well," Foyle said. "Let's see what we can do."

Ten minutes later they were standing outside the door of the dining room. Sounds came from within. Foyle frowned.

"Think he's got another live one, from the sound of it. Don't like it when that happens. Not cricket."

"Not what? No, never mind. This is how he renews himself, isn't it?"

"Yes. Revolting practice. Ran into a vampire up in the Torogurt Pass once, very similar sort of thing. But of course the Khan's survived for such a long time, he's very powerful."

"How does he bring them in?"

"Lures them through dreams, or has his men scout for them. Don't know how this one came in, on account of being shut up."

Zhu Irzh was entertaining thoughts of rescuing the current unfortunate, but it might already be too late.

"If you're hoping to hear anything revealing," Foyle whispered, corroborating that hypothesis. "I wouldn't bother. The Khan doesn't engage in light conversation—none of this explaining to victims why they're about to be slaughtered, or how he plans to do it. Just slits their throats and devours them."

From the noises coming from the dining room, Foyle was right.

"You stand a better chance with the war room," Foyle added.

"War room?"

"The Khan keeps a war room on the upper story of the villa. Like a library, but I've seen him planning strategy up there. Trouble is, Zhu Irzh, I can't do anything physical—can't turn pages or unfold maps. I have to go on what I hear or see. Damned inconvenient."

"Yes, it's a problem, being a ghost on the earthly plane," the demon said with sympathy. Foyle shrugged.

"Goes with the territory. Got used to it. But you—you're incarnate. Nothing stopping *you*."

"You'd better show me where this war room is," Zhu Irzh said.

"Right-o."

Zhu Irzh followed the ghost up a flight of stairs. The sounds continued from below, but there was no sign that anyone had heard them. Yet. He tried to be quiet, but even for a demon this was difficult: it was an old, creaky house and the floorboards had partially rotted through. The war room was situated at the end of the house, along yet another passage. With Foyle standing by, Zhu Irzh pushed the door open.

It reminded him of his father's study in the house in Hell: lined with books and with a huge table in the center of the room. Everything was covered with dust, except the table, which bore a number of parchments on which someone had scrawled sigils and lines that looked like hand-drawn maps. The air reeked of magic.

"Interesting," the demon murmured. He went further into the room to study a row of jars on an upper shelf. They contained what might have been fetuses, small curled ammonites in a dull orange liquid. "Foyle, do you know what these are?"

The ghost shook his head. "Not a clue, old chap. Some kind of sorcery. Tap the glass."

"Why?" But Zhu Irzh did as instructed. The fetus moved

within, a sudden squirm. "They're alive." He peered at the thing. It was blind, with small eyelids like shells. Its mouth opened feebly. "Yes. They've been here a long time. There were two fewer when I first came here."

"Hmm." If he was going to steal anything from this room, the demon thought, one of these jars would be a good candidate so far. He inspected the rest of the war room, finding that the books were all devoted to the subject of magic—at least, the Chinese editions. He couldn't speak for the many volumes in Arabic or other languages, but from the diagrams in a couple of the tomes, they, too, concerned the sorcerous arts.

"He's been looking for something," Zhu Irzh suggested.

"A way out. Power. A way to expand his influence. I've watched him, over the years."

The demon was not quite ready to tell Foyle about the reanimated Tokarians, but it seemed probable that the Khan had acted from this particular base of operations. "Have you seen him do actual magic here?"

"Oh yes, many times. The last occasion was just a day or so ago. I could feel it, not see it, because of being in the wall. But it was a big spell—made the whole building shudder. I don't know what its aim might have been."

"I think I do," Zhu Irzh replied. Foyle looked enquiring, so the demon said, "I'll explain later." He crossed to the table and started examining the manuscripts. Most of the papers made no sense, but then, toward the middle of the pile, he discovered something that did. It was in an unknown language, full of hooks and vertical lines, and someone had made notes in the margin. In Mandarin. Reading quickly, Zhu Irzh saw mention of "revivification."

"I think that's the spell," he said, and quickly explained to Foyle what had happened.

"Armies," the ghost said. "He's looking for an army. Years ago, it would have been easier to recruit—the situation was far less stable then, and some of the mountain tribes, who have traditionally done his bidding, were many in number. But now everyone's moved into the cities and the warriors are gone. The Khan needs men."

Or women, Zhu Irzh thought, remembering the shaman. Foyle turned, sharply. "What was that?"

A footstep on the stair, a distinct creak.

"Into the wall!" Foyle commanded, pointing to a second plaster rose amid the paneling. The demon pressed it and a panel slid to one side. He squeezed within and the ghost melted through the wall beside him. Zhu Irzh slid the panel back and heard the door to the war room open.

It was almost certainly the Khan. Zhu Irzh couldn't see out of the cramped, musty space in which he was hiding, but he could still hear and the muttering voice sounded familiar. He tried to keep as still as possible, hoping that the concealment spell would hold if the Khan took it into his head to investigate the wall. But why should he? the demon asked himself. As far as the Khan knew, Foyle was still a prisoner and the house was secure. He hoped.

Then the whispering began. It started as a murmur, so faint that Zhu Irzh wasn't even sure if what he was hearing was real. But the sound escalated, rising into first a litany and then a roar, until it filled the house and the demon had to fight not to cover his ears.

It was the Khan: not his voice, but his magic, and that magic was desperate. It reminded Zhu Irzh of some of the souls in Hell, the ones who hadn't yet realized how hopeless their situation was. These were the spirits who had been perpetually confined, not the human souls who would, in the fullness of non-time, be released back into the reincarnation cycle. You didn't come across them very often. They were usually to be found in the pits and dungeons of the Ministries, away from the mansions and homes of the rest of that level of Hell. And of course, one found them more frequently in the lower reaches of Hell, the endless lands where one rarely had a reason to venture.

The Khan was one such, and he wasn't even dead yet. It was the fear of that death that drove him; he had become pathological over the centuries. Zhu Irzh might be a demon, but he didn't like nutters. And now he was stuck here in the wall while the Khan's magic raved on.

Great. He didn't want to take a chance with the concealment spell, not with his inadvertent host in this kind of state. He'd just have to stay and ride it out.

15

Inari stared at the lovely, malignant figure seated before her. She'd never met the former Empress of Heaven, Mhara's mother. Although Inari had visited the Celestial Palace, the Empress had been deposed some short time before, having proved to be as mad as her late husband. Mhara would not, of course, have his mother slain, and Inari was not even sure whether this was possible—the death of the Imperial members usually meant that they were de-souled, cast from the Wheel of Existence itself.

Instead, Mhara had been faced with the necessity of his scheming mother's imprisonment and rather than having her jailed in Heaven, with the possibility that she might influence someone in the vicinity, he'd sent her into exile in the middle of the Sea of Night. Inari remembered Chen talking about it, though she had never felt able to raise the subject with Miss Qi or, of course, with Mhara himself: it would simply have been too tactless.

But now, here was the Empress, sitting like a black-eyed spider in the midst of her web, peering at Inari and Miss Qi.

"Who are you?" she asked. She had a beautiful voice to match her appearance: low and husky. "A Celestial and a demon. Have you come to visit me?"

Miss Qi dropped a perfunctory curtsey. "Madam. I'm afraid we are here by accident. Our vessel was caught in the winds of Earth and whirled here."

"Ah," the Empress said, smiling. "How unfortunate. Well, perhaps I may be able to help you. But first, will you have some tea?"

Inari was letting Miss Qi, a fellow Celestial, handle this one. She could sense Miss Qi's reluctance, but knew that the Celestial would accept, rather than risk offending the Empress.

"That would be most kind," Miss Qi said.

They settled themselves gingerly on the cushioned seats on either side of the Empress. The former ruler of Heaven wore a magnificent gown, with spreading skirts in pink and gold, like clouds, that took up most of the seating. The Empress smelled of jasmine, but there was something too sweet, too sickly about it, and Inari, used to far fouler odors, had to struggle not to recoil. The Empress raised a hand, in which was a small bell, and rang it.

It took Inari a moment to recognize the person who entered. She was slight, dressed in a formal gown, moving with small shuffling steps that suggested her feet were bound. She had a pale, oval face, the color of peach blossom, and huge, dark eyes, but both her mouth and her ears were missing and there was little expression in her limpid gaze. Across the room, Miss Qi stiffened in shock, but Inari thought only, *Clever Mhara.* Instead of supplying his devious mother with servants who might, even here, be suborned, or worse, sending her servants who needed to be punished and who would, therefore, resent their position, Mhara had looked to Earth for a solution. The mouthless drones who served the super rich had provided him with a way out. This thing had no proper sentience of its own, could not hear, and could not speak. From the distaste with which the Empress was regarding it, she did not appreciate its services.

"Tea," the Empress pronounced, bleakly.

Miss Qi and Inari murmured thanks and sipped hot oolong. Inari was becoming increasingly uncomfortable. It was clear that the Empress was both angry and mad, and despite her current status, she had once possessed a great deal of magical power. If she chose to exercise that on some nasty whim—

But then the Empress turned to Inari and gave a glacial smile.

"So. What is a demon doing in the company of a Celestial warrior?"

"Circumstances," Miss Qi said, firmly. "Much has changed in the last few months."

"It certainly has." The Empress looked at Miss Qi. "I rarely hear from my son, you know. How is he faring?"

"I have never met his August Serenity," Miss Qi said, lying with a smoothness that Inari could only admire. Deception didn't come easily to Celestials, whatever example the Empress herself might have set. "But I believe him to be well."

There was a glitter deep in the Empress' eyes. "He betrayed me, you know," she murmured.

"I'm sure he—"

"My own dear son sent me here to live. Forever." She turned to Inari. "Do you know how long forever is, little demon?"

"I—"

The Empress dropped her teacup and it shattered into a hundred shards on the wooden boards beneath her feet. Hot tea mottled the surface of her skirts like blood. The mouthless drone was instantly there, to sweep up the remains. The Empress, rising, struck the drone and sent it spinning to the floor. The drone shook its head with mechanical speed, and rose.

"I think we'd better go," Inari said.

"I agree." Together, they hastened out of the cabin, with the badger at their heels. The Empress gave a shriek of fury.

"Don't leave me!"

—but it was too late. Inari and Miss Qi sprinted down the passage and out onto the deck. To Inari's intense relief, the houseboat was still there, moored on the black heave of the Sea of Night, and within reach. Miss Qi helped her over the railing.

They stood looking back at the Empress' boat, rocking close by. Inari somehow expected the disgraced Celestial to hurtle after them, but the boat remained quiet.

"She's quite mad," Miss Qi said flatly. "I had heard the rumors, but I hadn't—well, I found them difficult to believe, even though I know the current Emperor could never lie."

"Sometimes I think we're better off in Hell," Inari said. "You expect that sort of thing."

Miss Qi looked askance. "How horrible."

"Well, it *is* Hell. And at least it comes as less of a shock."

"True enough."

One of the benefits of being on the houseboat was that they had plenty of food. With the stormy season coming up Inari kept stocks of noodles and dried mushrooms, tins of bean sprouts and water chestnuts in the kitchen cupboards. As supernaturals, she and Miss Qi could survive without food, but it was more pleasant with it and she found that cooking grounded her, providing a familiar activity in the midst of this limbo. Over a simple meal, wok-cooked on a conjured flame, they discussed their options.

These were, Inari reflected in dismay, somewhat worse than they had thought. They were stuck in the Sea of Night with the Empress' boat moored next to them, and Inari did not like the thought of such a mad and powerful neighbor.

"The trouble is," Miss Qi said, "there's nothing we can do about it. We can't move away. We can't erect a barrier, even. We've nothing to do it with and neither of us could sustain that kind of magic indefinitely."

"Mhara must keep an eye on his mother," Inari suggested. "Maybe he sends someone to check on her periodically. In that case, all we have to do is wait."

Miss Qi looked a little more hopeful at this optimistic idea, but then she said, "She must have had that boat steered next to us. I can't believe they just drifted together. That means she's plotting something."

"I agree," Inari said. "I think we should take it in turns to sleep tonight."

Miss Qi nodded. "A sound plan. I am a light sleeper. You need not fear that you will be unable to wake me up."

However, the Empress' boat remained quiet and still. Inari had offered to take the first watch, but Miss Qi would not hear of it.

"You need your rest, Inari. For the sake of the baby. Besides, if she's planning anything, it's likely to come sooner rather than later and I am a warrior. I have badger's help, too."

"I will not sleep," the badger declared. "I do not trust that woman."

"No one should," agreed Inari.

She was surprised to find, some hours later, that she had in fact fallen fast asleep. She went out on deck. Miss Qi was still sitting on the bench, staring at the Empress' boat with her bow in her hands.

"I woke up," Inari said. "I feel quite refreshed. You can let me take over the watch now, if you wish."

Miss Qi nodded. "Very well. If you're sure. Nothing's happened."

They swapped places and Miss Qi went below. Inari collected a book and took it out to the bench, while the badger remained on watch. The Empress' boat was as still as before. An hour or so passed. Inari began to concentrate a little harder on the book, rather than the boat. Then, she heard a sound. It didn't come from the boat before her, but from the cabin below. Perhaps Miss Qi could not sleep. The badger rose to his feet. "Something is wrong."

Inari could hear footsteps coming up from the cabin. They did not sound like the light, quick step of Miss Qi, but stealthy, as if the person was trying not to be heard. Very quietly, Inari rose from the bench and made her way along the deck, to hide around the corner of the cabin. The footsteps continued. She peered forward.

Miss Qi stepped out onto the deck, her bow clasped tight. Before Inari could sigh with relief, however, the Celestial turned and Inari saw that her face, normally so delicate and expressive, was somehow blank. It looked as though a grotesque mask had been placed over the Celestial's features. Beside Inari, the badger stifled a growl.

Miss Qi's head snapped up. In a second, the bow was up and drawn. She ran along the deck. Inari and the badger fled up the nearest means of escape: the ladder leading to the roof of the cabin, where Wei Chen grew herbs in pots. Inari crouched at the end of the roof. As Miss Qi, her face contorted, climbed onto the deck,

Inari stifled any misgivings and threw a pot at her. It missed, but Miss Qi dodged and in doing so fell off the ladder. There was a thud from below. Inari climbed down the ladder on the other side of the roof, heading for the kitchen, where there were pans and knives. She did not want to injure Miss Qi, but perhaps if she could stun her—

Just as she reached for the cupboard where the heavy iron frying pan was kept, an arrow sang past her and buried itself in the wall. Inari spun around. Miss Qi was notching another arrow to her bow.

This, thought Inari as she wrapped her arms around herself, *is going to hurt.*

16

This time, Omi did not have the luxury of closing his eyes. He had to keep them open, to steer the crane as it flew, according to the fragment of map given to him by the akashi. Now that Raksha had been left behind—waving from the acacia groves—Omi discovered that despite his mistrust, he now missed her. For all her strangeness, she had been a calm presence, curiously dependable. Thinking back, the fact that his grandfather had not appeared during his time with Raksha boded well. Had she been malevolent, he felt, Grandfather would have issued some degree of warning.

Assuming Grandfather hadn't been prevented from doing so.

Omi set these reflections aside and nerved himself to look down. Desert and more desert, much as it had been when he'd crossed its northern extent with Raksha. It was changing, however. The black sand and shimmering red cliffs had changed to a dusty gray. A tiny train trundled across the expanse, its tracks shining in the sunlight, and it seemed to Omi to form some demarcation line between the northern harshness and the true desert further south. What unfolded below was what Omi thought of as "desert"—high sandy dunes rolling away toward the horizon, interspersing flat expanses of sand. He grew more hopeful. He hadn't fallen off yet, and they were surely nearly there.

What would be found at the other end remained to be seen. He was ashamed of his hope, that a spell would be found, not for the sake of Raksha and the akashi, but for his own: that he would have aid and not be forced to undergo his trials alone. His grandfather and the sensei would have told him that there was no shame in seeking aid, but Omi was young enough to feel it all the same, and old enough to recognize it in himself.

He'd be glad when they landed for purely practical reasons, too. Magic had its limits. His throat was parched and his eyes tired from squinting into sun and dust. He was aware of a cramp too, but reluctant to shift about too much on the crane's back. So he concentrated on the land instead, and on the indigo-cerulean-sapphire feathers of the beautiful bird on whose spine he perched.

After a while, he began to fear that he'd missed the spot where the pagoda lay. The dunes all looked the same, and Omi had the dismaying impression that you could just fly round and round and never spot it. But then they passed over a high ridge of dune and the crane gave a croaking cry. A black spire rose from the desert, in front of a crescent lake of startlingly clear hue. There was a line of trees. It looked, in the middle of that dusty expanse, a cool and inviting place. Omi, overcome with relief, directed the crane downward.

Climbing from its back, he was immediately struck by the silence. There was no wind. The desert was completely still, not a grain of sand moving. Omi, enchanted by the quiet, walked down to the shore of the lake, which curled in its half-moon shape around the base of a dune. It was close to sunset now and the sky was a deep green, like water. Omi knelt and ran a hand through the water of the lake: it was cool to the touch and not at all stagnant. Toward the center of the crescent, a school of fish flicked and were gone.

Omi took a deep breath and released it. There might be enemies here, but he found it difficult to believe. He turned and studied the pagoda. Dark wood and stone, a sturdy construction. A white pennant, quite plain, drooped from its peak, and he glimpsed a great bronze bell. A long gallery led around the interior of the pagoda, surrounding what was obviously a courtyard. Omi walked toward the pagoda and just as he reached the oak doors which lay beneath the gallery, the bell clanged once, making him jump. His hand reached toward the bow, then away.

No voice spoke, and yet Omi knew that he had to explain himself. Aloud, into the desert silence, he said, "I have come from the akashi. I am in need of help."

The doors opened, creaking with age. Omi hesitated, then went inside. The courtyard was also quiet. An immense stone basin stood in the middle of it, and Omi could smell incense. He looked around the upper stories of the gallery but there was no one to be seen. Then a voice spoke, clearly, into his ear, "Come."

"Where are you?"

"Go up."

Spotting a flight of steps at the far end of the courtyard, Omi did as he was told and found himself on the wooden boards of the gallery.

"The third room," said the voice.

Very well. Omi walked along the gallery to the third door, and entered.

The room was empty. The door seemed to be its only entrance, for there were no shutters. Black-paneled wood shone in the light of a single lamp, casting shadows to all four corners of the room. A book sat on a small lacquered table, its crimson covers stiff with age.

Omi had not been trained for nothing. He said to the book, in amazement, "You spoke to me!"

"Yes," said the Book. "I am alive."

"Are you a book of spells?"

"I am a book of *making*," the Book said. "Why have you come here?"

"I'm looking for help," Omi said. He told the book about the Khan, about the akashi.

When he had finished, the Book said, "Sit down."

Omi did so, on a small bench to the right of the table.

"Do not touch me," the Book warned. "I can unmake you."

Omi, who would in any case have considered it an unpardonable liberty, assented.

"Lean forward," the Book said. "And watch."

Omi did as he was told. Later, he thought how naïve he had been, but it had not even occurred to him to disobey. He watched as the book's cover opened and he was, immediately, within the land.

It was as though he had been disembodied and stretched out. He was everywhere at once, standing on the glacial summits of the mountains above Urumchi, amidst the grit of the desert dust in the deepest Taklamakan. He was water in a pool in the Imperial palace, far to the east, and a spire of rock above a winding river. He was city and stone and forest.

When the Book snapped shut, Omi reeled back, gasping and fighting for breath.

"Now," the Book said. "Do you see what I am?"

"You're—everything?" Omi corrected himself. He wasn't thinking straight. "You're China?"

"I am the Book of the land, and of Heaven, which mirrors the land. I told you. I can make and unmake."

"How old are you?"

"I came into being when the land came into being. I have had other shapes," the Book explained.

"So—if you are the land, and you can—create it? You can change things, yes? Could you change a land-based spell?"

"If you want to do that," the Book said, "then you must enter the land and do so yourself. That is the price you must pay."

"How do I do that?"

"I will show you," the Book said.

He stood at the edge of the desert. It was night, and the stars burned and blazed like fire. Behind him, the little lake and the pagoda were invisible, but he knew they were there. Deep within, he also knew that he was still sitting in the third room of the gallery, while his consciousness ranged through the world that the Book contained.

"Choose your shape," the Book said.

"I don't—" Omi started to say.

Then there was a blur in the air and Grandfather was standing before him. He bowed—not to Omi, the latter realized, but to the Book. "Thank you for permitting my humble presence."

"You're welcome," the Book said mildly.

To Omi, Grandfather said, "Our ancestors came from the

north, from the mountains. *This* was their totem." He extended a hand and a snow leopard appeared, pacing.

"Then I choose," Omi said. Immediately he felt his muscles begin to shift and change, his face elongating, the bristle of fangs within his gums. His fingers prickled, became claws. Omi dropped to all fours.

"Now go!" Grandfather said. Omi raced out into the desert, splayed paws scattering sand. Even at the height of the sensei's training, he had never felt so connected to everything else: this must be what it was like to be an animal, a sense of place so strong that little else was needed beyond the basic drives of food and mating. Territory was part of this, and so was the maintaining of it. For the first time, Omi, with his remaining fragment of human awareness, understood that self-consciousness is a two-edged sword, dividing us from the world as greatly as it allows us to comprehend ourselves.

But leopards don't do reflection. Omi ran on and the landscape of the Book unfolded and flowed around him, coalescing and condensing.

He needed to find the spell itself, the spell that bound Raksha and the akashi to *place*. He didn't know what it looked like, or how it smelled. He would, the Book had told him, know it when he came across it, but Omi was doubtful. However it was not, he had been given to understand, in the caves where the akashi lived. It had been cast out, and then taken away, to make sure that they could not stumble across it, and reverse its effects.

But where? With all China to look in, Omi's spark of consciousness felt despair. He had to trust the Book to give him a clue, and indeed, the Book did. Coming up over the next ridge, Omi saw a forest spreading below and the distant gleam of mountains far beyond. Omi stood on the ridge and searched. An odd smell on the wind—magic?—and the glitter of light amid the trees. Omi headed down, bounding over the boulders to the treeline, and soon was among groves of trees he did not recognize. Orchids hung in clusters on the branches, and the stars shone high above, and yet somehow it was not a beautiful place, but sinister. It felt anomalous and wrong, inserted into the natural world of the Book like a page from another, darker text. Omi's fur prickled as he headed toward the light, and then he came out into a clearing. A building stood there: a squat stone temple. The statues of two demons stood by its entrance, scimitars upraised.

Except they weren't statues. As soon as they caught sight of Omi, they roared and charged forward. Omi, warrior though he was, might have been tempted to take flight into the trees, but not so his totem. He gave a snarl and threw himself under the nearest blade, catching the demon around the waist with his spiked paws. Disemboweling proved to be a brief and exhilarating process, Omi turning over as he'd seen the temple cats do. One kick and the demon lay still. That left the second one, and Omi made another choice. He snapped back into human shape, picked up the fallen demon's scimitar, and clashed blades.

The demon was massive, like a boar. Its tusked face snarled, its little pig eyes glinted. It gave a grunt as Omi's blade met its own. Its sheer strength made Omi stagger backward, catching his foot on a log. Rather than trying to save himself, Omi went down into a roll and then back up, just under the demon's blade. He scythed out with the scimitar and even at this limited range it bit through the demon's armor. Hissing golden blood spilled forth and Omi stifled a cry as it burned his hand. He feinted, the demon struck and the blade whistled past Omi's ear as Omi brought his own blade around and struck off the demon's head.

The demon chuckled soundlessly as his head flew across the

glade, scattering drops of gilded fluid, and kept chuckling when it landed. The little black eyes were still alive, filled with greedy humor. He watched Omi as the warrior ran toward the temple steps. Glancing from right to left, Omi sprang into the building.

Once inside, it took him a moment to find his bearings. The temple seemed much larger than it had from the outside, an echoing hall whose columns reached into the distance. Used to magic, Omi was wary but not deeply perturbed. He did not, however, know where to start looking. Now that his eyes had adjusted to the low light, he saw that it was less a temple and more of a library. Books lined shelves along both sides of the room, leather-bound texts and ancient scrolls and parchments. It even smelled like a library, despite the statue of a god at the end of the room. After his experiences with the last lot of statues, Omi wasn't going to take any chances. With the scimitar still in his hand, he made his way toward the god.

He was not very familiar with the Chinese pantheon, but there was something recognizable about the figure that sat on the plinth at the top of the hall. He'd seen it before—Omi searched his memory and at last recalled the occasion.

A side street in Singapore Three, a baking, broiling summer day. Omi had been sent to the city on a mission for the sensei and he was not enjoying the experience. It was a long way from the cool and the quiet of the mountains. With a sigh, Omi thought of the pine-scented breeze and the breath of snow, and as the heat and dust and the smell of badly maintained drains threatened to overwhelm him, he came across a temple.

It was a small place, much older than the city that surrounded it. Singapore Three had roared up in a handful of years, swallowing the little villages and townships that had scattered the shore, but fragments of them still remained, persisting in between the high rises and tenement blocks like old teeth in a row of gleaming new dentures.

This temple was no exception. Its façade was wooden, covered in bleached and peeling blue paint. But incense smoldered up from the little shrine by the door and there were fresh flowers in a vase. The temple was still alive. Omi thought of darkness and peace and pushed the door. It opened soundlessly, and inside were statues to two gods: the God of Writing and the God of War.

The deities glowered at one another, as if displeased at being obliged to share living space (later, Omi discovered that this actually was the case, and in the world-beyond, Writing and War rarely spoke to one another, one being in Hell and the other in Heaven, and then only under protest). Their sharing the temple had come about through lack of funds and planning permission, apparently, but whatever the reason, here the two were, glaring at one another.

Now, in another realm entirely, Omi found himself standing before the God of Writing, in his own lavish temple. He bowed.

"You fought my demons," the god said in a voice like a bell. "Impressive. Are you a warrior?"

"Yes. From Japan." Best get that out of the way immediately, Omi thought. He didn't know how a Chinese god would react to a Japanese warrior.

"And you are a cat?"

"It is my totem."

"I see. Why did you come here?"

"I came to search for a spell," Omi said. He explained.

"And you were sent by a *book?*" The God of Writing had a smooth bronze face, quite impassive. Omi could not tell where the voice was coming from, since the god's lips did not move.

"Yes."

"Very well," the god said. "I know the spell you mention."

"You do?"

"But of course," the god said, and though he did not move, Omi somehow had the sense that the statue had leaned forward and was wagging an admonishing finger at him. "However, I cannot simply let you have it."

Battling demons wasn't enough? No, probably not. Omi inclined his head. "I understand."

"Of course," the god echoed. "You are a warrior. But I shall not ask you to fight anything else. That would, I think, be too easy. You have an hour to find the spell."

"In here?" Omi faltered, looking around at the thousands upon thousands of books. *Demons, now! Bring them on!*

"Just so," the god said.

"But—" Omi began.

But the god was already starting to fade, becoming a bronze shimmer on the air. "Wait!"

The god was gone. And Omi was left in a library, with an hour's chance of success.

17

The Khan was never going to stop reciting his damned spell, Zhu Irzh thought. He was starting to feel cramped inside the wall and there was a shooting pain along the calf of his left leg, wedged into the paneling. Foyle didn't know how lucky he was, being a ghost. The spell went on and on and then, abruptly, someone screamed.

Zhu Irzh didn't think it had been the Khan.

The spell stopped, so suddenly that the demon could almost see a void opening up in the air, into which words had fallen.

If you could describe the Khan's recitation as "words." "Raving" would be more appropriate.

"Ah!" The Khan's voice was filled with satisfaction. Something had worked. Zhu Irzh dreaded to think what it might be.

The Khan said something unintelligible and then there was a curious change in the atmosphere, almost like a decrease in pressure, and the slam of a door.

"He's gone," Foyle said, materializing beside the demon.

"At bloody last!" Zhu Irzh hauled himself back through the panel. He might not have been able to see what had happened in this room, but it hadn't been pleasant. Someone had died. Blood spattered the walls and floor and was already beginning to attract flies. The whole place smelled sour, reeking of stale magic: as though the Khan had let all the spells that had ever been done in this room accumulate, building up like a residue.

Messy. "I'm taking these back with me," Zhu Irzh said. He picked up a fragment of parchment which still lay on the table, and one of the jars containing the fetuslike thing. He wrenched open the window and stepped out onto the balcony. "Foyle, look—I don't know if there's anything I can do. For you, I mean. I can't promise to help you."

"Perfectly all right, old boy. I know you'll do your best." Somehow, this breezy confidence in his willingness to help lodged in what the demon was displeased to call his conscience. He would do his best, he knew, just as he would for Chen, or for Roerich. Was this how obligation worked? Snaring you in its threads like a web? But Zhu Irzh could not bring himself to resent it too deeply. He supposed it was known as maturity.

"I'll—" What? Be in touch? "Hopefully, we'll meet again soon. In better circumstances." He swung one leg over the balcony rail and dropped into the shrubbery. A feral shrieking came from the jar. Holding it up, the horrified demon saw the fetus' mouth open wide and the scream bubbling up through the liquid in which it was contained. Zhu Irzh flung the jar into the bushes and ran. He had a last glimpse of Foyle's forlorn figure fading out of sight above him and then the ghost was gone. Zhu Irzh sprinted down the path and into the night of Kashgar.

"I was starting to get worried," Jhai said. She sat with her legs curled underneath her in one of the hotel's armchairs.

"Frankly, so was I," Roerich said. "You were gone a long time."

"I got—stuck. He was doing some sort of spell. I had to hide. There was a ghost there." Zhu Irzh told them about Foyle.

Roerich winced. "I doubt he's the only spirit who's trapped there."

"I'd like to help him, if I can."

"There are a great many people in need of help," Roerich said. He leaned forward and rubbed his forehead. "What else did you discover?"

Zhu Irzh explained about the parchment and the jar. "It was probably stupid to try to take it."

"That's the trouble," Roerich said. "The Khan uses ancient magic. It's hard to tell what's advisable and what's not."

"I did get this," Zhu Irzh said and held out the parchment.

"It's a reanimation spell," Roerich said, after a moment. "I think it's a translation. It doesn't look like Chinese magic to me. Something Central Asian, maybe."

"Wherever it comes from," Zhu Irzh said, "I got the feeling it worked."

Later that night, the demon found it impossible to sleep. He lay beside Jhai, staring into the dark and dreading more dreams. Roerich had departed, promising to return in the morning. Zhu Irzh wished he could talk this over with Chen, but all he could get hold of was the answering service, and Inari's mobile seemed to be switched off as well, which was unusual. He had Jhai, but she was no wiser than he was, having access to the same set of information.

So he was left with the night and his own thoughts. Years ago, he'd have shrugged off the actions of the Khan as yet another supernatural power play. It happened. It was just what people did. But now, it seemed like a violation. The demon was aware of an unfamiliar sense of anger—on behalf of Foyle, on behalf of the unknown person whom the Khan had murdered that night.

Eventually, thinking he might wake Jhai, he got up and went over to the window. The streetlamp outside poured in a sulphurous orange glow. A flicker of movement caught his attention and Zhu Irzh turned. There was something in the corner of the room—a rat? Zhu Irzh raised a hand, started to summon up a spell. Not a rat, but a little crawling thing with a tapering tail, its mouth gaping, showing sharp teeth—as Zhu Irzh threw the bolt of the spell, the thing leaped and as it did so, it grew. Zhu Irzh went down under a mass of claws and teeth and leathery wings. Cursing, he struck up at it, knocking the long, fanged head to one side. Then there was a roar from the bed and a tiger form threw itself on top of Zhu Irzh's assailant.

The creature screamed and black blood fountained from its slit throat. The tigress clouted it with a massive paw and it collapsed, shrinking into itself like a punctured balloon. Its blood hissed into steam. Soon, there was nothing left except a small, limp scrap on the smoldering carpet.

"What," said Jhai, sliding back into human form, her stripes fading, "was *that*?"

"That," Zhu Irzh replied, "was the contents of the Khan's jar."

18

Miss Qi, her bow notched and ready to fire, collapsed slowly onto the deck. Her eyes were quite blank as she fell face-down and lay still.

Inari stared. It took a moment before she saw what had stunned the Celestial warrior: a small silver sphere. It rolled to the side of the deck and lay against the railing. Inari looked wildly around, trying to trace where it had come from and who had fired it—for it was clearly a weapon. Nothing, and then there was a flutter of shadow high on the mast of the Empress' vessel.

Inari stared. The shadow was definitely moving.

"Who's there?" She ran across the deck to Miss Qi and hastily checked her. The warrior still retained her spirit and Inari felt a wash of relief that Miss Qi had not been sucked back to Heaven. Selfish, she thought, but at least Miss Qi did not appear permanently damaged. There was a flutter of night and someone descended to the deck.

"Who are you?" Inari asked.

"I might ask you the same," the figure said. It was hard to tell what it was: crimson eyes peered out from beneath a long hood, and the remaining garments looked as though they had been cut out of black mist. It was difficult to see directly. But the voice, unless she was greatly mistaken, was female.

"My name is Inari," Inari said.

"You're a demon. But she isn't—although she is possessed. She was trying to kill you. If I'd realized you were a demon, I might have let her."

"I'm glad you didn't," Inari said. "I've been killed once already in the last few months. Who are you?"

"I am Shoth." The figure shifted position and Inari saw that it was carrying a sling. "I am a guard of the Empress."

"We don't mean her any harm," Inari said.

"I'm not guarding her from other people," Shoth said. She pushed back the hood, revealing a face as black as her garments. She was like, and yet unlike, a demon. Long curving fangs extended over her lower lip and her red eyes had small black pupils. She was entirely hairless. "I'm protecting others from her."

"I hope I'm not being rude," Inari said, "but what *are* you?"

"The Emperor of Heaven called us in from elsewhere," Shoth said. "We were held not to have local loyalties."

"You're a mercenary?" Inari said.

"In a manner of speaking. Our own Empress, the goddess Oshun, is being rewarded for our work here. So, little demon. What are you doing here?"

Inari told her. On the deck, Miss Qi gave a groan and stirred.

"Stand back," Shoth commanded.

"Don't hurt her. She's my friend."

Shoth gave her a curious look. "A strange alliance."

"It's a long story."

"What—oh." Miss Qi sat up and put a hand to her head. "I remember being below, and then—"

"You were possessed," said Shoth. "How do you feel now?"

"Groggy. Who are you?"

Shoth told her, while Inari cast an uneasy glance at the Empress' vessel. "If you're the Empress' guardians," she said, "where were you when we boarded?"

"We were summoned away. There were pirates."

"There *are* pirates on the Sea of Night? I've heard of such a thing."

"They come in from other systems," Shoth said, as Inari helped Miss Qi to her feet. "They always make for the Empress' boat, believing it to contain riches. It doesn't, of course."

"If you're assigned to the Empress' boat," Inari said, "then maybe you could help us detach our own craft."

Shoth nodded. "You can't stay here. But equally, you won't be able to travel over the Sea of Night under your own power. Only we are granted that ability, and the ships of the Sea itself that travel between Heaven and Hell, and the pirates from elsewhere. Anything stranded here stays stranded."

"Then how are we to get out?" Miss Qi asked.

"The boat belonging to the goddess Kuan Yin is due shortly—it travels between the worlds, transporting souls. It might be able to tow you. You may end up going home the long way round, though."

"I don't really care," Inari said. "As long as we *get* home. Besides, Kuan Yin has helped us in the past—she was my husband's patron."

"*Was?*" Shoth said.

"He is now independent, but with her blessing. You may ask her yourself, if you choose."

"How long will the boat take to get here?" Miss Qi asked.

"Not long," Shoth said. She turned her red gaze on Inari. "You are pregnant. With a warrior."

Inari put a hand to her stomach.

"One of the warriors of the age," Shoth said. "A fighter in the coming war."

"Which war is that?" Inari faltered. Having recently emerged from a war between Heaven and Hell, she wasn't sure that the three worlds would survive another conflict.

"The great war, with the star people."

"*Star* people? Do you mean aliens?"

Shoth looked irritated. "I mean what I say. I'll send a message to the goddess' ship." She turned on a spiny heel and was gone in a shuffle of shadow.

Miss Qi put a hand to her head. "An efficient weapon, that sling. I think I'd better sit down."

Inari was relieved to know that they might soon be going home. "I'll put the kettle on," she said.

Three cups of tea later, Miss Qi spotted a sail. By now almost fully recovered, she ran across the deck, followed by Inari.

"Let's hope it's Kuan Yin's ship, not pirates."

"It is the goddess' boat," Inari told her. "I recognize it."

Even from this distance, the pale, shell-speckled shape of the goddess' craft was unmistakable. Fearing misunderstandings, they did not hail it, but waited until Shoth had come back on board. Inari was pleased to see her. She could still feel the malign, arachnid presence of the Empress, squatting at the heart of her web, spinning out spells. Kuan Yin's boat glided swiftly over the surface of the Sea of Night, trailing a phosphorescent wake behind it. Soon, it was rocking alongside the houseboat.

Shoth stepped onto the houseboat's deck while behind her, on the Empress' vessel, more shadows clustered and congregated. Red eyes glittered in the darkness. There was no sign of anyone on board the goddess' boat, but Shoth flung a line from the houseboat over its side and the line held taut.

"Are you ready, Inari?" Shoth called.

"I think so," Inari replied. She did not know how much she would have to steer, and she was expecting interference from the Empress' vessel despite the presence of the guards, but to her great relief they began to pull away from the side of the Empress' boat.

Miss Qi came to stand beside her as they sailed. "How are you feeling?" Inari asked.

"Pale," said Miss Qi, with a shiver. "I'm glad to be away from there." She looked over her shoulder across the black expanse, to where the Empress' boat still wallowed. "Being possessed was— not pleasant."

"It rarely is," Inari said.

"I could feel her in me," Miss Qi went on, after a pause. "She's *rapacious*. Like a vulture."

"She is quite mad," Inari reminded her.

"But that someone like that could be Empress of Heaven—" the Celestial warrior said, shivering again. "Inari, I cannot help thinking—what if this is something to do with the nature of the role itself?"

"What happened to the Emperor before last?" Inari asked.

"It was many thousands of years ago by human reckoning. I don't remember him, of course—I am not that old. He ascended peacefully off the Wheel of Existence, amid great honor."

"Well, there you are," Inari pointed out. "The Lords of Hell rarely last that long. They go up and down like yo-yos between the levels—there are constant coups."

"But—with all due respect to yourself, Inari—that is Hell. For Heaven to be so beset—what if Mhara—" She broke off, unable to continue.

Inari smiled. "I don't think Robin would let him," she said.

Kuan Yin's vessel sailed on, towing the little houseboat slowly behind it like a tug, reversed. The boat of the former Empress of Heaven receded into the distances of the Sea of Night and that was the last they'd see of *her*, Inari thought to herself.

She was, of course, wrong.

19

It was not so much like being in a library, Omi thought, as attending a particularly crowded party. Far from keeping their secrets locked between their covers, the books seemed to recognize that he was in need of help, and they all clamored at once—all offering advice, assistance, and aid. He could barely hear himself think in amongst the tumult.

He moved to the end of the shelves in an effort to be systematic, but it was not the end after all, although Omi could have sworn that when he'd entered the room, there had been a single rack of shelves running along the walls. Now, he found himself amid seemingly endless stacks, which receded into the distance. The library was a Library indeed. And he kept getting sidetracked by interesting volumes, which didn't help.

It would be an old text, he knew. Maybe not even a book at all, which narrowed things down. And often, libraries were organized in terms of age, with the older books at the back, in a more secure location. So this is where he headed, walking swiftly past books that, indeed, looked more and more ancient as he went. Then, with a mixture of relief and panic, he realized that he had come to a dead end. The stacks briefly opened out into a room, then closed again.

Here, there were cabinets, but only a few books stood within them. Encouraged and hopeful, Omi started to search, but the books and scrolls were all written in languages that he could not read, and unlike the texts in the main section of the library, their voices were silent. He tried, cautiously, to open one of the cabinets, but the lock would not budge.

Omi stepped back to consider his options. He went round the room again, hoping that this time, something would spring out at him, that there would be something he'd be able to comprehend. But there was nothing.

And then he looked up. Above the cabinets hung what he had originally thought to be pictures. But one of them wasn't simply a representation of trees, a river, mountains. It was a map, encased behind glass. Omi looked closer and, with a shock, saw the whole of his journey—not as a flat two-dimensional graphic, but as it had happened. The pavilion by the crescent lake was perfect in miniature. He could almost smell the breath of heat-soaked air, the coolness from the lake. There was Omi himself, a tiny leopard bounding through the convolutions of the forest, and here was the temple of the God of Writing. Omi reached out a hand, expecting warding, but the map allowed him to take it down from the wall and detach it from its case. It even rolled itself up for him, obligingly.

As soon as he tucked it inside his waistband, Omi had the disconcerting impression of being in several places at once. He was still in the library—he could see its outlines beyond the walls of the room in which he stood—but he was also aware of the forest, of the distant peaks, and then the great hum of the desert. The library was, he realized, contracting in upon itself, just as it had previously expanded, and that meant he had to get out of it.

Be careful, the map said in a small, clear voice, and he recognized it for the voice of the Book itself, speaking through the text he held. Did the Book somehow hold a connection to all books, a kind of ur-text? Or was it Omi himself who was the link? He did not know, and he realized that he did not have the time to find out. He sprinted back through the stacks, which were indeed contorting around themselves, and into the main chamber of the temple.

The God of Writing stood before him, blocking his way. The god held a book in his hands.

"Before you can go," the god said, implacably firm. "What is it that you have found?"

Omi was about to tell the god the literal truth: that he hoped he'd located the spell that held the akashi to one particular spot. But instead, there was a whisper in his ear: Grandfather's voice, a breath only, but Omi knew what his ancestor meant.

"Knowledge," he said. "The most valuable thing of all."

The god bowed his head and was gone, fading out into smoke and streamers of mist, and the temple was similarly evaporating around him, swirling up into the night sky.

Omi stood alone in the forest, clutching the scroll. But not alone after all, he realized over the course of the next minute. Something was coming through the trees, crashing through branches and sending pine needles in a shower ahead of itself. A second later, he caught the characteristic electric-spice odor of an ifrit. He put the scroll between his teeth and changed, narrowing and arrowing down into a snow leopard once more, and then Omi started to run.

20

Chen returned from heaven to Singapore three via Mhara's own temple, stepping out into thin, spring sunlight that was freshened with a breath of air from the sea. The colors of Earth always seemed wrong after those of Heaven, and Chen tried to work out why this was so: the Celestial Realms were rich, but mostly muted, and Earth seemed too garish, too glaring, too—*uncoordinated*. He blinked as he stepped into the temple's small courtyard, a place he could not now enter without a shudder of memory. It was here that Seijin, the Lord Lady assassin, had struck off Inari's head, and Chen doubted whether he'd ever recover from that particular shock. Things had come right again, but all the same . . . he was looking forward to getting home.

Robin, Mhara's priestess on Earth and de facto wife, was nowhere to be seen as he walked through the little courtyard, but just as he stepped though the gate which led to the city beyond, she appeared. She was a little spectral herself in the sunlight, slightly patchy. Quite often, Chen forgot that Robin was herself a ghost, and it felt odd to be reminded of this fact. She wore her usual temple whites, a loose shirt and wide trousers that reminded him of hospital scrubs. But the sneakers on her feet were contemporary and casual enough.

"Hi, Robin," he said. "Hope I didn't startle you—did the Emperor tell you I was coming back?"

"I've been trying to reach him," Robin said with a frown, "but no one seemed to know where he was."

"I think that was because we were in—well, anyway, we had some business to attend to," Chen amended. "Is something wrong?"

"Come back inside," Robin said, and Chen was aware of an all-too-familiar finger of ice beginning to trickle down his spine. He followed her back into the temple and then Robin closed the door behind him.

"Chen, I'm awfully sorry. Please try not to worry, but I don't have very good news."

"Inari?" the finger of ice felt more like a flood. "The baby?"

"They're missing," Robin said. "There's been a typhoon—the boat's disappeared."

"But when I left—"

"It blew up out of nowhere. Took the meteorological organizations completely by surprise and I didn't hear anything of it, either. Normally, we get to learn about untoward things before they happen, but this was so *sudden*, Chen."

"What do you mean, exactly—*disappeared*? Has it been blown out to sea?" His thoughts were racing. In that case, perhaps the coastal authorities—but Robin interrupted his train of reasoning.

"There's no sign of it. Inari must have been sailing it toward the typhoon shelter—there was helicopter camera footage of the boats. But then the chopper had to pull away—too dangerous—and when it was calm again, which apparently was literally within minutes, according to the eye witnesses, your houseboat was gone. They're certain it didn't sink."

"Then—where?"

"That's what we're trying to find out," Robin said. "If I can contact Mhara, I'm sure he'll be able to help." But Chen remembered as well as Robin did that, previously, on the occasion of Inari's killing, the Emperor had been as helpless as any of them.

"All right," he said, because Robin was only trying to help. "I ought to contact the station, speak to Lao and Ma. Maybe the authorities at the typhoon shelter could help. Lao might also be able to do a location spell."

"Do what you need to do," Robin said. "We haven't heard from Miss Qi, either. I think she must have been with Inari—I know she was planning to visit."

Robin pulled open the door to the courtyard once more and a pale green radiance, like watery jade, flooded in.

"What—?" said Robin, open-mouthed. But Chen knew at once who was standing in the sunny courtyard.

"It's you," he said. *Or, at least, an avatar of you.* The figure who stood before him was not quite the goddess he remembered. Still beautiful, still serene, and yet slightly changed, not diminished, but—just not the same. She blinked sea-colored eyes.

"Hello, Wei Chen," the goddess Kuan Yin said.

There was, it seemed, a considerable degree of etiquette involved in visiting someone else's temple. Especially, Chen reflected, a someone who was effectively your boss. Kuan Yin might have been an elder deity, but she was still subject to the will of the Emperor of Heaven, and it took a few moments of raised eyebrows and significant throat clearings before Robin took the hint and formally invited her over the threshold.

"I must apologize, my lady," Robin said, mortified. "We don't often have visitors of your stature."

"Not even gods can go exactly where they please," Kuan Yin said, with the faintest note of apology. She rustled into a chair proffered by Chen and accepted a cup of tea. She looked smaller than Chen had remembered.

"I have come because of your wife." Was there the faintest trace of disapproval in her voice? Chen could not tell: Kuan Yin, Goddess of Compassion and Mercy though she may be, still retained a capacity for expressionlessness that rendered her inscrutable. But she had withdrawn her support from him when Chen had married Inari, a clear and obvious sign of disapproval. One cannot expect one's patron Celestial to sanction marriage to a demon, after all. At this memory Chen, although he had understood at the time and still did so, felt a distinct twinge of anger, and at this the goddess glanced up.

"Inari's missing," said Chen, feeling hollow.

"In fact, that is not true," the goddess said, and sipped her tea. "She is sailing the Sea of Night, along with her own familiar and your Celestial friend."

"The Sea of—"

"I'm afraid there are forces at work which have conspired to snatch your wife from Earth," Kuan Yin said.

"My wife?" Chen asked sharply. "Or our child?"

"Ah," the goddess said. "She is safe, you should know that. There we come to the crux of the matter. Few might concern themselves only with a little demon. But Inari has contacts—" Here she looked at Robin, and Chen knew that she was referring to Mhara, "—and powerful ones, these days."

"Mhara," Robin echoed. "And Jhai, and Zhu Irzh—his stepfather's the new Emperor of Hell. I can see why Inari might be important as a game piece." She grimaced.

"Precisely so," the goddess said. "And I must tell you that there are also—intimations—of events to come."

"What sort of events?" Chen asked. He didn't like the sound of that.

"Rumors of war."

"With whom?" Robin asked in dismay.

"I do not know. Your husband will have heard of them, but even he may not know more. The rumors are very faint and do not originate in our own universe. They may yet come to nothing—such things have been known before. But your child, Wei Chen—your child will be a warrior."

"It's the same spirit, isn't it?" Chen asked, with a sinking feeling. "Seijin?"

"Not so much the same spirit. This is not a case of possession. It is more the role that gets handed down through the generations—a warrior for the world. Seijin occupied the last such role, but over the years became mad, unable to reconcile the male and the female self."

"That mustn't happen to our child," Chen said, but he didn't know if it could be prevented. "Are they always hermaphroditic?"

"Usually."

"So someone wants—what? The child itself? Or to make sure it doesn't come to term?" It seemed grotesque and awful to be discussing it in such cold and clinical terms, but he had to focus.

"I do not know."

"But you said Inari was safe?"

"Yes. The boat was found and my own craft has it in tow. It will have to go first to Heaven, that is where it is bound. Then we will see about returning it to Earth."

"But who abducted her?" Chen asked.

"The former Empress of Heaven," Kuan Yin said.

Robin's mouth dropped open. "My mother-in-law? But—we made sure she was closely guarded."

"She needs more guards, then," the goddess said. "Or guards of a different nature."

"These were the best Mhara could find. He doesn't trust his mother—can you blame him, after she tried to have him killed?"

Chen released a pent-up breath. "At least she's safe. Thank you so much."

The goddess inclined her gracious head. "You will need to wait, Wei Chen. The boat's voyage must be completed before we can return the houseboat."

Chen nodded. "I understand." It was frustrating, but there was clearly nothing else to be done.

"You can stay here," Robin said, reminding him that it wasn't just Inari, the baby, and Miss Qi who had been abducted, but also his home. "Much better than a hotel."

Chen agreed, and thanked her. "When will I know?"

"I will tell Inari where you are and she will call you herself," Kuan Yin said. "And now, I must go back." She put down the tea-cup and stood.

"Wait," Chen said. "What about the Empress?"

"Mhara's got to know," Robin said. Once more the goddess inclined her head. "Then I shall let you tell him." And with that, she was gone into a fading jade glow.

Chen stared after her. "She doesn't want to get involved, does she?"

Robin snorted. "Can't say I blame her. Have you *met* my mother-in-law?"

"Not as such. I've only ever seen her from a distance."

"Believe me, that's by far the best place from which to view her. Mhara couldn't bring himself to dispatch her—and given her status, it would be incredibly difficult to do that, even given what she's done and what he himself is. He had reservations about putting her on the boat, let alone anything more extreme."

"Maybe she needs to be imprisoned somewhere with even greater security," Chen said.

"Yes, but where? The Sea of Night is the only real option—other Heavens won't take her and we can't put her in someone else's Hell, she'd cause too much trouble. The Sea of Night is the closest limbolike place available to us, apart from Between. And look what happened with Seijin—the Lord Lady set up a separate palace and moved between the worlds at will. We couldn't guarantee to keep the Empress in there."

"I just wonder what she wanted with Inari," Chen said. He and Robin fell silent, in mutual acknowledgement that none of the options were good.

"At least she's under the protection of Kuan Yin now," Robin said.

"I wish I found that more reassuring."

21

"An Ifrit," Roerich said, straightening up from his examination of the stained hotel carpet. Jhai frowned.

"That's an Islamic spirit, isn't it? A kind of demon."

Roerich nodded. "A lower-level one. They don't have true intelligence—they're like an animal form, but vicious and predatory. There are other species—they come in a humanoid version, but that's rare in these parts, they prefer the Middle East, their true home."

"How common are these things here?"

"Pretty common. I've seen them many times out in the desert. Some say that they originate from here, that they were an early devil that got co-opted into the Moslem Hell. But no one knows for sure."

"Took some taking down," Jhai said.

"I'm sure," Roerich murmured.

"The Khan's using them," Zhu Irzh said.

"Yes, but that doesn't actually make a lot of sense. He's always deployed ifrits, but they're of very limited use. They're attack creatures, really, nothing more. Why would he have them in jars in what amounts to a lab?"

"Because he's experimenting on them?" Zhu Irzh said.

"It's got to be that, hasn't it? I wonder what he's trying to achieve."

"Sentience?" asked Jhai, who was, Zhu Irzh suddenly recalled, no stranger to experimenting on other life forms. *Oh well. We all need hobbies.*

"You might be right. Perhaps he's looking to the ifrits to provide an army . . . But it wouldn't be a very reliable one, if that's the case. They're very much a law unto themselves."

Jhai's features had taken on a look of distinct calculation that made Zhu Irzh nervous. "But if they could be *modified* in some way—" she began.

Roerich's head snapped up. "What was that?"

Something had moved outside the window and they were several floors up. Jhai and the demon flung themselves toward the glass, Jhai's tiger stripes standing electric against her skin. Zhu Irzh was expecting to see another ifrit, or some being conjured at the Khan's bidding. He wasn't expecting to be smiled at.

"It's quite all right," said the elderly Asian gentleman who floated just beyond the window. "I can see your wards. I don't expect you to invite me in." His black robe, decorated with a pattern of flying cranes, drifted in swirls around his feet.

"You're familiar," Roerich said, behind Zhu Irzh's shoulder. "Have we met?"

"Did you ever come to Japan in your many travels, Mr Roerich?"

"I visited many places throughout Asia," Roerich replied, with a slight smile.

"We were contemporaries all the same. I believe you know my grandson."

"You're Omi's grandfather?" Roerich asked, after a moment's pause.

"Just so. The boy does not, in fact, require much of a guiding hand—he seems to be doing quite well by himself. But he will need assistance in the time to come and I can't provide much in the way of tangible help—I'm a ghost, you see." He gave an apologetic smile. "Long dead, alas. But free at least to observe."

"A common problem," Roerich said with a sigh. "I think you'd best come in."

The old man sat a few inches above the surface of the chair, Zhu Irzh noticed. Perhaps he felt it was polite. He listened with careful attention as the demon recited the course of events so far and sat in thought once Zhu Irzh had finished.

"The connection with my own family is this," he said. "We have a charge to kill the Khan; the result of an ancestral bargain. Although we do not, obviously, come from this part of the world, we were invested with the duty of dispatching this particular spirit."

"Why was that?" Jhai asked. "What sort of bargain?"

"It's what my family does. The women as well as the men— my own grandmother was a formidable warrior. We have spirit blood, the blood of the ancient tribal spirits of Japan, and thus we are able to walk between the worlds to some extent. In the past, we have fought devil generals; we have sailed the seas of Japan to battle pirates from other dimensions; we have retreated into the mountains to fight possessed monks—just a few of the many tasks that have befallen us over the centuries. In return, we are given knowledge, and the powers that come from service."

"Most commendable," Roerich said. "I believe I've heard of you, and others like you. You are guided?"

"Yes, by one of the Eastern Masters. He rarely appears in tangible form, but we hear his voice. Omi has only encountered him once, at my grandson's initiation."

"And where is Omi now?"

"Ah," said the old man, "this is what I have come to tell you. He has had a task to perform, and has now carried it out. We are to meet him at a particular location, if you so choose."

Zhu Irzh leaned forward. "Frankly, Nicholas, I think it might be prudent to get out of Kashgar. I don't hold out much hope of another raid on the Khan's villa."

"You may be right," Roerich said, to the demon's relief. "We stand a better chance if we join forces."

"Could I have a word?" the demon asked. "In private?"

Behind the bathroom door, he said, "Are you sure we can trust him?"

Roerich nodded. "His story is easily verified. I can contact the Master in question, I think—or at least, others who may know him. Leave it with me. I'll be back first thing in the morning."

The old man received this news graciously. "I will leave you, too. You young people don't want a ghost hanging around your bedroom all night."

"What's left of it," Jhai said, as the ghost slowly faded and Roerich left on a mission of his own.

22

Inari didn't feel entirely comfortable venturing on board Kuan Yin's boat: the goddess had been kind enough in giving them a tow but Inari didn't think Kuan Yin would welcome the presence of a demon on board—particularly the demon who had caused so many problems for the goddess' own acolyte Chen.

"She's not like that," Miss Qi protested. "I'm sure it would be all right."

"No, I don't feel right about it," Inari said. "*You* go, Miss Qi. They are your kindred."

"I'll stay here with you," Miss Qi replied firmly. "Unless—you would be happier with me gone?"

"I am just glad that you're not seriously hurt."

"I feel such a fool. Letting myself be possessed like that."

"It wasn't your fault," Inari said. "The Empress is obviously still powerful. Mhara will have to know, when we get back."

Ultimately Miss Qi stayed on board the houseboat. They made endless cups of tea, and played mah jongg to while away the tedium. Inari had never spent so long on the Sea of Night and it was quite remarkably boring. Kuan Yin's boat wallowed ahead, slow and ponderous. Inari took to looking out for the shore of Heaven at every opportunity, and failed to find it. Eventually, they decided to rest.

Inari did not think she would sleep, but she must have been more tired than she had realized, for when she next opened her eyes, Miss Qi was shaking her awake.

"Inari . . ."

"What is it?"

"We've stopped."

Together, they hurried on deck. The scene was the same as before: featureless Sea, starless sky. Kuan Yin's opalescent boat rocked a few yards distant, the rope between the two craft hanging slack. There was no sign of life on deck.

"I shouted," Miss Qi said, "but there was no reply."

"We could try again," Inari suggested, but there was still no response from the other boat.

"I don't like this," Miss Qi said.

"Not after what happened earlier." Inari surveyed Miss Qi anxiously. "Do you feel any different?"

"No. I can't sense anything."

"I could go," said a voice at Inari's ankles. She looked down to see the badger.

"That's a good point, actually," Miss Qi said. "If you don't mind?"

"It is what I am for. I can run along the rope if you hold it tight. I do not like to swim."

In the Sea of Night, Inari thought, the badger was more likely to simply sink and re-emerge in another galaxy somewhere. She shivered. They caught the rope and stretched it while the badger scrambled across onto the neighboring deck, then they waited anxiously. Just as Inari was thinking that they'd have to go in search of her familiar, the badger reappeared.

"Is everything all right?" Miss Qi asked, once the badger had come back onto their own boat.

"No, it is not. There are people on board—Celestials, maids, and crew—but I cannot see the goddess Herself, and all the others are asleep."

"Asleep?"

"Or entranced. Their eyes are open, but I cannot attract their attention."

"It's the Empress," Inari said. "She's put them under a spell."

"Also there is someone below deck," the badger said. "I could hear them moving about, but I do not know who it is."

"Maybe that was Kuan Yin?" Inari ventured.

"It was not. I am familiar with her energy—I have seen her before. This person felt different."

"What sort of different?"

"Not good."

Miss Qi looked at Inari. "I've got a nasty feeling we're back where we started."

"We can't just sit here," Inari said. "And where's the goddess Herself? Could the Empress have—?" She found that she did not want to continue.

"I don't know what the Empress is and isn't capable of, after all this," Miss Qi said blankly. "She's supposed to be powerless but she obviously isn't."

They waited for a while, but the opalescent boat did not

move and no sound came from it. At last Miss Qi and the badger took hold of the rope and, hauling hard, pulled the boats closer together. They had agreed to go together, just like last time.

The goddess' boat gleamed like moonlight as they set foot on it. Inari did not feel comfortable here—it was one thing being friends with the kind Miss Qi, whom she felt to be a kindred spirit, but another exploring the boat of the goddess. Inari did not belong and she knew it. Within her, there came a faint twinge of discomfort, as if the child, too, knew that this was not its place. Inari put a hand protectively to the base of her abdomen and kept close to the Celestial warrior. They moved through corridors glittering with pale jeweled tapestries, past elegant furniture. It made the houseboat feel homely and squat, but Inari thought she preferred it all the same. The air smelled faintly of perfume—jasmine, perhaps, or sandalwood. In one of the cabins, they came across a maid, frozen in the act of pouring tea. Her stiff skirts fanned out around her and although she had been arrested in motion, the tea had not: it pooled over the surface of the table and dripped down the legs. Inari, who liked order, had to stifle the urge to seize a cloth and mop it up.

"You see?" the badger said.

Inari nodded. She passed a hand across the maid's eyes but the woman did not blink. Her face had a glassy, glazed expression— an ivory statue.

"At least she doesn't seem to have actually possessed anyone," Inari said doubtfully.

"Not yet." Miss Qi turned to the badger. "Where did you hear this sound, then?"

"Down the stairs."

Leaving the maid, they followed the familiar down the stairs and into another maze of passages. Despite the beautiful decoration, the boat felt claustrophobic and cramped. The badger paused outside a door and waved a paw for silence. Inari and Miss Qi listened. At first, there was nothing, but then they heard a distant scratching, like a mouse. Had it not been for the unusual circumstances aboard the goddess' vessel, Inari might have suspected a more prosaic explanation, like vermin, but the frozen maid told a different story.

The door was open a crack. Miss Qi put her eye to it, but withdrew with a shake of the head.

"Can't see anything," she mouthed.

There was a brief, odd moment, almost as though an electric current had passed through the ship. Inari felt a tingling along her nerves; her scalp prickled.

The doorway erupted into movement: whirling limbs, a golden-black glitter as if some vast insect had whistled into view. Inari screamed as a bright edge swept down toward her; she threw herself to one side. Across the passage, Miss Qi was a blur, her own blade striking out. There was a cry, cut short. She could hear the badger growling. But Inari's vision was filled with black and gold as she was picked up and turned upside down.

"No!" she cried. "Be careful! I—"

Too late. Her abductor was running down the corridor. She could see the floor and the whisking end of a brocade tail-coat. Behind her, someone—Miss Qi?—gave a sharp short shout. She glimpsed figures. Then they were onto the deck. Up and over, with Inari's head bouncing painfully from side to side—but at least it was still attached to her shoulders, she thought. They must have come up along the far side of Kuan Yin's boat: she caught sight of a towering mast and hanging sails like rags. Inari was flung face down onto the deck and her wrists and ankles bound. She felt the boards of the vessel shudder beneath her. Squirming around, she saw that they were already moving, though there was no wind in those limp black sails. Then the world was suddenly bright. Inari saw something descending from the night skies, gleaming pale like a diamond star.

Kuan Yin was coming back at last. But before Inari could feel the faintest trace of relief, the boat beneath her speeded up, the incorporeal substance of the Sea of Night splashing soundlessly over the rail. The darkness opened up and the boat was gone, swallowed by a maw of air.

23

Chen and Robin did not discover what had happened until later that evening, when, without warning, Mhara appeared in the middle of the temple. His manifestation was sufficiently sudden for Chen to blink and step back.

"Mhara!" Robin said. "I've been trying to contact you."

"I was in the Book room," the Emperor said. "Chen knows."

"Kuan Yin was here earlier. I'm afraid there's a problem," Chen began.

"I know. My mother." The Emperor's serene face took on an expression of unfamiliar unease. "She's missing. I'm very sorry, Chen. Your family seems continually to be caught up in my own problems." He paused and Chen realized that he was ashamed: it seemed unnatural, to be facing the Celestial Emperor when the Emperor himself was in the wrong. "She's taken Inari with her."

"How did you find out?" Chen and Robin said simultaneously.

"Do you know where she's gone?" Chen then asked.

"Kuan Yin returned to find pirates ransacking her vessel," Mhara said. "Her crew was frozen, but remained aware. One of her maids saw Inari being taken. Miss Qi was with her, and the badger. She is not alone. I know that isn't much comfort."

Chen took a deep breath. "It's somewhat reassuring. I know there are supposed to be pirates on the Sea of Night, but—"

"These weren't local."

"Then—"

"These people came from somewhere else. Another sea, in another Hell. There are such."

"I thought the worlds were supposed to be sealed off from one another," Chen said. "Unless—" Zhu Irzh had recently managed to get snatched into a Hindu Hell, after all.

"Unless one is venturing in lands where many different cultures have strong religions," Mhara said. "Even then, one tends to find oneself only in the realms belonging to one's own particular faith. There is a certain amount of bleed—Between was such an area—but the Sea of Night is not such a place."

"So what does this mean?" Robin asked. "That the walls between the worlds are breaking down?"

"I can't think what else it would mean," Mhara said. "Somehow, against all magical logic, it seems that my mother managed to contact someone outside the Sea of Night."

"Or someone contacted her," Chen said. "She's still powerful, isn't she?"

"Yes, she's still powerful. And she wants revenge for what she sees as my slights."

"I can't just sit here," Chen said.

"No. But equally, you can't go to the Sea of Night on your own, with no clue of who these people are or where they've come from. We know roughly where they entered the Sea. I will send you a boat, Chen, if you wish."

"I'd like to take Zhu Irzh with me," Chen said, "but I haven't been able to reach him."

"I think you'll find that Zhu Irzh has a task of his own," the Emperor said.

The "boat" the Emperor sent was a warship, which Chen had not been expecting. It did not look like something that had come from Heaven. It was high and black and blunt, not modern. It lay at anchor just off the coast of Singapore Three, not far from the typhoon shelter and the place where, until recently, Chen's own home had been moored.

"Can anyone else see it?" Chen asked Mhara as they stood at the harbor wall, looking out. The boat, silhouetted against a fiery sunset, was the color of ink: a medieval engraving. Its sails billowed gently in an otherwise unnoticeable wind.

The Emperor laughed. "Only a few. It won't show up on naval radar, if that's what you mean. Quite invisible."

"Who's the captain?"

"You'll meet him." Mhara pointed. A skiff was setting out from beneath the shadow of the war-junk, moving swiftly over the gleaming water. Chen could see a small figure hunched in the prow, but no one seemed to be rowing the craft. They climbed down the harbor steps to meet it and as the skiff slowed, the Celestial in it stood. He reminded Chen of Miss Qi: another heavenly warrior, pale-faced and sloe-eyed. He bowed his head as he neared the Emperor.

"Majesty."

"Don't bother with all that," Mhara told him. "It's good that you're here."

"I've come to collect Master Chen," the young man said. He extended a guiding hand, but Chen climbed on board without aid, nodding his thanks.

"I have to return to Heaven," Mhara said. "With my mother missing, I need to be there, but I've placed troops on the borders."

"You think she's trying to raise an army?" Chen asked.

"I think she wants Heaven back," Mhara said. He raised a hand in farewell as the skiff set off again, a smooth, invisible glide. Chen watched the Emperor's tall figure recede against the lights of the city, until suddenly it was no longer there. He sighed. He wished that he could believe Mhara to be wrong, but a maternal plan to reclaim Heaven sounded all too plausible.

But what did she want with Inari? And where was Zhu Irzh? Chen told himself not to fret as the black bulk of the war-junk drew closer. Then they were alongside the ship and a rope was tossed downward. The pilot seized it and held it taut while Chen scrambled up onto the deck. The sails belled out over his head and all at once the city was falling fast behind. They came out of the harbor mouth, speeding past the place where Chen's house-boat had been moored, and then toward the hummocks of the islands, whalebacks against the still-red sky. As they passed the last rock, with the towers of Singapore Three glittering in the distance, Chen felt the world shift around him. He gripped the rail. Beside him, the pilot of the skiff gave him a sympathetic glance. Chen looked back. The city was no longer there. Ahead, lay the yawning dark expanse of the Sea of Night.

24

The forest shifted and warped around Omi's fleeing form, the trees changing as he ran. It was hard to tell, out of the corners of his eyes, but he thought they were shifting into words: huge flickering characters written on the air. The world was rewriting itself, Omi realized, perhaps transformed by the contents of the scroll that he now carried carefully between his cat-jaws. Different tastes—blood, jasmine tea, snow, metal—touched his tongue and the scroll seemed to be singing, a small joyous voice that spoke in a language he could not understand.

Behind him, however, he could still hear the ifrit, crashing through the trees. Ifrits, Omi reminded himself, can't read. He was confident that he could outrun it and if not—well, then he would simply have to turn and fight. But he was worried about the scroll, wanting to keep it safe, hoping that he could make the oasis before—

And there it was, whirling through a wall of words and symbols, the startling blue crescent of the moon-shaped lake with the pavilion beyond.

Omi conjured a last burst of speed from his limbs and was out once more into the desert. The ifrit gave a shriek, perhaps rage, perhaps despair. But Omi was already bolting across the harsh shiver of the sands toward the lake. He shot through the gate and as he did so, was jarred forcibly back into his human form. He just managed to catch the scroll before it hit the stone flags. Turning, he saw the ifrit hurtling toward the gate, its narrow, leathery head outstretched. Half phoenix, half pterodactyl, it struck the air of the gate and exploded in a shower of blood and fire. Omi shielded the scroll under his coat as blazing fragments fell all around the courtyard and the air was filled with the reek of burning demon.

Inside his head, the Book said, *"Well?"*

"I got it!" Omi said aloud, exultant.

"So you have. Well done. Bring it to me."

Omi took the stairs two at a time and found the Book, not unexpectedly, sitting where he had left it on its pedestal.

"Open the scroll," the Book instructed him. "Read it to me."

"I can't," Omi said blankly. "I don't know what language it's written in, and anyway, there's not much writing on it as far as I can see—it's a map."

"That doesn't matter. Just open it."

Doubting, Omi did so and experienced a curious sensation, as though the top of his head had been lifted off. He felt words entering his consciousness, unfamiliar, unrecognizable, and he spoke.

When he had finished, he stared. The spell hung before him in the air, its letters glittering like fire. But it was not just a spell. The words snaked into configurations of their own, forming constellations in the dim air of the library.

"It's still a map," Omi said, peering.

"Yes. Words that formed the world," said the Book. "And if you could look within me, you would find part of me missing."

"The scroll was taken from you?" Omi asked.

"Stolen from me. Stolen, and used to rewrite the rules of the land. It must be restored and I must be restored with it."

"How is that to happen?"

"I must be taken back to the place where this began. I must be allowed to rewrite the world into its correct configuration, to reknit the text into its original and proper form."

"What place is that?" Omi asked.

"The deep desert—not the desert of the physical world, but of time. The world of the Taklamakan and of the Tokarians."

"We need to go back into the past?" Omi gaped at the Book.

"Back, and remake it. You must carry me, but it is too dangerous for you to go alone. I have sent for help," the Book said.

A man stepped out of the shadows, making Omi start. He had no indication that the man had been there, and this was bad, for a warrior. The stranger was tall, bald, dark-eyed, and carried a palpable weight of experience.

"Omi," he said, and bowed. "My name is Nicholas Roerich."

"I've heard of you," Omi said.

"I work for the Masters, just as you yourself do. And I knew your grandfather, both in life and in death." Roerich smiled. "The latter condition does not appear to have greatly altered him, as a matter-of-fact."

"He didn't really see any difference between the two," Omi concurred.

And it was true. He had not.

Later, Omi stood with Roerich on the parapet of the pavilion. The desert lay beyond and the dunes hummed, singing in the dying light with a strange, deep boom.

"They're gathering," Omi said. He pointed to where the ifrits wheeled over the sand, avoiding the lake, which now gleamed golden under the sunset.

"Yes. They'll stop us if they can. The Khan's controlling them; he seeks to breed them afresh."

Omi looked at him askance. "Can he do that?"

"He has a lab, of sorts. The . . . man we'll be traveling with discovered it."

Omi was not sure whether he had imagined the tiny hesitation before the word "man," but decided not to press the point, for now. "What else did this man discover?"

"Ghosts in the walls. The spirits of the murdered."

"My grandfather was one of those."

"I know. But your grandfather is free, Omi." Roerich amended this. "Free to move, at least, if not free from duty."

"The Book says we need to go back in time," Omi said. The idea filled him with disquiet. Once, he might have welcomed the adventure; but this did not please him.

"So we do. But you know that you will not be going alone." Roerich spoke quietly and did not look at Omi; the latter knew that he was trying to save the younger man face and was grateful. "I will be going with you, as will the other."

"The—man—who discovered the Khan's lab?"

This time Roerich smiled. "Just so. He is not a human, Omi. He is a demon, from the Chinese Hell. He works as a policeman in Singapore Three. You will find him helpful, in a number of ways."

Whatever Omi had been expecting, it was not this. "A *cop?* But—"

"Wickedness is, I have found, at least partly in the eye of the beholder," Roerich said. He pointed to the wheeling ifrits. "Those, for instance. If they could be free to have a real choice, what do you think they would choose?"

"Evil," Omi replied promptly. "I do not like to think in black and white, Roerich. My grandfather taught me not to do so, and so did my sensei. But ifrits are predators, and mindless."

"Even so," Roerich said, "perhaps even they might one day surprise you." He sighed. "I have walked the face of this world, Omi. In life, and now in death. I have seen a great many things that surprise me, and more that may yet do so."

"This policeman," Omi said after a pause. "When can I meet him?"

25

The badger was nuzzling her face, muttering as he did so. Inari stirred, feeling hard wooden boards beneath her, and sat up. They were moving: up and down in a gentle rocking motion that suggested they were on water. Light filtered into the dim chamber, startling after the Sea of Night. Across the chamber, Miss Qi lay in a pale huddle of garments.

Inari's hands went to her stomach, but there was no sign that anything was amiss and she breathed a sigh of relief.

"We are afloat," said the badger.

"Have you been on deck?"

"No. The door is locked." Scratch marks at the base of the wooden door told Inari that the badger had made considerable attempts to break free. "I can smell salt. This is a proper sea."

"Maybe we're back on Earth?" Inari said hopefully. She went across to Miss Qi and knelt by the Celestial warrior's side.

"What—?" asked Miss Qi. She blinked.

"Are you all right?" Inari said.

"I think so. I don't remember what happened. I was fighting, and then—" She frowned.

"I remember being carried off," Inari said. "There was another ship. We're on it, presumably."

"But where *are* we?"

High on the wall, there was a little window, without glass. The badger might have squeezed through it, but the window was too small for either Inari or Miss Qi. They managed to look through it, however, by dragging a bench to the wall and standing on it on tiptoe.

"It *looks* like Earth," Miss Qi said. An expanse of glittering blue sea, bright sunlight, and a warm, spicy breeze lay beyond the window. In the distance was a little hummock of an island, clad in dark green foliage. Inari could hear the snapping of sails above her head.

"It does look like Earth," Inari agreed, "but I don't think it is."

Miss Qi looked at her curiously. "Why do you say that?"

"I don't know. It doesn't—feel right." All of her life on Earth had been lived on the sea, after all, even if it had been the edges of it, close to shore. The light was a little too vivid, the sea slightly over-aquamarine.

"Maybe it's just a different place on Earth," Miss Qi said.

"Maybe." But Inari didn't think so and could not say how she knew.

They got down from the bench and worked at the door. But though it looked old, the wood salt-rotted and stained, it would not budge, even with the badger's solid weight against it. Eventually they sat back down on the bench.

"They can't keep us in here forever," Miss Qi said. "Someone will come eventually."

"I don't like being kidnapped," Inari said. "Especially by mad empresses."

"This isn't the Empress' ship."

"I know. And that worries me."

But Miss Qi was correct. It was not long before the door was wrenched open. A man stood in the opening: not human, Inari's senses told her, but she did not know what manner of being he was. Tall, dressed in cerulean blue robes and turban, with skin the color of soft brown earth. Indigo spirals circled his cheeks and brow and his eyes were the same color as his robes. He smiled, displaying sharp golden teeth. He carried with him a smell of cinnamon and ginger.

"Ladies! And beast! Good afternoon."

Miss Qi was frowning again. "You are a djinn."

The man, or djinn, laughed. "Indeed so. You are well-traveled, warrior."

"I saw a documentary," Miss Qi said, surprising Inari.

"My name is Banquo," the djinn said. "Welcome to Hell."

"Ah," said Inari. "That's where we are. Whose Hell? It's not mine."

"It is the Hell of the Moors. Only a little Hell, I'm afraid. It didn't have a very long existence and yet, we endure."

"Did the Empress hire you?" Miss Qi asked.

"Yes. But she has not kept to her side of the bargain." Banquo's golden smile widened. "We were not paid the price we requested. In fact, we were not paid at all. And so, my dear ladies, you must remain here until we can find someone who will ransom you."

"The Emperor of Heaven will do that," Miss Qi said.

"Are you certain of that? You seem very confident. And yet one of you is a demon."

"The Emperor is my friend," Inari said. The blue eyes widened.

"Is that so? How unusual."

"Nevertheless," Miss Qi said firmly. "Send word to him. You'll find that we speak the truth."

Banquo gave a bow. "I shall do so. Until then, you will be my guests. We'll leave the door unlocked. You may have the run of the ship. Don't entertain any thoughts of escape. There's nowhere to go."

"I am," Miss Qi said balefully, "an excellent swimmer."

Banquo gestured toward the door and they followed him onto the deck. The heat hit Inari like a fist. One of the warmer Hells, evidently. And not, at second glance, all that unpleasant, with the gleaming heave of the sea and the little islands. Then Banquo pointed over the side.

The sinuous black bodies of over a dozen sharks circled the boat. Their sharp fins broke the water and as Inari peered over, one of them looked up. Its eyes were not the eyes of a shark: they were aware, alive with a malign intelligence. And they were hungry.

"A good swimmer, you say? So are they."

26

Omi watched the demon cautiously. He did not want to be seen staring. In a varied career, he had encountered the denizens of the Chinese Hell only at the end of bow or sword, but never over tea in a dingy hotel room. And the woman with him—she wasn't human either, unless Omi was greatly mistaken. But he didn't know what she might be.

"The thing is," Zhu Irzh was saying, with a languid flick of the hand, "the Khan's obviously our main foe. But what about this book? Can it be trusted?"

Roerich leaned forward. "Absolutely."

"But where does it come from? I've never heard of such a thing."

"The Book is itself a Master," Roerich said. "It comes and goes as it pleases."

"And why should it help us?"

"I think you will find," Roerich said, "that it has its own agenda."

"That's *not* reassuring." The demon looked as close to unnerved as Omi had ever seen a demon look.

"Whatever that agenda is," Roerich reminded him, "it would appear to have chosen you."

"Myself *and* Omi here," Zhu Irzh said, looking across at Omi. The golden gaze was itself disconcerting. Omi was used to battling demons, not negotiating with them.

"I might say," Omi said diffidently, "that the same applies to yourself, from my point of view. How do I know I can trust you?"

"You can't."

"Can't know, or can't trust?"

"I'd like to say that you can trust me, but you can't know that. I got roped into all this—I didn't volunteer. It seems that events have selected me and I don't like it—I'd bail out if I could, but I know how these things work. Once you're involved, you have to see things through." He looked genuinely unhappy, Omi thought. There was no sense of anything amiss, and Grandfather had effectively approved . . . Grandfather should know. But Omi himself had been wrong before . . .

"We have to act," Roerich said. "The Khan's gathering strength. His ifrits are massing."

The demon rose abruptly. "Then let's do it. What did the Book say?"

"The spell needs to be taken into the desert, taken to the land. It will know what to do once it's there."

"All right." The demon turned to the woman, Jhai. "There's no need for you to come with us."

"But—"

"No need."

After a moment, Jhai gave a reluctant nod. "I'd like to. Don't like to miss out on an adventure. But I suppose I ought to get back to business."

Unless Omi was once more greatly mistaken, he thought, Jhai had agreed a little too easily. Up to something? She was the kind of woman who would be.

Several hours later, Omi, Zhu Irzh, and Roerich stood on the edge of the desert. Behind them Kashgar shimmered, a mirage-oasis. Omi could hear the boom and shift of the sands. It was close to dusk now, with a bloom falling over the eastern sky and a small, hard moon riding up above the shoulder of the dunes.

"What now?" the demon asked. With his long coat billowing out around his heels, Zhu Irzh looked like a sliver of shadow.

"We start walking," Roerich said.

Soon the lights of the city faded into the heat haze and were gone. The desert lay all around them, the high waves of the dunes reminding Omi of a static ocean. An owl glided low over the sands, casting a moon shadow before it, and looking up, Omi was somehow surprised to see the tiny cross of a jet moving over the sky and leaving a contrail behind it, rosy in the reflected light of the sunken sun. When he next looked up, a moment later, the plane and its wake were no longer there, and Omi repressed a shiver. It was as though the desert was watching him now, rather than the other way around.

"You all right, Omi?" the demon said.

"I'm wondering when we are now," Omi replied in a low voice. "I'm wondering whether we've slipped in time."

"Why?"

Omni told him about the plane.

"I didn't see that," Zhu Irzh said. "But you could be right. The stars would be the same, wouldn't they?"

"More or less."

"I've gone back in time before," said the demon. "To a village. But that was north of here."

"Time seems very loose in the desert," Omi said. "I suppose we'll just have to live with it. I'm more worried about the ifrits."

"I haven't seen any so far."

"I know. That's what worries me."

After his previous experiences, the desert seemed too quiet, too peaceful—and yet there was still that air of waiting, as though they walked through something that was itself alive. Omi kept expecting ifrits to come shrieking over the next dune, but all he saw were long-tailed desert vermin and the occasional silent glide of owls. After three hours or so, during which Omi's companions spoke little, Roerich suggested that they camp for the night. They set up a rudimentary encampment around a fire at the base of one of the dunes. It felt too exposed to Omi, but there was no other choice.

When they had gathered enough scrub for a blaze, the demon reached out a hand, but Roerich stopped him.

"Wait. Don't do magic here. It's too risky."

"Okay," Zhu Irzh said, peaceably enough, and produced a cigarette lighter from his pocket. They sat around the little fire, which flickered blue in the moonlight, and ate some of the bread that Roerich had brought with them. The fire might have been produced by ordinary means, Omi thought, but it wasn't behaving like a proper fire. The demon eyed it uneasily.

"We'll take it in turns to keep watch," Roerich said.

"I'm not tired. I'll take the first stint," Omi offered.

"You're welcome to it," said the demon, yawning. He lay back into the embrace of the sand, crossed his legs at the ankle, and appeared to go straight to sleep. Roerich glanced at him with evident amusement, then said to Omi, "I'll leave you to it. I might be dead but I still have to conserve my strength. Wake me in a couple of hours. Since our demonic friend is out for the count, I might as well take the second watch."

But in the end, everyone was woken.

Omi had anticipated an ifrit attack. What he had not expected was to see the ifrit flapping over the edge of the dune like a windswept umbrella. It tumbled down the dune, sending sand cascading in all directions, emanating a thin shrieking. By this time not only Omi, but also Roerich and the demon were on their feet and Zhu Irzh had drawn his sword.

The ifrit reached the bottom of the slope and lay still. Close to, Omi could see its prehistoric origins in the line of wing and the tiny, useless claws that lay at the tip. These creatures were ancient, summoned from some unimaginable but mortal past by desert mages, also in the very-long-ago. Ancient or not, Omi wished they had been allowed to become decently extinct.

Zhu Irzh poked the ifrit with the toe of his boot before Omi could stop him. It did not move.

"Be careful," Omi said. "They're cunning."

"So am I."

Roerich sat on his heels a short distance from the ifrit, and studied it. "No, it's dead," he said, after a moment. "It's beginning to disintegrate."

He was right. Seconds later, the ifrit was no more than a bundle of leathery gristle, and a minute after that, even less. Soon, a sparse pattern of dust lay on the desert floor and Omi caught sight of the ifrit's vestigial spirit ascending into the heavens, a single spark, soon gone.

"Well," said Roerich, straightening up. "Whoever did that knew what they were doing."

"And whoever did that," Omi murmured, "isn't far away."

They fanned out, taking care not to lose sight of one another. Omi himself went up and over the dune, sidling sideways like a cat against the slippery sand, while Roerich and Zhu Irzh went along its sides. Omi's shout, however, soon brought the others running.

"What the *fuck?*" Normally soft-spoken, even Omi was driven to profanity.

"Where did it come from?" Zhu Irzh said, wild-eyed. "I didn't see that when we camped."

The city lay on the other side of the dune: immense, reaching as far as the eye could see. Its marble walls shone in the moon's glow; its turrets towered toward the stars. Banners fluttered from their pagoda-summits, and from the highest tower a call rang out over the city like a night-bird's cry, warning and shrill. The city faded, as if summoned back into the substance of the sands, and then there was only the empty desert air. Omi stifled a cry of protest, but it was too late: the city was gone.

"Agarta," Roerich said, with a hint of satisfaction.

"What?" said Zhu Irzh. "Never heard of it."

"One of the great lost cities of the Gobi," Roerich said. "Built before the Tokarians, before any of the current desert peoples. Its twin was Shambhala."

"I thought that was a myth," Zhu Irzh said.

"People would say the same about you."

"It was beautiful," Omi breathed.

"Yes," Roerich said. "Men have spent their lives craving Agarta after a single glimpse of its towers, have laid down their bones in the desert in search of it. Don't be one of them, Omi."

"So why did it appear now?" the demon asked.

"I suspect the ifrit blundered into it. It comes and goes. Like its twin, it's woven into the fabric of the desert's landscape. But they know how to deal with ifrits in Agarta."

"Somehow," Zhu Irzh said, "I doubt I'd be welcome in those marble walls."

"You might be surprised. It's the home of the Masters, or one of them. They tend to see beyond normal distinctions."

For Omi, sleep was out of the question after that. Rather than reviving the dying fire, they buried the ashes and moved on. By this time, the short desert night was almost over and the eastern sky was glowing bright indigo. The city did not reappear.

27

It was difficult to stop staring into the shadowy expanse of the Sea of Night as though it contained answers. It did, just not in the way that Chen wanted it to. The Celestial crew of the war-junk worked with quick, grim determination, hauling on the junk's insubstantial sails to keep it tacking on a course that Chen estimated to be directly into the middle of the Sea—if it could be said to have a middle. Chen waited impatiently until a faint shout from the crow's-nest indicated that Kuan Yin's ship had been sighted. It weighed anchor in the billowing clouds of the Sea, ghost-white.

The goddess herself was waiting on the deck.

"Wei Chen." She gave the slightest inclination of her head, a sign of apology. Chen didn't expect this from a goddess, and it was gratifying.

"Goddess."

"We've traced them," the girl standing next to Kuan Yin said. For a moment, Chen thought it was Miss Qi who stood there, then realized that she was another Celestial warrior.

"Good. Where are they?"

"They've traveled through a rift in the Sea of Night. They're in another Hell, but we don't know which one."

"That's—not good," Chen said. There had to be thousands of Hells, some of them no larger than a single person. He'd heard of such things.

"But you can follow them through. If you wish to take the risk, I mean—"

"I'll take it," Chen told her. He'd gone further than this for Inari. And Mhara had sanctioned it—even when he'd already signed Chen up for another job. The Emperor must be impartial, and this suggested to Chen that Inari, or rather, their child, had become a priority.

Once more, the goddess bowed her head. "Very well. I cannot go with you. We must go on, to the shore of Heaven."

"What happened to the Empress' boat?" Chen asked.

"Gone."

"Do you know where?"

"It may be that it has traveled to the same place."

"We're going to need the warship," Chen said.

Standing on the prow of the war-junk, he watched as the rift grew nearer. It had only recently become visible, expanding through the cloudy shadows as a line of light, and Chen's heart had leaped when he saw it. The warrior who captained this ship, Li-Ju, came to stand by his side: a tall man, armored, with a drooping iron-gray moustache.

"I have sailed the Sea of Night for over a hundred years by human reckoning and I've never seen anything like this."

"I've only traveled on the Sea on a few occasions," said Chen, "but neither have I. It seems the walls between the worlds are breaking down."

"Is that surprising?" Li-Ju remarked. "With war between Heaven and Hell, and even trouble within Between, one cannot wonder that the fabric of the weave is becoming torn. Previously, all believed as the Emperor Himself believed; all was seamless and whole. Now, the universe mirrors our disagreements."

Chen looked at him curiously. "You don't agree with what the new Emperor is doing?"

"I question the wisdom of the action," Li-Ju said, after a pause, "not the wisdom of the Emperor, but I think it is necessary all the same."

The rift was widening, as if reflecting Li-Ju's thoughts. Through it, Chen could smell spice, a warmth.

"You must strap yourself down!" Li-Ju called. "This could be rough."

Chen seized a rope and with the captain's help, they lashed themselves to the railing. Now the rift was directly ahead and Chen could see sunlight, a welcome change from the shadows of the Sea of Night. But the junk was starting to plunge and list like a bolting horse, and a moment later Chen glanced over the side to see the clouds of the Sea pouring down through the gap like rapids.

"Hang on!" Li-Ju cried. Along the deck, crew members were scrambling about the rigging, securing themselves with ropes and making sure that the sails remained as steady as possible. One of the booms swung free, hurtling over the deck, which was mercifully unpopulated. Chen tasted a different air, so strong that it was like a mouthful of wine. Then the light was all around them as they shot down the rift and into another world.

The sense of violation was unexpectedly powerful. Chen knew, at some fundamental level of his being, that this should not be possible—or, if possible, should not be allowed. It was similar to the sense that he'd had on entering the realm of Between, that liminal place that was neither Heaven nor Hell nor Earth itself: a transgression, that might in some manner be reflected in his own soul, a tear, a scar.

The junk was shaking as if it might rip itself apart and Chen was conscious of a flicker of fear: normally, he was not afraid of death (difficult, when one has visited all the places that one is likely to end up in the afterlife), but he did not like the thought that if he were to expire, his soul might be trapped in this other Hell. One could trust Kuan Yin to help only so much and it seemed that the goddess had distanced herself from the situation, Grimly, Chen clung to the rope and looked back.

The war-junk was almost through the gap. As Chen watched, the rift in the air began to close, first slowly, and then with appalling speed. Seconds later, it was gone and there was only serene blue sky.

"Well," said Li-Ju at his side. "We're still in one piece." Crew members were running about, checking that the junk was intact.

"And nothing waiting for us on the other side," Chen added.

"Nothing *yet.*"

Indeed, the sea that surrounded them was as empty as the Sea of Night itself. Unlashing himself from the rail, Chen went around to the other side of the ship. There was an island, a little round curve arching up out of the sea. Unconsciously echoing the earlier experience of Inari, Chen knew that although this might look like Earth, it was not.

"I think we should make for land," Li-Ju said. "Wherever the Empress has gone, it seems the most likely objective."

Chen was not sure that he agreed with this conclusion, but it was not his boat. He inclined his head in agreement and waited, tense, as the crew hauled the great sails around and the warship headed for the island.

28

Banquo was a solicitous host, but Inari found herself fretting. She was worried about the houseboat, about Chen, but most of all, about the baby. What if no one could find them? What if Banquo could not, despite his protestations, get a message through to Mhara? He said that a message had been sent, and when Inari had asked how this had been done, the pirate captain had informed her that it had been sent by bird.

"We tend to rely on email," Miss Qi said, gloomily.

Banquo laughed. They were sitting in the captain's cabin, around a table that was strewn with maps. Inari tried to get a good look at these, as much out of interest as self-preservation, but the maps were strange: their content altered from moment to moment, coastlines shifting and changing as she watched. A tiny line-drawing of a sea-serpent swam up through blue-stained parchment and was once more gone.

"We have no such technology here," he said. "We have no need of it."

"My own Hell develops constantly," Inari told him.

The pirate grimaced. "A Hell indeed. We prefer things as they are."

"Those sharks," Inari said. "Are they the souls of men? In my home, I've seen fish that were the souls of businessmen."

Banquo smiled. "Reduced to fighting for crumbs? The Chinese always were a subtle people. Here, things are more obvious. You are right, of course. This was a Hell for marauders at sea, for slave traders. For human sharks, one might say. But they're not just confined to the ocean. The islands are overrun with them, too."

"What, with sharks?"

"On land, they take the form of men. Well, more or less. They still retain . . . certain aspects."

Inari did not think she wanted to find out what aspects those might be. Miss Qi stirred, restlessly.

"When is this bird likely to return? Do you know how long it will take to deliver a message to the Emperor?"

"I do not. We have not dealt extensively with your world." Banquo stood, bowing. "We must hope that it will not be long."

Back in their assigned cabin, Miss Qi paced the boards while Inari sat on one of the cots, hugging her knees. "This is frustrating. It's not even as though we've been properly kidnapped. Just pushed onto someone else because the Empress couldn't cough up."

"Yet she went to all that trouble," Inari said. "Why would she do such a thing and then not pay?"

"Maybe she was prevented from doing so," Miss Qi said hopefully. "Maybe the Emperor has found out what she's been up to."

"It's possible," Inari said.

Then, her voice changing, Miss Qi said, "We're very close to that island."

"Are we?" Inari got up to look out of the porthole. The cabin was considerably better appointed than the chamber in which they had originally been dumped; Banquo was evidently confident that they wouldn't try to escape. But Miss Qi was right. The island, which until now had been nothing more than a blot on the horizon, loomed above the ship. They were perhaps a quarter of a mile from shore, close enough to see the dense forest that ran down to a half-moon of sand. High on the summit of the island ran a ridge of rock, and Inari could see birds wheeling above the treeline.

"They're enormous," she said.

"I don't like the look of those. They're shaped like vultures."

"Vultures and sharks," Inari murmured. "Whoever constructed this Hell didn't waste time."

The island was drawing closer. "I think I'd like to know why we're heading there," Miss Qi announced.

They made their way back to Banquo's chamber, but the captain was nowhere to be found. Nor was there any sign of the crew.

"Remember Kuan Yin's boat?" Inari whispered. "Everyone frozen? If the Empress is here—"

A sudden slithering noise made her break off her speculations. "What was that?" Miss Qi whispered into Inari's ear. The badger hastened forward to peer around the corner of the cabin and just as quickly shuffled back.

They still retain . . . certain aspects, Banquo had said and now Inari could see exactly what he meant. The thing that stood before them was tall, sinuous, gray-skinned. Its long face grinned, rimmed with triangular teeth, but its legs were human enough, though ending in flipper-like feet. It wore a loin cloth and carried a short, serrated spear.

"I've come to find you," the shark-demon said, and grinned wider.

Miss Qi smacked the wall with the flat of her hand, a gesture that Inari did not associate with the calm Celestial. However, she knew how Miss Qi felt. Without actual confirmation they could not say for certain, but both were sure that the shark-demons were in the Empress' employ.

"Even if Banquo's still—well, not alive, as such, but able to operate, he's unlikely to come looking for us," Miss Qi said. "It's just easier for him to go out and get new hostages."

"I agree. Ones who are less trouble."

"I'm tired of being taken prisoner," was Miss Qi's next comment. "It's such a waste of time."

"Well," Inari said, "in that case, we need to escape."

They had already made a thorough search of the room. At least, Inari thought, they had a reasonable idea of where they were being held: the shark-demons had taken them at spear-point off Banquo's ship, rowed them in a small craft to shore, and then marched them up a narrow track between the trees. The look and the sounds of the forest were unfamiliar: strange red-fronded ferns, fleshy fat plants which oozed a glistening fluid, and a smell of lushness and rot. Finally they had been shown into a rickety wooden building at the summit of a pinnacle of rock, reached by a swaying plank and rope bridge.

Getting out of it was, however, something of a problem. The stone escarpment below them was almost sheer, ending in a ragged ravine, and the only obvious way out lay across the bridge. To reach it, they would have to break free of the room.

The badger had been rooting and snuffling at the bare boards. He scraped with an experimental claw.

"This is old wood."

"Do you think you can break through it?" Inari asked.

"They'll hear him," Miss Qi pointed out.

"If anyone's listening."

"The Empress has gone to some trouble to seize us a second time. I doubt she'll be as careless as she has been."

Inari was inclined to agree, but she did not want to discourage the badger. "Do you think you can dig quietly?" she asked him.

"I can try." The badger began to claw at the boards.

"Banquo said that this was a Hell for many people," Inari said thoughtfully.

"What do you mean?"

"Well, Banquo and his crew clearly aren't in league with the Empress as such. They're just for hire. The same probably goes for the shark-demons. They've got no natural link with the Empress, have they?"

Miss Qi gave a delicate shudder. "Hardly."

"Then if the pirates and the shark-demons are their own entities, what about those birds?"

Miss Qi looked at her. Then they went to the window and looked up. The huge fringed wings were still circling the peak of the island, floating lazily on the thermals. There was no way that Inari and Miss Qi could be seen from below, unless someone was hiding in the ravine.

Inari tore the single sheet from the bed and they bundled it out of the window. It was much too short to make a rope, but could, perhaps, be waved. They did so.

"Pity we can't call out," Inari said as they flapped the sheet.

"They'll probably just think it's someone doing the washing," Miss Qi said.

"I doubt whether shark-demons do laundry, somehow."

They waved the sheet until their arms grew tired, while the badger continued to scratch at the rotting boards. But the great birds continued their endless procession around the summit, gliding like distant clockwork toys. Eventually Inari and Miss Qi gave up and sank back on the bed, clutching the sheet. The badger roused himself from the floorboards and shook his head like a dog. He had made a small hole.

"Mahogany," he said. "Old, but still tough."

"Maybe we could have another go at bribing the shark-demons," Inari suggested. They had already attempted this once, during the climb up the hill, but the demons had only grinned wider and shaken their arching heads.

"One could almost feel sorry for them," Miss Qi said with disdain. "I doubt the Empress will be able to recompense them any more than she could pay Banquo."

"Perhaps they'll find that out and let us go," Inari said, but she was not hopeful. Something about the way in which the shark-demons had looked at them, a cold glimmer in their unnatural eyes, had suggested that something more like dinner might be on the menu. Inari might not be able to die as such in this particular Hell, but she did not like the thought of being eaten.

A shadow fell over the window, abruptly cutting out the sunlight. Miss Qi was on her feet and Inari looked up to see a long, bald head peering in. Its feathers were bronze and black and green, so hard and sharp that they might have been real metal. And its eyes were human, too, like those of the shark-demons: set in wrinkled folds of goose-pimpled flesh.

"Aha," it said, in a man's voice. "So this is what all that flapping was about."

29

After the appearance of the city of Agarta, Zhu Irzh found that the dynamic between the members of their little team had changed somewhat. Roerich, though the instigator, had previously taken a back seat, allowing Omi to become de facto leader. And the young warrior had risen to the challenge, scouting ahead amongst the dunes and suggesting possible directions in which to travel. But since the city had risen out of the desert air, Omi had become distracted and preoccupied. Twice, Roerich had to repeat a question and eventually Zhu Irzh saw him give a little nod, as if a suspicion had become confirmed. That night, when they again made camp, Roerich drew the demon aside.

"You mentioned folk who became obsessed by this place," Zhu Irzh said. He looked to where Omi was gazing into the fire. "Is this what's happening to him?"

"I'm afraid it's the only conclusion I can draw," Roerich said. "I hope I'm wrong. But Agarta—it's a cursed place as well as a blessed one. Only the Enlightened are allowed within its precincts and yet it calls to the best among us, as though its purpose is a magnet of goodness."

"I suppose that makes me safe," the demon said.

"I told you. Don't be so sure. Agarta sees things in us that we do not necessarily know are there. But in the case of Omi—"

"Do people ever—just get over it?"

"Not really. I'm worried about his performance. Longing can sap the will."

"I can see how that could happen," Zhu Irzh said. "Is there anything we can do to snap him out of it? Given the ifrits and all that, we need him at peak capacity."

Roerich sighed. "I don't think we can just 'snap him out of it.' It may be that he'll come through it on his own. He is experienced in meditative disciplines."

"But you're not hopeful," Zhu Irzh said.

"No, I'm not."

"If this city is appearing to us," the demon said, "what does that mean?"

"It means Agarta is on the move," Roerich said. "That doesn't happen without good reason. You must understand, Zhu Irzh, that the city is itself an entity, just like those who live in it. The city council includes the city as a member and it has its own agenda."

The demon was growing used to inanimate objects that weren't. He merely nodded. That night, however, he was not surprised to find himself being shaken awake by Roerich.

"Omi's gone."

"Oh great. To look for his city, no doubt."

"He's had at least two hours head start," Roerich said,

"assuming that he took off at the start of his watch. I've only just woken."

"We can't have this, Nicholas. What if we'd been attacked when Omi was supposed to have been keeping watch?"

"I know." Roerich said nothing more.

The good thing about sand, even the gritty, stony soil of the Taklamakan, was that it still carried the traces of footprints. Omi had set off in a northeasterly direction, toward the heart of the desert, and he had moved with certainty. There was nothing faltering about the footsteps, which appeared with swift precision over the soft dunes. Roerich and Zhu Irzh, saying little, followed them, but there was no sight of the young warrior in the expanse of the desert ahead. Small hares danced in the moonlight, and whenever the demon glanced up he saw the moon itself, with the rabbit inside it, mocking him like an eye.

Omi had taken the scroll with him. Without that, the demon knew, all of their journey would be useless.

"If we can't find him—" he began.

"We will," Roerich said, and then, as if trying to reassure himself, echoed, "we *will*."

They had been walking for perhaps an hour when the demon first noticed it: tiny balls of sand scuttling beneath his feet. He stood still and listened. The distant boom of the dunes had been joined by a new sound, faint at first, then growing louder. It was a susurrus, a murmuring like the sea. Zhu Irzh's hair was stirred by a breath of wind and his coat ruffled in the sudden breeze. Then, with a cold clutch of fear that was an unfamiliar sensation to him, he knew what was happening.

"Roerich! Sand!"

"We've got to find shelter," Roerich said. The demon could see it now, a glaze over the dark distance of the desert. Sandstorm, and coming fast. He could taste grit on the wind.

He might not be able to die, but the prospect of being buried beneath a thousand tons of sand was horrifying. With Roerich, he bolted down the side of the dune, but he knew it was useless. There was nothing here apart from the roll of the dunes themselves; no canyons, not even a boulder behind which to cower. And the sand was roaring on, the wind whipping at the hem of Zhu Irzh's coat and filling his mouth with dust. As he had done before, he flung his sleeve in front of his face, trying to keep the sand out of his eyes, but the fringes of the storm were upon them now. He remembered what the policeman had told him back in Urumchi, about sandstorms so vicious that they were able to blast holes in parked cars. He had no problems believing it. For a moment, he glimpsed Roerich's hunched form against a swirling backdrop of particles, then it was blotted out.

"Nicholas!" he cried, and again, "Nicholas!"

The first time, the name was swallowed by the howl of the wind. On the second occasion, it rang out into a sudden silence.

"Roerich?" Zhu Irzh said aloud. He lowered his arm. The sand had gone. Only a faint shower of dust from the sleeve of his coat pattered to the floor. Zhu Irzh looked up at a towering marble wall. He stood on flagstones, so tightly joined together that you could not have slipped a hair between them. The air smelled of roses, and somewhere, like the sound of a fountain, someone was playing a lute.

He had found his way into Agarta. Or, more likely, Agarta had rescued him. Zhu Irzh breathed a sigh of uneasy relief. But what about Roerich, and Omi? There were signs of life, anyway, and even if he'd somehow been saved from the sand by accident, he'd still been saved. This was a city of the Enlightened: Would they know what to do with a demon in their midst? Feeling out of place, Zhu Irzh started walking in the direction of the lute.

After perhaps ten minutes' walk, he could see why the city had exerted such a hold over Omi. It was far beyond the merely pretty. Everything seemed perfectly proportioned. There were no awkward angles, no out-of-place vistas. The eye was led harmoniously from one splendor to the other and yet it was never dull. Roses were everywhere, cascading down the sides of the marble turrets. As Zhu Irzh walked, a nightingale began to sing, tremulous at first, and then with more confidence. Above, the sky had started to lighten. The demon made his way into a courtyard, reached through a round moon-gate under a fall of blossoming jasmine. The sound of the lute was growing clearer and then he saw the lute player: a middle-aged woman in a blue robe that fell like water around her feet. She did not look up as the demon approached, though his feet rang out on the flagstones. She finished her piece with a calm flourish, then said, "Seneschal Zhu Irzh."

The demon blinked. "You know who I am?"

"Why, of course," the woman said. It was hard to place her. Her hair was a steely gray, bound in a long braid, and her flat, calm face and folded eyes could have been Chinese, or something entirely different, Siberian, perhaps, or Native American. "The city told me you were here."

"There was a sandstorm," Zhu Irzh explained. "I was with someone—a man. Nicholas Roerich?"

"I know him."

"We were separated. I'm worried about him."

"The city will have collected him," the woman said. "The desert is riven with storms—some natural, some not."

"What makes the unnatural ones?"

"The ifrits conjure the sand."

"But someone conjures the ifrits, am I right?"

"You are not wrong."

"If Roerich's here," Zhu Irzh said, "I'd really like to speak to him. And there was someone else with us—he went missing." Perhaps not tactful to mention that he'd done so because he'd become besotted by the city itself. "A young warrior, named Omi."

The woman gave a slight frown. "If he is here, the city has not told me."

That defused the demon's suspicion that this person might *be* the city, an avatar, but maybe she was dissembling. "I need to find him," Zhu Irzh said.

"Why?"

"He has something that's important to me." Zhu Irzh didn't want to tell this woman any more than he had to—from what Roerich had said, the city was clearly on the side of light, but that didn't mean they shared an agenda. It felt weird to be here at all; it didn't make him as uncomfortable as being in Heaven had done, but it was certainly similar.

"I will try to find him for you," the woman said. "But for now, come inside." She rose in a watery swirl of robes and led the demon into a small pavilion. In it was a table, set with a number of plates and a large metal jug.

"Tea?"

Tea. In a supernatural, timeless city in the middle of the night. What the hell. "Shall I pour?" asked Zhu Irzh.

It occurred to him that it might not be wise to eat or drink anything. Mythologies of all the lands cautioned against doing so, and the fear that one might be trapped in such a world, anchored by physical desires. But Zhu Irzh had not heard of demons being so snared, and anyway, he was thirsty after all that sand. He sipped his tea, which was perfumed with jasmine, and waited while the woman went off on some unknown errand. Though she knew his name, she had not given him her own. Perhaps she did not have one.

Then someone walked quickly through the hangings of the pavilion and the demon looked up to see Roerich.

"Nicholas!" It surprised him a little to realize how pleased he was to see the man: it was like having Chen around, the feeling that somehow, everything would be all right.

"We seem to have been taken on board," Roerich said. "Omi is here."

"Is that a good thing? I mean," the demon said hastily, "obviously I'm glad he's okay. But isn't it a bit like giving someone a drug to which they're addicted?"

"I don't know how it will affect him," Roerich said. "I share your unease. It's more likely to be a problem when he has to leave, but we'll cross that bridge when we come to it."

"Where is he?"

"He's at the Council chamber, apparently—I haven't seen him yet. We're to join him there."

"The Council?"

"The Council of the Masters. Which includes Mistresses, by the way—you've met one of them, Nandini."

When they stepped outside the pavilion, Zhu Irzh saw that it had become significantly lighter, with a morning softness to the air. "Nicer than the desert," he remarked, as they walked through the rose garden.

"It's got its own microclimate," Roerich said. He pointed to a distant turret. "That's the Council chamber."

Now that dawn was coming, the demon was able to get a better sense of the city itself. Its harmoniousness was still evident, but its construction was certainly curious: it possessed no one form of architecture, but seemed assembled from all manner of buildings. Low-roofed cottages sat side by side with towering fortresses; pagodas sat next to humble dwellings. It should not have worked and yet, it did.

"The Masters are from all over the planet, remember," Roerich said when the demon pointed this out. "They have the homes they knew in life." He gestured to a temple held up by Grecian columns. "It mirrors our own history."

"Weird." But it worked, which was more than Zhu Irzh could say for Hell.

The way to the Council chamber led down a long, narrow street lined by marble walls. At the end of this, steps climbed in a semi-spiral up toward an ancient door: it looked like the medieval turrets Zhu Irzh had seen in pictures. Nandini stood on the steps, smiling.

"You've found it, good. I'm glad my instructions were adequate, Nicholas."

Zhu Irzh was aware of a sudden, acute nervousness, occasioned, he was sure, by being in the wrong place. He told himself that he'd hung out with the Emperor of Heaven; after all, they were friends. So why feel so uncomfortable now? Nandini was watching him with a penetrating dark stare.

"You can't help what you are," she said. "You can help what you do with it."

"Did you just read my mind?" Zhu Irzh demanded.

"I didn't need to. It was clear from the expression on your face," she said gently.

That obvious, eh? But the demon felt that whatever he tried to hide, these people would see through it. Nandini was different from the Celestials he had met—sharper, despite her outward serenity. More human, probably. Just be honest, the demon told himself. It didn't come naturally, but anything less would be a mistake.

"Are you ready to go in?" Roerich asked.

"As ready as I'll ever be."

It was hard to see, at first. Nandini led them up a wide stone staircase, plain and without ornamentation, and this was clear enough. But then they were shown into the Council chamber itself and Zhu Irzh found it impossible to focus on any one thing. Later, in memory, it became a little clearer. He thought there were tall windows, arched and looking out onto a vista of snow-capped mountains, even though he knew that the city had been sitting in the middle of the desert. He thought, too, that there had been stone flags beneath his feet, and a round table, surrounded by high-backed chairs. And he seemed to remember that sitting in the chairs had been a variety of people, of many races and ages, but in memory their faces were blurred, like the photos used in news reports to protect people from being identified.

Nandini was clear enough, and so was Roerich—and so was Omi, sitting in a chair beyond the Council table, underneath an open window. He approached Zhu Irzh, smiling, and the demon was surprised to discover how relieved he was to see the young warrior.

"I owe you an apology," Omi said in an undertone. "I shouldn't have gone off like that—I put you both in danger."

Zhu Irzh could tell that the young man was genuinely ashamed, so to save Omi face he said, "No worries. It turned out all right in the end. And if you hadn't gone off, then we might all be under several feet of sand by now. Who knows?"

"Even so," Omi said, but fell silent at a glance from Roerich. Zhu Irzh blinked, ducked his head, but still could not see the Council properly. He felt suddenly very small, like a child allowed at an adults' dinner party. It had been a long time since Zhu Irzh had been a small child—several hundred years, in fact—and he did not relish the sensation.

A voice came from the Council table. "Demon, ghost, warrior."

"That would be us," Zhu Irzh said, overcompensating for nerves by flippancy.

"You're carrying a spell," the voice said.

"I won it in a fair fight," Omi said, defensive.

"Can you help us take it to its rightful place?" Zhu Irzh said.

"You don't understand," Nandini said. "You see all that is around you, and you know that we saved you from the sand. But our power is limited."

"That wasn't what I understood," the demon said.

"That is because you don't know the wider picture. We are being rewritten."

"What?"

"The Book of Heaven has come to Earth," Nandini told him. "Omi has spoken to it, done its bidding."

"Was that wrong?" Omi asked. "I thought it was helping us against our enemy?"

"It is. But it has its own agenda. It has become displeased with its home in Heaven. It thinks that things need to be—revised. The spell that you're bearing will accomplish that—when you release the spell, it will enter reality and change it. Like throwing a stone into a pond—ripples will spread outward through time. The Khan may be removed, he may not, but what is certain is that the relationship between the worlds will be altered. The free concourse between the worlds will no longer be so open. You're likely to find yourself back in Hell." This last comment was directed at Zhu Irzh.

"Let me get this straight," Zhu Irzh said. "This spell is our best chance of defeating the Khan, and you're telling me that it's likely to permanently alter the entire world?"

"Effectively, yes."

Across the room, Omi shifted uncomfortably.

"Great. You said it could close the 'concourse between the worlds.' Why would this book want to do that?"

"Because Heaven's become corrupted," Roerich said. "The Book is one of Heaven's guardians."

"But I *know* the Jade Emperor. He's a friend." Too late it occurred to Zhu Irzh that having a demon as a personal acquaintance might not reflect all that well on Mhara, in the view of either the Book or Council. "Anyway, whatever. He's an exceptional person."

"But he has changed things," Nandini pointed out. "And the Book doesn't seem to approve of change."

"Neither did the old Emperor. Look what happened there." The demon stole a look at the Council, but found that his gaze slid off them, as if gliding on ice. His thoughts were moving too quickly for him to organize them properly, but one thing seemed relatively clear. "If the spell will have the effect that you think it will, then we can't use it. We'll have to think of something else."

Without your help. Zhu Irzh had the wit not to express this thought aloud, but the whole situation reminded him of Chen's dealings with Kuan Yin, in the earliest days of their working partnership. Then, Chen had only recently been cast out from the Goddess of Compassion and Mercy's protection—a punishment for marrying a demon—but it seemed to Zhu Irzh that it was a similar issue. All of these deities, these masters and mistresses, wanted you to do their dirty work for them, without actually sullying their pristine hands. And if you failed, or didn't conform to the strict dictates that they set, then you were history, even if it hadn't been your fault. Hell was at least more honest, the demon thought, as he had considered on a number of occasions before.

Roerich wasn't afraid to get his hands dirty, though. Zhu Irzh turned to his companion. "Nicholas. What do you think about all this? The best thing would be not to use the spell, yes?"

"I'd have agreed with you," Roerich said unhappily, "if it hadn't been for the fact that, as Nandini has just informed me, it's already too late."

30

"You're sure that's it?" Chen lowered the telescope from his eye. The war-junk rode at anchor, behind the lee of a reach of rock.

At his side, Li-Ju nodded. "I've only seen it once before, but it fits the specifications. It's the Empress' ship."

Chen didn't have a problem believing this. The black boat slid over the sparkling surface of the sea like a spectral vessel. Even in what was clearly a Hell, it did not belong in this world of sunlight and ocean. If he squinted slightly, it was almost possible to see the islands through its form.

"She's found a way out," he remarked.

"Yes. But with what end in mind?"

"She's also found allies, it would seem," Chen said.

"Or coerced them."

"Inari's on that ship. And Miss Qi, and the badger. We need to have a plan of action." It was all Chen could do not to suggest that they immediately storm the vessel, but impatience had proved the parent of disaster on more than one occasion. They needed a strategy.

"Not knowing the lay of the land—or sea, in this case—makes things difficult," Li-Ju said. "I suggest we follow, at a safe distance. If we can do so out of sight then so much the better."

"If she does see us," Chen asked, "is there anything that will mark this as a Celestial boat?"

"No. We stripped it of its banners before setting out from Heaven."

"So unless she's got someone on board who knows all the craft of this Hell, this could be just another ship," Chen said, aware of the triumph of hope over experience. They were clearly a warship, after all.

"Only one way to find out," Li-Ju said, with a fierce and un-Celestial grin.

They kept close to the shore, hugging the island as closely as they could without running afoul of the sharp rocks that fanged out from under the surface of those deceptively calm azure waves. The black ship sailed ahead, also curving close to shore. Chen wondered what its ultimate destination might be. The island itself showed no signs of habitation, although a skein of immense birds wheeled around its craggy summits. Had the Empress found her way here by chance, or had she sailed here by invitation? There was nothing about the ship's course to indicate where it might be bound.

Then the black ship started to tack out from the coast, her sails veering into the wind. They had a choice: either skulk beneath the cliffs and hide, or follow her out into the open ocean. Li-Ju chose to follow.

"The boat's not armed, although the Empress has her own spellcraft."

"Have you taken precautions against that?"

"Yes. The boat's heavily warded. But then, so was Kuan Yin's boat. This is a warship, however, and has more effective protection."

At least, we hope so, Chen thought. They pulled out from under the cliffs, fully visible now. But the black ship did not falter in her course. She continued to tack out into the wider ocean, her sails hissing in the wind of an unknown Hell.

31

"A land of our own," the Roc said. "Or it's no deal."

"I can't promise you that," Inari told it, leaning perilously out of the window. She did not like being so close to the Roc's ferocious bronze beak; nor did she like the gleam in its molten eyes. But the great bird was, thus far, their best chance of getting out of captivity, if not this Hell itself, and it had proved more willing to negotiate than the shark-demons.

The Roc ruffled its metal plumage. "In that case . . ."

"Wait," Inari said, anxious that it would simply take off and not return. "Don't go. We can't contact our friends. But I am close to the Jade Emperor. My husband's colleague is the stepson of the Emperor of Hell and about to marry a demon who has connections with the Hindu levels. She's also wealthy in her own right," Inari added, thinking of the acres that Jhai owned in China, the places where her secret labs were said to be situated. "Why, even now she's in Western China, buying land."

She did not hope to convince the Roc, but it seemed that she'd done a better job than she'd thought.

"Indeed?" the bird said, with bright-eyed interest. "In that case . . . They will be happy to have you back, will they? They didn't decide to dispatch an inconvenient little demon down to somebody else's Hell in the first place, did they?"

"Certainly not! We were kidnapped," protested Inari, but Miss Qi added icily, "Besides, I am a Celestial warrior. If you know anything of my kind, you know that we cannot lie. My friend is telling you the truth."

"I'll need something in writing," the Roc said.

"I don't have a pen."

"Blood will do."

They had no weapon, and neither wanted the potential bondage of a touch from the Roc's razor claws, but the bird dived in a clatter of wings and plucked a thorn from one of the bushes in the ravine below. Inari and Miss Qi drew a drop of blood from each wrist, then watched as the liquid hissed into a word upon the air and faded. Inari had seen enough to know that although it had left no trace, it was as binding a promise as any inscribed upon a piece of parchment.

"Now," the Roc said. It stretched its wings, a twenty-foot span or more. "Let's ride."

Scrambling out of the narrow window and bundling the badger through the gap, Inari was sure that the shark-demons would not be far behind them, but the building lay in silence as the Roc rose up, spiraling on the warm wind. The hut soon fell away beneath them, revealing a courtyard that they had not seen on the way in: pillars, and half-rotted statues of misshapen forms.

"It's a temple!" Inari said.

"To sea demons," the Roc told her over its shoulder. "Things come here when their worship on Earth is long forgotten."

Well forgotten, Inari thought, glancing back. She did not like the look of those gaping piscine mouths, too reminiscent of the shark-demons. Perhaps they worshipped themselves.

"And you?" Miss Qi asked. "Who worshipped you?"

The Roc's beak yawned, in what might have been a laugh. "I was not worshipped, though maybe I wanted to be. I do not remember. I was a political adviser to a well-remembered dictator. A world of car bombs and hand grenades, not swords and bows. I am not long dead. I was sent here, in the form of a rapacious, predatory bird. No doubt I deserved it."

Inari was silent. No doubt he did.

"I should like the same kind of power, without the risk," the Roc went on. "My colleagues—I cannot call them friends—would agree."

"In this form?" Miss Qi asked, and Inari knew that she was wondering what kind of creature they might be unleashing upon some unsuspecting realm. "This one, or another?"

"Let's see when the time comes," the Roc said smoothly, and winked a glowing eye.

Over the ocean, and beyond. No one came after them. Inari, who did not like heights, forced herself to look down on a couple of occasions as they flew, and saw boats as tiny as matchstick vessels, sailing upon that endless sea. But there was no land other than islands: this Hell was, in its way, almost as featureless as the Sea of Night. At last, though there was no visible curve to the world before them, a dusky twilight began to fall.

"Heaven's too far," the Roc said. "Earth will have to do. It will be interesting to see Earth again. I doubt it's changed much."

Inari doubted that, too. "If you can just fly to Earth," she asked, "why haven't you done so before now?"

"Because I couldn't. The key is your blood. Someone had to freely pay, in blood, to liberate me. People weren't exactly queuing up."

"Glad we could help," Inari said, looking down again. The sea had darkened, until it truly resembled the Sea of Night. Then she realized that it actually *was* the Sea of Night: somewhere back there, they had left Banquo's Hell behind and were heading into the realms between the worlds.

"Ah!" said the Roc, in a gasping cry. "Earth is waiting!" And there was a gap in the clouds ahead, with light pouring through it.

32

In Agarta, Omi replayed the memories over and over again. He knew he should not have left his companions, but the call of the city had been too strong. Omi barely realized when he rose quietly from his watch-place by the fire and headed out into the desert. The stars ahead spun in their courses, moving too fast and too far, and the air slammed into his lungs as he stumbled up and down the dunes. It was like being drugged, or losing one's mind. Occasionally, memories of Roerich, of the demon, of the spell that he still carried inside his coat rose to ambush him with guilt, but Omi thrust it aside and carried on.

Halfway up the next dune, he saw his grandfather standing at the summit. The old spirit was insubstantial: Omi could see the stars through his body.

"Omi, what are you doing?" Grandfather said in distress.

"This is not where you should be. What about your friends, your mission?"

Omi's mouth opened, but no words came out even though he tried to speak. He gaped like a fish, gasping for air, struggled on up the sand. He pushed his way through Grandfather's form and the old man's body dissipated in rags and tatters onto the desert wind. Only then did Omi cry out. He knew that Grandfather was a ghost, but what if he had hurt the old man so greatly that he would not want to return? Omi fell to his knees at the top of the dune and put his face in his hands. When he next looked up, there was an oasis below him.

It was like, yet unlike, the oasis of the crescent moon lake. There was a pavilion—a much smaller one—and a low pool of water, but the place smelled stagnant and dead, and there was no sign of movement around it. The scroll that contained the spell leaped inside Omni's pocket, and for a moment he forgot the city. His vision sharpened and cleared. Somewhere, he thought he heard his grandfather's voice, but when he looked round, no one was there. The scroll was speaking, however, strongly and without words, a liquid fountain-fall of sound, and it impelled him into movement. He sprang up and ran down the dune toward the oasis.

When he reached it, Omi became even more aware that something was obviously wrong. The trees that surrounded the pavilion were stunted, their leaves withered, and the pool was almost dry. The pavilion itself was scoured and bleached by the sand, until the wood of which it was made looked ancient and rotted. There was a skitter of dust down its steps, sparkling in the moonlight.

The spell leaped again, whispering. Omi took it from his pocket and without stopping to think, opened the scroll. Immediately images poured out upon the air, flickering like flame and causing the world to stop. The dust paused in its tracks, the little breeze that had rattled the dry leaves stilled and died. Omi watched as the lines that had made up the map on the scroll sank into the dry earth and disappeared. There was an electric second of waiting. The dust on the steps began, so slowly, to move again. Life spread outward from the place where the spell had sunk in. Under the moon, the dry leaves lifted and grew green again. Water rose within the pool, ebbing up from deep beneath the surface of the sand, and the pavilion gleamed as if freshly painted. Omi felt a spring of hope: he had acted rightly, after all, and the memory of Agarta hung before him in the air. But then the dust on the pavilion steps swirled upward. Omi watched as it started to spin, whirling and whistling around the oasis and drawing more sand up with it until the oasis was surrounded by a twisting wall of sand. More spread outward until Omi could no longer see the stars, could no longer see the desert beyond, could see nothing except the pavilion itself. And then the sand turned inward and Omi flung himself up the pavilion steps and hammered on the unyielding door until he was unable to see or breathe and the world went dark.

When he woke, the city had come. It lay all around him, and once he had risen to his feet and breathed in its perfumed air, it was, Omi discovered with a cold pang of pain, no longer what he wanted.

33

"So you just—what? Activated it?" the demon asked. They were out of the Council chamber now, to Zhu Irzh's relief, and standing on a circular landing. Nandini was not with them, but Zhu Irzh had not seen her go.

"Yes." Omi looked down at the flagstones. "I can't tell you how ashamed I am, Zhu Irzh. I will be honest. You are a demon, out of Hell, and I am a sacred warrior. And I am the one who—" He paused.

"Fucked up?"

"Yes. I can't make excuses for myself."

"Actually, I think he can," Roerich said. "The pull of Agarta is legendary. I explained to you, Zhu Irzh, that it has driven men mad before now. And I'm not convinced that Agarta didn't somehow persuade him into releasing the spell. Or the spell into releasing itself. Whatever the Council says, it doesn't always know the mind of the city."

"I'm not blaming him," the demon said. "I know how you can get sucked into things. It's unfortunate. But we'll just have to deal with it."

"The question is how."

"Do you have any ideas?"

"No," said Roerich bleakly, "I do not."

They could stay for a day, Nandini told them. After that, the city would expect them to move on. The demon greeted this instruction with a mixture of trepidation and relief. He didn't relish the prospect of getting back out into the desert, given the possibility of radical change, but neither did he want to stay: Agarta had started to give him the creeps. City of the Enlightened Masters it might be, but he didn't like the feeling of continually being watched, even though no one was in sight.

With Roerich and a silent, withdrawn Omi, he dined in the little pavilion on an exquisite vegetarian dinner. They were shown chambers in a nearby tower, by Nandini. Zhu Irzh, more fatigued than he'd realized, fell asleep immediately.

He didn't know what woke him, but once roused, he was instantly and fully awake, senses jangling. He got off the bed and crossed to the window. Beyond the glass, the sky was filled with stars. Agarta was on the move: the city was flying. He was looking out across a galaxy. The demon gaped open-mouthed for a moment, then ran to rouse Roerich.

But Roerich wasn't there. The bed in which he had been resting was empty, with no sign that anyone had ever slept in it. With growing apprehension, Zhu Irzh went in search of Omi and discovered that the young warrior's bed was also vacant.

Zhu Irzh stepped out onto the landing. "Nandini?" he called, aloud. Somehow he knew that she'd hear him, but no answer came. He ran back down the stairs and threw open the double doors at the base of the hall, to stand teetering on the threshold.

The street wasn't there, either. Instead, the door opened onto star-filled darkness, even though Zhu Irzh had seen the city below only minutes before. It reminded him of the Sea of Night, but this galaxy-whirl was alive, just as the city had been. The demon slammed the door shut and stepped back against the wall, his thoughts swirling as fast as the stars. A voice said out of nowhere, calm, verging on amused, "It's only you I'm taking."

"You're the city, aren't you?"

"That's right."

"Where are we going?"

"Back."

"What do you mean: 'back'?" Zhu Irzh asked.

"Ah," the city said. "You've been there before."

The demon knew where it meant. "To the Tokarians?"

"That's when things started to fracture," Agarta said. "The Book has rewritten things now. But the Book no longer has that authority."

"Somehow," Zhu Irzh told it, "I got the impression that you were working with the Book."

"We had a deal," said the city. "I was to help you, to set the spell. But the Book, it seems, had other ideas."

"It stabbed you in the back?"

"That is too Hellish a way of putting it. It has changed matters."

"Maybe that's a good thing?"

"I am here for humans," Agarta said. "The Book isn't."

"Ah." There was a pause. "Whose agenda *is* it running, then? Its own?"

"The Book made Heaven. Perhaps more than one Heaven—it's far older than I. My age was after the Ice Age; the Book dates from long before that, from the lands beyond the Northern stars."

"The Book wants Heaven to withdraw from the human world," Zhu Irzh said.

"And so it has rewritten the world to make sure that this happens." Involuntarily, Zhu Irzh glanced toward the tall, arched windows along the hallway. All he could see was the calm, marble street outside, but he knew that if he opened the window, he would once more be looking upon a starfield. And beyond, on Earth, just what the hell had the Book *done?* It was beginning to hit home that the Book had done something genuinely huge. "Has it changed the whole world? Or only a bit of it? Only China?"

"I don't know. Whatever it's done, it's removed me from Earth."

This hadn't occurred to the demon. "*You* can't get back?"

"I can return, but only to the point when the world changed. That's when I'm taking you."

"Why me? Why not Roerich?" were Zhu Irzh's next questions. "Surely he'd be a better candidate?" He'd have suggested Omi, but the warrior was clearly susceptible to unfortunate influences and maybe it was better that he was out of it.

"Roerich is not entirely of the world, being dead. You are."

"I'm not really used to saving the world," the demon said. "That's my partner's job."

If a city can be said to smile, then this was what Agarta did. "You had better accustom yourself to the notion, then."

34

Li-Ju's celestial warship rode at anchor, close to a half-moon bay. The Empress' vessel had disappeared, heading swiftly and unhesitatingly up a narrow creek. Li-Ju was reluctant to follow her, fearing a trap, and Chen was compelled to agree with him.

"It's too narrow," he said, looking at the mouth of the creek. A thin tongue of mud unfurled into the clear water of the bay and the sides of the creek were gnarled with roots. "If we go down there and something comes up behind us, we'll be stuck."

"It's bad enough in the bay," Li-Ju said. He cast an uneasy glance behind him.

"So what do we do? I'd suggest going in on foot." Chen turned to the Celestial captain. "I'm prepared to go in alone. I can't ask anyone to risk themselves. And if I'm not back by an agreed upon time, then go on without me."

"The Emperor sent us to help you," Li-Ju said. "And that's what we'll do. You and I will go."

"Very well," Chen said, slightly ashamed of how relieved he felt.

Li-Ju ordered a small boat to be slung over the side, then they climbed down into it and rowed in silence toward the mouth of the creek. Chen, armed with one of Li-Ju's bows and a sword, kept a close eye on the water beneath, just in case. But though the water of the bay remained clear, once they traveled into the creek itself the water was too murky to get a proper view. They proceeded cautiously, until they had moved so far along the creek that the bay and the warship were no longer visible. The creek narrowed, the branches almost meeting overhead, until they rowed down what seemed like a long, fetid green tunnel. There was no sign of the Empress' ship, until they rounded a bend and saw it ahead, startlingly close.

At once Li-Ju took the little boat into the side of the creek, under the root growth. Like being in a cave, Chen thought: the great roots arched and curved overhead. He didn't like the idea of what might be living in amongst those roots, either. The underside of the boat scraped mud, but the creek itself must form a deep channel, for the Empress' boat was able to travel down it.

"Do you think we've been seen?"

Li-Ju peered out between the roots. "There's no sign of anyone."

A voice spoke out of midair, making Chen start. "Captain! There's a ship approaching."

Celestials do not usually curse, but Li-Ju looked as though he might be on the verge of doing so. He spoke into a small mirror, carried in one of his long sleeves. "Can you take evasive action?"

Over the captain's shoulder, Chen glimpsed the agitated face of the crewman in the mirror. "Doing so now, sir!"

The mirror blurred and went dark. "They're changing position," Li-Ju said. Mentally, Chen wished them luck.

"Look," he said. "We're close enough to go in on foot."

"I agree."

Together, Chen and Li-Ju clambered out of the boat and up through the tree roots onto the bank. It was dense jungle at this point, and not easy going, but they scrambled through the undergrowth until they came level with the Empress' vessel, then they climbed up one of the broad tree trunks and onto a thick branch. Disregarding the insects that crawled in and out of its bark, Chen began to inch forward along the branch, hoping that the ship wouldn't suddenly surge forward. They were close to the side of the ship now. The voice spoke again from Li-Ju's mirror.

"The boat's coming down the creek, Captain."

"Did they see you?"

"We don't think so. We're behind the headland."

Chen glanced up at the birds that still circled the peak. Spies? The prospect that they had been watched all along, but not from the sea, was a dismaying one, but it obviously could not be ruled out. He continued his slow progress along the tree branch, trying to avoid the sharp spines that periodically protruded from the bark. He was over the water now, close to the deck of the boat and at an angle to be able to see into one of the cabins. There was not, as far as he could tell, anyone there, nor could he glimpse anyone in the wheel-house.

Behind him, Li-Ju said, "Ready?"

"Ready." They dropped down onto the deck, landing with more noise than Chen was comfortable with. He drew the sword and ducked behind the side of the wheel-house, with Li-Ju close behind. They waited, but there was no sound from within. The silence was beginning to give Chen the creeps, as though there

THE IRON KHAN

was no one at all on board, the boat traveling under its own voli-
tion. Then Li-Ju nudged him.

"Look!"

Another ship was edging its way up the inlet. Chen thought it
was the vessel he'd seen earlier, heading out into the open sea. It
was hard to tell, as the ship's sails were furled. The mast brushed
the treetops, but only by a few inches: this boat was made to fit
this world. It was being rowed, the creak of the oars and the splash
as they hit the water were the only sounds he could hear.

Next moment, he dragged Li-Ju back into the shadows of the
wheel-house. A figure strode past: black-armored, with a high
plait of red hair.

"That's—" Li-Ju started to say, then bit it off. There were footsteps overhead, clattering down the steps. Three more figures, of
near-identical aspect, ran past Chen.

"Who are they?" Chen whispered.

Li-Ju was frowning. "They're the Empress' guards."

"They don't seem to be doing much guarding."

Peering round the corner of the wheel-house, Chen saw that
the new arrival was bearing down fast on the Empress' ship. Its
sails were still furled, but its oars had stopped their motion and
Chen could not see how it was still coming on. Magic? No doubt.

As the craft approached, one of the guards gave an ear-splitting
scream: Chen had never heard a more obvious war-cry. The guard
drew her scimitar; moments later, a man dressed in blue with a
cutlass between his teeth leaped over the side from the oncoming
ship and hit the deck with legs braced. More men followed him
and soon the deck was filled with fighting, struggling crew members. But it was evident to Chen that the struggle was unevenly
matched. One of the Empress' guards struck off the head of an
attacker and Chen winced. The head, grinning, flew through the

air, but before it could strike the water it disappeared in a plume
of fire. At once, it was back on the neck from which it had been so
recently severed. The guard went down under a swift stroke of the
cutlass and vanished, but she did not reappear.

"Sent back to her own place," Li-Ju said.

"Which is?"

"Another Heaven. They were hired from there."

They did not, Chen thought, seem to have been very effective.
But he was wasting time, watching a battle in which he had little
part. He had someone to find.

With Li-Ju close behind, he ducked into the empty wheel-house.
A narrow flight of steps led down into the depths of the ship. Chen
dropped down the steps and found himself in a passage.

This had clearly been a Celestial vessel. Once upon a time,
anyway. Now, the wooden panels were eaten and eroded away,
covered in cobwebs and a curious black film. Chen touched it,
cautiously, and it came away, staining his fingertips like soot. Yet
it felt soft, not at all gritty.

"If you ask me," Li-Ju whispered in his ear, "that's what the
Empress has exuded."

"*Exuded?*"

"Yes. The evil that she contains, breathed out into the air so
that it does not stain her soul. Or so she hopes."

That was a lot of evil. Never mind, Chen thought grimly. He'd
met worse.

Hastily, they searched the ship as the fighting raged overhead
on deck. There was no sign of Inari, Miss Qi, or the badger. But
one of the doors showed signs of abuse, as though something had
tried to break through it. A badger's claws? Chen was willing to
put money on it. And attached to a splinter in the wall was a single long strand of pale hair.

"Miss Qi," Chen murmured. More than the signs of hair and claw, however, was the twinge that told him of Inari: a flutter across the surface of his soul. "She's been here."

"Not here now, though," Li-Ju said.

"No. So where is she?" The emptiness of the vessel, the presence of the possessed or manipulated guards, was beginning to get to Chen. And there was something else, as well. Something waiting.

"This way," he said, and they sprinted down the rotting passageway.

35

With Miss Qi and the badger, Inari clung to the Roc's back as they flew onward toward Earth. The bright gap in the sky was widening and she could see land ahead.

"Singapore Three," the bird said over its shoulder. Miss Qi craned her neck.

"I can't see it."

"This is where we are headed," the Roc said.

"It might be where we're headed," Inari replied, "but where *is* it?"

No towering apartments were visible. The red Jaruda symbol of Jhai's company, Paugeng, no longer lit the sunset sky. The harbor was there—a wide muddy inlet—and Inari could see a huddle of huts on the banks of a river. But the dome of the Opera House, the mass of government buildings, the temples, and avenues—none of these were there.

"Where is it?" Miss Qi asked, blankly.

"Look!" Inari said, pointing. "There's the Night Harbor!"

It had never been a place for which she had held any affection, being the gateway to both Heaven and Hell. But now the sight of its oblong black form made it feel like an old friend.

"I thought this was a city?" the Roc said.

"It was. Where have you taken us?"

"This is Earth!" the Roc said, clearly as surprised as they were. "You can feel it."

The bird was right. If Inari reached into herself, her core—further even than the child that swam, dreaming, in her womb—she felt Earth there, the pull and weight of the human world. It was more than instinct; it was knowledge.

"But where's the city?" echoed Miss Qi.

Clinging to the Roc's metallic feathers, they circled the place where Singapore Three had been. It was definitely the right location; Inari could tell this from the underlying geography. But something—not just the lack of the city—was different.

"Magic," Miss Qi whispered.

"Yes, but what kind of magic?" Looking down from the Roc's back, she could see the air sparkling, a fine dust permeating the atmosphere, but visible from the corners of the eyes, not when studied directly. Inari knew it for the aftermath of magical work, on an immense scale. She'd seen such work before, but only in Hell.

"Yes," Miss Qi said, when Inari pointed this out to her. "Someone must have stolen the city."

"Or destroyed it." Inari could still feel Singapore Three, but it was like an echo, or a fading dream.

"I don't think it's been destroyed," Miss Qi said. "I can sense it, but it's in the wrong place. That's what made me think it must have been stolen."

"But who would steal a city? And why?" The main problem with Miss Qi's hypothesis, Inari thought, was who would *want* it.

"I grow tired," the Roc said, and soared downward toward the little hummock of an island.

"Wait!" Inari commanded. "Land on shore. Please. We need to find out what's happened." This new shore might prove to have unknown dangers, but they stood more chance of discovering the truth about the changes if they weren't marooned.

"I could just turn around and take you back to my Hell," the Roc pointed out. "Since there appears to be little for me here."

"You said you wanted land of your own," said Inari. "Maybe this is your chance to take it."

"Yes," said Miss Qi, with a cunning that Inari had not expected in her. "There might be new prey."

The Roc did not reply, but their comments had evidently given it food for thought, because it glided over the islands and headed for the coast. Inari looked down as they passed above the harbor: no boats now rode at anchor in the bay, nor was there any sign of the typhoon shelter.

"There's a plane!" Miss Qi said, suddenly. Inari looked ahead. The Celestial warrior was right: a jet was streaking across the sky, leaving a vapor trail behind it. With the Roc still circling, they watched as it headed downward to a flat piece of land close to the bay. This was not, Inari knew, where the airport was situated in her own day.

"That doesn't look like a fighter plane," Miss Qi said, frowning.

"It isn't." Inari didn't know much about aircraft, but she recognized this one from the red symbol emblazoned across its fuselage. It was one of the Paugeng jets; Jhai's private craft. She leaned forward in excitement.

"The woman who owns that plane has a lot of power. She's the one I was telling you about. Can you land us near it?"

"Very well," the Roc said, in slightly more conciliatory tones now that there was a chance of getting what it had come for. It headed inland, toward the rudimentary landing strip. The plane had landed now and was slowing. The Roc took them down to a slight rise and Inari scrambled gratefully from its back. The badger shook himself. Miss Qi took Inari's arm.

"Are you sure that Jhai's in there?"

"I can't be sure." Inari looked around her at the desolate coastline. "Things have altered so much . . ."

But she had to take the risk. Leaving the Roc ruffling its feathers on the rise, they headed for the aircraft, which had now taxied to a halt. It was with considerable relief that Inari saw the door open and Jhai herself swing down a ladder to the ground.

"Inari! What the hell?" Jhai spotted her Celestial bodyguard. "Miss Qi! And what's that bird doing there?"

"We were kidnapped. Ended up in someone's Hell. Got rescued," Miss Qi said. Jhai appreciated brevity, Inari knew.

"Oh. Sorry to hear that. I've just been working, out West, then in Beijing. Had to leave Zhu Irzh—he got involved in a case. Left Beijing airport earlier and as we were halfway here, something happened."

"The city's gone," Inari said, feeling that she was stating the obvious.

"Let me tell you, it's not the only thing that's disappeared. The whole of China's changed. One minute I was looking out of the window at urban sprawl, the next, it wasn't there."

"Is this really Earth?" Miss Qi asked. "Or some kind of parallel world?"

"That would seem to be the obvious explanation," Jhai said. She looked up, to see a passenger jet heading over the hills. "Anyone up in the air seems not to have been affected, though. I've tried to get hold of Zhu Irzh but I can't reach him."

"And Wei Chen?" Inari faltered.

Jhai shook her head. "I'm sorry, Inari. No sign of him. But this world isn't entirely empty. As we flew in I saw villages—even some little towns. So it isn't completely unpopulated."

And as if to punctuate her words, her cellphone rang.

36

Zhu Irzh watched the stars as they flew, galaxies whisking by. The city was speeding up, taking him into the past: he could feel the years rolling back, affecting him at the cellular level. This was not the subtle transition that he'd experienced when he'd first slipped into the Tokarian village, but was swift and brutal. It took him a moment to realize that the city had stopped moving, and then he felt windswept and breathless.

"Are we nearly there yet?"

The city did not reply. Instead, it began to fade, the stars flickering out one by one, the walls folding down into themselves. It was a calm process with an air of unstoppable authority about it: Agarta had done this before. It reminded Zhu Irzh of watching a computerized image slowly dismantle. When it was over, he stood alone in the desert, a bright sun golden above him and the scent of incense on the light breath of the wind.

The demon followed it. Whereas the southern part of the desert had featured those huge dunes, this terrain did not: it looked more like another planet. Black grit crunched beneath Zhu Irzh's boots and a line of old red hills broke the horizon. Then he heard singing. It was so unexpected that Zhu Irzh stopped dead and listened.

It wasn't human. He could tell that much. And it was coming from above. The demon looked up. Overheard, perhaps at a height of some thirty feet, a group of women soared in flight. Their long, trailing garments floated around them as they flew in brightly colored streamers and each one wore a conical hat, like a small beehive.

Then one of them spotted Zhu Irzh. She gave a scream and a second later, all of them were drifting down to cluster around him.

"Ladies, *ladies,*" the demon said, not displeased. "There's no need to be quite so enthusiastic."

"But what *are* you?" There didn't seem to be any linguistic barrier, although Zhu Irzh could tell that he was not speaking, or hearing, his native tongue.

"I am a demon. From Hell."

One of the flying women frowned. "I've never heard of such a place."

"I can assure you it exists," Zhu Irzh said, conscious of some unease. Perhaps it no longer did, in this timeline, or perhaps its gateways were much less clearly marked than they were in his own world. "And you—you are akashi, aren't you?"

"Yes." There was twittering, and a certain amount of giggling. "How did you know?"

"I've—met your kind before." But he was not sure whether this was really true. None of them looked quite like the akashi he had encountered, and so maybe none of them were. Could the spell alter appearance in addition to—well, everything else?

The akashi laughed behind their hands, which were slender and clawed. "Are you going to visit the Enlightened One?"

"Who is he?" Then Zhu Irzh hastily amended, "Or should I say *she?*"

More laughter. "*He* lives in the cave. Over that ridge."

Well, why not? It wasn't as though he had a clue what he was doing, after all. "I'll go there, then," the demon said.

The akashi rose into the air in a flock, like birds, their streamers fluttering around them. Zhu Irzh watched them go with a faint regret. Maybe they'd come back later. In the meantime, he might as well see who this Enlightened One was.

Over the ridge lay a grove of acacia. Wherever he was in this timeline, he didn't think it was where he'd been previously. He could see what were clearly caves: a long, high line of rock, interspersed with dark hollows. But the air was sparkling. A crystalline stream ran between the trees.

It felt like Heaven. And that made Zhu Irzh nervous. He kept walking toward the caves and as he did so, he became aware that there was someone within. He was being watched. At the foot of the cliff face, he paused and looked up.

"I am here," someone said.

"Are you the Book?" Zhu Irzh asked with some trepidation. He wasn't sure that he could give an account of himself to that particular entity.

"Which book is that? We have many books here. Come and see for yourself."

"How?" The cliff face rose sheer before him.

"Step upon the air," the voice said. Frowning, the demon did so and found himself hovering a foot or so above the ground.

"I've never done that before!" Perhaps this was how the akashi managed their flight: an invisible staircase. Experimentally, he continued to climb and found himself standing in front of a narrow ledge, some hundred feet up the cliff face. He stepped onto it and said aloud, "Where to now?"

"Here." There was a cave entrance some few yards along the ledge. Inside, it took the demon's eyes a moment to adjust to the dim light. Then he took a step back.

The face was huge and golden, the eyes elongated. It was smiling.

"Buddha?"

"One of my avatars."

"Wait a minute," Zhu Irzh said. "You were a living being, weren't you? And as far as I remember, you weren't contemporary with the Tokarians—they were much earlier."

"That is so. But in fact, my spirit has always been around, staking a claim on certain places. This visage you see before you is not me as I truly am, but only the face that humans have put upon me."

This was something that Zhu Irzh understood. He nodded.

"You, however," the Buddha said, "truly do not belong."

It was said courteously, but with a query. And the divinity had not known about the Book. Zhu Irzh decided to explain.

"I have never heard of such a thing," the Buddha said, wonderingly. "And you are a demon."

"Ah, yes. That." His origins had embarrassed him before, Hell knew, but rarely so much as now. Then he remembered that Agarta had taken him in and he stood a little straighter. "But I am not on a demonic errand."

"You're speaking the truth," the Buddha said. "I can hear it. How odd."

"I need to find the Tokarians," Zhu Irzh told him. "Can you help me?" He didn't see why the Buddha should do so, but it couldn't hurt to ask.

"One of the girls will take you there," the Buddha said.

Zhu Irzh perked up. "Fine with me."

He didn't expect her to be a deer, but in retrospect, it made a certain amount of sense. The akashi, she explained, were animal spirits: deer and birds and butterflies, anything gentle and lovely. It reminded him of the Indian Hell belonging to Jhai's cousin, from which he had recently been obliged to escape.

"And you can go where you please on the face of this world?" Zhu Irzh asked, just to make sure.

"Yes, of course. Often, we go to the mountain forests to visit our friends the tiger spirits."

Tiger spirits. Hmm. Best not mention that other close encounter with tiger spirits, or even that he was engaged to one.

"How nice." It *was* just like Heaven, Zhu Irzh thought. No matter how long ago this might be, he didn't think Earth had ever been so pleasant. He wondered what else the Book had managed to achieve. The deer skipped ahead, darting through the long grass. It might be that this was simply her natural form for a journey, or that the Buddha had asked her to take this shape to remove temptation from visiting demons. Easy to be cynical. Easy to be right, though.

"Is it very far?" he asked.

"A little way, but the journey is so pleasant," the deer replied, pausing to munch on some flowers. This was not like the desert he had known, either: closer to steppe, with miles of gently waving grass dotted with spring blossoms. The air smelled sweet and fresh.

Zhu Irzh sighed. It was like stepping into Disneyland. Despite the charms of this place, he preferred the Earth as it had been, in all its multifarious complexity. And if the Tokarians were as pleasant as the akashi, would they actually be any help? He might have to end up frightening people to get answers out of them, and in that case, would the Book's new rules simply write him out of existence?

These questions reached a head of concern as they stepped over the next rise and a small settlement came into view. There were vestiges of the village which Zhu Irzh had so briefly glimpsed before the sand came in and he and Nicholas were rescued. It was low, but the defensive clay wall that had protected it from enemies and the desert was no longer there. Sheep grazed on sloping pastures and a child was running down the slope. Her fair hair streamed out behind her like a banner; it seemed the Tokarians—if these were indeed they—still retained their Celtic appearance.

"Here we are," the deer said, unnecessarily. "Do you need an introduction?"

"That would be helpful," Zhu Irzh said. He didn't think the sudden manifestation of a demon in their midst would please the villagers all that much. But if he was in the company of a friend of the Buddha . . .

"Then I will go with you," the deer said, scampering ahead. Sighing again, the demon followed.

The villagers came out to meet them as they approached. One woman—a tall girl with long, light brown braids—bent to speak to the deer and the akashi metamorphosed back into her human form, streamers twirling. But when they saw Zhu Irzh they grew silent and fearful.

"It's all right," the akashi reassured them. "He was sent by the Buddha."

"I'm looking for something," Zhu Irzh told them. "A book."

"What's a 'book'?"

Ah. He'd been afraid of this.

"Something that's written down."

"Written?"

Whatever form the Book had taken on its return to this time, it wasn't the one he'd been hoping for. Damn. Zhu Irzh decided, uncharacteristically, not to engage in subterfuge. He seemed to be growing more naturally honest as the years went by. Another of those depressing signs of maturity and age, no doubt. "What I'm actually looking for is a piece of magic. Creation magic."

The woman with the braids was frowning. "You'll need to talk to the shaman, I think."

"Is he available?"

"She." And at this Zhu Irzh's heart gave a bound. If this proved to be the woman he'd last seen perched on the edge of a parapet, about to leap onto a crane's back . . .

And when they took him in among the huts to a low cottage near the well, his hopes were realized.

"It *is* you!"

The woman crouching over the fire looked up and frowned. "Have we met? Oh. You're not human." She straightened up and ran a hand through indigo hair.

"Can we talk?" Zhu Irzh said, with a glance at the woman with the braids. "Alone?"

After a pause the woman nodded. "You can go, Cealta," she said. The braided woman was clearly reluctant, but after a sharp glance from those blue eyes, she did as the shaman wished.

"You ride a crane," Zhu Irzh told her. "I last saw you many thousands of years in the future. You'd been brought back to life by a man who calls himself the Khan."

The shaman was staring. "This is an extraordinary tale. But you are right about my crane."

"I know it sounds odd." Then Zhu Irzh gave her a brief account of events.

After he had finished, the shaman sat staring into the flame for a moment. Then she said, "You're telling the truth. The fire says so."

That was a relief, at least.

"But here, things are well. I have visions that they have not always been so. Visions that I don't understand. This is a healed world, but I don't know what it has been healed from." Then, as if the word had been forced out of her, she added, "Almost healed."

"Almost? Are you sure?"

"There is one remaining wound," the shaman said slowly.

"A wound?"

"In the world. It is recent, too."

"What do you mean by a 'wound'?"

"I'll show you," the shaman said. "My name is Raksha. Or at least, that is what you may call me."

"Zhu Irzh. I'm—of supernatural origins."

"That," Raksha said, "is fairly obvious."

They rode on horseback to the place that the shaman spoke of as a wound. Zhu Irzh's mount was nervous: with a demon on its back in this revised paradise, he could not blame it. Nor could he see any sign of anything amiss—the steppe was a peaceful place, with a serene blue sky and clouds floating overhead. Raksha spoke little, but spurred her horse on at a swift pace. At length they came to a narrow valley, winding between low hills, and Raksha brought the horse to a halt.

"It's here."

The demon looked down the valley, but could see nothing wrong. "Where?"

In answer, the shaman dismounted and led him into the valley, to a spot that overlooked the wound. As she did so, a cloud passed over the sun and the valley fell into sudden shadow. Even the scent of fresh grass seemed muted. Zhu Irzh could hear running water. A small spring bubbled up, halfway along the slope, and spilled down onto the valley floor. Close to it, there was a gouge in the earth.

At first, it looked as though someone had drawn a plough through the soil. It was perhaps ten feet long and a foot wide. Zhu Irzh stepped closer but Raksha grabbed him by the arm. "Be careful."

"What made this?"

"I don't know."

As he drew closer he could see that there was, indeed, something very wrong. The sides of the gap looked more like flesh than soil, and a stench rose from it that made even the demon blanch. "What the hell—?"

Something fluttered up from the depths of the crevasse, something small and scattered. Black moths? Or flakes of ash? Whatever it was, there was nothing natural about it.

"When did this first appear?" the demon asked.

"Only a few days ago. I will tell you honestly, when I first set eyes on you, I thought you had come from the gap. But the fire told me otherwise."

"To be brutally frank," Zhu Irzh said, "it's possible that the gap leads to my home. Or somewhere very similar. I'll need to take a closer look."

"Be careful," the shaman said again.

Zhu Irzh went up the slope to the beginning of the rift. He wasn't foolish enough to stand over the gap itself—things had been known to reach up and pull you in under similar circumstances—but there were ways of telling whether the rift went all the way down to Hell. He held out a hand and, mindful of the fact that this was a different world, spoke a spell.

According to the dictates of this kind of magic—a simple locator spell—an image should now unfold itself in front of Zhu Irzh's eyes, depicting the gap itself and its origins. What happened was somewhat different.

The earth beneath Zhu Irzh's feet began to rumble and growl, a tiger sound. The shaman gave a warning cry and Zhu Irzh leaped backward down the slope, stumbling a little as the earth began to crack under his feet. The gap was widening like a maw. Behind him, one of the horses screamed, and he turned to see that Raksha had caught both of them by their plaited leather bridles.

"Quickly!"

Zhu Irzh was more accustomed to leaping into a car than onto a horse's back and his mount did not appreciate him scrambling onto it: the beast gave an angry whinny and shot off across the steppe.

"Hang on! Slow *down!*" Zhu Irzh cried, struggling to stay mounted. The shaman galloped up beside him just as Zhu Irzh managed to rein the horse in a little. He glanced over his shoulder.

Streaming out of the gap in the earth, they came: a long line of black-clad horsemen. At their head rode a familiar figure, wearing red leather armor and with a curious, pointed helmet.

"I mentioned the Khan?" Zhu Irzh shouted to Raksha. "That would be him."

The Khan gave a roar as he spotted Zhu Irzh and the shaman. He motioned to one of the horsemen behind him and the man notched an arrow to his bow and let fly. The arrow shot past Zhu Irzh's ear and buried itself in the grass. Raksha cursed. She leaned back in the saddle and raised a hand. A white-hot bolt of energy whipped out and knocked the horseman out of the saddle. The Khan laughed, showing golden teeth. His horsemen surged forward, toward the demon and Raksha. Zhu Irzh, realizing that they were hopelessly outnumbered, kicked his horse onward but it was too late. The faster he tried to ride, the more the world slowed down around him, until Zhu Irzh felt as though he were inhabiting one of those dreams where you walk through treacle. Beside him, Raksha called out, and he turned to see her horse crumple beneath her. The shaman went down into the grass and struggled to rise, but it was as though someone had clapped an invisible jar over her. She mouthed something to Zhu Irzh which he could not hear.

"Shit!" His own horse was folding and Zhu Irzh leaped clear. Then it was as if the world was contracting down into itself. He threw out a hand but encountered resistance. His limbs felt heavy, gravity dragging him down, and then his knees buckled and the world turned to cloud and cotton wool.

37

As soon as they stepped through the door, a black stickiness fell all around Chen. He swore, making a swift invocation, but in this Hell his magic did not work. The spell fell apart, pattering softly to the floor like rain. Then the web held him in its grip. Behind him, Li-Ju spat something in the Celestial tongue and the web began to disintegrate.

"Unwise, Madam," the captain said coldly, "to rely on Heaven's magic in another world's Hell. Oh, wait. I forgot. It isn't Heaven's magic, is it? You renounced that some time ago."

The Empress, squatting at the center of the room, hissed at him. Li-Ju leaped forward, sword drawn, as the Empress rose, with surprising speed given the weight of her skirts. She cast a spell toward Li-Ju, but it fizzled out like a damp firecracker.

"Oh no you don't!" said a voice behind Chen. He turned to see a figure in a robe the color of a summer's sky, striding down the corridor, followed by an armed group of demons. The blue-robed person was grinning a sharp-toothed grin. "So, Madam. It *is* you. You owe me a debt."

Li-Ju had tried to explain, but it seemed that the pirate Banquo was having none of it.

"Doesn't matter to me. One Celestial's much the same as another, regardless of any feuds. Sorry about you," he added to Chen as he shut the cell door, "humans tend not to fare all that well in Hell. Still, you must have known the risk."

"We came looking for someone," Chen said through the grille. "Two women. A Celestial and a demon. Have you seen them?"

"Ah." Banquo turned. "Indeed. Two most decorative and enterprising young ladies. They had some sort of animal with them. Not only have I seen them, I've taken them prisoner. Twice, in fact. On the second occasion, they managed to suborn a native and escape. For obvious reasons, I've no idea where they are now."

"Why were they held prisoner?"

"I was hired to take them. By Madam, there." He pointed across the cell to where Mhara's mother sat sullenly in a pool of her skirts.

"And what happened to them then?"

"I told you. They escaped, on the back of a bird, I believe."

"On the back of a—?"

"Anyway," the pirate said briskly. "I can assure you that they are not here now. And if you're thinking of attempting a similar route out, I wouldn't. There are no Roc this far down in the forest and the shark-demons want for nothing and thus cannot be bought."

"So what are you going to do with us?"

The pirate grinned a golden grin. "I have a large ransom in mind."

Then he was gone in a swirl of blue robes. Across the cell, the Empress had begun muttering. It might be preferable to be ransomed, Chen thought, than be subjected to whatever the Empress had in mind as an escape route, if indeed she did so.

"Madam, be quiet," Li-Ju said sharply.

"I will not!" A small but potent darkness was gathering in the corner of the cell, conjured by the Empress' murmuring. Chen did not like the look of it, or the smell. Then the darkness was abruptly cancelled out, sizzling into nothingness like an evaporating stormcloud. The Empress swore. Borrowed magic, it seemed, had its limitations.

38

"Where are you speaking from?" Jhai cupped a hand to her ear. Evidently it was not a good line. "What? What are you doing *there?*"

A crackling on the other end of the cellphone, like distant bees. "Roerich?"

Miss Qi turned to Inari. "Who is she talking to? Do you know?" But Inari shook her head.

"Never heard of it. Is it near Lhasa?" A pause. "Oh, I see. Well, sort of. Look, what the hell's going on, Roerich? I'm standing on what's supposed to be Singapore Three and there's no trace of it."

More squawking. Jhai listened intently.

"What, the whole lot? Outside China?"

Then she added, in more pragmatic tones, "Okay. So what do you want me to do?" Roerich replied at length and Jhai said, "I don't know whether I've got enough fuel. I'll have to check with the pilot. There's no sense in flying out to Tibet if we—what? Where's Zhu Irzh?"

The conversation ended and Jhai snapped her phone shut. She did not look happy. She said, "That was—a friend. At least, I think he's a friend. Says he's in a floating moveable city in the middle of Tibet and my fiancé's gone back in time to try and sort things out. We're in trouble."

Inari did not know whether Jhai was speaking generally, or in direct connection with Zhu Irzh's apparent involvement. "Did he say anything about Wei Chen?" she asked.

"No, and I'm sorry, Inari." Jhai put a hand on her arm. She might even have meant the apology. "I didn't ask."

"But where *is* everyone? Are they dead?"

"No," Jhai said slowly. "It's apparently more accurate to say that they were never born."

"What's that?" Miss Qi asked. They looked in the direction of her pointing finger. On a slight rise, some distance from the shore, stood a white-domed building. It was so small that it was almost invisible against the gray-green-brown of the hills, but Inari recognized it at once. How could she not? It was the place where she'd died.

"Mhara's temple!"

It made sense, Inari thought. If anyone survived this changed, denuded world it ought to be the Emperor of Heaven.

"Do you have a number for Roerich?" she asked.

Jhai examined her phone. "No. And somehow, I'm not sure he was using an actual phone."

"I don't know this man," Inari said uneasily. "I'd rather go where it might be safe." An odd term to use for a place where you'd been decapitated, and yet somehow she knew it to be the right choice.

Jhai shrugged. "Fair enough. If Roerich wants to track us down, I have a feeling he will anyway."

She spoke at length to the crew and pilot, who elected to stay with the jet. They could survive for some time on aeroplane food, they said. But Inari felt that the presence of Mhara's temple was an indication of some kind of life, unless this world had changed so radically that the temple was inhabited by something else entirely. One never knew, but one had to take the risk anyway.

She set off, with Miss Qi and Jhai. The Celestial warrior was nervous and kept glancing around her, but apart from the plane crew, there was no one else in sight. Inari, however, respected Miss Qi's instincts.

"Can you sense anything?"

"Many things," Miss Qi said with a shiver. "Ghosts of the might-have-been, perhaps."

"What caused this?" Inari asked. So Jhai explained, and the story took them more than halfway to Mhara's temple. Inari was relieved to see it so close at hand. She kept trying to trace the lines of non-existent streets, seeing from the corners of her eyes the shapes of buildings that were no longer there, and in this reality, had never been. The sun was going down now in a calm burn of gold beyond the shore and even if this was a worldly paradise, as Jhai had suggested, darkness was still dark and things still lived in it.

The temple was still, its roof turned to gold by the sunset light. The doors were closed: they walked up the front steps and knocked. Inari expected the door to remain bolted, but it did not: Robin stood in the entrance, gaping at them.

"Inari! Miss Qi! You've come back!"

Inari was so relieved by this apparent lack of change that she went weak at the knees. Robin hastened them inside.

"Things," said Robin, "have changed."

"You said they came back," Jhai said sharply. "Did you know they'd been away? Or were you referring to something more general?"

"No," Robin said. "These two went missing in the typhoon. Chen's been here, Inari, looking for you, and he's gone after you. I don't know where Zhu Irzh is. But Kuan Yin came here and told us what had happened." Her slightly spectral face was creased with worry. "Then I got up in the morning and—this had happened. The whole city's gone. The worst thing of all is that I can't seem to contact Mhara."

"Do you think the spell—edited him out?" Inari faltered. She did not like to think of that level of power.

But Robin shook her head. "Why would it do that, and leave me here—I'm his priestess as well as his girlfriend, after all. Why not just write me out of the equation? No, I think it disrupted communication somehow, or stranded him in Heaven."

"If the aim of the spell was to set Heaven and Earth in their rightful place," Jhai said, "then maybe there's no need for direct communication between the two."

"But what is Earth's 'rightful place'?" Robin asked. "Looks like it's a world with no one in it."

"Maybe that's the idea," Inari said. "And what about Hell?"

"If we could find a spot that connects to Hell, maybe we could find out," Jhai said. She sat down on a low bench, brow furrowed. "Of the three worlds, that's the least likely to have been affected by the spell, one would have thought. I spoke to the pilot—there's not enough fuel to get us back across China. But if we can travel through Hell, and meet up with Roerich . . ."

"There's the Night Harbor," Inari said. "That's still there."

"Wait until morning," Robin advised. "We don't know what's out there."

Halfway through the night, Inari woke with a start. She'd been dreaming—of Seijin coming through the door with a sword in hand, of that moment of sudden stunning silence when Inari's head fell to the floor. But the room was empty and the silence within it was simply that of the depths of night. Yet something had woken her, all the same. Inari got to her feet and, clutching Robin's borrowed night robe around her, went into the temple.

Robin knelt before the altar. Her head was bowed and, for a moment, Inari thought that the ghost was weeping. Then Robin raised her sleek dark head and Inari saw that the expression on her face was one of intense concentration.

"Can you hear me?" Robin asked, and Inari bit back a reply. Robin was not talking to her; the ghost's face remained fixed on the altar. There might have been the faintest whisper across the air, or perhaps it was only the draft. Robin waited, but there was nothing more.

Inari meant to go back to her room but Robin turned.

"Inari! Sorry, I hope I didn't wake you."

"No, it's okay. I often wake in the night. I heard something, that was all."

"I was trying to contact Mhara," Robin said, rising from her knees. "Still nothing."

Inari sighed. "If you cannot get in touch with him here, then you are unlikely to be successful anywhere else."

Robin grimaced. "Someone in Heaven once told me that this was how it was long ago. The three worlds separate, with spirits passing behind a veil that none could penetrate. Perhaps that's how it's supposed to be."

"And yet the Night Harbor is still here," Inari said. She did not like the idea of traveling back through Hell: most journeys took one across the Sea of Night, and Inari did not care if she never set eyes on that Sea again.

Jhai drove a hard bargain. Inari had known this, but she had never had reason to be so thankful for it. The clerk at the Night Harbor was not someone Inari had seen before: a small, wizened individual of indeterminate sex.

"We don't get many folk through here," the clerk was saying, as though Jhai and the rest of her party had proved a gross imposition. "Especially not headed for Hell."

"I don't care whether we pass through Heaven or Hell," Jhai snapped. "We just need transport."

The clerk peered more closely. "One of you is a ghost. Two of you are demons, and one—a Celestial."

Miss Qi stepped forward. "We are obliged to travel to another point in this world. To do so, we must pass through another realm, or start walking. I will act as a personal guarantor for these women, if you let us travel through Heaven's domain."

"I cannot do that," the clerk said. The wizened face grew grim. "Each must pass through her own realm."

"Look," Jhai said. She leaned forward. "I'm sure some arrangement can be made."

"What kind of arrangement?"

"Perhaps a token of our appreciation for your help?"

"My help will be considerable," the clerk warned.

"So will our appreciation."

39

Zhu Irzh came round to find that his hands were bound behind him. He sensed warmth, and wriggling his fingers received an answering response. Blinking, he saw that the flickering light in front of him were the flames of a fire.

"Raksha?"

The owner of the other hands replied, "Yes. I was beginning to think you'd never wake up."

"Where are we?"

"At the world's wound." He could not see her, but Raksha's voice was grim. They were bound on opposite sides to a stake—in a valley, a basin between low hills. Not far away, voices hissed in exultation.

"Who *is* he?"

"He is the Khan." Zhu Irzh thought he knew what had happened. The spell had indeed revised the world to its current paradisiacal state, but it had been incomplete. Perhaps it was easier to create from fresh cloth rather than to revise: Zhu Irzh knew little about building worlds. But it was both encouraging and problematic to know that gaps remained in the fabric. Given that the Khan had ridden through one of them.

He tested the bonds. Strong, and yet Zhu Irzh thought he could work his way through. Cautioning Raksha to silence, he started to rasp at the rope with a sharp nail; at least the bonds were not made of metal, in this bucolic age. A whoop from the Khan's encampment signaled some kind of action and Zhu Irzh rasped faster.

At last, to his intense relief, the rope started to fray. There was movement, somewhere over to the left. Zhu Irzh couldn't see what it was from this angle, so he concentrated on the rope and it snapped and sagged. He felt Raksha clutch it, to preserve the illusion of bondage. She might be the product of a paradise, but she had a good grasp of the essentials, he thought.

"Wait," he murmured.

"I think the Khan is coming."

A moment later, this hypothesis proved correct. A striding, helmeted figure came into view.

"So!" the Khan cried. "We have visitors!"

He thrust the point of a short sword into the earth and the soil split and fractured like glass.

"Not for long," Zhu Irzh muttered. "Raksha, get ready to run."

"Where is the brushwood?" the Khan snarled. A man ran forward with an armful of broken wood, the scrublike saxaul of the steppe, and threw it in front of the stake.

"Supper!" The Khan was gleeful.

Oh great. The Khan's habits clearly hadn't been modified much over the intervening centuries. More brushwood was brought, and Zhu Irzh pretended to sag in his bonds, his head drooping. The Khan continued to stride around the growing pyre, and once the wood had been assembled to his satisfaction, he called for a torch.

"Now!" the demon cried, as the Khan set the flame to the pyre and the sparks leaped up from the dry branches. Zhu Irzh leaped over the pyre and struck the Khan a blow to the jaw. The man's head snapped around, then back again. Zhu Irzh could have sworn that he'd felt the Khan's jaw shatter, but the terrible, leathery countenance was as masklike as before. The Khan swung his sword and Zhu Irzh jumped back. More warriors were running forward: he could not take them all. Raksha cried out and there was a whistle of wings as her crane swooped down from the sky. Zhu Irzh found himself seized unceremoniously by the waist and dragged upward.

The Khan gave a shout of fury, but Zhu Irzh and Raksha were already ascending, spiraling quickly into the evening sky. Stars spun, dizzyingly close, and the demon was reminded of Agarta and the constellation field. He felt a moment of relief, then Raksha swore.

Zhu Irzh looked down. There was still enough residual daylight to see the Khan's warriors swarming like ants beneath them. But from this height, he had a far better view of the sylvan hills of the steppe. From that gash in the earth, from which the Khan and his men had sprung like some unnatural seed, a sequence of spiderweb cracks were radiating out across the land. More evidence that the spell had worked, but incompletely.

And from the center of the cracks spread a thin, towering black column. It took the demon a moment to realize what he was seeing.

"Ifrits!"

"What are they?" Raksha asked over her shoulder.

"Devils." I should be the one to talk, the demon thought. The crane had seen them, too, and its heavy wingbeats quickened. It swooped low over a grove of trees, leaving the Khan's troops far behind. Glancing back, Zhu Irzh saw the ifrits coming onward, gaining ground.

"Head for the Buddha!" he urged Raksha, but the crane was already veering to the east. Zhu Irzh clutched the shaman as the bird turned, and he felt the power starting to grow inside her. Instinct told him to leave her to it: it was her world, after all, her magic. Instinct was right, as the thunderbolt which shot past his ear consequently proved. Behind, he saw the ifrits scatter. A smoldering body plummeted into the trees. Ahead, the cliffs of the Buddha rose up. The crane headed straight for them, wind whistling past its wings, and Zhu Irzh felt a palpable impact as they hurtled through the invisible barrier that protected the cliff.

They were safe, but behind them, the ifrits gathered like a stormcloud on the other side of the barrier, shrieking with frustration and rage.

40

Inari looked down at the loop that bound her wrist. The thin cord that depended from it extended a short distance into the air before disappearing. Inari gave the cord a slight tug and, a moment later, felt an equal return pressure on her wrist.

"Can you hear me?" she asked, feeling foolish, as though she were a child speaking into one end of a tin-can telephone.

A moment later, Miss Qi's whisper came out of nothingness: "Just about."

It had been the best that the clerk could do. "I cannot give you passage together throughout the realms. But I can ensure that you are joined." The clerk held up a cord, twisted with silver and glowing with the faint light of a spell.

"Is that possible?" Jhai asked, frowning.

"Unusual. But certainly possible. Remember how the three

worlds are configured: they are folded in upon one another, with points that overlap. Essentially, you are moving through different layers of the same space."

Remembering how such places as Kuan Yin's temple and the Opera House on Earth had analogies in both Heaven and Hell, Inari understood.

"All you have to do is to maintain the link given to you by the cord," the clerk had said, binding the wrists of Inari, Jhai, Robin, and Miss Qi. The latter would, obviously, travel via Heaven, while Inari and Jhai took the route of Hell. Robin, meanwhile, would accompany Miss Qi: although she was a spirit, the marks granted to her as the consort of the Emperor were sufficient to allow her Celestial passage.

None of them liked the idea of separation. "We'd be stronger together," Jhai said. "But if this is the only way . . ."

It seemed that it was. They walked through the doors of the Night Harbor, linked by the silver cord like dancers in some rite, and then Jhai and Inari had turned to see that their companions had vanished.

Every time she had come to Hell, in these recent years, Inari had gone by various routes. Now, with the dispensation given by Jhai's generous bribe (claimed via the Bank of Hell), Jhai and Inari stood on the summit of a high bluff. The lights of the city, Hell's analogue to Singapore Three—when still in existence—sparkled in the distance. Inari did not understand how the city could remain in Hell, and yet be absent on Earth. Jhai thought Singapore Three had somehow been shunted sideways by the spell, moved into some separate dimension. But they did not know for sure, and there was nothing for it but to wait for the transport that had been arranged for them. Somewhere in Heaven, no doubt, Miss Qi and Robin stood upon a pleasant rise, looking out over orchards or meadows. Inari, looking at the rugged red landscape of Hell's plains, sighed. Jhai showed no such regrets.

"Did that clerk say when our transportation was likely to show up?"

"It didn't say." Inari knew only that they would be traveling by train. Zhu Irzh had enthused about Hell's new railway network after his last trip, and even Chen had been cautiously impressed: trains like silver bullets, speeding through the sultry airs of Hell, slick and quick and luxurious. Almost something to look forward to.

Except that Chen and Zhu Irzh had been guests of the Ministry of War on that particular occasion, whereas the train that now approached the platform on which they stood was heading into the equivalent of Hell's West; not, Inari belatedly recalled, the most sophisticated part of the realm, any more than Western China might be.

The train was rusty. It chugged, spurting black smoke into what passed for Hell's atmosphere. It looked as though its multiple wheels might be about to drop off and spin across the plain. Jhai was staring at it with undisguised horror.

"That's *it?*"

Inari reflected that Jhai, Paugeng's scion, was unlikely to have traveled anywhere in anything less than first class or in her own private jet since infancy, if that.

"I'm afraid so."

"Right," Jhai said, recovering quickly. "Better get on with it." She put out a hand and the train slowed, then ground to a halt with a great creaking and groaning of gears. There was no sign of a driver, though coals burned and sparked in the cage of the engine. A series of doors along the sides of the train looked rusted shut, but Jhai wrenched one open. With more consideration than Inari would have expected from her, Jhai reached down and extended a hand.

"Be careful, Inari."

"Thanks." The cord from her wrist was stretched briefly taut, then slackened again. Presumably Miss Qi and Robin were undergoing a more pleasant version of the same experience. Inari stepped up beside Jhai, finding herself in a narrow corridor, and shut the door behind her. The train pulled slowly away, picking up speed in a cloud of red dust as the rails took it across the plain. Soon the platform was left far behind. Inari and Jhai made their way down the corridor, which like many of the constructions of Hell, was awkwardly shaped. Jhai made a clicking sound with her tongue.

"Why is this so *constricted?*"

Inari sighed. "So that we don't enjoy it."

"How typical." Jhai opened the door to the first carriage they came to and discovered it was already occupied, if not full. A sullen range of faces turned in their direction and stared.

It was some time since Inari had visited her native realm and after the uniformity of human countenances, she found the diversity of Hell had become disconcerting. Flat, squashed faces vied with long, pear-shaped ones. Crimson, yellow, and jade eyes regarded her with substantial disfavor. And the carriage smelled even worse than Singapore Three, which might generally be described as ripe. The odor of stale sweat and dried blood rose to meet her. Pregnancy made one nauseous, Inari discovered, or perhaps it was simply the unfamiliarity lent by distance. She had not remembered Hell as smelling quite so rank. Meanwhile Jhai's elegant nose was also wrinkling.

"Delightful. Mind you, I've seen worse. I hardly dare ask whether they serve food on this train."

Inari stared at her companion in horror. "You can't be hungry!"

"I had some congee at Robin's. That's it. What can I say? I'm a carnivore. Let's find a seat, Inari. Then I'm going in search of the buffet car."

They found two adjacent places, sitting opposite an elderly spirit in a hat. She gazed at the two visitors for a moment, then busied herself by rummaging in a capacious handbag. Inari slid gratefully into her seat and pressed her face to the grimy window. Hell's plains slipped away in a blur of dust; Inari closed her eyes and thought of the child within.

When she opened them again Jhai was shoveling sticky rice into her mouth with a pair of chopsticks, and the landscape of the plain had changed to a rockier, wilder scene, with mountains rising shadowy in the distance.

"Want some?" Jhai asked, pointing to the rice. "It's not bad."

"No thanks," Inari said automatically, but she thought she might see if the buffet car served tea. Jhai offered to go for her, but just as she was rising from her seat a spirit appeared at the front of the carriage, shoving a large and ancient cart before her. Served tea without having to move cheered Inari up somewhat.

"See if you can speak to Miss Qi," Jhai suggested sourly. "Ask her if they'd be willing to do a swap."

Inari laughed. "I doubt it. Even if it was possible." She took a sip of strong tea. "How long was I asleep?"

"A couple of hours. It's difficult to tell here." Jhai leaned across and looked out of the window. "On Earth, it would take a couple of days to reach Tibet from where we are. Here, it's harder to say. The trouble with the other realms is that they're folded in a way that Earth isn't."

"Those are quite high mountains," Inari ventured. She had visited relatively few places in China itself, and those had mainly

been on the South Coast, although Chen had once taken her to
Hawaii. Inari heaved a nostalgic sigh.

"Yes, they are. Not the Himalayas, though. But I don't know
whether they'd look—ah!"

"What have you seen?"

"I thought those were clouds. They're not. They're peaks."

Inari craned to see. Jhai was right. Behind the shadow hills lay
a line of whiteness in the sky, and when she scrubbed at the filthy
window with her sleeve she was able to see that this was, indeed, a
line of glaciers. Shortly after this, the train began to slow and then
pulled into a remote halt on a high platform of rock.

"Is this it?"

"You want Tibet?" the old person sitting opposite them asked.

"Yes."

"This isn't the border yet. You'll know when you come to it."
She gathered up her numerous bags and got up. "Hope your documents are in order, young ladies."

Inari hoped so, too. She helped the elderly person off the train
with her bags, earning a suspicious glance and a muttered, grudging thanks. Here, the air was colder: almost Earth-normal, and
unimpeded by the grubby glass, the sky was a pure, chilly aqua-
marine. Not very much like Hell at all, Inari thought, and her
spirits rose.

When she got back to the carriage, slackening the cord between
their wrists, she found Jhai speaking into it.

"Heaven's transportation system is apparently delightful," Jhai
informed her with a roll of the eyes. "Miss Qi and Robin are pro-
gressing across flower-strewn meadows and almond groves in a
carriage pulled by does."

"Lucky them." Normally made happy by the happiness of
others, Inari felt that there were nonetheless limits on one's

charitableness. Jhai gave a sardonic grin. The train roared on, into the darkening evening.

Toward what Inari estimated to be midnight, they reached the border. The train stopped for an hour, with no sign of action, then a pair of guards got on. Scions of the Ministry of War, they had bristling, tusked faces and carried assault weapons rather than the more traditional swords and spears. Tibet had such an unfortunate relationship with China on Earth that Inari wondered what the state of the place was in Hell: not good, from the look of things.

"Papers," the guard demanded. Jhai shoved them forward, giving the guard a glittering smile. Inari felt a brief pang of envy: she was too shy to flirt like that. The guard preened. "In order, madam. By the way, should you grow bored during the night, there's a card game in carriage three. We'd be happy to welcome you to it."

"I might just join you," Jhai said. "Thanks."

Thus the border was crossed without incident and the train speeded into the mountains. Inari dozed. She woke once, to find that they were crossing a narrow bridge of rock over a great chasm. A river snaked far beneath, lit by glancing fires. There was no sign of Jhai; presumably she had sought the buffet car once more, or perhaps the card game. Inari shut her eyes again.

When she next woke, it was close to Hell's vague dawn. Jhai was back in her seat, curled neatly asleep. The train was trundling around an immense bend. Inari looked down and wished she hadn't. The drop fell away beyond the thread of the rail, thousands of feet to an invisible below. The mountains were all around, the icy summits looking close enough to reach out and touch, and far across the chasm Inari spotted the first sign of life, a tiny temple, perched doll-like on the side of a cliff. She wondered if this, too, had its counterpart in the world of Earth. Then the train whisked around the curve and the temple was gone.

Jhai blinked awake at a tug on the cord. Miss Qi's voice came faintly out of the air. "Our guide says we're nearly there."

"Thank god," Jhai muttered. She stretched, stiffly. "I could do with a wash. I hope Roerich's city has running water."

After a sojourn in Hell, Agarta sounded like paradise indeed, no matter what its hygiene might be. Jhai and Inari got to their feet and made their way to the door. The train was pulling into the side of a temple complex, Inari saw, that stepped up the steep mountainside in a series of levels. It did not look like a building of Hell and this in itself was hopeful. Once on the platform, she watched the train haul away without regret.

"All right," Jhai said into the cord, "what now?"

It was the temple of a shepherd god, appropriate in this mountainous region. When they walked through the door, Inari turned to look back, and had the sudden disorienting vision of a mountain pasture, soft with blossoms. A high-sided carriage stood beneath a flowering tree. Miss Qi was talking to a golden-horned deer—and then both Miss Qi and Robin were standing by her side. Inari blinked. The pastoral scene, a dusty hillside, and the sharp terrain of Hell were all visible, overlayed upon one another, glimpsed from the open doorway of the temple. Deliberately, Inari turned her back on the triple scene and followed her companions through to the courtyard, where a man was waiting by the side of a fountain.

"It will come to us," Roerich explained. He smiled at Inari. "No more traveling."

"I'm not sorry."

"I am—but not for your lack of journeying. It's in part due to my negligence that has led you to these straits."

Inari smiled back at him, feeling safe with this calm-faced, austere man. "I don't think you can blame yourself too greatly, from what you've told us." They were sitting in a side chamber of the monastery. Roerich had drawn the shutters closed against the triple view and the room was plunged into a comforting, cool gloom.

"Besides," Miss Qi said, "we were in enough trouble of our own already."

"You didn't see your boyfriend when you were in Heaven, did you?" Jhai asked Robin.

The ghost shook her head. "No. It was like traveling through a channel. Everything on either side was just mist. Anyway, I have the feeling that if we'd sought Mhara out, you'd have found yourselves in the middle of Hell's capital. I've never journeyed when connected like this."

Inari repressed a shudder. At least they'd stayed together, in a manner of speaking.

"And now," Roerich said, "I need to summon Agarta."

41

Chen and Li-Ju had spent the night patiently examining every inch of the room, while the Empress continued to glower in the corner. There was no obvious way out: Banquo was, it seemed, taking no chances. Toward morning, Chen became aware of a further disturbance from the corner: the Empress was mumbling again.

"What's she up to?" Li-Ju whispered, uneasily.

"I don't know." It sounded like the earlier spell, but Chen could tell that this one was of greater potency. The words sizzled through the air, striking sparks from the paneled wood. A faint smell of burning became evident.

"If she sets fire to the room—" Li-Ju began.

Quietly, Chen started to form the beginnings of a counterspell, one against fire. His own magic was not strong enough to break out of a room, but it had some impact, all the same. Something water-summoning . . . Just as well they were on a river, although Chen did not like to think of what he might be bringing up alongside the spell.

But it seemed that destruction was not, after all, the Empress' intent. The sparks fizzed out, hissing into spirals of smoke, which began to thicken.

"Madam—" Chen warned, but the Empress was not listening. Through the thickening smoke he could see her eyes roll back into her head, making the beautiful face look even more mask-like. Her mouth fell open as though her jaw had become suddenly unhinged. Beneath Chen's feet, the boat gave a violent lurch. Thrown to one side, he grasped the windowsill. Through the tiny porthole, a treetop sailed by.

"My god! We're *flying!*" Li-Ju breathed.

Rather than escaping from her prison, it seemed that the Empress had simply decided to steal it. Footsteps thundered down the corridor and the door was flung open.

"*What—?*" Banquo roared. He hurled a spell at the Empress, a glistening conjuration of gold-and-blue, but it was too late. The Empress was changing, no longer a statue-still, disdainful figure, but a spinning confection of magical threads, weaving out from her form like a spider. The room reeked and stank of magic, something truly ancient, from a time of sacrifices and war. Chen coughed as rancid spellwork tore into his throat. The river was now a line of dull green far below, the trees themselves left far behind. The boat was spiraling up through the rainforest canopy, passing the distant summits with their spinning coils of birds, up into the blueness of sky. Ahead, as the boat turned, Chen could see a thin, dark crack.

"What's that?" Li-Ju asked. Drawn by the motion of the Empress' magical engine, the boat was speeding up, no longer turning like a twig caught on an eddy, but arrowing straight for the gap.

"I don't know." Yet Chen thought he did. The boundaries between the worlds were breaking down, allowing magic to bleed between systems, allowing rifts and ruptures. The pirates had taken advantage of one such, and now their captive was turning the tables on Banquo and his crew.

But where was she heading? Surely not back to the limbo of the Sea of Night? And Heaven would hardly welcome her. That left, to Chen's mind, a handful of unappealing alternatives.

It wasn't long before they found out. The boat sailed straight for the crack and as it approached, there was a roll of thunder. Lightning shot out from the crack, forming a web in the heavens and merging with the threads of energy generated by the Empress. She was drawing her power from somewhere, Chen realized: this was more than she could possess herself. Besides, it felt different—more like the magic of Hell, but with an added foreign quality that he was unable to place. All he and Li-Ju could do was hang on while the boat hurtled through the lightning storm. Beside them, Banquo was cursing.

The gap now filled the air ahead. Through the little window, Chen kept getting glimpses of its darkness, shot with lights: scarlet and jade and a fiery white. Then the world beyond the window was blotted out as they soared into the gap.

Immediately, all the sound and fury ceased. A vast quietness fell upon the boat. The Empress, now a wadded mass of magical threads, continued to spin like some silent generator. Li-Ju turned to Chen and spoke, but no sound emerged from his mouth. Chen felt as though his ears had been packed with cotton wool. Inside his chest, his heartbeat slowed to a painful, thudding pace. His breath seemed to be congealing in his lungs.

"What?" But he couldn't even hear his own voice.

Gradually, the circle of darkness that was the window began to lighten. Chen saw a drift of cloud, then a strip of sky in between the swirling mist. A moment later, the Empress' gyrating figure began to slow down. Her eyes reappeared within the mass, two malevolent black sparks. Far beneath the boat, a green curve appeared.

It was Earth, and yet it was wrong. As soon as they were through the gap, Chen knew that he was back home, but there were subtle differences. Nothing obvious in the air through which the boat was descending, no clue in the land below them—but the magic was wrong. Or was that—right? Chen felt a surge of unfamiliar power through his fingertips, as if a bolt of lightning had arced up from the earth itself. He felt connected; he could almost have described the land that was now speeding by under their feet even if he was still unable to see it.

Across the room, the Empress' eyes widened. The spell came to Chen's lips almost before he had time to think about it. He threw out a hand, a gesture which was normally accompanied by slicing a spell into his palm. But now the magic shot through him effortlessly. He had a sudden, disconcerting vision of himself from the outside, a figure of light, one hand outflung, and then the magic was coursing out of him and striking the Empress full on.

It sent her into a spin and the boat spun with her. Chen reached down into the land, found the threads that made the link, pulled, tugged, twisted . . .

Li-Ju and Banquo were staring at him wide-eyed.

"What the hell are you doing?" the pirate demanded.

"Taking us in," Chen said, humming with magic. He spread his fingers wide, pointing away from his adversary now and taking the boat into a long glide. They were now perhaps twenty feet above the ground. A grove of trees rushed past. Chen took the boat lower until the grass brushed its sides, and then he stopped it. The boat sank to a gentle, lurching halt.

Immediately the Empress rose in a rustle of skirts and magic and rushed at the door.

"Oh no you don't!" Banquo said. He reached for her but Chen was quicker. He picked up the trailing threads of the Empress' magic and bound them around her. The Empress toppled like a cut sapling, hobbled by her skirts and the remnants of her power. Banquo hauled her upright and bound her hands behind her with a fragment of rope. The Empress cursed and spat, but suddenly she grew limp and sagging in the pirate's grasp.

"Where are we?" Li-Ju threw the door wide and started down the corridor. Chen followed him, ignoring the pirate.

The grasslands stretched as far as the eye could see, a soft rolling land starred with flowers in all shades of yellow and mauve, blurring the landscape into an impressionistic watercolor. A few groves of low trees broke up the steppe. In the distance a herd of what might have been deer grazed peacefully.

Li-Ju was staring, with a frown. "This is Earth. But it feels like Heaven."

"Earth's changed," Chen agreed. He was still aware of the aftermath of unaccustomed power; aware, too, of the force of it coursing underneath his feet, as swift and smooth as uninterrupted water, there for the taking. Quickly, he brought Li-Ju up to speed.

"And you don't normally have that kind of power?" the captain asked.

"No. All my magic has been hard won," said Chen. He saw no need to be macho about it, not at this stage of his life. He gripped the rail of the grounded boat, looking out across the sea of grass.

"I had to study hard. It didn't come naturally. The only time I've ever had that sort of magic available so readily was when I was still under Kuan Yin's protection and that was just borrowed. It wasn't like this."

More out of wonderment than need, Chen reached down into the ground with his senses and pulled up a handful of power. It sparked and sparkled through the air, changing into a swallow and shooting off across the grassland. They watched it go.

"So," Li-Ju said, after a weighty moment. "Earth, but not Earth."

"Yes. We need to find out what's happened. And we need to do something with the Empress. I don't trust the pirate not to cut some kind of deal."

But then Chen was staring in amazement out over the grass.

"What's *that?*"

42

It was not like watching a plane descend, or a spaceship—the nearest thing, Inari decided, to what it actually was. Rather, the flying city of Agarta arrived by degrees, like a palimpsest: first a shadow on the morning air, then a firmer image which blurred the mountain wall, and finally its full self, hanging against the bulk of the rocks. Inari had never seen anything like it. Even Jhai was silent.

"Thus it comes," Nicholas Roerich said, with quiet satisfaction. A bridge was spinning itself weblike across the air, joining the gap between Agarta and the wall of the temple. It looked too delicate to bear any human weight, a gossamer confection of silvery threads. Above it, Agarta's turrets towered.

"You spoke of the Masters," Jhai said. "Where are they?"

"Within." Roerich took a step onto the bridge. "Follow me. You'll be quite safe."

"I'll go first," Robin said. "I'm already dead, after all."

"I've died once before," Inari murmured, but she let the ghost go ahead of her. Stepping out onto the bridge gave her a moment of extreme disorientation, but mindful of Jhai and Miss Qi close behind, she tried not to hesitate. And indeed, once she was actually on the bridge, she discovered that it felt quite solid and safe, as though she could not fall off, despite its fragility and the depths of the gaping air beneath her. A minute's confident walking later, and she was stepping off the bridge again into Agarta.

It did not feel as though it welcomed her, nor repelled her. Instead she had the distinct sensation that she was being watched and evaluated. Beside her, Jhai gave an uneasy start. "I'm not sure this place likes me."

Miss Qi and Robin, predictably, seemed to have no such qualms. "What a lovely place," the Celestial warrior said, striding forward to examine a lily. Inari, looking back, saw that the temple was fading away behind them. The bridge had disappeared, separating them from the land, and within moments the temple had become no more than a shadow. The mountains, too, seemed different: more solid, lit by shades of green as far as their pale summits.

"Where are we?" But she quickly answered her own question. "We're back on Earth, aren't we?"

Roerich nodded. "Earth-the-Changed."

The mountains were folding around them, shifting as Agarta moved.

"We're flying!" Inari said.

Jhai turned to Roerich. "Where to now?"

"Your fiancé's gone back in time," Roerich said.

"To do what?"

"He's looking for the Khan."

"I thought," said Jhai, "that the Khan was looking for him."

Inari wandered around the narrow streets of the city. She had been left to her own devices and she felt safe here, although she still did not feel that she had been wholly accepted. The city was judging her, seeing whether she was worthy of acceptance. It made Inari nervous, but she was damned if she was going to beg for its approval. She had Chen's approval, after all, and that was all that mattered. She had been given a chamber, a room high in a tower from which she could view the changing, rushing world, but Inari, strangely restless, preferred to walk.

Roerich had explained what had happened, that his young acolyte, Omi, had accidentally released a spell from the remaking Book of Heaven. And this new Earth was what the Book had created, but it was incomplete, somehow fractured. Inari could have told him that already, for Hell had appeared unchanged. Perhaps the sad old world was too much now for even the Book to unmake and it had simply displaced it, papered over the cracks, created an illusion.

The mountains underwent one last fold and were left behind. Now Agarta skimmed over seemingly endless plains, and the sweet smell of empty grassland filled the air. Once Inari looked up to see a white horse running toward her, its mane flying behind it. Then, with a flare of its nostrils, it was gone. She wondered what it had seen. But Agarta was slowing down now, the grass below visible as more than a pale wheat-green blur. Inari went to a low wall and looked over, parting a curtain of cascading roses.

There was a curious thing: a boat, marooned on a hillside, miles from any waterway that Inari could see. And standing on the deck was someone who was not at all unfamiliar.

Inari rarely raised her voice, but her shout echoed across the steppe. "Wei Chen!"

Several reunions later, Chen, Inari, and her companions sat in a round chamber high above the city, with Roerich and the Enlightened woman named Nandini. Inari had the impression that there were others in the chamber, too, but when she tried to look at them directly, no one was there.

"The world is breaking apart." Nandini spoke calmly, but Inari could see the tension in her face.

"Do we know what's happened to the cities of Earth? To the people?"

"We believe they have been shifted to the place known as Between," Nandini said. Inari had visited Between, while dead. She had not thought all those people would fit. Perhaps it was bigger than it looked.

"So they have not been—unmade?" Chen asked.

"No. Whichever way you look at it, altering the timeline would effectively have resulted in wholesale murder. So the Book seems merely to have moved them at the times at which it decided to change things. Don't ask me how this affects folk who are already dead: presumably their spirits reside in Heaven or Hell or in their reincarnations."

"And Zhu Irzh?" said Chen.

"Somewhere. *Somewhen.*"

Agarta might be home of the Enlightened Masters, Inari reflected, but it seemed that not even the Enlightened knew everything.

"What happened to the Empress?" she heard herself say. Years ago, Inari might have been too timid to raise her voice in such august company, in case she caused them to lose face, but those days were long gone, eroded by experience and time and the child growing within her. The Empress had struck out at Inari once, and the baby, and Miss Qi, and badger. Enough was enough; Inari would not tolerate it again.

Chen turned to her reassuringly. "She's incarcerated here in the city. As soon as things are set right, she'll be returned to the Sea of Night."

"Speaking of which," Robin said, "has anyone heard anything from *my* fiancé?"

"We have sent dispensation to the Night Harbor," Nandini said, rather stiffly, "petitioning to enter Heaven."

Jhai snorted. "Might I suggest a large bribe?"

"Agarta does not encourage corruption," Nandini replied, now icy.

"Whether you encourage it or not," Jhai said, "even in this remade world, it would seem that the Night Harbor remains reassuringly the same."

Nandini was too serene to glare, but she came close to it.

Inari was still thinking about the Empress. She'd broken out of the Sea of Night, and then Banquo's capture. Inari did not think that these calm rose-growers were likely to hold the Empress hostage for long, whatever Chen may think. Then, ashamed of her own disloyalty, she told herself that Chen was no fool and had defeated the Empress once already.

"Agarta is at its limits," Nandini said now, as if reluctant to admit such limitation. "We can travel no further. The Book has circumscribed our world."

"But the Book has been unsuccessful," Chen argued.

"I agree," Jhai said. "You said yourself—the world is breaking down. Why not test those limits? You're the only one who believes in them."

Nandini was silent.

Inari saw that Roerich was staring at Nandini, his dark gaze unblinking, and it was as if she had read his mind. *The Masters want others to act for them, now. Agarta's time is passing.* Then, with a sigh, Roerich spoke.

"You have to try," he said.

43

The swarm of ifrits still circled at the boundaries of the cliff. How did the spirit that was the Buddha see them? Zhu Irzh wondered. As gnats, or fleas? Or, in his limitless compassion, simply as themselves?

But the demon didn't really care what the Buddha thought of them. They were vermin and enemies, and he wanted them gone. Frustrated, he watched them circle against the velvet sky. Raksha had spoken of another way out of here, and he was waiting for her to return. The shaman had taken to adversity with surprising effectiveness for someone raised in an earthly paradise: perhaps she retained memories of her alternative Tokarian self, the one in his own timeline. Mulling it over, Zhu Irzh decided that he preferred Earth as it had been; it kept you on your toes, somehow. Heaven seemed to make you either soft or mad.

Raksha materialized at his shoulder, coming cat-footed out of the dark.

"Any luck?"

The shaman assented. "There's a tunnel which runs through the cliff—looks like a natural cave." She looked out at the ifrits, eyes narrowing. "Do you know much about those things? How good is their sense of smell?"

"I've no idea. I wouldn't put much past them, though. They're predators. Where does this tunnel come out?"

"Into the grassland somewhere."

"The wound in the world," Zhu Irzh said. "I think that must be where the spell was activated."

"It's a place where something is badly wrong," Raksha agreed. Zhu Irzh sighed.

"A good starting point, then." Even with the Khan and his troops milling around. Now that Zhu Irzh thought back, out of the mists of panic, there had been something odd about those warriors: not men, he thought, but if not, then what? Had the Khan been recruiting in Hell? "We have to find out what the Khan is planning to do."

And hopefully, reverse a paradisiacal spell.

The tunnel was bone dry and dusty underfoot, running in a series of twists and turns beneath the hill. Even down here, Zhu Irzh could sense the presence of the Buddha: a great calm pervading the place like the hush and rush of the sea. Not quite calm enough, however, to stop him from worrying about what might be waiting for them at the other end.

Raksha was silent. The demon had no idea what was going through her head, but he was grateful for her presence. Not to mention her abilities. He wondered about the others—where Roerich might be, or Omi. And then there was Chen—had he been edited out of this revised future? Zhu Irzh was aware of a substantial indignation. He was tired of people playing God. Even if they *were* gods.

The tunnel was widening. Raksha carried a small torch, a flaring thing of pitch, but unless it was his imagination, the light was growing. Next moment, Raksha caught him by the arm.

"We're coming to the end of the tunnel. Be careful."

The demon did not need telling twice. He flattened himself against the wall at the end of the tunnel as a draft of cool, grass-scented air blew inward. There was no sound from outside. Zhu Irzh checked his instincts: they were telling him it was safe. Cautiously, he peered around the side of the tunnel.

Outside, the land sloped gently down to the gleam of water. A stream snaked between low, grass-fringed banks. Above the hills, the moon hung huge and golden. No sign of the Khan or his men, yet the demon's senses told him that the land was not as empty as it looked. Next moment he darted back as something sprung out of a thicket of scrub.

Raksha, however, didn't hesitate leaving the tunnel.

"So, it is you!" she said.

"It is I," the hare said. It sat back on long, folded legs and gazed up at her with eyes like the moon. "There are strange things out in the grass."

Looking at the hare, Zhu Irzh caught the fleeting shadow of a girl, golden-eyed, with long fawn hair. Human and animal had not been so distinct once in the world's history.

Raksha sat down on her heels, making herself level with the hare. "What kind of strange things?"

"Men. Or not men—I do not know what they are. There is one with them who smells of blood."

"Where are they?"

Zhu Irzh cast an uneasy glance at the sky, but there was no sign of the ifrits, only the round moon riding in clear air.

"At the bend of the river. They have made a camp. The place stinks of blood." The hare shivered. Raksha turned to Zhu Irzh. "What is your plan?"

Ah. That plan thing. "I need to find out what the Khan's doing, and then find this spell. Or maybe the other way around." The trouble was, even if he located the spell and managed to reverse it, he had no way of knowing whether it would set the world back to the way it should be. Maybe the Tokarians would be as they had been before, eking out an existence in the bleak expanse of the desert, or maybe you couldn't switch these things back once they'd started, and an entirely different world would result.

"The Khan's camp is some distance from the wound," Raksha said. "It would be safer to find this spell first."

Cowardice was, frankly, a greater compulsion than strategy. Zhu Irzh was not eager to face the Khan, and anything that served to put that off for a bit, perhaps indefinitely . . .

"All right," the demon said with sudden decisiveness. "Let's revisit the wound."

It looked different under the moon, less of a gaping mouth, more of an ancient scar. Perhaps this revised earth healed swiftly, or perhaps time worked in a different way. Or maybe it was nothing more than moonlight. He said as much to Raksha as they peered over the top of the bluff, down into the dark rip.

"It is *wrong*," was all that the shaman said. Zhu Irzh agreed. Now that they had time to consider the wound in calmer circumstances, the smell of magic surrounding it was strong, and it was no magic that the demon recognized. It did not taste either of Heaven or Hell, nor of anything earthly, and he supposed that this was a function of the Book, so much older than the world around it.

"We need to get closer," Zhu Irzh said.

They followed the river, keeping close to the trees that banded it. The hare came too, bounding along beside, a creature of silver and moonlight.

"How will you reverse the spell?" Raksha breathed into Zhu Irzh's ear. Her apparent confidence in his abilities appalled him.

"Not quite sure what I'm going to try yet," he told her, attempting to sound as if he knew what he was doing. In fact, he had no idea. The magic around the wound was making him dizzy. The only positive note was that there was no sign of the Khan, or his warriors, though distant cries suggested to Zhu Irzh that they could not be far away.

Who are you?

The voice, when it entered his ear, was startlingly loud, making the demon jump.

"What was that? What did you say?"

Raksha eyed him askance. "Who are you talking to?"

"Did you say something?"

"No."

"Nor I," the hare said.

"Well, *someone* did." He looked suspiciously around him, but there was no one to be seen.

Who are you? It was more insistent this time; the kind of voice that demands answers.

"My name is Zhu Irzh."

Raksha was staring at him. He made an impatient gesture, motioning her to silence.

What kind of thing are you? The voice sounded bemused.

"I'm a demon." No point in lying. Instinct told Zhu Irzh that fabrication would not be wise. "From Hell."

What is a demon? And where is Hell?

It was impossible to tell who the voice belonged to. The wondering note in it sounded like a child, yet there was a timbre and quality to it which suggested a far greater age. It was more male than female, but this, too, could have proved mistaken.

"Why don't you come out and take a look at me?" Zhu Irzh suggested. "Then you can see for yourself." *And we can see who you are, too.*

I cannot move.

"Why not?" And then the demon suddenly realized who he was talking to. "It's *you!*" he said inanely. "You're the spell."

My name is Book.

This was not, Zhu Irzh realized, wholly true. "Book" was the word he understood, but the word that had been spoken was different. He remembered Roerich saying that the Book was far older than printed text—could only be, in fact, since the word came from humans and Celestials, and this thing had appeared before both; it was the creator of all.

"I'm coming down," the demon said.

"Be careful," Raksha hissed, and the hare's long ears flattened in alarm. Zhu Irzh broke cover and set off down the hill toward the wound.

When he reached it, he saw that it pulsed faintly, as if alive. The demon frowned: it was disturbing, somehow, to witness this gentle heave of the land. He'd had too much experience of earthquakes . . . Memories of chunks of masonry hurtling into the streets of Singapore Three were still vivid in his memory. He might be supernatural, but even the demonic prefer not to be flattened. Or buried alive.

A thread of magic, a thin filament, coiled out from the dark maw in the earth. Zhu Irzh willed himself to stay put and not run: this was a test, a probe, not an attack. He hoped so, anyway. The thread snaked around his head; he felt it poking into one ear. Not a pleasant sensation, and the demon gritted his teeth as the thread filtered through his mind, observing with a distinct sensation of curiosity the demon's powers and memories. Then, suddenly, it was withdrawn.

Interesting!

"Well?"

I do not understand you.

"I thought I spoke clearly."

I have never seen such a thing as you. Except—

"Except?"

Except those that have come through me.

"Do you know what you yourself are?" the demon asked.

I am Book. I am the beginning of things.

"Take a look into my mind again," Zhu Irzh said. "Look at my memories of you."

Again, the thread probed; again, his memories were gently raided.

I am not as I was, the Book said.

"No. You tried to put things back to the way you thought they should have been. But something's gone wrong. You spoke of the things that came through you. What you've done is caused the world to crack. Things are bleeding through it and unless you reverse yourself, further chaos will result."

I cannot do that.

"Cannot, or will not?"

The Book was silent. Then it said, *I do not know.*

"Let me take a look at you," Zhu Irzh suggested, feeling like a doctor and speaking with an authority that he did not feel. For a moment, he thought the Book was going to refuse, then it said, *Very well.*

"All right," the demon told it, though he had no idea how he was going to proceed. "How are we going to go about this?"

You must enter me.

Disturbing. The demon disliked dark holes in the earth; positive things rarely emerged from them. With a sigh, he sat down on the lip of the maw and inserted his boots. He thought he heard a stifled exclamation from Raksha and flapped a hand, again motioning her to silence.

Next moment, he was somewhere else entirely. The grassland around him and the sky above disappeared. Zhu Irzh was standing in a room, among stacked shelves of books.

Another has been here, the Book said, its voice echoing all around him.

"Who?"

A human. Young.

"Was he called Omi?"

I think—yes, that was the name. He took the form of a great cat.

That was news to Zhu Irzh.

"So, which one of these are you?"

I do not know.

Zhu Irzh gave a sigh of pure exasperation. "What do you mean, you don't know?"

I am one and many. The Book sounded genuinely puzzled, and Zhu Irzh began to wonder whether he had inadvertently struck the heart of the problem: that in revising the world, the Book had succeeded in revising itself as well, perhaps—horrible thought—erasing vital parts of its functioning. Seeing the Book as a computer seemed to make more sense than regarding it as a textual entity, although Zhu Irzh's understanding of information technology was patchy at best.

"Okay," he said aloud. Best not to share his internal speculations with the thing: it seemed confused enough already. "Why don't I start looking?"

Omi had told him that the spell had been found among the scrolls, rather than the books, and this made sense. He strode through the stacks, searching for anything that resembled the scroll that Omi had carried with him, before Agarta had come and caused him to act so disastrously. He rifled through shelves and ledges of scrolls, desperately seeking. He didn't want the Book to change its mind about allowing him in here and it appeared unstable enough for anything . . .

It had been a parchment, stained as if a myriad of teacups had been placed upon it. He remembered that it had been tied with a scarlet ribbon, tightly bound at each end with wax—and *here* was something, right at the back of the rack, where one might expect the most ancient scrolls to lurk. Holding his breath, Zhu Irzh held it aloft. "Do you know if this is the spell that you are? Do you recognize it?"

I think it is so, the Book said doubtfully.

Good enough for me, the demon thought. He broke the seal at one end and unscrolled the parchment. As soon as he opened it, the room grew quiet and dim and Zhu Irzh felt a twinge of magic, deep inside.

"This is it, I'm sure of it."

He held the scroll open, attempting to read it the wrong way round. Symbols poured off the page to hang brightly in the air. Each one glowed like a firefly and then, one by one, they went out. The room grew even dimmer, the stacks of books lost in shadow, and the demon felt an almost imperceptible shift, as though a vast hand had reached out and moved him sideways.

"What—"

The room was melting, fading as mist fades at the coming of dawn, boiling away into evaporation. Sand crunched under Zhu Irzh's feet; he tasted grit on the wind. As his vision cleared he found himself standing in the desert, under the same swimming moon. But the endless grassland had disappeared: this was the Taklamakan as he remembered it, and the small, huddled fortress of the Tokarians was visible once more across the river, now more of a muddy stretch. A woman was walking down the slope: Raksha, still with the hare at her heels.

"I think I did it," Zhu Irzh said. He looked around him, finding no sign of the world's wound.

Raksha was frowning. "I remember—like a dream. This was a sea of grass. And you—"

Zhu Irzh blinked. The moon, which had ridden above him like a great round eye, was now a sliver, a crescent in the west. The shaman was quicker to understand.

"We've *moving.*"

"Not just us," Zhu Irzh said. He'd already heard the hammer of hoofbeats across the steppe. "Quickly!" Grabbing Raksha by the arm, he hustled her up the slope into the comparative shelter of the rocks. The trees were gone, although he could still see the silhouette of branches above the walls of the village. A moment later, the Khan appeared, riding hard out of a dustcloud. In the trace of moonlight, his face was set. His warriors rode at his heels and underneath their helms Zhu Irzh finally glimpsed their faces—long, leathery countenances, almost beaked, with small black eyes as hard as stones. Kin to the ifrits? Zhu Irzh would have put good money on their being of the same species.

He opened his mouth to tell Raksha to keep her head down; when the horsemen swept by, Zhu Irzh felt himself pulled in their wake like a leaf sent spinning by the passage of a speedboat. He saw Raksha beside him, her eyes wide, and then they were torn away from the world and that time, under the dizzying orb of the swiftly changing moon.

44

The world changed in the blink of an eye. Where the grassland had been, there was now only the desert sand, fawn and black and gold, with the distant red line of the mountains beyond.

"God! He did it!" Jhai said, as her cellphone rang. "Hello? Yes, this is Jhai. Who are you?" She listened for a moment, then said, clearly thinking quickly, "No, I'd intended to come back on the jet, but something came up here and we needed to send a few things back. Not good for the carbon footprint, I know, but I'll sort something out at this end." She snapped the clamshell shut. "That was Paugeng, asking something boring. Thank *god*. Didn't seem to notice anything had changed."

Inari exhaled a sigh she did not know she'd been holding. "Then everything's back to normal?"

"Yeah," Jhai said, looking disparagingly around Agarta. "If you can call *this* normal."

"So where's Zhu Irzh?" Chen asked. They clustered around Jhai as she phoned.

"Nothing. He's not answering."

"Is it ringing?" Chen asked.

"No."

Chen sighed. "Typical." He turned to Roerich. "Sometimes, it's important to focus. I was originally hired to find the Book of Heaven. When all this began, that was Mhara's original request."

Roerich smiled. He and Chen were very alike, Inari thought approvingly, even though they looked so different: one Russian, one Chinese. And yet their spirits were similar; a blind person could have told that.

"And so you have been successful," Roerich said. "At least in part. I will speak to Nandini, ask if Agarta can take us to the temple of the Book. It isn't so far, after all. Then you can question your suspect directly."

"Good enough plan," Chen said. "I wonder whether it's the same entity, or whether Zhu Irzh has managed to do something to it. He usually has a disastrous effect on these things."

Later, Chen gripped the wall of the city and looked out across the desert. Agarta was still stationary, hovering a hundred feet or so above the black sands of the Gobi. *What a wasteland,* Chen thought. Fascinating to be so far west, although he'd generally considered traveling by more conventional means.

The relief that had filled him on seeing Inari, safe and sound and waving to him from the improbable vista of Agarta, had been so great that Chen had been compelled to sideline it—as though there was a box in his head marked "RELIEF" into which such emotions could be placed, and examined later. Now, with Inari resting in the tower chamber, he allowed himself to experience that relief and it nearly brought him to his knees. The desert below swam into sudden darkness and he clutched the wall more tightly, bowing his head for a moment to let the blood supply resume.

Roerich was still in consultation with Nandini, which Chen thought might take a while. He still had not worked out Agarta's place in the scheme of things: Roerich had said something earlier that suggested the agendas of the city itself and those of its inhabitants might differ, an unnerving thought. Chen looked down at the stone beneath his hands, wondering if it was alive. Despite Agarta's beauty and calm, he did not like the sensation of being so dependent on such a powerful enterprise: it was the same disquiet as when he was caught in Heaven's mills. Had Robin been able to contact Mhara yet? She'd said she was going to try.

With these thoughts running through his mind, Chen reached down and casually drew up a thread of power from the black sands. Earthier and harsher than the magic of the lost grasslands, it settled into his palm like a lump of lead. Experimentally, and with a mental apology to the city, Chen cast it outward and a crow swooped down over the sands, disappearing against the shadows of the dunes.

Interesting.

The world that had given him this power was gone, illusion briefly created and as swiftly dissipated, but whatever it had changed in him remained. Chen wondered whether it was some lingering effect, whether it would fade. He was not afraid of power, but there were always ramifications to these things, always a price to pay. In recent months, it felt to him as though Inari had been the one to bear the brunt of that price and at this thought, Chen's lips thinned.

He was intending to return to the tower room and see how Inari was, but at that point, Agarta began to move.

45

It was like watching a movie, ratcheted up to impossible speed. Rather than the sensation of falling, after the initial pull, Zhu Irzh felt as though he was standing still while the world whisked past him. Fragments and snatches of scenes whirled by: cities built and ransacked, armies on the move, forests growing and dwindling as the desert sands took hold. Beside him, he thought Raksha might be screaming, but he could not be sure.

Then it all stopped. Heat was beating down on his skin, and a yelling man was swinging a sword at him. Startled, Zhu Irzh brought up a reflexive hand and cast out a spell. His assailant burst apart in a shower of fire. Alongside, other warriors paused for an astonished moment, then resumed their battle. Raksha had picked up the fallen man's sword and was swinging it with grim determination. She might have come from a pre-Iron Age culture, but she'd got the hang of more modern weaponry with commendable speed and enthusiasm. Another warrior went down in a fountain of blood as Raksha decapitated him. Might as well leave her to it, the demon thought, and concentrated on blasting opponents apart until enough of a path was cleared for him to grab the shaman and haul her onto a nearby rise.

From here, they found themselves looking down onto a battlefield. For some half-mile distant, warriors in pointed helms hacked and slashed at men armed with short swords and what looked like farm implements.

"This is carnage!" Raksha spat in disgust. Zhu Irzh agreed. The Ministry of War might have approved, but the sight did not bring its reluctant scion any pleasure. From the layout of the battlefield, it was easy enough to see what was occurring: invaders from elsewhere, sweeping down onto the city, which, taken by surprise, was being inadequately defended.

Inadequately and, Zhu Irzh could see, with futility. Lines of horsemen, in the same leather armor, riding fast, tough ponies swept around from the east of the city. Zhu Irzh could see structures rising over the city wall: huge blue domes swimming in the heat, like a mirage. He turned to a panting peasant who had joined them on the hillside, hoping whatever translating magic had been with them was still in place.

"What's that city?"

"Samarkand," the peasant said, giving the demon a curious glance. "You must be from a long way away, if you don't know that."

"We've come very far," Zhu Irzh agreed. "And these warriors— who are they?"

It was clearly not the time for a social chat, but the peasant was winded. Between heaving breaths, he said, "These are the hordes of the Khan. Timur the Lame, cursed be his name."

And all at once the ground shifted beneath the demon's feet, as though the mere utterance of the name had been enough to cause the earth to shake. He was standing directly in the path of a horseman and threw himself to the side as the man bore down. He glimpsed a harsh, set face, the mouth twisted in a snarl, and then the horseman rode past, the iron sword slamming down.

Timur the Lame. Not the Khan he'd seen: a later version, perhaps, in the same mold—but then the demon turned and saw the Iron Khan. The man—if one could call him that—wore blood-red armor. His face looked as though it had been carved from bone, bearing little flesh. He was staring straight at Zhu Irzh and his rictus grin was worse than Timur's snarl. He raised a hand and Zhu Irzh felt a wash of magic that was so old and powerful that his knees started to buckle. The demon rarely felt weak—as a denizen of Hell in a world full of humans, he was not often at either a physical or a psychological disadvantage. But faced once more with the Khan, he felt as though he'd been caught in some magical riptide. It rolled him over and under. When it finally washed him up, Raksha was back by his side, spitting curses.

"Zhu Irzh!"

They weren't alone. Some two hundred people stood with them, bewildered. Almost all were the attackers: Timur's men, though after a cursory glance, Zhu Irzh did not think that Timur himself was among them. All carried bloodied swords.

The blue domes reached up into an equally cerulean sky. Ahead, Zhu Irzh saw an arch: suns and golden tigers and striped deer cavorted across an azure background. It reminded him of the scenes in the Buddha's cave, innocent and joyful and a realm away from the blood-soaked man who now roared in triumph, raised his sword aloft, and caused the world to change once more.

The steppe, and a curve of a river, somehow familiar and yet unknown. The part of Zhu Irzh's mind that still remained intact to himself told him that this was generic recognition, not somewhere he had previously been. He smelled fresh grass, something spicy, something piercingly sweet, with the dank odor of the river running underneath it all. Then all of this was blotted out as Master rode by, turning the black pony fast along the lines of warriors, and the demon bowed his head, along with his companions, including the black-haired woman whose name he no longer knew.

You bowed your head or you lost it. By now, a day after the battle of Samarkand, Zhu Irzh had learned that much and so had the others.

"We ride on!" Master cried. His teeth were bared in a fierce grin, exulting. That little separate part of the demon's mind, raging with frustration, told him that the Khan's great plan was moving toward fruition. Freed in time by the imperfect actions of the Book, the demon thought, the Khan had seen his opportunity and snatched it: traveling forward from that initial point, gathering an army as he rode. Was his ultimate destination the present day, or some other time? Zhu Irzh did not know, and again he bowed his head.

He also did not know whether this was the original time of the grasslands. There was something eternal about the steppe with its unceasing cycles of winter and summer, as though the grasslands were a liminal space, untied from the temporal world. This, and the desert, were where the Khan had come from; almost as if the Khan himself had been conjured from the substance of the land, stone and bone and dust.

There would be more fighting soon, Zhu Irzh understood. Only the elite had horses, the half-ifrit cavalry whom the Khan had summoned with him from the very early days, but Zhu Irzh had been issued a bow and a quiver full of arrows. The idea was to kill those who could be killed, leaving a quota of the rest. They themselves, untied from time, could not die, and they would take the new warriors with them when they moved on.

The black-haired woman, frowning, turned to Zhu Irzh and said something, but he did not understand her. A moment later she, too, looked confused, and then her face cleared suddenly, leaving a blankness in its wake. She turned expectantly toward the Khan, waiting for orders.

They were not long in coming. Minutes later, the first wave of horsemen swept over the hill.

46

"It's changed," Roerich said.

"How so?" Chen was standing with Roerich at the summit of one of Agarta's turrets. In the near distance, the dunes boomed and roared like the sea. Agarta's breezes—the city's own microclimate— were saving them from the worst of the sun, but out there in the Taklamakan, it looked as if you could fry an egg on the sands.

Roerich pointed. "That lake. It's usually full of water. But now look at it."

Chen raised a pair of borrowed binoculars to his eyes and surveyed a muddy, crescent-shaped puddle. "I see what you mean. Doesn't look healthy."

"And those trees are normally in full bloom despite the heat. The temple protects them, you see, just as this city protects us. Now they're no more than desiccated twigs."

"Maybe something's wrong with the Book," Chen suggested.

Roerich shot him a quick, appraising glance.

"That would seem to be the most likely hypothesis. Are you up for taking a look?"

"It's what I was hired for." Even though Chen's Imperial employer still wasn't within hailing distance, apparently. Roerich thought that might have something to do with the nature of the city itself; when discussing the subject with Robin, Roerich had mentioned Agarta's proclaimed neutrality, that it must remain separate from all the various Heavens and Hells, being dedicated to human affairs and run by humans, however ascended.

"Does it work?" Robin had said, her spectral face skeptical.

"Not very well," Roerich admitted. "But they like to claim it does."

Chen could understand why: the whole point of being an Ascended Master (or Mistress) was that you had attained another plane of existence without the inconvenience of dying first, thus bypassing the Night Harbor, limbo, purgatory, or whatever system one's religion had set in place.

A sort of esoteric version of Switzerland, with similar degrees of prettiness and organization. But then, Chen didn't think Switzerland had all that much clout in real terms, either.

Now he said to Roerich, "Well, then. Let's go."

Close to, the temple was even more dilapidated than it had appeared from the city. Roerich and Chen approached with some caution across the shifting dunes. Rather than entering the front of the temple, past the stagnant lake, they deemed it best to go around the back, and see if there might be another way in.

"The trouble is," Roerich murmured, "I don't know what defenses the Book might have erected."

"Nor I," Chen said. Back in the city, Robin was still arguing with Nandini about contacting Mhara; Chen hoped she'd be successful. He thought that the Emperor had a better chance of making the Book see reason than either himself or Roerich.

The back wall of the temple was a blank: a high palisade of weathered stone, scoured by the wind and the sand. There was no obvious way of getting inside. As they approached even closer, however, a black gap opened in the wall and something shot out of it, a shrieking bolt. Immediately Chen cast a spell and Roerich, too, raised a hand. Intermingled magic sparked red and glowing green, then fell uselessly to the ground. Chen and Roerich ducked as the thing sped toward them, hurtling through Chen's outstretched arm and vanishing.

"Illusion," Roerich said grimly. "But the next one might not be."

"What was it?" Some kind of demon, Chen had thought: leathery and winged, with gleaming red eyes.

"It was an ifrit. I'd be surprised if the Book was recruiting them. They're the creatures of the Khan."

That raised unpleasant speculations. "Perhaps they're preventing people from going in."

Roerich gave a curt nod. "Be on your guard."

In the absence of any access, they made their way to the front of the building. Roerich was attempting magic, Chen could tell; some kind of concealment spell. But it wasn't working and eventually Roerich gave a snort of annoyance and gave up. The temple lay before them, its lacquer peeling in the sunlight.

"Very well," Roerich said, tight-lipped. He raised a hand. "Book! Can you hear me?"

Silence, so resounding as to be a noise in itself.

"Book!"

At last, a whisper on the desert air, a thin, frail sound. "I hear."

"Where are you?"

"Where I have always been."

That was not true, but perhaps the Book knew no differently.

"Can we enter?"

"Yes. But there are presences." And now the Book sounded fearful. With a glance at Chen, Roerich stepped forward.

Even if he had been so blind as not to notice the state of the place, Chen would have been able to tell that something was badly wrong. The aura of rank magic, as stagnant as the sad little lake, hung heavily in the air, making it suddenly difficult to breathe. Above him, the sky dulled, a sultry, thunderous shade, and the heat was stifling.

"This has changed," Roerich said, unnecessarily.

"I can tell." Chen glanced around. There was no overt sign of the ifrits, but when he looked over his shoulder, he could see a flickering in the air beyond the temple, the beat of wings visible from the corners of the eyes. Something was waiting and he did not understand why they had not attacked again. Perhaps Roerich had been correct and these things were no more than illusions, but even so . . .

Roerich's head went up, like a lean hunting dog. "It's up there."

Chen followed him up the rickety stairs of the temple, trying not to put a foot through the rotten wood, and onto a narrow parapet. The stink of magic was strongest around the door to a middle chamber. Together, Roerich and Chen looked inside.

There was the Book, setting on its plinth. Flies and wasps buzzed and hummed around it and the smell of ageing meat was overpowering. Chen clapped a hand to his face.

"I'd have said it was well past its sell-by date, Nicholas."

"Book," Roerich said, into the fetid gloom, "what has happened to you?"

"I wanted to restore things," the voice said, faintly. "To what they should have been."

"You are a creator." Roerich's tone was gentle. "Not a sustainer. You don't have to hold constant what you make. That's other people's job."

"I thought I did. But it was imperfect, incomplete." The Book sounded desolate.

"Things go as they were fated to go," Nicholas said.

"But what am I to do now?"

"Your place is in Heaven," Chen said. "You would be welcomed home. Interwoven, once more, with Heaven's fabric."

In fact, he had no idea whether this was the case or not. He prayed that Mhara would understand. Whatever the case, Chen's conscience gave an uneasy twinge and he told it to be silent. Roerich was listening intently.

"I do not know," the Book said, and indeed, it sounded unsure.

"Come," Roerich said firmly. "You know where your rightful place should be. Look around you. Does this seem right, this rotting room, these odors and this decay? Let your temple be restored, if you can restore nothing else. Go with Wei Chen."

"I must consider it," the Book said, and despite the wan sunlight beyond the window, the chamber in which they stood grew cold and dark. In unspoken agreement, Roerich and Chen backed out of the door and waited on the balcony.

"I'll be honest with you, Nicholas," Chen said. "I don't know the best way to handle this thing. It's obviously unstable."

"We'll just have to hope that it has enough self-preservation to allow itself to be returned to Heaven," Roerich told him.

"It's always hard to tell how things experience the world," Chen mused. "From a human perspective, it can't have been much of a life for the Book—stuck up there in what amounted to a sealed chamber."

"The trouble is, we don't understand how these things view time. What might be aeons to us could have seemed no more than a few seconds to an entity of this longevity. It's very difficult to see things from their perspective."

Chen was about to reply, but his attention was caught by a sudden disturbance in the sky above him. "What's that?" For a moment, he thought it was one of the ifrits, broken through the protective barrier of the temple, but then he realized that it was a single curl of paper, white as a dead leaf against the sky. It sailed down, joined by further sheets of parchment, until they were falling as a single scroll. Chen held out his hands just in time for the Book to fall into them.

"I have decided on this form," the Book said. "It may make it easier for you to transport me."

Back at Agarta, Chen and Roerich stood looking down at the temple. The ifrits were still visible, but shadowy: flickering in and out of human sight.

"I don't understand why they didn't attack," Chen said.

"Perhaps they *are* no more than illusion after all."

Chen once more checked the leather tube in which they had placed the Book. He had a feeling it was going to be a movement that would become familiar, if not obsessive. The tube now hung from its strap across his chest, easily defensible. The Book itself was silent, maybe out of contemplation, or perhaps because its consciousness had passed into whatever realm it normally inhabited. Inari had greeted Chen with relief when they returned from their mission, but Jhai and Robin were nowhere to be seen.

"They're with Nandini," Inari said, "working on a way home." Her brow was creased with worry. "I think this is a beautiful place, Wei Chen, but it makes me nervous. Maybe it's because I'm a demon, but—"

"I don't think it's just that," Roerich reassured her. He paused. "There's such a thing as becoming inhuman, when all you were aiming to do was to enhance your humanity." He broke off as Robin and Jhai appeared at the end of the terrace.

"You're back! What happened?" Robin asked. Chen told her and she visibly relaxed. "That's wonderful. At the very least, if we get the Book back where it belongs, it can't do any more damage."

"What did Nandini say?" Roerich asked.

"They still won't have any truck with Heaven. Or with Hell, for that matter. I argued and argued, but it didn't do any good. What they have agreed to do, however, is to transport all of us to a temple of Mhara's in the mountains near Urumchi, and then we can contact him there. That's the best Jhai and I could do."

"It's enough," Chen said, and Roerich nodded.

At least they could relax, somewhat, now that they had the scroll. All Chen had to do was wait for the city to move them, and get in touch with Mhara at the other end. A simple matter, he thought, and then reflected on the nature of famous last words.

47

Zhu Irzh paused for a moment in the midst of the fighting. The body of a young man sprawled at his feet, eyes glazing in death. The demon could not understand why this should disgust him so much: he'd seen enough killing, surely, as a warrior of the Khan. Dim memories of another place, a red sky, a mansion black as iron, filtered through the haze and he thought he remembered a city, too: a world of high towers and screaming sirens.

. . . sitting on the deck of the houseboat at sunset, nursing a cold beer in one hand and. . .

. . . the police precinct's dreadful tea, grown cold as he worked late on a case where . . .

. . . a cool breeze stirring the blinds of Jhai's bedroom in the middle of the night . . .

Zhu Irzh blinked. Suddenly, it was all back, his life, waiting patiently where he had left it for the wandering warriorhood of the Khan. Whatever spell had held him had broken, whether due to imperfection of its casting, or age, or simply as a result of the bloodshed, Zhu Irzh did not know.

"I'm back!" he said, and then, *"Raksha!"*

He found her across the battlefield, sheathing her short sword in earth. He took her by her shoulders, claw-tips cutting into the leather armor, and called her by her name. But her face remained as blank as before—as blank as his own must have been, an hour or so ago.

"What are you talking about?" she asked impatiently. "Look— they're calling us in. We have to go."

"No. Wait. *Listen* to me."

"It's all right," said a new voice, a familiar one. "I haven't cast the breaking spell on her yet."

The demon turned to see a young man staring at him with sad patience. "Omi?"

"I found out a few things," the warrior said. "Zhu Irzh, you need to stand back."

Zhu Irzh did so, watching as Omi spun a handful of glittering green sparks out of the ground. With practiced movements, he wove them together in a net and cast them toward the shaman. She gave a cry of fury but before she had time to react or counter- attack, the sparks sifted down through the air and vanished around her head. One glowed green for a moment, hovering in front of her heart, and then it, too, was gone. Raksha's mouth fell open in wonderment.

"I—I remember you. What happened? Where are we?"

Urgently, Omi said, "You must pretend that nothing has changed, that you are still in the thrall of the Khan. Otherwise all this is for nothing."

"Omi," the demon asked. *"When is this?"*

The young warrior looked drawn, Zhu Irzh thought. He did not, even now, find it all that easy to discern human emotions but there was a tension to Omi's face that had not been present even during their mission in the desert and its disastrous aftermath, and the demon knew that Omi's life had not been so easy before that, either.

"You're at the time of the great hordes that swept across the steppes of Asia. This was a battle that is barely mentioned in history: a war between neighboring tribes as the Golden Horde rode toward Russia. The Khan is collecting soldiers."

"And how have you come to be here, Omi?" Raksha asked.

"My grandfather," Omi said, and bowed his head in shame. "I have been traveling alongside, with the help of the Buddha. In another time, I took a drop of the Khan's blood—that's the spell that broke the magic that bound you."

He cast an unsettled glance toward the gathering line of warriors. "You'd better go. You'll be missed. I will be watching. I shall not be far away." Then he melted into the gathering dusk as Raksha and the demon made their way back into place alongside the other warriors.

Now that he had been freed from the Khan's spell, Zhu Irzh found it easy to see what had been done to his colleagues. Bonds and swathes of magic hung about them in pulsating silver ropes, shot with a bloody light. All of these webs snaked their way back to a focal point: a band on the wrist of the Khan, so that although the bonds themselves were cobweb thin, the Khan looked, from a distance, as though he was holding the leads of a thousand hunting hounds. He still wore that savage grin, which increased in satisfaction as he surveyed his troops.

"Welcome!" he cried, mocking, as some two dozen men were

brought before him. An overseer in a pointed helmet forced each of them to their knees and as they knelt, the Khan made his way along the line, casting magic from his outstretched hand. Soon the kneeling warriors, too, were enmeshed in magic. It hissed and spat, meeting lines of force in the land. Zhu Irzh strove to keep his face blank: this must have been what was done to him and Raksha. Not a happy thought, and what was worse, he had no recollection of it. He could feel this magic, too, tugging and nagging at his awareness, sending out tendrils in an effort to bring any strays back into the fold. He hoped the Khan wasn't paying attention to it, and in desperation he thought of Omi, keeping his promise and not far away, the demon's unlikely talisman.

To his surprise, it worked. The tendril snaked away, approaching one of the other warriors with greater confidence, and eventually withdrawing. The Khan made a sweeping gesture, both arms up toward the sky.

"Come! Rise in the presence of your master!"

And the new warriors did so, their faces as slack and expressionless as those around him. The Khan gave a crow of triumph. "Excellent. And now, we ride!"

It was much later in the day. Demons have greater stamina than humans but even so, Zhu Irzh was exhausted. Beside him, Raksha's beautiful face was also haggard. He wondered what kind of toll this was taking on her, snatched and whirled far from her own time. And what had happened to the woman he'd seen perched high on that balustrade in Urumchi? Was this the same Raksha, her existence somehow temporally folded so that it was the identical girl who now traveled time? Or would she meet herself, if the Khan took them back to the twenty-first century? Difficult

THE IRON KHAN

questions, which the demon did not feel equipped to answer. The whole thing was making his head hurt. Chen was usually better at this sort of philosophical issue, but even Chen had his limitations. And what of Roerich? Where was he now?

"I'm out of my depth," Zhu Irzh confessed in an undertone to Raksha. She gave him a troubled glance.

"You think I know what *I'm* doing, then?"

"Well, no. I guess we're just along for the ride." He looked down at the city that sprawled across the plain, far below them. They had come out in a narrow gorge, a very different country from the roll of the steppes. Crags towered above them, greened with scrub and a thin scattering of grass, and the air smelled fresh, of fir and pine. The demon had no idea where they were. The city itself was big, but not modern. Low buildings were surrounded by a thick brick wall, a massive fortification. Surely the Khan wasn't planning to attack that? It looked as though it would withstand everything except heavy mortar fire, and the Khan had no war machines with him, no trebuchets or even, as far as Zhu Irzh was aware, a battering ram. A city like the one below was constructed to withstand concerted assault, and long sieges.

Beyond the city, Zhu Irzh could see something else: a village, perhaps. But it didn't look quite like a village.

"Can you see what that is?" he whispered to Raksha. The shaman squinted against the sunlight; shading her eyes would have betrayed independent thought and neither of them wanted to risk that.

"I can't—wait a moment. It looks like a palace. Yes, I think it is. A palace surrounded by gardens—I can see a lake. And there's a hill not far away, with some kind of terrace built around it."

Now that she'd filled in the picture for him, Zhu Irzh found it easier to see. "Why isn't it inside the city?" he asked. "It doesn't

285

make sense to have those fortifications and then build your palace outside it."

"I don't know," Raksha said. "I don't understand it either."

"I suppose we'll just have to wait and see what happens," Zhu Irzh said.

The contingent to which he and Raksha had been assigned was in the process of setting up camp. The warriors moved with mechanical precision; Zhu Irzh and the shaman joined in, doing their best to mimic the jerky movements of their colleagues. Soon a blaze was leaping up into the evening air, redolent of pine resin. Zhu Irzh found it easier to think, as though the fragrant smoke cleared his head, but it didn't seem to have the same effect on the others, still deeply enmeshed within the Khan's spell.

"I have an idea," the demon murmured to Raksha, as a warrior doled out dollops of porridge and dried meat. "I can't see Omi anywhere—I hope he's made it along with us—but what do you think about my trying to eavesdrop on the Khan? Find out where we are and what he's up to?"

"Do you think he discusses this with anyone?" Raksha asked dubiously.

"I've seen him talking to one of the ifrit-types," Zhu Irzh said. "The one in the general's helmet. He seems to be functioning as a kind of second in command."

"It's worth a try," Raksha said. "As long as you're not seen. Do you want me to come with you?"

"No. If anyone seems to notice I'm missing, try and create a diversion." He nearly said: *Take your clothes off or something,* but thought better of it. As Raksha kept watch on the rest of the cohort, Zhu Irzh slipped like a shadow amongst the pines.

The Khan's own encampment was some distance away, centered on a cave in the rocks. Zhu Irzh planned to approach it via a circuitous route, coming up through the trees and along the side of the cave. He moved as silently as he could, with the soft carpet of pine needles serving to cushion his footing. It was a shock, therefore, when a hand fell on his shoulder. Zhu Irzh spun around, striking out, and Omi stepped quickly back.

"Sorry! Didn't mean to startle you."

"God, you move quietly!" Demons didn't tend to suffer from pounding hearts, but if he'd been human, he thought, it might have been enough to finish him off. He leaned against a nearby pine. Omi laughed.

"Good training. My apologies."

"It's okay. I'm glad you're here."

"I came in your wake," Omi said. "If I can tap into the right current, I'm able to follow the Khan."

"I was spying," the demon said, and explained.

"Might be worth it," Omi said. "Shall I come with you?"

Zhu Irzh nearly told him that if he could move with that degree of stealth, he was welcome to go in the demon's stead. Together, they crept through the forest. It was a remarkably silent place, Zhu Irzh thought. Normally this kind of woodland would be filled with night sounds—the call of owls, the whirr of nightjars. But this wood was as quiet as though a lid had been placed upon it. He whispered as much to Omi.

"I think it's the Khan," the young warrior whispered in return. "I've noticed it before. He has an inimical effect on life."

They were nearing the cave now. Zhu Irzh could hear the sound of voices and the crackle of flames. With Omi close behind him, he edged around the side of the rocks and peered out.

The Khan was seated squarely in front of a campfire. He held his hands out before him, as if warming them, but when the demon shifted position he saw that the Khan's hands were directly in the fire itself. Zhu Irzh's eyebrows rose. A human's fingers would be crisped within seconds, given the level of the blaze, but the Khan's hands were steady. His face was lit by the fire, giving him a livid countenance. The scarlet streaks of the flames made him look as though he had been flayed.

"What's he doing?" Zhu Irzh murmured.

"I think he's drawing power from the fire."

Zhu Irzh thought that Omi was right. The Khan was growing in stature, swelling like a frog. A moment later he let his hands drop and the fire abruptly went out, extinguished as though someone had doused it with water. Only a handful of coals, glowing like an ifrit's eye, remained and one by one winked out. The clearing in front of the cave was lost in shadows and smoke. The Khan rose and strode down the path toward the forest. The ifrit general followed, at a gesture from his leader.

"Where's he going?"

Omi and Zhu Irzh slid through the trees at a safe distance. Unlike them, the Khan did not seem to care how much noise he made. He crashed through the undergrowth, unheeding of whatever lay in his path. At first the demon thought he was heading for the main encampment, but it soon became evident that the Khan was, for once, not concerned with his warriors. Through the gloom, the demon could still see the magical threads by which he held them, snaking around one thick wrist and extending out into the darkness, a spidery web of power.

The Khan was now heading straight down the mountainside, making it difficult for even Zhu Irzh and Omi to follow him. Both needed to be careful of their footing, and Zhu Irzh started to worry that they would lose sight of their quarry. He was also concerned that someone might be following them, and kept casting glances over his shoulder. There was no one to be seen, but Omi had managed to creep up on him and Zhu Irzh was by no means confident of his own abilities.

There was something up ahead. Zhu Irzh strained to see, but it wasn't clear—some kind of building? But who would put any construction on such a steep hillside? The first heavy rain would wash its foundations away. Then Omi gave a little indrawn breath of understanding, and Zhu Irzh understood, too.

"It's a portal!"

A black square in the air, distinct even against the shadows of the trees. A darkly glittering outline betrayed its extent. The Khan stepped through it, accompanied by his general. Omi and the demon glanced at one another, waited for a second, and then they followed.

48

Inari stood at the window of her turret in Agarta, watching as the steppe sped by. Agarta was, so Nandini had told her, legendary for its serenity, the peacefulness which it bestowed upon its inhabitants, and this had been something which Inari had experienced for herself. So why was she now aware of such a tension in her stomach, the baby turning uneasily within, and a band like a strap of steel tightening around her head?

Chen was down in the Council chamber with the Book, talking to Nandini. Inari knew that it was a good idea to try and get some sleep, but she was too restless. Maybe this was just some symptom of pregnancy; perhaps going for a walk would be a good idea . . .

With that thought in mind, she went through the door and down the stairs, heading for the ramparts. But before she reached them, there was a curious vibration in the air. Halfway down the stairs, Inari nearly fell. She clutched the banister for support and regained her footing.

Agarta was shuddering. The staircase on which Inari stood began to creak, a sound she did not think stone was capable of making. Alarmed, Inari hastened down the stairs, gripping the banister in case the shuddering came again. It did not and she was beginning to feel that it had been nothing more than a temporary perturbation when she reached the bottom of the steps and the city gave a great groan like an animal in pain.

Singapore Three had been subject to earthquakes: some naturally generated, some not. Living on a houseboat, this had been a constant fear, but Chen had also told Inari what to do if a quake hit while she was out in the city. She was, she understood, safer outside than in, and although this did not really apply to the self-contained Agarta, she didn't like the idea of all that stone tumbling down the stairwell on top of her. So she bolted as quickly as she dared toward the door and out onto the ramparts.

There, she collided with Jhai, emerging just as rapidly from another doorway. The two women clutched one another.

"What—?" Jhai stared at the thing rising up ahead of them, across the rampart. It took a moment for Inari to recognize it, accustomed as her eyes had become to smaller structures. Even Agarta's towers were dwarfed by this building.

Jhai pointed a trembling figure at the monstrosity. "That's *Paugeng*."

She was right. The skyscraper rocketed into the heavens, with its red Jaruda bird symbol blazing at them over the edge of the rampart. Inari could see a strip of sea through a gap in the clustering buildings, and the lights of the city beyond. From forty stories up, late in the evening, the skyline of Singapore Three was an impressive sight.

"We're home!" Jhai sounded more appalled than relieved.

"But I thought Agarta wasn't able to travel outside the west of China?"

"So did I. Maybe it's changed its mind." But the agonizing creaks and groans that were resonating throughout the city's structure suggested a different tale to Inari. Now Nandini ran out onto the terrace. Her impassive, remote serenity was gone: her face was distorted and she was wringing her hands. Jhai seized her by the arm.

"What's going on?"

"Agarta has been hijacked! We have been wrenched out of our path, stolen away!"

"Who'd hijack a flying city?" Jhai asked, but Inari, with an awful sinking in the pit of her stomach, found that she already knew the answer to that question.

"The Empress! Where is she?"

At this, Nandini rushed off, looking even more panic-stricken.

Chen had been in the main chamber of the city when the shift had occurred. Nandini, obviously closer than Chen to the city's own soul, had screamed and run from the room. This change in her was almost more startling than their sudden alteration in location. Chen and Roerich, with a horrified glance at one another, rushed to the window.

"The city's in pain," Roerich said. "I can feel it."

"It shouldn't be here," Chen said, the policeman in him coming to the fore. "There's helicopter traffic at this level—and if we go any higher, we'll be in the flight path." Paugeng wasn't so close to the airport, but it was still within crashing distance, and after that episode in New York all those years ago, the combination of flight and large buildings was not an appealing one. Just as this thought struck him, Agarta shot upward at dizzying speed. Both Chen and Roerich were thrown against the wall.

"First flying boats," Chen said through gritted teeth, "and now flying cities." He'd not counted on such an aerial week. Below, the vast tower of Paugeng was receding fast. Around it, the towers of Singapore Three were approaching the dimensions of pins. The shattered stumps of those buildings that had been demolished in the last, goddess-induced quake were clearly visible, with the cranes around them looking like small pecking birds.

"What is Nandini thinking?" Chen asked.

"I don't think this is Nandini's doing," Roerich replied. "I think the city is panicking."

Looking down at the vertiginous view, Chen agreed. He was about to suggest to Roerich that they go in search of Nandini, when Agarta veered sharply to the left and soared out across the bay. Suddenly looking down on water was slightly better than the concrete jungle below, but the harbor was conspicuous now, and so was the empty space where Chen's houseboat should have been. Another thing to worry about, but at the moment, his main concern was Inari.

As if he had read Chen's thoughts, Roerich said, "If you need to look for your wife, Chen, please do so. We'll find her first, and then go in search of Nandini."

"I'd appreciate it," Chen said, and headed for the reeling stairs.

By the time he reached the ramparts, the city was once more coming back over Singapore Three. Someone had, by now, noticed that local airspace was being occupied by an unauthorized visitor, and as Chen approached the bottom of the stairs, a jet streaked past, flying low over the harbor and coming back around across the hills. Agarta was, so Chen had been told, supposed to be invisible to the eyes of unenlightened mortals but unless the Chinese air force was suddenly embarking upon a particularly tricky set of maneuvers, he had the feeling that the city was, by now, all too visible.

Just as he stepped out onto the ramparts, Inari appeared around the corner, with Jhai in tow.

"We think it's the Empress," Jhai told him curtly.

"Seems like the most probable candidate. Does anyone know where Nandini was holding her?"

Jhai shook her head. "No idea. But if it is the Empress, she doesn't seem to have much control over her latest acquisition."

"No, she doesn't," Chen agreed, as the city lurched back over the skyscrapers. "Inari, wait here. Hang onto something!"

"I'll try not to fall off," his wife wryly remarked. As she braced herself against one of the pillars, Chen, Roerich, and Jhai pelted down the stairs.

"Does Agarta have dungeons?" Chen shouted to Roerich, against the sudden roar of the wind in the narrow passages. It looked as though the city's internal climate was breaking down and that wasn't good news: the non-humans could probably cope but at this altitude, anyone else was likely to freeze. And Agarta didn't seem like the kind of place that would possess dungeons.

"I think there are rooms on one of the lower levels," Roerich called back, confirming his fears. "But they're not really cells. Agarta doesn't often take prisoners, as you can imagine."

They reached a wide platform and Chen, startled, saw that the center of the city was almost hollow. Parapets circled an echoing space, filled with dim light. He felt as though he had stepped into the presence of some vast entity, not a god, but a living, thinking being, and a moment later realized that this was precisely what had happened. They were at the heart of Agarta, the source of the voice Roerich had mentioned.

But there was something in the midst of the light that clearly did not belong. To one side of the door from which they had emerged stood a small chamber, a honeycomb cell in the substance of the city. As Roerich had said, it looked more like a monk's meditational cell than a prison, but its door had been blasted off its hinges and now hung awry. The origin of that disharmony was floating in the middle of the light, staring at them with cold, black eyes.

Roerich stopped dead, staring ahead. "Majesty," he said at last. Chen had only set eyes on the former Empress of Heaven on a couple of occasions, but he had no difficulty in recognizing her. She looked exactly the same, her masklike face lovely in repose and yet somehow hollow, as if the evil behind it had eaten it away, corroding it over the long years until this was all that was left. Her garments floated round her like streamers of cloud, drifts and eddies of rose and gold.

"I don't know you," the Empress said. Her voice, too, was still lovely, and yet it grated. Roerich gave a small nod. The Empress floated closer. "And Detective Inspector Chen. What a surprise. You appear in the most unlikely places."

"One might say the same of you, Madam," Chen said. There was the faintest flicker of anger across the Empress' smooth countenance, like a distant bolt of lightning.

"Empress," Roerich told her. "You must relinquish control of the city. Even if you care nothing for its inhabitants, or for the people in the buildings below, you must be aware that if we crash, you are likely to return to the Sea of Night, where your prison is waiting for you."

"Oh, I know that," the Empress said. "My son was very careful. And I am learning to be careful, too."

"Not fast enough," Jhai said. "This thing's already missed a couple of passenger aircraft and you damn near took out the upper story of my offices."

"And what do you propose to do about it?" the Empress said, still sweet. "The Enlightened Masters have been incarcerated— it proved very easy, once I'd freed myself. And with them taken, the city itself was willing to bow to my will. I suppose limitless compassion doesn't really equip you for battle, does it? I wish I'd remembered that during all those insipid centuries."

"Power's addictive," Chen said. The Empress laughed.

"Do you speak from experience, Detective?"

"You must stand down," Roerich repeated.

"I don't think so," the Empress told him. "I've come too far to back down now. And what kind of existence would be waiting for me if I did? As you so kindly reminded me, the Sea of Night and that cursed boat? Oh no. If you're not happy with the way things are, my enlightened friend, then why don't you just leave?"

She raised a hand. The city canted over on its side, sending Chen and the others sliding down the parapet toward the emptiness of its interior. Chen scrabbled for a handhold and succeeded only in clutching Jhai's sleeve. They went down into air, falling through sudden light, and out of Agarta.

The cold knocked the breath out of Chen's lungs. He thought: *Inari!* as the cityscape of Singapore Three spun up underneath him. The lights were so bright: he could see the length of Shaopeng, all the avenues that led out in a wheel from the district of the Opera House. From this height, it looked remarkably like Hell. He couldn't even muster the breath to scream. Turning in the air he saw Agarta hanging like an inverted chandelier above the bay—and then his vision went black as something came up fast beneath him and Chen hit solidity.

"Are you all right?"

It was Inari's voice. Chen blinked. The sky swam. It didn't make sense, that Inari should be speaking to him so urgently now.

"*Wei Chen!*"

Her face came into focus: the huge dark-red eyes, filled with fear and concern in the pale oval of her face. His head was thumping, a rhythmic beat like distant thunder. He must have been stunned—and yet there was no pain. It took him a moment to realize that the sound was coming from outside his own skull.

"*Jesus,*" said Jhai's voice. They were moving. With difficulty, Chen sat up and found something soft underneath his fingertips.

"What the hell—?"

Immense wings rose up, fell, rose up, beating as smoothly through the sky as a spoon through cream. Bronze pinions caught the lights of the city and glittered into cold metal. From ahead, a chilly voice said, "I've been waiting for you to come back. Best that you keep your promises, this time."

49

A rushing, gushing magic that reminded Zhu Irzh of water filled his senses. A moment later and it was gone, sucked back into the portal behind them. Omi and the demon stepped out into a dank, dark place, smelling of earth and mold. Zhu Irzh looked a question at the young warrior, but Omi shook his head. They could hear the footsteps of the Khan and his general receding up ahead. Once more, they followed.

After a short distance, the earthen floor and walls gave way to polished stone blocks. Whoever had built this place really knew how to construct a fortress, the demon thought: the blocks were massive, but fitted together so tightly that he could not have slid a razor blade between them. The smell of the place changed, too: soil and damp giving way to incense. Thin veils of smoke hung in the air and they did not come from the sconces of burning tallow that lit their way.

This was familiar. He'd been somewhere very like this before, so many times that it had burned its way into the marrow of his bones. This was Hell, Zhu Irzh knew, and yet his magical senses still told him that he was on Earth. Perhaps this was a gateway, like the temples of Singapore Three. The presence of the portal suggested as such. He wondered, if they passed into Hell itself, which region they'd find themselves in.

Omi interrupted his speculations, putting out a hand to halt the demon in his tracks. Ahead, the footsteps had stopped.

"Ah!" the Khan said aloud. "So he has done my bidding after all."

"Did you think he would not?" The ifrit general had a rasping, rattling voice like a bird. Zhu Irzh could almost see the Khan's grin.

"Can never be sure, you see, when it comes to the mad. Who knows what they might choose to do?"

The general laughed. "Who indeed?"

The Khan should certainly know, Zhu Irzh reflected.

"But it's more the span of time," the Khan mused. "The years pass by, messages sent back through time become warped and changed."

"What was the original request, Lord?"

"Ah," the Khan said again. "I asked him to build me an army. And as you see, he has."

Zhu Irzh heard them heading away, their voices dwindling. Something about "the river" and "taking care." With another glance at Omi, the demon went after them.

He had seen some remarkable things on this particular trip, he thought, as he stared down from the parapet, but this really beat everything.

"My God," Omi breathed beside him. The demon turned to his companion.

"I must have seen them a thousand times. In magazines, on TV. And yet they're still extraordinary."

Under the flickering light of the sconces, the army spread out into the distances of the cavern. Archers knelt, with bows drawn. Cavalry officers sat upon stiff-legged horses, awaiting orders. Ahead, the infantry stood in rigid rows. In the torchlight, their faces looked more like flesh than terracotta, the red glow lending animation and life to clay features.

The terracotta army, creation of the mad First Emperor Shi Huang Di. Buried for over a thousand years, Zhu Irzh recollected, discovered by a farmer in the 1970s who had been trying to dig a well. He'd found a lot more than he bargained for.

It was hard not to feel as if the army was looking at him. There was something unnervingly human about the faces, each one with a slightly individual cast, as though humans had been changed to clay . . . The demon was struck by a disturbing suspicion, which he decided not to voice. Omi nudged him.

"They're over there."

They were standing on a narrow walkway, a raised earth bank which led two-thirds of the way around the perimeter of the cavern. At the far end of the chamber, the stocky figure of the Khan and the attenuated form of the ifrit general could be seen, making their way through an open iron door.

Once Omi and the demon reached this point, the way ahead was not clear. The door led into a further sequence of passages, twisting and turning in so confusing a manner that Zhu Irzh began to wish he'd tied a bit of string to the entrance: if they got lost in here, they might never find their way out again. He whispered as much to Omi, who confessed that he'd had the same fear. "But I have been counting the turns."

"Where do you think he's going?" Zhu Irzh hissed. "We're a long way from the army now."

"How much do you know about this place?"

"Not a lot. I know we're in Xi'an, so that means we're quite a long way from the desert. I've read a few articles on the subject."

"Well, it isn't just the army that obsessed Shi Huang Di. He also had a huge mausoleum constructed for himself, in the shape of a map of China—with himself at the center, of course. In fact, it does bear some relation to the reality of the geography—we must be close to the middle of the country. The mausoleum's never been found, but it was supposed to be filled with precious metals and rivers of mercury." Omi hesitated. "He's also supposed to have set a lot of traps in the entrance passages to the tomb—like the ancient Egyptians with their pyramids. Disease was among them."

Zhu Irzh was not tactless enough to say that this was more a problem for humans than demonkind, but he'd had run-ins with the Ministry of Epidemics before and he didn't like the idea of a replay. "Maybe he hasn't completed it yet," he said, hopefully.

They went on, by now unsure whether the Khan was ahead or not. Then the passage came to an end: a further open door. Once more the demon stepped out onto a parapet and he nearly gasped.

"Precious metals" had been an understatement. The entire cavern glittered from floor to ceiling with gold and silver. Rubies winked red from the rolling ground beneath, denoting on the map the presence of Beijing, and the great centers of medieval China. A glistening river poured across the expanse to a silvery sea. At the center of this huge map sat a throne, and on the throne someone crouched, knotting his hands and laughing.

"Mercury poisoning," Omi whispered, as he and Zhu Irzh drew back against the sanctuary of the door. "Not very good for you."

Another considerable understatement, Zhu Irzh thought. He'd seen madmen before, but few so obviously demented as the creature who huddled on the throne.

"*Emperor!*" thundered the Khan, and at once the giggling idiot became a stern-faced warlord, who rose from the throne and marched across China to where the Khan stood.

"My lord, you are finally here! You see that I have done as you asked. The army is almost complete; all that is required is the animating spell and your clay warriors will rise up and go forth to fight for you. They will be invincible—my magician has imbued them with great strength, with lunatic courage; he has hardened their surfaces so that spears will glance from them!"

"I suppose," Omi whispered to the demon, "that he has no direct experience of mortar fire."

"They had gunpowder in these days, though," Zhu Irzh whispered back. "After all, we invented it. Or rather, the Ministry of War did, and made sure humans got hold of it."

"Maybe his magician has been liaising with the Ministry of War," Omi suggested.

"Frankly, that's all too probable."

Looking at the lunatic ahead of them, Zhu Irzh saw something familiar about him: the demon could not place the memory, but he was sure he'd encountered this man before, in Hell. Since they had traveled back in time, this was possible. But which of the Ministries had it been? Epidemics, or War? Zhu Irzh was fairly certain that it had not been Lust. Whatever the case, it suggested that Shi Huang Di's spirit had not been reincarnated in human form but had remained in Hell, and that wasn't a good sign. For anyone except perhaps the Khan.

"So!" the Khan now boomed, all menacing jocularity. "My army! When can they be mobilized?"

"Tonight!" Shi Huang Di's face was lean and eager, alight with fanaticism. "My magician will arrive shortly, summoned from the far west. Then we will begin."

"I'll call down the troops," the Khan said. "We will be ready and waiting for our journey."

"We need to stop this," Omi murmured to Zhu Irzh.

Indeed, thought the demon, but how? Their main focus must be the magician, and to attack him, they would need to remain here, close to the army. He said as much to Omi and the young warrior nodded.

"We ought to go back," Omi added. As silently and swiftly as they could, they made their way back through the maze of passages, with Omi in the lead. To the demon's surprise and relief, they soon stepped out into the cavern that contained the army. Lines of terracotta eyes stared into the flickering light and once again Zhu Irzh felt that these images might already be alive.

Their concern now was to find a place to hide. They found this behind a row of barrels to one side of the chamber. There was no way of telling what these contained: the lids were nailed tightly shut. Zhu Irzh hoped they held something innocuous. Then, cramped, hungry, and nervous, they waited for Shi Huang Di's magician to arrive.

Zhu Irzh had lost track of time. Despite the constricted conditions, he must have dozed, for he came awake with a start. Omi was crouched close by, his eyes intent and gleaming. He put out a warning hand as the demon shifted position.

"Something's happening."

Zhu Irzh heard voices, and footsteps. They were too far away to identify, but he thought one of them was the voice of the Khan. Then, suddenly, the cavern was filled with magic: the same rank sorcery that he had sensed throughout his dealings with the Khan. Had the Khan brought it with him from the past, or had he learned it along the way from people like Shi Huang Di's magician? Zhu Irzh did not really want to know.

"I can see him," Omi whispered. "Come here."

Zhu Irzh moved closer so that he could see past Omi's shoulder. The magician was standing in a small knot of people: Shi Huang Di and the Khan himself, while the ifrit general stood guard. Zhu Irzh could not see very clearly but the magician was old, stooped, wizened. He wore Qin dress and a thin white beard, but when he turned and the demon was able to catch a glimpse of his face, he saw that the magician's countenance was as flat as a plate, his eyes hard little pebbles.

"Uighur," Omi said. "Or one of the western tribes."

"Are you ready?" That was the Khan, his voice booming out into the chamber. Zhu Irzh could not hear the magician's reply but it must have been in the affirmative, for the Khan hissed, "Good!"

The magician raised his arms, and Zhu Irzh felt a sudden surge of power beneath the ground, summoned up from the land around the cavern. Earth magic, and yet there was something wrong with it: it was not a pure earth current, but had something twisted and unnatural within it. And moreover, it lacked power. Whereas earth energy could be used for many ends, this felt flaccid, like a slack rope.

"Not very good, is he?" Zhu Irzh whispered hopefully. But in the next moment, he realized what the Khan was about to do.

There were five captives, perhaps representing each one of the elements. Four were men, and one was a woman.

"Damn," Zhu Irzh heard Omi murmur. The woman was Raksha. Her head was drooping, like those of the men, but when the magician turned his back she glanced up and he saw the sudden determination in her face. The shaman was neither drugged nor enspelled. Then the magician drew a circle of power around the five humans. It glowed in the air, a vivid, hectic scarlet. A second later, it was joined by another shade of red as the magician, without ceremony, slashed the throat of one of the captives. The man crumpled without a sound, his windpipe severed.

"We've got to get her out of there," Omi said. He notched an arrow to his bow and raised it, angling to get a clear shot past the barrels, but the magician was behind Raksha, walking around the perimeter of the bloody circle and chanting. By now, power was humming through the chamber like an incoming tide, making the demon's head swim. Then the magician moved beyond Raksha's drooping form and Zhu Irzh hissed, "Now!"

The arrow sang through the chamber just as the magician slit another captive's throat. Omi's aim was good. The bolt struck the magician in the chest, but it did not kill him. Magic sizzled through the magician's body, lightning bright, earthing itself through the floor of the cavern and spreading out. Zhu Irzh felt it pass through the floor, quivering and alive. The Khan gave a great howl of rage. Raksha's head snapped up.

Not far away, across the line of barrels, the eyes of a terracotta warrior blinked open and Zhu Irzh thought: *Oh shit.* Blood-magic to energize an army of earth, and it seemed that the blood of a magician was worth any number of mortal captives.

50

The Roc soared downward, its broad wings spread wide like a fan, catching and riding the thermals that spiraled up between the skyscrapers of the city. Looking back, Chen could still see the inverted cone of Agarta. He fumbled at the strap around his neck, checking that the Book was still intact and had not fallen out into the depths of Singapore Three. But the scroll was still safely stored in its case.

"Bird!" Jhai shouted, scrambling forward. "Can you take us *there?*"

There was Paugeng, coming fast up ahead. Chen had never thought that he'd be so pleased to set eyes on Jhai's slightly sinister headquarters.

"Very well," the Roc said, and veered.

"What is that building?" Roerich asked.

"It belongs to Jhai," Chen said. "It's pretty secure."

Although if the Empress decided to do something really rash, like crash Agarta into the city, he doubted that even Paugeng would be secure for long. He could see from the thoughtful look on Roerich's face that the Russian was entertaining similar doubts.

The Roc soared downward and came to light on the roof of the corporation. Up here, so many stories high, it was almost cold. Chen helped Inari down from the Roc's back; she looked exhausted. Security guards were running toward them, weapons drawn.

"Hey!" Jhai shouted. "It's me." Within minutes, she had everyone organized: Inari was led down to Jhai's own apartment in order to get some rest, and the others to a boardroom. Before she left, Jhai spoke to the Roc, urgently and at length. To his regret, Chen was too far away to hear what she said, but it seemed to satisfy the bird, for it dipped its bronzed head in acknowledgement and flapped up to perch patiently on a stanchion.

"What did you say to it?" Chen asked, as they made their way down the stairs.

"Promises," Jhai said curtly, and would not elaborate.

In the boardroom, Chen looked at the faces around him. Jhai, Robin, and Roerich. It was a reassuring sight, but he missed Zhu Irzh. He'd grown so used to having the demon around that his absence felt like a spat tooth. And what had become of the badger? Chen could count on the ability of Inari's familiar to look after itself but there were limits. Not to mention the houseboat . . . At this thought Chen sighed and turned his attention back to the matter in hand.

". . . best I go now if you can arrange transport," Robin was saying.

Roerich leaned across the boardroom table. "Where is the temple located? Is it close by?"

"No, it's across the city. I'll get you a car—"

But just as Jhai spoke, the air on the other side of the board-room started to shimmer. It glowed blue, a Celestial azure, and for a moment Chen thought the Empress had found them. Then the air solidified into a familiar figure and Mhara stepped into the room.

Robin ran to him without a sound. They did not embrace but took hands for a moment, then Robin stepped back. Chen could almost see the mantle of the priestesshood fall over her, like a veil. The Emperor of Heaven turned to Chen.

"My mother."

"Yes, we've had a few problems," Chen said.

Roerich bowed. "But Chen has secured what you sent him in search of."

Mhara smiled. "Do you mean Inari, or the Book?"

Chen returned the smile. "Both, in fact. Inari's resting. The Book is here." With relief, he unhooked the strap from his shoulder and handed over the parchment in its case. As soon as he did so, there was a change in the entity. From being an inert object, it returned to life; Chen could feel this, as though the Book had pulled a thread which bound them.

"I am in another place," the Book said wonderingly. "But I know you."

"Yes. I am your Emperor," Mhara said. "You have been on a long journey, haven't you?"

"I tried to mend things." The Book sounded regretful.

"Go back," Mhara said, and reached out a hand. He drew a gate-way in the air and held the Book out to it. "When all is well again, I will come and talk to you. We'll discuss your unhappiness."

"Thank you," Chen heard the Book say, but it was already fad-ing and in another moment it had disappeared through the air.

"Good," Mhara said. "Back where it belongs."

"I'm profoundly glad to be rid of the thing," Chen said.

"Yes, it's caused enough trouble. Well done, Chen."

"It's my job. And anyway, I had a lot of help. Do you know what's happened to Zhu Irzh?"

"I have no idea. This omniscience thing—it's not all it's cracked up to be, you know," Mhara said ruefully. "But in the meantime, we need to deal with my mother."

"This floating city," Jhai said. "I'm assuming we can't just shoot it down out to sea?"

"Quite apart from any ethical considerations," Roerich said, "the resulting tidal wave would cause as much havoc as anything the Empress is planning."

"I'm surprised she's managed to take over the city so quickly," Chen said.

"The trouble with Agarta," Roerich said, "as we found with young Omi, is that people become beguiled by the city. But like all spells, it's reversible. If the Empress found a way to reverse it, it may be that the city has become besotted by her."

"The power of the Imperial Court is often one of glamour," Mhara pointed out. "My mother was once beloved of all Heaven. And she's had quite some time, alone in her prison, to work on her magic. Her power might be decaying, but if she's found a way to gain back even a fraction of what she had, it could be enough."

"Inari told me that when they first came across the Empress' ship, her guards were absent," Chen said. "I got the impression that they had too much to deal with—that the incursions into the Sea of Night were increasing. We know that the barriers between these various Hells are breaking down."

Mhara sighed. "I'm responsible for this. I thought we were keeping a close enough eye on the situation, but I became distracted when the Book went missing. I should be the one to shoulder the blame. Besides, she's my mother."

Chen was about to reply when a sound shrilled through the boardroom. Jhai jumped up. "What the—that's the alarm!"

Footsteps were already thudding along the hallway outside the boardroom. Chen and the others rushed outside to see a security detail heading down the stairs. Jhai grabbed a guard.

"What's going on?"

"Incursion in the atrium, ma'am. We've had to shut down the elevators."

"For god's sake," Jhai muttered. "Can't get a moment's peace."

"In the event that it's Mother . . ." the Emperor said, and next moment Chen was standing by Mhara's side in Paugeng's large atrium. Ferns fronded the entrance, almost hiding the reception desk from view. But behind it, the receptionist was screaming. A brief rattle of gunfire came from the courtyard of the atrium. A Celestial warrior was striding through the atrium: a male presence, of similar pallor to Miss Qi. Chen's first thought was one of relief: Mhara had managed to summon backup. But just as Chen started to step out, the Emperor caught him by the arm. The warrior raised a spear and sent out a bolt of energy to the far end of the atrium. There was the sound of gunfire again, but the bullets clattered harmlessly to the floor.

"*That's* the incursion?" Jhai cried.

All the Celestials Mhara had sent to Earth, Chen thought, all those heavenly presences who were now in residence in Singapore Three. Miss Qi had told him that the Empress had taken control of her on the Sea of Night. It looked as though she'd tried the same trick again. And succeeded.

Beside Chen, Mhara raised a hand in turn. The warrior halted in his tracks. An expression of bewilderment crossed his face.

"Hold your fire!" Jhai snapped to an unseen guard. A sensation of peace and calm washed over Chen, something that had become entirely unfamiliar in recent months. It was coming from Mhara: Heaven's energy, channeled through its Emperor. It struck the warrior like a soft blow and he fell to his knees. Chen saw a small dark thread recoil from the top of the warrior's head, snapping like elastic and then shooting away out of the door. The warrior blinked, the Empress' hold on him broken.

"All well and good," Mhara said grimly, "but what about the rest of them?"

51

The cavern was falling down around Zhu Irzh's ears. With Omi, he cowered behind the barrels, waiting for rocks to stop falling. Above the racket, the Khan's voice was thundering in a rage-induced spell and the demon could hear laughter, too—the mad Emperor Shi Huang Di. It could be no one else.

At last the noise stopped. The pale sky of dawn was now visible through the shattered roof. Zhu Irzh peered cautiously over a barrel. The terracotta army stood where it had stood before, its lines unharmed. But the army itself was stirring: sword arms flexing, bows becoming strung. Zhu Irzh stared. The terracotta warriors did not look human, but neither did they appear to be made of clay, either. Their skins were a reddish, ruddy color; their eyes small black slits. Despite their earthy origins, they moved with an unnatural fluidity which reminded Zhu Irzh of demonkind. Possessed, but by what?

The Khan gave a roar of triumph. He raised his hands high above his head and cried, "Onward!" Ignoring the remaining human captives, he stepped over the bloodstained body of the magician and beckoned to the army. "Move!"

And the army did so, striding forward across the floor of the cavern toward the collapsed wall. It poured through the gap and the Khan marched beside it. Once he had passed through the gap Zhu Irzh and Omi ran out from behind the barrels and cut Raksha's bonds, then, as a matter of principle, freed the other warriors, who rose stiffly and followed the Khan with blank expressions.

"Thank you," Raksha said. "Who were those warriors?"

The demon attempted to explain, as they followed the army. The Khan was wasting no time. As they emerged into the dawn light Zhu Irzh saw the animated army marching through another black portal in the air.

"Now that he's got his warriors," Zhu Irzh said to Omi, "where do you think he's going?"

"There's only one way to find out," Omi answered.

As they stepped through the portal, Zhu Irzh realized for the first time the extent of the army. The ifrits had been joined by the warriors from Samarkand and the steppes, and these in turn by the terracotta soldiers. In all, the demon estimated, there must have been several thousand individuals, all under the will of the Khan. At the other end of the long line rode the cavalry: human and clay, the terracotta horses prancing with eager life. They rode toward a square of light, which the demon assumed to be another portal.

Another moment—and then the square flooded open. Zhu Irzh, briefly blinded, threw a hand up to protect his eyes and felt himself being whisked forward. He stumbled out onto concrete.

Familiarity. He knew this place, the smell of the air: cooking and the harbor and inadequate drains. A little like Hell, but uniquely its own self, and the demon was surprised to find how much it felt like home. The Khan had taken his troops to Singapore Three. Omi, wide-eyed, said, "This is—"

"I know. But why are we here?"

Omi's eyes widened yet further. "I think *that* might have something to do with it."

The demon followed the direction of his gaze. They were close to the Opera House, the army spilling out into the wide area in front of the domed building. The wide avenue of Shaopeng led down toward the harbor, and at the end of it Zhu Irzh could see a strip of sky with something like a chandelier hanging in it. At first, with a distinct sense of disbelief, he thought he was looking at a UFO. Then he realized that this, too, was familiar.

"Agarta," Omi breathed, but with more dismay than any other discernible emotion.

"What's it doing here? I thought it couldn't travel beyond the West."

"Neither could the Khan."

That was true enough. The Book's attempts to change the course of history seemed not to have been final—the existence of Singapore Three, as dissolute, stinking, and hectic as ever, was the final proof of that for Zhu Irzh—but it had certainly shaken things loose.

Raksha was glancing about her, her arms wrapped tightly around herself. Her expression—fear, wonder, and something that might almost have been amusement—was enough to give her away to anyone who might be watching. Zhu Irzh seized her by the arm and pulled her into a nearby alleyway.

"Time to leave the military," he said. Ahead, Agarta was beginning to move.

52

Miss Qi would go with the security detail, Mhara informed Chen, as she knew how to handle her fellow Celestials. He did not want casualties, but under the circumstances, they might be difficult to avoid. Jhai was making her own plans. But they *all* decided it would be best for Inari to remain at Paugeng. The Emperor would have offered the sanctuary of his own temple, Chen knew, but recently it had hardly proved such for his wife, given that the temple had been the scene of Inari's own death. As for Paugeng, it wasn't ideal but at least it was reasonably defended. And present in this dimension.

"What about you?" Chen asked Mhara.

"I'm going to try to get onto Agarta. But at the moment—it's shutting me out. Roerich has some ideas which we're going to try."

"I'll stay with you," Chen said. Inari's safety was paramount, but after that, he needed to look after his city and the best chance of that was by helping Mhara. He started as his phone rang and an unknown number appeared on the screen.

"Yes?"

"Chen! It's me!"

"Zhu Irzh! Where are you?"

"Here, in the city," the demon said, speaking hurriedly. "So is the Khan. So is an army."

"What kind of army?"

"All sorts—warriors from the steppe, horsemen, and he's brought the terracotta army with him."

For a moment, Chen didn't think he'd heard properly. "The what?"

"That army that mad warlord had made," Zhu Irzh said. "The one in Xi'an, to accompany him into the afterlife. The Khan's animated them."

"I see." Though he didn't, exactly. "All *we've* got to deal with is a rogue flying city, the demented former Empress of Heaven, and some possessed Celestials."

"Yes, I saw Agarta," Zhu Irzh said. "What's it doing here?"

As briefly as possible, Chen brought him up-to-date. "We're in Paugeng. Jhai's here, too." The demon hadn't actually asked after his fiancée, Chen noted: perhaps he'd automatically assumed that Jhai was fine. One tended to, somehow.

"Then we're heading over," Zhu Irzh said.

"Be careful," Chen told him. "There's been one battle in the hallway already."

He had not, the demon said later, encountered too many problems.

"Met a Celestial but she seemed stoned rather than aggressive. Other than that, the Khan's army is congregating around the Opera House."

"I know," Chen said. "I spoke to the precinct. The army's been drafted in."

"I don't know how much to worry about it," Zhu Irzh said. "On the one hand you've got horsemen and clay zombies. Against the Chinese infantry, even in the middle of a city, you'd think it would be no contest. But then again, the Khan's behind them." He looked suddenly somber, an unfamiliar expression on the normally upbeat demon's features.

"He's really got to you, hasn't he?" Chen said. Both Roerich and Jhai had spoken to him of the Khan, but this was the first time that Chen had been able to see for himself how greatly the warlord had affected the demon.

"Yeah. I don't know why. Nicholas said he'd marked me but I don't know why. He had me under a possession spell for a while but Omi managed to break it, otherwise I'd be standing outside the Opera House now waiting for orders."

"Well," Chen said firmly, "you're free and that's all that matters."

"What's happening with Agarta?"

"See for yourself."

They were now in Jhai's private apartments, high up in Paugeng. From here, they could see a huge swathe of the city. Agarta hung like a lantern directly above the Opera House itself: the gilded dome of the Opera seemed to be trying to reach up and touch Agarta's base, as though the two were mirror images of one another.

"What's the Empress up to?"

"I don't know," Chen said. "But I'd be very surprised if it turned out to have nothing to do with the Khan."

*   *   *

Inari luxuriated in the wide bed, appreciating Jhai's Egyptian cotton sheets and the dim, soothing lights. It was somehow more comfortable than even beautiful Agarta: perhaps because this was a demon's home, after all, and not the province of the more morally elevated. And in a wider sense, the city was *her* home as well: an imperfect one, to be sure, with many dangers, but still more her place of sanctuary than anywhere else. Now that she finally had some peace and quiet, she could tune into the child within her. It turned slowly, not kicking, just moving in its watery casing like a small seal.

"Who are you?" Inari whispered aloud, and the child replied with calm certainty, utterly serene, completely secure, *I am the bridge.*

"What do you mean?" Inari asked, but the child said, with perhaps a touch more urgency, *Someone is coming.*

Inari sat up. A figure was forming out of a cloud of mist in the far corner of the room, shadowy and vague. Black and red tendrils snaked out from it, but Inari did not need to see these to know who it was.

"Empress!"

"You," said the Empress with an absolute malevolence at odds with her usually saccharine voice, "are coming with me."

The Empress drew a gateway in the air, but Inari retorted, "I don't think so."

She threw a warding hand outward, drawing on what she thought at first was the power in Paugeng, but then realized it came from a different source entirely: the child in her womb. There was a sudden surge and the Empress reeled backward, but the gateway remained. Inari braced herself for another bolt, but the door flew open and Chen was there, with others behind him.

The Empress, taken by surprise, faltered for a moment but the gateway was already starting to glow.

Enough, the child said inside, with sudden impatience. Inari remained rooted to the bed as the Empress, and Chen and his companions, were pulled through, leaving Inari clutching the sheet to her throat and staring at empty air.

Chen staggered against the wall. He'd been here only a short while before, fleeing while the city rocked around him, but this was greatly changed from the Agarta he'd known then. Dark threads covered its walls like a spiderweb, pulsing with faint crimson magic. In an impressively short space of time the Empress had converted the city into her own personal lair. Chen did a quick count: Roerich and Zhu Irzh, those who had come with him when he'd felt Inari's distress and the cry of his child. Unnerving, to be suddenly summoned by one's own unborn offspring, but Chen found it encouraging that the Empress could be distracted enough to screw up: it suggested that her power was not, after all, omnipotent.

"Where now?" Zhu Irzh asked.

Roerich pointed to the threads. "Those are growing more thickly further up the passage. I suggest we follow them."

They did so, but it was not easy. Chen was reminded of a recent—and unwelcome—sojourn in the Ministry of Lust, in Hell, a place that was also alive, but in a more unpleasantly organic and fleshy way. This had something of the same feel to it, a sign of how far the Empress had fallen. They moved through air that had become stagnant and fetid, over floors that were covered in a soft powdery dust, like moldering fungus.

"So great a change in so little time," Roerich said unhappily. "I'm appalled that she's achieved so much."

"She was an Empress," Chen said. "Her husband was even more destructive, believe me."

Agarta's windows were also filmed, with a faint black slime, making it difficult to see where the city was currently located. Eventually Chen managed to make out the long reach of Shao-peng: it seemed that the city was still where they had last seen it. But he was distracted from the view when something rushed at them out of thin air, a swift and hideous shape. Roerich, with an exclamation, struck it aside and it swept screeching into a corner in a tangle of leathery wings. At once, Roerich was upon it, blasting it into an ashy outline with the force of a spell.

"What was that?" Chen asked. "Ifrit?"

"Ifrit." Roerich's dark eyes were narrowed. "And that means the Khan."

"Wonder who's the paymaster?" Zhu Irzh said.

"We might soon find out."

The threads led them upward, winding around one of Agarta's spiral stairs until they came out onto the summit of a landing. Here, the grime was so thick that Chen could see nothing from the little pointed window. Roerich turned to him. *She's here*, his expression said, more eloquently than words.

The door before them was locked and the threads seemed to have welded it to the lintel. Roerich tugged, but soon stepped back. Chen was about to suggest alternatives, when the Empress evidently decided to take matters into her own hands. The door melted away before their eyes, leaving Chen unsure as to whether it had been an illusion in the first place.

Within, the Empress sat in state, enthroned on a black mass that reached up over her head. Like the threads, it, too, seemed almost alive: a series of arcs and spines that moved faintly in crustacean motion. From the top, a point coming down over the Empress' head, a thick twisting rope of darkness sank into the middle of the Empress' skull. She was smiling. Chen had no idea what this thing might be—something from the depths of the Sea of Night itself?—but he could hear it whispering. Beside him, Roerich gave a murmur of revulsion.

The Empress reached out a hand and the black mass convulsed. A bolt of energy shot along the Empress' arm, pulsing with blue light, and Chen threw Roerich back against the wall as it shot past, leaving a scorched patch on the stones opposite. Beneath his feet, Chen felt Agarta writhe in agony.

"I need you to help me," Roerich said urgently as they cowered behind the lintel. "I think I can help the city to eject her, but I need to ground the power in someone who is actually mortal."

"Best if I do it," Zhu Irzh said. "No offense, Chen, but demons are tougher."

"I'm afraid by 'mortal,' I meant 'human,'" Roerich said. He looked at Chen. "Are you willing?"

"I don't feel that I have a choice." Now that they were finally facing their foe, Chen once again felt that curious feeling of calm, a Zen-like bow to inevitability that he had experienced before at moments like this. Perhaps to someone of a different culture, the attitude toward choice would be different; to Chen, it seemed that it had to be a question of fate. Roerich appeared to recognize this in him, for he nodded.

"Very well." He touched Chen lightly on the shoulder and together they stepped into the shimmering doorway.

53

"What's wrong with him?" Huddled in a borrowed robe of Jhai's, Inari stared down at the prone form of the Emperor. Mhara, floating in midair, looked as serene as a person asleep, his arms resting by his sides and his blue eyes closed. The light that surrounded him was very faint, yet it had pushed Inari away when she tried to touch Mhara, a gentle, but irresistible force.

"I don't know." Robin's spectral face was creased with concern. "I've never seen him like this before."

"It doesn't look bad," Inari ventured.

"Whatever the case," Jhai said flatly, "he's not going to be battling his mother anytime soon."

"What if this is just his body and his soul is elsewhere?"

Robin sighed. "It's not that simple. When he became Emperor, he essentially fused into a single entity—he doesn't really have a soul, he *is* a soul. So what you see here is Mhara himself; there isn't anything else."

"So we now have the question of whether he's done this to himself," Jhai said, "or whether someone has done this to him."

"I am certain of this," Robin told her. "Mhara wouldn't save himself and leave us at risk. That suggests that this is enforced from outside."

"The Empress is the most likely suspect," Jhai said. She crossed to the window and raised one of the blinds. Over her shoulder, Inari saw the cone shape of Agarta, still hanging over Shaopeng. But something had changed.

"It's spinning," she said.

The cone was beginning to revolve like a gigantic top. Dark threads spun out from it, as though the city was weaving. Within Inari, something twinged.

I have taken measures, the child said.

"What are you talking about?" Inari asked it aloud.

Jhai gave her an odd look. "I didn't say anything."

"I'm not talking to you." She didn't want to sound rude, but since the child had once more started to communicate . . .

The Emperor cannot be risked, the child said.

"I don't understand."

There was a feeling like a sigh: exasperation, perhaps. *Oh Mother.* As if talking to an idiot, the child said, *He cannot be risked. I have placed him under my protection.* This more than anything else scared Inari. The fact that her baby was able to affect the existence of the Emperor of Heaven was alarming in the extreme.

"The baby's done it," she said.

Jhai and Robin stared at her as though she'd gone mad. Maybe she had, Inari thought. It would explain a great deal. "It's just told me," she said.

"Well," Robin remarked after a moment, "someone's certainly done something."

Agarta was revolving. Chen still could not see out of the windows, but he could feel the motion of the city underneath his feet, and within himself, too, via his magical senses. The Empress' teeth were bared in a feral grin. She cast bolt after bolt of energy, which jolted through Roerich and down through Chen's boots. Roerich himself was doing nothing, either protective or offensive, and Chen had decided to respect his decision. If everyone started going off on their own track, things tended to get messy.

He was not sure whether the Empress' attacks were causing the new movement of the city, either through reaction on the part of Agarta, or direct control on the part of the Empress. But if he was not greatly mistaken, the Empress' triumph was starting to waver, as Roerich took hit after hit without flinching. Chen did not know, however, whether he himself could withstand this indefinitely, and from the unfamiliar look of worry on Zhu Irzh's face, he must look worse than he felt. Which wasn't great, quite frankly. His skin was beginning to prickle as if bitten by a hundred mosquitoes and the place on his shoulder where Roerich was touching him had begun to burn hot. Then his knees buckled and he almost went down.

Roerich, whispering a spell beneath his breath, cast a fleeting glance at Chen, who saw him grow pale. Then everything started to pulse, as if they fought beneath a strobe light. The only constant that remained was the Empress' eyes, like two black sparks in a psychedelic fog. After a moment, Chen realized what was happening: Agarta had begun to spin in earnest and they were being whipped around like a top. The window shattered, blasted outward. There was a thin, high keening sound—the Empress, screaming. Chen considered that to be positive, at least. He and Roerich were flung against the wall, breaking Roerich's grip on his shoulder. The demon swore. Chen grabbed at the rail of the landing, feeling himself being sucked across the few feet to the window. Suddenly, his hands still gripping the rail, he was airborne, feet flying up into the miasma emanating from the Empress' chamber. From the broken window he caught a glimpse of nothingness, lit by a dim swirl of lights, instantly recognizable as the stretch of the Sea of Night. Beside him, Zhu Irzh and Roerich were hanging on for dear life. The black threads which had filled the halls of Agarta were the first to go, swept up like cobwebs into a vacuum cleaner, leaving cool clear stone.

"Chen."

He looked to see Roerich's dark gaze. Roerich extended a hand. "Can you?"

"I will." Roerich's touch was like fire, filled with borrowed power. Chen gritted his teeth, forcing the power down through his hands since his feet were not in contact with the earth. He saw the surge pass through Roerich, illuminating him in a brief instant into a skeletal negative, bones and skull and teeth outlined in a lightning flash, and Chen knew he looked the same. Through the open doorway he saw the Empress blasted off her unnatural throne. She clawed, clutched, screamed—and then was gone, sucked through the window into the Sea of Night. Chen had one last glimpse of her spinning figure, growing tiny against the backdrop of the Sea, before she disappeared.

The throne itself scuttled out, claws rattling for purchase. A scorpion, lobster, centipede: all of these things. Chen saw revulsion fill Roerich's face and the Russian opened his mouth for a final spell, but it was not needed. The creature followed its mistress into the depths of the Sea of Night.

From deep within Agarta came a soundless cry of exultation. The Sea of Night vanished. A huge salt wave splashed up against the turret and in through the open window, narrowly missing Chen and the others. It raced down the staircase, washing the city clean. Agarta spun again and Chen briefly blacked out with the sudden momentum. When he opened his eyes once more, the city hung in a clear sky, with the towering peaks of the Himalayas beyond. The sun touched the long lines of the glaciers, spilling into icy fire. Roerich's face was filled with peace.

"She's gone," was all he said.

But Chen could hear moaning. With Zhu Irzh, he ran to a door set in the wall, close to the main parapet of the city. When they wrenched it open, they found Nandini crouched behind it. Her face was in her hands.

"Come on," the demon said. "It's okay. You can get up now."

Nandini turned a traumatized face toward him. "How could this have happened?" she whispered.

"The city's become too far removed from the affairs of men," Roerich said. "Men, and other things—it's become too distant from Heaven and Hell. You've so little experience of evil now, so little memory of it, that you don't recognize it when it appears and all your defenses are as dust. That has to change. Either that or you simply keep the city here, amongst the high pure peaks. It's your choice." He looked up as he spoke, glancing past Nandini, and for a second Chen saw the other Enlightened Ones. A woman in a headdress of peacock's feathers, a tall, stern man in blue, a Chinese sage amid the throng. But Roerich, unintimidated, went on: "But if you do choose the world of ice, it is my opinion that the city will start to wither, be blasted at the root. It needs the conflict and tension of the other realms in order to thrive, for its role is balance."

"We will give thought to what you say," said a voice from the air, and Chen did not think it sounded pleased. But whether or not this was the case, the grudging note in it suggested that Roerich's words had left their mark. Roerich bowed.

"I thank you," he said. And before the words had left his mouth, the room around them had changed. The Himalayas disappeared. They were once more standing in the boardroom of Paugeng, with Jhai and Robin and Inari staring at them across the floating body of the Emperor of Heaven.

Omi ran down alleyways, ducked under awnings, dodged parked cars. The ifrit veered ahead, its wingspan so wide that it had to tilt in order to fly. Omi, with a brief prayer for forgiveness, leaped onto the roof of someone's Mercedes and drew his bow. The arrow struck home; the ifrit fell from the air like a downed pterodactyl and burst into flames.

It was raining. The downpour had started around dawn, with thunder that seemed trapped over the city, rolling around and around and out across the bay. Now, five hours later, the Khan had still not made a move, but the ifrits were pouring into the city like the rain itself and Omi could not think that they were unconnected. A bold move on the part of the Khan, Omi thought. The incoming ifrits were keeping the army occupied and the government had called off the air force: too many tall towers. Shots fired at the Khan had whizzed harmlessly into vapor, and still the Khan sat upon his pony as if carved out of iron indeed, and smiled. Omi jumped down from the car and left its alarm shrieking behind him.

He was, as yet, unsure of what his role would be. He had spoken to Chen's department, been introduced to one Sergeant Ma and a demon hunter out of Beijing. Omi and the demon hunter had eyed one another appraisingly, like an evaluation, and come to a tacit mutual regard. The hunter, No Ro Shi, had then introduced him to the departmental exorcist, Lao, a gaunt and acerbic man who had nonetheless welcomed Omi and then told him that he was more or less useless.

"Your most valuable asset as far as I'm concerned is information," Lao said. "That's not to say that we don't value your skills as a warrior—far from it. But we have got to look at the wider picture and we've already got enough firepower. For what it's worth." Lao looked momentarily sour. "It'll be magic that will win this war, mark my words."

He was right, Omi thought. He could take out ifrits with a bow, but they did not respond well to bullets: modern technology had not built its own relationship with them, whereas the ancient ways, in some curious sense, had. So, after a thorough debriefing in which he had told Chen's department everything he could think of about the Khan, he had gone scouting.

The main influx of ifrits had slowed now, with only sporadic flocks coming into the city. Looking up, Omi could see them massing, a dark tornado cone against the blackness of the storm-clouds. He had once heard it said that ifrits feed off lightning, and watching the flickering lances across the cloudscape, he did not find this difficult to believe. The mass of ifrits hovered just above the Khan himself: Was he, in turn, drawing power from them? An odd symbiosis, Omi thought, and not a fortunate one for Singapore Three.

Magic. Grandfather had not reappeared since Omi's transgression over the matter of Agarta, and Omi was resigned to this, though his heart hurt every time he thought of it. If he had not been so weak, such a fool—as shameful as if he had been seduced . . . but it was useless to entertain such regrets and he knew his grandfather would tell him so, were he here. He needed to learn from it and keep on the right path from now on. He was a warrior, not a magician, but he needed to remember what Grandfather had told him about the Khan and magic: the Khan had existed all those years by draining the power of the land. Was that why the Gobi was as it was, a toxic desert? Could one necromancer achieve so much? Perhaps so, given sufficient time, and the Khan had certainly had that in abundance. And now the Khan, freed from his geographical chains, had been able to come here. What energy there was in this city, Omi thought, what vitality. The energy lines themselves were still repairing after an unfortunate incident some years ago involving the Feng Shui Practitioners' Guild, but there was plenty here for the Khan to occupy himself with.

And with that thought, Omi came back out of an alleyway and found himself opposite the Opera House. The Khan's army stood in their clay and human lines, implacable, impervious to all that the city had thrown at them. Behind a row of police cars and tanks, Omi glimpsed the attenuated figure of Exorcist Lao, who seemed to be in the middle of giving directions. Omi sidled around the square to join him.

"Ah, it's you. Any luck?"

Omi shrugged. "Some ifrits down. I can't do much." Frustrating, but true.

"Who can?" Lao cast an uneasy glance toward the army. "I can't understand what he's waiting for."

"Where's Agarta?" Omi asked. Deep within him, something wailed, bereft.

"It disappeared. God only knows what's happened to—"

Lao was interrupted by a sudden roar of fury from the Khan. It echoed around the square like the thunder itself, an ear-splitting cry of rage.

"Something hasn't pleased him," Lao said, eyebrows raised.

The Khan raised his sword. Lightning ran up it and shot into the heavens, bringing an answering increase in the force of the rain. Lao opened his mouth to say something to Omi but whatever it had been was forever lost as the army started to move. It surged forward out of the square, the clay horses bounding over the cars and tanks, trampling anything in their path. Bursts of gunfire from the direction of the troops did nothing to slow them down. Lao raised his arms, uttering a quick, firecracker spell, but Omi could see it fizzling out like sparks in the rain.

He ducked as a clay horse leaped over him, leaving a surge of power in its wake. There was a sharp peal of sound to his right; Lao spoke urgently into his cellphone and immediately Omi's ears pricked up.

"Chen! We're having—what did you say? Yes, he's with me." He turned to Omi. "Chen's on his way. Says the Empress is gone."

Omi felt a wave of relief. One down, one to go. "Where are they going?" The army was sending out tentacles from the main mass, which still occupied the Opera House Square. Horses thundered down the alleys and streets, heading in different directions.

"I don't know." Lao looked baffled. "I don't know *what* they're attacking." The Chinese troops seemed almost incidental to the Khan's concerns, as small a distraction as a gadfly. Lao and Omi crouched behind a tank, watching and waiting.

The normally immaculate and florally scented Miss Qi looked close to disheveled, Zhu Irzh thought. To his mind, it made her rather more appealing, but Miss Qi evidently did not agree. She was frowning.

"I've spoken to a few of them. They don't remember anything."

"The Empress must be dead," Chen said. "Or at least, the equivalent." He had told them how the Empress had fallen into the Sea of Night, how Agarta had cast her out. No loss, Zhu Irzh thought, and everyone else seemed to agree. But Mhara was still in his weird floating trance—which had something to do with Inari's baby, apparently—and nothing seemed to be capable of breaking it.

"We're just going to have to proceed without him," Chen said.

"We've managed okay so far," Zhu Irzh replied. Typical of gods. They'd let you do all their dirty work and then wake up. It was, he considered, the story of Chen's life. At least, according to Miss Qi, the Empress' hold on the Celestials present in Singapore Three was now broken, which left only the Khan. He started to say, "We might as well let him rest in peace," when Mhara's prone form gave a blue shimmer and disappeared.

"What—" Chen began, but Robin answered.

"He's in the temple. Don't ask me how I know—I can feel it."

"Why has he gone there?" Chen turned to Inari. "Darling, did the baby say anything?"

"No, not a word."

But Lao's urgent voice on the other end of Chen's cellphone confirmed that the bulk of the Khan's troops were heading for Mhara's temple.

"It's not just here," Chen said to the demon, some while later. They were standing outside the familiar confines of Mhara's temple, white on its slight rise. It was still raining, drops as hot and heavy as blood. "I've been listening to the police radio—the Khan's soldiers have been congregating on entry points throughout the city. Kuan Yin's temple is also surrounded."

"So what's he planning?" Zhu Irzh asked. "He's focusing on entry portals to Heaven and Hell—assuming Mhara's temple has an analogue in Hell." It seemed unlikely, but stranger phenomena had happened.

"He's already raided history for an army," Chen said. "And now he's got one. He surely can't be planning to launch an attack on Hell or Heaven? Either one is too heavily defended and with his ally the Empress gone . . ."

"Don't know." Zhu Irzh squinted through the binoculars at the temple. The Khan himself was clearly visible, mounted on his pie-bald pony, as expressionless as a stone. But he was staring directly at the temple and there was no doubt as to where his attention lay. "What happened to Robin?"

"She tried to get in there but she can't. Whatever magic the Khan is using as a barricade is extremely potent."

"What kind of spell was it that you used to defeat the Empress?" Zhu Irzh asked Roerich. "Could you do the same thing again? Without Chen, this time."

Roerich shook his head. "The Empress was drawing power from the Sea of Night—that thing you saw was a denizen of it. I earthed her power via Chen through Agarta itself. But the Khan is a part of this world, even if he's out of his own time and territory. He's drawing on the power of the land here, not something eldritch elsewhere."

But that power was strong. Zhu Irzh could feel it pulsing underneath him. The energy lines that congregated on Mhara's temple were being sapped, like someone tapping into an electricity supply. The Khan seemed to grow—not in his actual physical size, but in his magical aura, which swelled as the power surged through him.

"We've got to stop this," Chen said. He turned to Omi, who had joined them in the company of Exorcist Lao. "Is there anything you can do?"

Omi's face was drawn; he looked far older than his years. "It's my job," he said. "But I don't know how to carry it out. My grandfather's gone. You can't help me, can you, Nicholas?"

"No. My plans for defeating the Khan didn't work out, if you remember."

"Something's happening," Zhu Irzh said. All the power summoned by the Khan was coming to a point, building up like a thunderhead. Zhu Irzh's head felt as though a storm was about to break, and the next moment, it did. The Khan took all the power he'd gathered and launched it at the temple: the demon could see this, not through his physical senses but in his mind's eye, a great arrow of lightning directed at the modest white building before them, striking through the rain.

The temple remained, but Zhu Irzh could not see how it still stood, for the strike blasted all the ground around it so that the temple hung in empty air above a great gaping abyss. Behind it, the demon glimpsed the Sea of Night, a thin black line, and beyond, the bright shore of Heaven and the livid one of Hell. It was like glimpsing the universe in miniature, but there was more to come. A series of glowing cracks appeared in the abyss, fracture lines between the worlds, and Zhu Irzh understood how it was that Chen and Inari and the others had passed so easily through. The universe was indeed breaking down. The nearest crack was splitting apart, growing so that the world it contained filled the gap. That world was like the Taklamakan: somewhere bleak and arid and blisteringly hot. But this was a land in which no human could survive: Zhu Irzh's demon senses told him as much.

And within it were armies. Legions upon legions, iron-armored, fire-eyed. Zhu Irzh glimpsed swords and spears and more complicated, arcane weaponry: massive trebuchets with creaking metal cogs, huge rusted catapults with flames flickering along their sides, tanks painted in all the colors of destruction. At the front, on a great red horse, rode a figure in a helmet, his face concealed, a broadsword hanging by his side. Something about him was familiar and with a shock, Zhu Irzh realized who he was: this was Tamurlane's spirit—Timur the Lame in an earlier time—endowed by all the powers of a Hell that was not home. He was looking at the Hell to which the Khan was spiritually linked: a desert realm, a land of fire, and through the coalescing ether he thought he smelled the Khan's fear.

The Khan, Zhu Irzh knew, had no intention of dying, of entering that Hell. Instead, he planned to bring its armies here. Then, beside him, the demon heard Omi say, "I'm going in."

Despite all they had been through together, Omi was still surprised to find Zhu Irzh beside him.

"You're coming with me?" Omi asked.

The demon gave him a slanted glance. "Gotta face your demons, you know. The Khan and I have unfinished business. Besides, it would be a shame not to see how things turn out."

"Thank you," Omi said, and meant it.

"Do you happen to have, you know, any kind of *plan?*"

Omi smiled. "No. Just an instinct, that this is what I have to do. But I don't know why, Zhu Irzh. You can walk away now if you choose."

"I'll see how it goes," the demon said.

Together, they walked toward the breach in the fabric of the universe. Omi saw the others—Chen, Lao, Roerich—fall back as they came on, as if it had been acknowledged that this was now their rightful place. Ahead, Mhara's small temple floated high above the ground, suspended like a toy. The breach was growing and out of the corners of his vision Omi saw all manner of things begin to appear at its edges: ships and barques and galleons, all the predators and pirates of the voids, gathering to see what pickings were to be had.

Suddenly, Omi's boots were no longer ringing on concrete, but on baking desert earth. He gasped for breath and the demon pulled him back.

"Not too close."

"Can't avoid it." And he couldn't: someone else's Hell was closing around him and its airs were toxic and fire-filled—Omi's throat closed and he started to choke.

"Shit!" he heard the demon say and then his senses were filled with cool water and the scent of endless grassland. A breath of wind brushed his face. He looked up. The blue crane hovered above him, wings beating like a huge fan.

"Raksha!"

The shaman smiled. "Here I am." She rode the crane with customary ease, a short spear in her hand, and the light of battle in her eyes. "It's time," she said, and Omi knew what she meant. He turned to Zhu Irzh.

"Thank you again for walking with me. But you've come far enough now."

"Hey," the demon said, surprised. "You don't want me with you?"

"It's not that. I might need your support here, to hold the gate open. But she and I must go on alone." Raksha was waiting. He climbed onto the crane's blue back and it bounded upward.

Omi looked down. At the entrance to the abyss stood the

demon, a small, dark figure against a wasteland of sand and fire. Omi could see the outline of the gateway before him, a portal to the world of a different Hell. It glittered faintly, betokening activity. Within it, the vast army waited. The Khan spurred his pony forward. Omi had a good view of him from above, and he could see how careful the Khan was to keep away from the portal. Unlike Zhu Irzh, he was afraid. And that, Omi thought, gives us our principal advantage. He tapped Raksha on the shoulder.

"You know what we've got to do, don't you?"

"Yes." She touched the crane's neck, in turn. Omi glanced through the gateway and saw that the army was beginning to move, slowly at first, the front ranks hammering across the desert, then the surge of the tanks and troops behind. Something swung dangerously close to Omi's head; he ducked.

"What was *that?*" He looked back. An anchor hung in the air, attached to a thick iron chain. Its pointed ends moved to and fro like a pendulum. It was attached to a ship, riding high in the clouds and flying a black flag.

Omi had not anticipated having to deal with flying pirates when all this began. He swore.

"Don't worry," Raksha shouted above the wind. "We're too small to bother with."

Omi was not sure she was right about that. The appearance of the anchor had seemed a little too deliberate. Maybe they were just playing. The Khan's pony wheeled below, galloping up and down in front of the portal and the slight rise on which Zhu Irzh stood. Omi saw the demon raise a hand and give a cheerful wave to the Khan.

"Closer," Omi breathed. "Closer . . ."

An ifrit dived, screaming. They'd spotted the crane. If the main flock took an interest, he and Raksha would be torn to pieces. Omi drew the bow and fired, spearing the creature through its nominal heart. There was a shriek from the flock. The crane dived with a speed that ripped the breath from Omi's lungs.

Zhu Irzh stepped back a pace. Through the portal the army thundered on. Omi caught his breath. Then Zhu Irzh took a scroll from the pocket of his coat. He held it high, shouted something. Omi was too far up to hear the words but he thought he knew what the demon was calling.

"Here's what you want, Khan. Come and get it!"

The crane was still swooping downward. Omi glanced back over his shoulder and saw a line of ifrits pursuing them. They were ten feet or so from the ground, closing on the Khan, who was riding toward Zhu Irzh. The demon stood firm, still holding the scroll. The Khan's sword flashed up and Zhu Irzh threw himself in a roll under the screaming pony's hooves.

Raksha and the crane swept alongside the Khan. As they did so, Omi reached out and seized the man around the waist, dragging him from his mount. The Khan shouted but the crane was hurtling on, with the Khan dangling from Omi's grip. The bird could not, however, take the new weight; its flight was dipping and an ifrit snapped at its tail feathers. The crane squawked.

"Go, Raksha, go!" Omi shouted, and the shaman threw herself off the crane's back, landing safely amongst the scrubs. Omi caught a glimpse of her sword as she came up fighting. Then that terrible smack of heat was once more striking him as he flew through the portal itself.

This time, however, Omi found he could breathe. The same magic that had protected him from the freezing altitude during that first flight was still in effect, protecting him from the worst ravages of this new atmosphere. Now that they were through the portal, the Khan's struggles had redoubled. He clutched at Omi's throat. Omi struck him back, slamming his fist into the Khan's face but it was like hitting a bag of rocks. Omi struck again, feeling the jolt all the way up his arm, but the Khan lashed out. The back of his hand connected with Omi's jaw and he felt it dislocate. The Khan's hand hammered back and Omi lost his grip on the crane's neck feathers. Locked with the Khan, he fell off the crane's back. The ground hurtled up to meet them, some twenty feet below.

Immediately Omi was gasping for breath, released from the protective field of the crane. He landed flat, managing to break his fall somewhat, but the Khan was on top of him. The Khan's hands around his throat. Omi had a nightmare glimpse of the Khan's face above him: the bulging, reddened eyes, the leather-and-bone countenance. He punched the Khan again and again, but it was no use: the breath was going out of Omi and his vision was turning black.

Then—not black anymore, but red. In his last instant of vision, Omi saw the figure riding up behind the Khan on his rust-red horse—Tamurlane's spirit: the pointed helmet, the glaring gaze, teeth sharp as a tiger's; his eyes were gold. He brought down his scimitar and struck off the Khan's head.

Warlords don't like competition, was Omi's last thought before he passed out. And they don't like being forced to do someone else's will. The Khan should have remembered that—and then there was nothing more.

"We're trapped," Roerich said. Chen looked back and saw a second wave of the clay warriors riding up behind. An archer drew a bow and let the arrow fly: Chen shoved Roerich to the ground. From a grove of trees to the left of where Mhara's temple stood, a Celestial fired back, but the arrow burst into flames as it flew and crumbled into ash.

"Stay down!" Roerich yelled, and he and Chen flattened themselves against the earth as the wave of cavalry leaped overhead. A sword cut downward; Chen cast his rosary upward and shouted a spell.

He did not expect it to work. The rosary struck the sword halfway up its length and the blade shattered, then the hand and arm that wielded it, and then the body of the warrior. The horse was the last to crumble, covering Roerich and Chen with dust. Along the ranks of the cavalry, horses and warriors were following suit.

Roerich spat soil. "Chen! What did you do?"

"I don't think *I* did anything," Chen said, rising shakily to his feet. He looked across the mounds of broken pottery, where horses and soldiers had been so brief a time before. An ifrit fell from the skies at Chen's feet. A second followed, but high amid the main flock the ifrits were turning to ash and blowing away on the wind.

"I think the Khan's finally dead," Chen said. At the portal, there was no sign of Zhu Irzh. Chen swore.

"Where's he gone *now?*"

Omi opened his eyes. Everything was white, swimming with sunlight. His head felt as though it was about to burst. Hands reached down and placed something wet and cool and sweet-smelling over his brow. The pain receded.

"He's coming round," a voice said.

"Concussion," someone else said, calmly. Omi's eyes opened wider and he sat up.

"Grandfather!"

The old spirit smiled. "Omi. I thought it best to leave you to find your own way for a while. The old tend to think that they always know best."

Omi grimaced, remembering mistakes. "In your case, you usually do."

"That is very gracious of you, my grandson. But I am as much to blame as you. I failed to foresee certain contingencies."

"If you're all right now," the demon said, "I ought to be getting back." Zhu Irzh, still in his long coat, was perched on the side of the bed.

"Where are we?" The room was whitewashed and simple, with a small window and thick walls. Rushes lay across the floor. Omi lay beneath a handwoven blanket.

"This is the village of the Tokarians," Raksha said. "When you passed out, the crane came to sit by your side. It tells me that Tamurlane saw only a bird and a human, who would soon be dead. Not worth his while, so the crane waited while he rode away, back into the Hell which he now rules."

"What's happened to his army?"

"They are all gone. The clay warriors have returned to dust, without their captured spirits. The others have returned to their original times. The ifrits are in Hell, along with the Khan. His spirit is under Tamurlane's rule now. Omi, you are welcome to stay as long as you wish. Your grandfather has spoken to the spirit—the one you call Buddha. But the work of your family is done."

"It is for you to choose," Grandfather said. "Stay here, or return to Japan and the present day."

"I'll think about it," Omi said. Looking up at Raksha, he was uncertain. There was a connection, but he did not know yet what form it would take: learning, under the shaman's tutelage, or something else? And he knew that at the end of it, he would be going home. The family's task may be done; his ancestors were avenged and the Khan was dead, but there was still work to be carried out in the world and Omi thought he would like to be part of it.

The Emperor of Heaven was as close to annoyed as Chen had ever seen him. "It's not so much missing out on the action," he told Chen and Robin, "as not being able to help."

"This is my fault," Chen said. One could not let the Celestial Emperor lose face, after all. "At least, partly."

"No, it's mine," Inari said anxiously. "I'm carrying this baby, after all."

"Your child would seem to have significant abilities," Mhara said. Chen was not sure that the Emperor approved. "Perhaps I should make it my godchild, when it finally makes its entrance into the world."

"When will that be, Inari?" Robin asked.

"It's due in another couple of months. Seven weeks, as far as the midwife can estimate. Demon gestation is—oh." Inari put a tentative hand to her stomach.

"Inari? Are you all right?"

"I don't—oh dear." An expression of alarm crossed Inari's pale face. "I don't think it's going to be another couple of months after all."

"It's not that I mind you borrowing the jet," Jhai said, sitting by Zhu Irzh's side as the expanse of the desert once more unscrolled below. "It's just that I'd quite like to know where we're going."

The demon smiled. "Surprise."

"I could just ask the pilot myself, you know."

"You could. Take a look out of the window."

Jhai did so. Zhu Irzh followed her gaze and saw icy summits, impossibly high against a blue sky. Somewhere close, an invisible sentient city floated, thinking about its mistakes.

"That's Tibet," Jhai said.

"Yes, it is."

"So the nearest airport in China is probably—ah. Kashgar."

"That's right."

They touched down around midday and took a taxi to their destination. Zhu Irzh clutched the spell in his pocket as they drove through the hot dusty streets. Roerich had been extremely helpful, but he had admitted that this was not his area of expertise. The demon was not sure what he was expecting as they approached the Khan's villa. Perhaps his journey would be unnecessary—after all, the other spirits that had been ensnared by the Khan were now free.

But as soon as he got out of the car and walked into the grounds of the villa, he knew that this was not the case. There might not be the same sense of hideous oppression—that had gone with the death of the Khan. But the place was still warped and haunted and filled with a terrible sorrow. Zhu Irzh stepped up to the door and went in.

"Foyle?"

There was no reply. Zhu Irzh waited for a moment, then took the spell from his pocket. Roerich had translated it into Mandarin: the demon read it carefully aloud, sending it forming into the air. No bloody incantation, this, no iron spell of death, but something calm and quiet and peaceful. Zhu Irzh watched as it hung in the air for a moment, then the words faded to a single point of light. The demon took a step back as the light started to grow.

It was a portal, but to a very different world than the one which the Khan had opened. Zhu Irzh saw a green lawn, a terrace with topiaried shrubbery in pots. The air smelled of roses, and a yew hedge grew, dark against a bank of trees. There was a sharp clicking sound from behind the hedge: a croquet mallet, perhaps. On the lawn was a table and around it sat three women, blonde-haired and wearing long, full dresses. They were drinking tea.

As the demon stared, one of the women looked up and waved. "Rodney! Where have you been, dear? We've been waiting ever such a long time for you!"

"We saved you some cake," one of the other women said.

"Coming, Mother!" Beside Zhu Irzh, Foyle's ghost had stepped out of the wall. Other shadows followed him, passing swiftly through the light to other destinations. Foyle paused, to seize the demon's hand and pump it. He felt quite solid, apart from a slight chill to the flesh. "Zhu Irzh, old chap! Splendid job. Knew you'd come back, though some of the other lads had their doubts. Knew when you'd got rid of the Khan, too."

"That wasn't me, actually." Zhu Irzh was rarely overtaken by modesty, but something in Foyle's manner seemed to bring it out of him. "Glad to help."

"Marvelous! Well, mustn't keep the mater waiting." And with that, Foyle was through the gap and walking across the lawn to an afterlife of polite teas and cucumber sandwiches. He'd earned it, Zhu Irzh thought, and watched until the portal closed and he was standing alone in an empty, echoing old villa on the outskirts of a desert town.

"At least we've made the most of it," Zhu Irzh said a day later, as he and Jhai walked up the steps to the airport. They'd had a holiday of sorts, even if it was only a twenty-four-hour break. But the

343

phone call telling the demon that Inari had gone into labor was enough to bring both of them home.

"True. I'll be back at the end of the month, though. The chemical plant's going into production then. It should be—" Jhai hesitated, eyes narrowing.

"What is it?"

"Those guys at the end there," Jhai said in an undertone. "I've seen them somewhere before."

Zhu Irzh looked over at the neatly clad Chinese men. There were three of them and Jhai was right, they did look familiar. "Just suits," the demon said, but it wasn't until he was walking up the steps of Jhai's own aircraft that he remembered where he had set eyes on them before: during his rescue attempt in the plane to Kashgar, when the pilot had locked himself out of the cockpit. The suits had seen him then and he was pretty sure that they'd spotted him this time, too. Just airline security, or something more? Time will tell, the demon thought. Time will tell.

ABOUT THE AUTHOR

Liz Williams is a science fiction and fantasy writer living in Glastonbury, England, where she is codirector of a witchcraft supply business. The author of seventeen novels and over one hundred short stories, she has been published by Bantam Spectra and Night Shade Books in the US, and by Tor Macmillan in the UK. She was a frequent contributor to *Realms of Fantasy*, and her writing appears regularly in *Asimov's* and other magazines. She is the secretary of the Milford SF Writers' Workshop and teaches creative writing and history of science fiction.

THE DETECTIVE INSPECTOR CHEN NOVELS

FROM OPEN ROAD MEDIA

 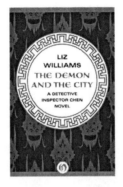 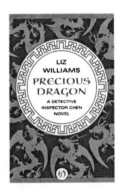

 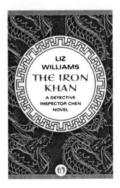

Available wherever ebooks are sold

OPEN ROAD
INTEGRATED MEDIA

Open Road Integrated Media is a digital publisher and multimedia content company. Open Road creates connections between authors and their audiences by marketing its ebooks through a new proprietary online platform, which uses premium video content and social media.

CPSIA information can be obtained at www.ICGtesting.com
Printed in the USA
BVOW04s1848220913

331848BV00001B/9/P